Don't Even Think About It

Daisy Dexter Dobbs

Published by Department of Daydreams, LLC, 2023.

DON'T EVEN THINK ABOUT IT

First edition. April 4, 2023.

Copyright © 2023 Daisy Dexter Dobbs.

ISBN: 978-1587850905

Written by Daisy Dexter Dobbs.

Dedication

This book is dedicated to everyone, past, present, and future, who has enriched my life with humor. To the comedians, humorists, entertainers, writers, artists, friends and family who have generously spread the healing power of laughter throughout the world. Thank you!

A few of my favorite quotes:

"It's your outlook on life that counts. If you take yourself lightly and don't take yourself too seriously, pretty soon you can find the humor in our everyday lives. And sometimes it can be a lifesaver."

–Betty White

"You know what it's like having five kids? Imagine you're drowning. And someone hands you a baby."

–Jim Gaffigan

"From there to here, and here to there, funny things are everywhere."

–Dr. Seuss

"I have seen what a laugh can do. It can transform almost unbearable tears into something bearable, even hopeful."

–Bob Hope

"I want to be silly, and that's being authentic just as much as being open and honest. It's authentic to make weird clown horn noises when it strikes you."

–Tig Notaro

"The one thing you're most reluctant to tell. That's where the comedy is."

–Mike Birbiglia

"If you're quiet, you're not living. You've got to be noisy and colorful and lively."

–Mel Brooks

"I'm a very observational type of comedian that points out everyday absurdities."

–Sebastian Maniscalco

"I've had great success being a total idiot."

–Jerry Lewis

ABOUT THIS BOOK

~<>~

After months of being subjugated, Mindy von Grettle's epiphany finally surfaces the night she accidentally overcooks her husband's steak. Edward's verbal tirade is coupled by physical abuse. All because his goddamn steak isn't still mooing.

Food becomes Mindy's only solace, with the tranquilizing effects of chocolate topping her list of caloric sedatives. The fatter she gets the less Edward touches her—the only benefit of watching herself morph into a bloated, lethargic caricature of her former self.

Eighteen months of painstaking work and resolve transforms Mindy into a stunner. Completely revamped, she's eager to exact revenge on her abusive, cheating ex. But the SOB robs Mindy of her well-deserved retribution by having a heart attack—in the act of cheating on his new wife.

Paying her final *disrespects* at the funeral home, she meets a man so breathtaking she's half-tempted to jump his bones right there in the mortuary. But once Mindy discovers vintner Archer Priest's connection to the she-devil she caught in bed with her husband, Archer is taboo.

Her meddlesome but well-meaning boss and best friend, Leo, is determined for Mindy to find the happiness she deserves. Ignoring her protests, Leo concocts cringeworthy attempts at playing matchmaker for her and Archer, planning on hot, steamy, spicy consequences. Instead, his meddling results in a series of embarrassing mishaps, misunderstandings, and a ridiculous masquerade.

Beyond mortified, Mindy, of course, decides *chocolatcide* might be the only way to manage her topsy-turvy life with as much grace and composure as possible.

Deserving mistreated heroine, charming good-guy hero, loveable trouble-making gay boss, mishaps and misunderstandings, snappy banter, sexy inventive scenes that sizzle, plenty of naughty words, and Cadbury the dog in a standalone HEA hilarious spicy-hot screwball romantic comedy.

Chapter 1

MINDORA VON GRETTLE advanced closer to the pearly gray casket and peered down. Yup, no doubt about it, it was really her ex-husband stretched out on all that creamy pristine satin. And he was really dead. That's what the obituary in the Chicagoland papers said: *Prominent Kentloe, Illinois, real estate broker, Edward von Grettle, age 45, dies of heart attack.* But Mindy had to come to the funeral home to see the evidence with her own eyes.

There he was, rigid, supine, and still flaunting that damned arrogant smile. An unwelcome shudder rippled through her. How the hell the mortician managed to affix that smile intrigued Mindy enough to want to poke Edward in the ribs. Just to be sure. Judiciously, she overcame the urge. A quick glance to either side ensured no one was in earshot.

"You robbed me, you sonuvabitch," she accused under her breath. "You had to die and cheat me out of my moment of glory, my sweet revenge, and I'll never forgive you for that, you bastard."

Standing over the bloodless corpse that had once been the man she loved, she tried to feel some emotion, any emotion other than bitterness, anger and loathing. Nothing. It just wasn't there anymore. Not after he'd physically abused her, and broke her heart, methodically stomping on it until it became a tattered clump of raw meat.

Success had always been important to him, to the exclusion of most anything else in life. Edward von Grettle had scored a palpable victory when he succeeded in obliterating every last ounce of love or compassion Mindy had ever felt for him.

It wasn't that she was happy to see Edward dead. Well, actually, she *had* wished him dead more times than she cared to remember. In fact, she'd often fantasized about plotting the perfect murder, killing the bastard off and reveling in a naked dance of joy on his grave. Cringing at the morbid recollection, Mindy bit back the trickle of guilt threatening to surface.

It's just that, if Edward had to go and die, couldn't he have had the decency to wait a little while longer? Just long enough for her to exact a teensy bit of well-deserved retribution?

Selfish in life, selfish in death, that was Edward. What a great epitaph. The thought teased Mindy's lips with a smile, which she immediately expunged, reminding herself that nice ex-wives shouldn't revel in such nasty thoughts about their dead ex-husbands.

Especially when the ex-wife was standing over her not-so-dearly departed ex's casket.

The mood in the room wasn't exactly one of bereavement, which helped to ease Mindy's less-than-sorrowful mindset. There were no inconsolable family members. The only blood relation Mindy spotted was Harry von Grettle, Edward's oily buffoon of a cousin. The best man at their wedding, he'd done his best to stick his tongue down Mindy's throat after the ceremony, while pinching her ass at the same time. Clearly seeing Edward's wake as a stellar networking opportunity, Harry glibly passed out business cards, schmoozing with Edward's smiling coworkers.

There were no grief-stricken friends in attendance either. Edward had never bothered cultivating friendships. It was unproductive. He viewed people as potential clients, competitors, or females he'd like to fuck. The only reason he ever turned on the charm was to reel in prospective customers or, at least in Mindy's case, prospective wives.

With another quick glance, she ensured no one was in hearing range.

"You were always a movie buff," she murmured. "There are so many apropos movie quotes I could choose from right now, like *yippee ki-yay, motherfucker*...or *adios, motherfucker*...but your final words to me during our divorce proceedings still ring in my ears. Remember, Edward?" When he didn't respond, she continued. "It was a quote from Terminator 2. And now, dear Edward, I repeat Schwarzenegger's words right back to you." Affixing the same sneer she'd seen on Edward's face when he'd delivered the words, Mindy said, "Hasta la vista, baby."

Expelling a sigh, she gave Edward's pasty remains one last, narrow-eyed, glimpse before turning to leave and finding herself face-to-face with Britney Priest—the anorexic-looking redhead who was once Edward's mistress and now his *grieving* widow.

Mindy took in Britney's overstated mourning garb with a knowing smile. The tight black dress stopped at mid-thigh, where it was met by sheer black hose and black stiletto heels. A profusely veiled, wide-brimmed black hat, fashionably slanted over her long, brazenly *out-of-the-bottle* red locks completed the ensemble.

If there were a Widow's Weeds magazine, the widow von Grettle could easily be voted playwidow of the month. And if there were a Tramps R Us magazine, Britney Priest von Grettle would be the sleazy publication's all-time favorite cover girl.

Fighting the urge to succumb to an emerging head-to-toe shudder, Mindy hiked back her shoulders, elevated her chin, and looked the widow von Grettle right in her heavily mascaraed eyes. Her lashes looked so chunky it was a miracle she could keep her eyelids from drooping shut.

It was clear Britney didn't recognize Mindy. And why should she? Eighteen months had passed and more than a hundred pounds of fat had been painstakingly shed from Mindy's frame since she last saw Britney, or Edward for that matter. Compared to her mortifying high of just over three hundred pounds, Mindy was positively svelte now.

That wasn't all that had changed in the last year and a half. Gone was the limp, drab-brown hair and in its place glistened bouncy blonde curls, the color of sunlit honey. Granted, Mindy's golden locks were also straight out of the bottle, but at least they *looked* as though they could have been God-given, unlike Britney's clownish red-orange hue.

Now when Mindy looked in the mirror, instead of chubby chipmunk cheeks, she saw an elegantly sculpted face, with blessed little hollows under newly visible cheekbones.

The chalky pallor resulting from the no-makeup, natural look she'd dutifully adopted according to Edward's wishes during their ten-year marriage had been trashed. Instead, Mindy's attractive features were flawlessly accented with makeup. In fact, the only original telltale visages left were her large blue eyes and full, generous lips.

Today, doing her best to exude the allure of a *Vogue* model, she wore a superbly tailored black wool suit—just slightly snug. So proud of the fact that it came from an upscale department store's misses section rather than a plus-size store, Mindy had been half-temped to wear it inside out so everyone could see the garment tag and size.

A wicked bit of scarlet lace from her camisole peeked out at the v-neck closure. A slash of crimson lipstick, garnet earrings and a red silk carnation on her lapel completed Mindy's carefully chosen *farewell and fuck you* outfit. The beautiful, ultra-chic woman who stood before the widow von Grettle was a deliberate, painstakingly designed creation.

So what if that creation's heart was playing a frenzied game of ping pong inside her chest? As long as Mindy played her cards right, no one, especially Britney, would ever suspect that Mindy felt like a frightened, intimidated, overwhelmed little girl inside. Or that she was on the verge of crying, breaking out in hives, and throwing up. All at the same time.

Clearly clueless as to Mindy's identity, Britney Priest von Grettle rendered a bland, obligatory *hello* as she extended a limp hand. "Thank you for coming," she said, giving Mindy the same compulsory little welcome speech she'd no doubt given everyone else who strode by Edward's casket that morning. No, there was still no seed of recognition apparent. The widow von Grettle's kohl-rimmed eyes were glazed over with disinterest as she rattled off her apathetic little spiel.

Disregarding the handshake overture, Mindy relished the moment, squelching the burgeoning urge to smoosh her hand into the woman's face hard enough to send Britney careening backward, ultimately landing her on top of her dearly departed husband.

"Hello, Britney," Mindy hissed, hoping she'd managed to keep the nervous quavering in her voice to a minimum. It was only after hearing Mindy speak that Britney's detached gaze crystallized, widening in shocked disbelief.

"You!" Britney furrowed her eyebrows and stiffened. "What the fuck are *you* doing here?" The once-over she gave Mindy was so caustic it could have cut through hardened enamel.

Fortifying herself with a deep breath, Mindy resolutely maintained her poise as she mustered the courage to converse with the woman she despised above all others. She'd waited a year and a half for this opportunity, ingesting little more than salad, steamed veggies and skinned chicken. And now Mindy was terrified she'd get cold feet and the words she'd rehearsed so carefully would stick in her throat like peanut butter.

Mindora von G, don't you dare even think about chickening out now! Holding her head high and beaming a narrow-eyed glare straight into Britney Priest's dog-poop-brown eyes, Mindy cleared her throat, ignoring the thunderous thumping of her chicken-shit little heart.

"After all, Britney dear, Edward was my husband before he was yours," Mindy managed matter-of-factly. Fluffing her hair in a calculated manner, she conjured a coy little smile.

Never breaking eye contact with her nemesis, Mindy swallowed the lump in her throat. Her thoughts raced as she mentally urged herself to continue, to override the commanding case of nerves gripping her. It wasn't in her nature to be deliberately cruel. Forcing out the acerbic words she'd planned to say to Britney was harder than she'd expected. But if she left without saying them, she knew she'd regret it.

"By the way, is the rumor true?" Mindy said nonchalantly. "I hear Edward keeled over with a heart attack smack dab in the throes of passion. With another woman. A much *younger* woman, in fact."

Pausing for effect, Mindy studied Britney's deliciously livid reaction. If the widow von Grettle's eyes grew any wider, Mindy feared they'd pop right out of her skull, bouncing down the red carpet runner that led from Edward's casket.

Satisfied her words had generated the desired effect, Mindy found new courage and continued. "My, how distressing that must have been for you, Britney dear. Why, I can't possibly imagine how embarrassed you... Oh!" Mindy touched her fingers to her mouth, tittering a demure little laugh.

"Silly me," she went on. "But *of course* I can imagine it. How foolish of me to forget that I caught you screwing my husband right in my own bed just over eighteen months ago."

Mindy finally released the wicked smile that had been clawing at the inside of her face, begging to escape. "Well, as they say, Britney, what goes around comes around. Now if you'll excuse me."

Oh God, oh God, oh God, she'd done it! She'd said it all without keeling over in a dead faint.

Now all she wanted to do was get the hell out of there and away from the mountain of painful memories cascading over her like an avalanche.

As Mindy sidestepped, Britney grabbed the sleeve of her suit.

"Not so fast, you little bitch."

Damn.

"*Little*?" Batting her eyelashes, Mindy's her hand flew to the base of her throat. "Why thank you for the lovely compliment, Britney. I'm truly flattered."

A depraved smile crept across Britney's hollow-cheeked features as she gave Mindy a piercing appraisal. "I don't care how much weight you lose, Mindy. You'll always be a cow as far as I'm concerned," she snarled through clenched teeth. "A big, fat, frumpy, repulsive heifer."

Licking the angry spittle from her stoplight-red lips, Britney clearly strained to keep her voice a near whisper. "Let me see...what was Edward's favorite pet name for you again? Oh yes, his little warthog." Scrutinizing Mindy as if she were fly-larva, Britney tapped a finger against her angular chin in an assessing manner. "Yes, even with the weight loss, the term definitely still fits."

"At least I'm not a devious, henna-headed, husband-stealing, belly-crawling viper," Mindy calmly countered with a half-smile. Her gaze fell to Britney's chest and Mindy almost laughed. "With ridiculously huge fake tits," she added. The little bee-stung breasts she remembered eyeing eighteen months ago had been replaced with so much plastic and silicone Mindy was amazed Britney's scrawny frame didn't topple over.

Tightening her grasp on Mindy's sleeve, Britney yanked her closer. "Nobody had to steal Edward from you, Mindy. You and all that disgusting flab of yours pushed him away. I just happened to snag him as he was trying to escape from that repulsive mountain of flesh, that's all." Britney flashed a sinister smile.

Mindy fought to keep the rising tide of old insecurities from making her cower.

"Sure, Mindy, you can get thin, dye your hair and slap makeup all over your plain-Jane, farm-girl face but you know what they say...you can't make a silk purse out of a sow's ear. And in your case..." Britney jutted her chin high, uttering a deep guttural laugh. "We're talking about more than just a sow's ear. We're talking the whole fucking sow. Oink, oink." Her sharp cackle curdled in Mindy's ears. "It's no wonder the thought of sleeping with you made Edward's skin crawl."

Her stomach roiling from a wave of nausea that wasn't helped by the cloying stench of Britney's cheap perfume, Mindy yanked her arm away, brushing at the bunched fabric.

The woman's spiteful comments scorched like a jalapeño pepper poultice over an open, albeit old, wound. Mindy was angry with herself for allowing it to hurt so damned much. For an instant she found herself wishing she could glom onto some chocolate and find a nice hole under the mortuary floorboards to crawl into where she could feed her face and escape having to deal with Britney. But she'd come too far and worked too hard to let herself crumble now.

Whatever you do, don't let Britney see you flustered. Remember, you're cool, slender and sophisticated now. You've had eighteen months of practice, Mindora von G...you can do this. You. Can. Do. This.

With a quick look left and right, Mindy straightened her shoulders, elevating her head proudly as she spoke down to Brit the Bitch. "It must be terrible for you to have to bury your husband, Britney," she said quietly. "Did I mention how truly sad it makes me that you can't join him?"

If anyone had been within hearing distance Mindy knew damned well she'd come off sounding like a cold, callous, unfeeling bitch. Hell, she even sounded like one to herself, but both she and Britney knew better.

Once again, Britney's eyes grew so wide Mindy half-expected they'd pop right out of their sockets, dangling from little springs.

"Why you-you," Britney sputtered. "You contemptible, wretched little cunt. You listen to me, Mindy von Grettle," she jabbed a bony finger at Mindy's breastbone, "this is *my* day. You don't have any business being here." Britney's face became a kaleidoscope of colors that Mindy had never remembered seeing before on a human being all at one time.

"If Edward could get up out of that coffin," Britney spat, "he'd kick you out himself. So why don't you just haul your fat ass out of here?"

"On the contrary, Britney," Mindy countered. "If Edward could get up out of that coffin, the first thing he'd concern himself with is finding a bouncy little twenty-something to hump one last time before they put him in the ground."

Britney opened her mouth to speak but before she had a chance to retort she and Mindy were joined by a man so striking, tall, and remarkable he stole Mindy's breath away for a moment.

Suddenly aware her jaw was slack and she was in danger of drooling—which might discredit her sophisticated, cool-as-iced-vodka performance—Mindy snapped her mouth shut. Her gaze scanned his princely frame crisply tailored in a charcoal gray suit. While exuding rough, raw animal magnetism he still managed to look polished, refined. Confident. Powerful. He veritably glistened with style and class.

This was the too-perfect, too-gorgeous, too-sexy kind of man who'd always intimidated the hell out of Mindy.

"Britney, aren't you going to introduce me to the lady?" He flashed Mindy a dazzling smile, seemingly unaware the women were in the throes of a seething verbal joust and fiercely glaring at each other. Britney stammered, obviously at a loss for words. With an outstretched finger she frantically gestured toward Mindy but still no words came forth. Finally, expelling an exasperated grumble, she threw her hands into the air, spun on one stiletto heel and marched off.

The impressive specimen of man turned to watch Britney parading determinedly toward the coffee room and Mindy seized the opportunity to inspect his backside. Mmm-hmm, his ass was definitely squeeze-worthy.

"Well," he shrugged, "it appears Britney is somewhat, uh...distraught. Understandably, of course." He motioned toward the casket and shook his head in an *isn't-it-a-shame-about-the-dead-guy* gesture.

"Oh yeah, of course," Mindy huffed through a sneer. "The poor grieving widow and all that." With a flick of her wrist she tossed off an acerbic laugh. When the handsome stranger slanted her a curious look Mindy realized her response may have smacked of a bit too much contempt.

Embarrassed, she cleared her throat. "I'm sorry. I, uh, I guess we all handle grief in different ways." She offered as contrite a smile as possible. "I'm not real good at these things," she said, motioning toward Edward's casket.

"Sure, I understand," the hunk said softly, with a smile that was scintillatingly sexy and compassionate at the same time.

It was at that precise moment Mindy noticed he had the most beautiful brown eyes she'd ever seen. Like two big, glistening chocolate chips. And he smelled fabulous. Of fresh soap and spring mountain air. His thick shock of hair, the color of dark-roast Sumatra coffee, with its errant lock lingering just above his eye, begged to be ruffled. Good God, what an absolutely delicious-looking confection he was.

Mindy felt her shoulders slump as realization set in. Tall, gorgeous and great-smelling or not, there was absolutely no way she had any interest in getting to know any of Britney Priest von Grettle's...*friends*. Even if the grieving widow's paramours *were* impossibly handsome and forty steps up the evolutional ladder from Edward. Of course, there was always the slight possibility Mr. Tall, Dark and Handsome was one of Edward's acquaintances and not Britney's. Mindy decided she owed it to herself to find out.

"So, you and Britney know each other?" she asked with a trickle of hope.

"That's an understatement." A chortle caught in his throat. "Oh yeah, we know each other all right. I guess it looks like we'll have to take care of the introductions ourselves." He extended his hand. "The name's Archer. Britney and I are—"

Former lovers? Current lovers? Sexting buddies? Eeew, eeew, eeew. This definitely wasn't something Mindy wanted to hear.

Expelling a sigh of regret, she interrupted. "Look, I'm really sorry, Mr. Archer." She pumped his large hand once before releasing it, surprised at the spark of current that seemed to arc between them. "I don't mean to be rude but I really need to get some fresh air. *Now*." Flashing a half smile as she brushed by him, she ignored the saucy little tingles teasing up and down her spine and lingering between her thighs. She hurried to retrieve her coat and scarf from the back of the viewing room.

Sprinting after Mindy as she entered the main lobby of the funeral parlor, the Adonis-like Mr. Archer asked, "Are you all right? Can I give you a lift or anything?"

"I'm fine. Just fine," she said, turning to walk backward. *I just need to get the smell of death and the odor of that nauseating bitch*

Britney out of my nostrils, she wanted to say but thought better of it. "Thanks for the offer though."

Probably an afternoon of tooling around in a car sitting next to a gorgeous hunk of man would do her a world of good but there was no way in hell Mindy wanted anything to do with any of Britney's leftovers, regardless of how meaty and appetizing they might be. Shuddering at the unsavory thought of sharing yet another man with Britney, Mindy waved and turned forward, quickening her pace.

She couldn't get out of that place fast enough. Being surrounded by people grieving for their loved ones laid out in the various visitation rooms at the funeral home made her feel uneasy and guilty. Really, really guilty. She tried, she honestly *did* try to remember the good times with Edward and treasure those memories. But those moments were few and far between, almost as if they'd happened to another woman. In essence, they had.

As Mindy bolted for the great double doors, one thought overruled all others... *Good Lord, I'm in serious need of a mega-chocolate fix.*

Exhaling the dead, stale air of the mortuary, Mindy filled her lungs with the sunlit, crackling-cold January air.

"Yeah, yeah, I know chocolate won't heal the hurt," she grumbled. Flicking her hand through the air as if to banish the intruding thoughts, Mindy audibly argued with the flourishing inner voice of her chastising conscience. "But it'll be an unbeatable temporary Band-Aid." She laughed and licked her lips as she sprinted to her car.

"Just when I thought I was becoming a real tough cookie, I let my eggshell-plated ego get deflated by a few crass remarks from that detestable bitch. Well, I refuse to let that skinny, venomous crone succeed in shattering my ego." With a broad smile she nodded with firm resolve. "Take a deep breath, Mindora von G...everything's going to be okay."

Once in the car, she dabbed at the nervous perspiration that had formed above her upper lip. The winter breeze was cool and brisk so it certainly wasn't from the heat. She was immensely glad she'd switched days off at the travel agency so she could have the rest of the day to herself. She needed time to patch her jumbled thoughts together.

What in the hell would she use for motivation to lose those last sticky twenty pounds now that Edward was dead? She'd had it all planned. It would have been exceptionally perfect.

As soon as she got down to a sleek just-this-side-of-emaciated single-digit size, Mindy would have arranged an *accidental* meeting with Edward. She'd show up swathed in something dangerously provocative. Of course, with Edward having been a breast-man, she'd have her already ample bosom flared up and out to its absolute maximum potential by wearing one of those amazingly engineered bras.

When Edward got a load of how sensationally sexy, ultra-sophisticated and knitting-needle-slender she was, that sucker would have been down on his knees, tripping over his tongue, begging, pleading, beseeching to have her back.

And then, as the smarmy bastard knelt at her skinny feet, simpering without an ounce of pride, Mindy would laugh in his face. Laugh! Tell him she found him pitifully revolting. Rest her five-inch stiletto heel on his face, push him to the ground and stroll off to link arms and lock lips with the incredibly gorgeous muscle-bound hunk hungrily panting for her just a few steps away from Edward.

The only glitch was that Mindy didn't have any gorgeous hunks panting in the wings—hungrily or otherwise. Her only viable options were to contact some rent-a-stud agency and pay through the nose, or talk her boss, Leo, into setting her up with one of his splendidly put together body-builder friends from the gym.

The fact all of Leo's buff-buddies were gay was a minor technicality as far as Mindy was concerned. As long as the guy looked like a Greek god and put on a good enough show to convince Edward that Mindy was his sex goddess, that would do the trick.

It would have been her ultimate triumph. Her magnificent grand finale. And then the rat bastard had to go and shoot her neat little plan all to hell by dying and cheating Mindy out of her well-deserved, long-awaited moment of blissful revenge.

Selfish, thoughtless sonuvabitch.

About a mile from her townhouse, her car somehow shifted into automatic pilot, magically transporting her to a favorite bastion of chocoholic bliss, Butterball Bakery. Her amazing wonder car had spontaneously delivered her to similarly calorific spots over the years.

Even with the car's windows closed, the glorious aroma of chocolate infused the air, causing Mindy to salivate. Putting her magic transporter in park, she swallowed hard and went inside for the first time in eighteen months.

Blissfully enveloped in the luscious, sensuous bouquet of chocolate, Mindy's educated gaze darted from one groaning bakery case to the next. The familiar aroma was like a comfortable old afghan, begging to blanket Mindy's wounds and offer a magical, albeit temporary, respite.

Artistically embellished creations seemed to frolic behind the glass bakery cases imploring Mindy, *Pick me! Please take me home with you*! It was the same gut-gnawing feeling she got when visiting the dog pound. She wanted to take all of them home.

Inhaling long and slow, as if to permanently imprint her olfactory nerves with the heady scent, Mindy closed her eyes for a moment. Exhaling, she felt her features relax into a serene smile. The sensational scents, the appetizing aromas, were enough to satisfy her. She could turn around and march right out of there now, feeling appeased and content.

"I'll have one of those nut-studded, caramel-topped fudge brownies," she said, surprising herself, but feeling downright virtuous and proud for resisting the urge to buy out the place. One little brownie wouldn't hurt anything. It's what any average woman might order.

"Anything else?" The dour-faced middle-aged bakery clerk asked. How anyone working in such glorious, intimate proximity to chocolate could possibly remain so thin, not to mention sport such pruney expression, was beyond Mindy's comprehension.

Nope, that'll do it. All I need is this one satisfying little morsel of chocolate to fully quench my emotional hunger.

"Yes. I'll take a chocolate éclair...and one of those mousse-filled cupcakes with the chocolate shavings and whipped cream."

Flabbergasted, Mindy whipped her head around, wondering who the hell had just spoken. More than a little dismayed to discover she was the only customer in the bakery, she blurted, "Oh my God, that was me!" Slapping her hand over her mouth, she peered up at the clerk, who eyed her warily as she assembled a small bakery box. All Mindy could do was offer a sheepish smile.

"Huh? I didn't get that last part," the cheerless clerk said. Shifting her weight to one side, she faced Mindy with a balled fist planted at her hip. "Was there something else you wanted to add to your order?"

No. Absolutely not. No way. Not on your life. Just wrap up my shameful chocolate indiscretion in a plain brown paper bag and let me get the hell out of here.

"Yes, I'll take half a pound of those chocolate-filled butter cookies, and a couple pecan-encrusted chocolate-rum truffle balls."

Breathing in an audible gasp, Mindy's heart raced as her brain tried to tell her something she most definitely did not want to hear.

Mopping the perspiration from her forehead and upper lip, she said, "I, um, I think that should be enough...for my guests. You see, I'm having a luncheon for several friends and want to be sure I have enough goodies for them." She glanced at the woman behind the counter, who had discarded the small box in favor of a more substantial one befitting an out-of-control chocoholic's purchase, and wondered if the woman knew there would be no guests.

Old habits die hard. Mindy suspected that, when she weighed three hundred pounds, food clerks knew damn well the guest list included no one but Mindy. But maybe now that she blended in with people of more normal weight, they might buy it because she didn't *look* like a binge eater.

"Of course," Mindy babbled through nervous laughter, "I can't touch this stuff myself. Diet, you know. Yup, it's just going to be raw veggies with fat-free dip for me." She couldn't stop her giddy laughter. "But I know my guests will enjoy these treats."

Offering an indifferent glance, the clerk shrugged and continued to pack the gargantuan bakery box.

Oh for God's sake shut up and quit your incessant babbling, Mindora! After all, it wasn't as if old prune face behind the counter gave a damn if Mindy had a hundred people coming over or if she planned to stuff every last morsel into her own greedy little face.

Mindy sucked in a deep breath. "Just add one of those chocolate croissants and a small slice of the flourless chocolate torte and that'll do it."

Once at home, Mindy lowered the garage door before exiting her car. There was no reason the neighbors had to glimpse the remnants of the bakery box she'd savagely torn open in the car. The news would travel the neighborhood grapevine at breakneck speed.

Yup, knew all along that bubble-butted von Grettle woman would bulk up again—just like two pounds of sausage in a one-pound casing.

She cringed at the all-too-real likelihood. "Will you *puhleeze* get a grip! Nobody gives a damn if you decide to feed your face non-stop from now until doomsday. Stop feeling so guilty about one lousy little chocolate binge for chrissakes."

Her beautiful black wool suit was powdered with confectioner's sugar from the half pound of butter cookies she'd already scarfed down on the short ride home from the bakery. Rolling her eyes skyward, she brushed at her lapels. "Nice going, greedo," she chastised herself. "At least you could have waited until you got inside the house."

But then bakery cookies always tasted better when eaten in a moving vehicle. There had always been something wantonly sinful about gobbling down food in the car. Like other dieters, Mindy had somehow reasoned the calories were negated if the items were eaten while in motion.

Heaving a tuneful sigh as she entered her townhouse, she struggled to hold the torn bakery box together. In an instant, a gleeful little brown dog scrambled around the corner to greet his mistress, and investigate the wonderfully odoriferous cardboard container. Depositing her dilapidated chocolate treasure box on the kitchen counter, Mindy bent to gather the frisky pup in her arms.

"Hey there, Cadbury, how's my best buddy today?" The sprightly mutt, named after one of her favorite chocolate brands, sniffed the air while licking his chops. Slanting Mindy his most charming expression, he gave a little whimper.

"Nope, sorry, Cad." She wagged her finger. Chocolate's poisonous for dogs." She went to the cupboard and withdrew a plastic container filled with her own homemade dog biscuits. Cadbury went wild, temporarily forgetting about the bakery box.

Giving Cadbury the command to stay, Mindy held a biscuit under his nose. "There's absolutely nothing wrong with my freely giving in to this well-deserved little chocolate binge and enjoying every last sugar-laden, fat-drenched crumb, is there, Cadbury?" As she waved the dog biscuit from left to right his head instinctively followed, resulting in what looked like an agreement on the dog's part.

"Good boy." She tossed him the biscuit. "You're one of the only males I can count on to give me a sensible, unbiased opinion." Smiling, she scratched her adorable rescue dog behind the ears. He immediately rolled onto his back, presenting his belly for attention.

Wrinkling her nose, Mindy sniffed the air. "Good grief. What is that foul stench?" As if he understood, Cadbury stopped pumping his legs and slanted his mistress a wide-eyed, muzzle-licking expression of dread.

Patting his belly, Mindy chuckled. "Don't worry, little buddy. It's not you. You're a good boy." Bounding to his feet, the little dog raced to the sliding glass patio door, fixing a deliberate expression toward Mindy. "Gotcha. You want to make sure you stay a good boy, right, Cad?"

Once Cadbury was in the yard tending to his business, Mindy resumed sniffing, recoiling when she got a whiff of her sleeve where Britney had grabbed her. "Ugh! That's Britney's putrid perfume!" Hastily shrugging off her powdered sugar and now dog-hair-covered jacket, Mindy held it at arm's length. "Can't have that offensive odor intruding on my chocolate indulgence, now can I?" Curling her lip, she whipped the jacket into the utility room and closed the door.

When Cadbury returned, Mindy gifted him with a new rawhide bone to distract him. Giddy with anticipation, she turned on the TV, going to her DVR recordings and selecting one of her favorite old romcom movies, Rock Hudson and Doris Day cavorting in *Pillow Talk*. Nearly crazed with chocolate anticipation, she plopped onto the cushy family room sofa and proceeded to ply herself with her precious cache of bakery goodies.

She could always depend on chocolate to provide a satisfying, all-encompassing rush, probably like the high cocaine addicts got, she imagined. Except snorting cocaine didn't put fat on your hips. Of course, she could always try snorting cocoa powder. If desperate enough, a raging chocoholic might very well entertain such a manic idea.

In what seemed like the blink of an eye, she was done bingeing, and facing Cadbury's eager prancing as he sniffed the leftover tidbits. Glancing at the clock, Mindy saw just over forty minutes had passed since she'd attacked the chocolate goodies with a vengeance. Patting the sofa cushion, she invited Cadbury to join her, enticing him with one of the dog biscuits she'd pocketed earlier.

Watching the tall, dark, handsome Rock trip over himself to win back Doris' affections in the latter part of the movie, Mindy heaved a sigh. "Why isn't real life like that," she asked Cad. "What's a girl gotta do to find herself a drop-dead gorgeous hunk of man who'll cherish her forever, hmmm?"

Drawing the furry pup against her aching, bulging stomach, Mindy bellowed a mighty yawn, sank against the paisley pillows on her couch and fell asleep.

Monet-like impressions floated across her mind, creating improbably wild dreamscapes.

Decked out like a fluffy ballerina from *Swan Lake*, Mindy's frolicking feet tiptoed across meadows of chocolate daffodils carrying her to Edward's grave, which was littered with used condoms and an array of women's panties.

There she stripped off her garments, revealing the flawless, worship-worthy body of a goddess. Cavorting breezily in the nude, she nibbled on the daffodil petals, while kicking the panties and condoms aside. She lifted her voice to the heavens, singing *ding-dong, the bastard's gone*, with gleeful abandon.

Her conscious mind intruding, Mindy shifted in her sleep, becoming vaguely aware of the offensiveness of her act. Soon the naked Mindy-ballerina pirouetted away from the gravesite and into the waiting arms of Rock Hudson, who morphed into the unbearably handsome Mr. Archer instead. He wore nothing but a loincloth. While she didn't remember any fierce Tarzan types in *Swan Lake*, the brief scrap of suede suited dream boy to perfection.

Clad only in pink satin toe shoes, Mindy offered the ultimate token of friendship a chocoholic can bestow—to share her chocolate daffodil. Scooping Mindy into his powerful arms, the muscled, chocolate-drop-eyed hunk nibbled on Mindy's ear, which had somehow turned into chocolate.

"If you like that, Mr. Archer, I have something else you might like to nibble on," the carefree, brazenly bare Mindy offered in a sultry tone. She nailed him with the hottest come-hither look she could manage, while skimming her body with her hands, molding her breasts, waist and hips as she worked her way down to the vee between her thighs.

As if she weighed no more than a dainty Snickers bar, her buff dream man lifted her into the air, high enough to align her pretty pink lady parts with his mouth.

"Oh yes," she told him. "Closer...closer...you're almost there."

Just as he was about to swipe his tongue over her eager flesh, a bony, ghoul-like apparition of Britney Priest von Grettle pranced through the air toward them from Edward's grave.

Her scraggily red locks transforming into hissing snakes, Britney erupted with cackles sharp enough to crack glass blocks. Spitting venom and fire, with a wave of her gray-fleshed hand,

Britney turned all the opulent chocolate daffodils into doll-sized replicas of Edward who were actually squirming squids in disguise.

Horrified, Mindy locked her arms around Mr. Archer's brawny neck only to discover that the stud had morphed into the mighty squid king. Dropping Mindy like a weighty sack of rotting potatoes, he propelled himself to Britney's side, groveling adoringly at her skeletal feet.

Waking up with a start, Mindy jettisoned the tattered remains of her bakery box against the TV, smacking Rock Hudson squarely in the kisser.

Chapter 2

INFUSED WITH A mega-chocolate hangover, Mindy crawled out of bed an hour early to get ready for work. Several brisk facial attacks with an ice-cold washcloth did little to hide the puffy, telltale traces of yesterday's calorie-packed indiscretion. Dispirited, she let out a sickly groan upon discovering every outfit in the whole damn closet seemed to fit too snug.

Left with no choice, she invaded the *just in case you become a big fat ass again* boxes of multi-sized clothes stored under her bed. The navy blazer and slacks she settled on were a roomy one size bigger.

"It's just about that time of month," she announced, studying her bloated reflection in the bedroom's full-length mirror. "So it's because of PMS." A creeping sneer emphasized the fact that her valiant attempt at being convincing was failing miserably. "It has nothing whatsoever to do with the fact that I stuffed my face with a month's worth of chocolate in one sitting."

Crossing her hands over her puffed-out belly, a sigh of disgust escaped Mindy's sneer. As she performed a final mirror check, sucking in her gut so hard she almost passed out, she noticed Cadbury assessing her while he sat with his head quizzically cocked to the side.

"Yeah, I know," Mindy said. "Your mommy's not a very pretty sight this morning, is she, Cad?" Responding with a mournful whimper, the pup turned on his heels and scampered away. Laughing, Mindy returned her attention to her reflection. Curling her lip, she heaved a dispassionate shrug as she slapped her hand against the wall, flicking off the light switch.

Her thoughts were such a blur, Mindy barely remembered the drive to work. All she could focus on were the chanting chastisements from her ever present know-it-all conscience. Damn, how she wished she could ball up that sanctimonious goody-two-shoes inner voice and hurl it from her car window, then back over it a few times just for good measure.

Once settled behind her desk at Persimmon Travel agency, Mindy attempted the near impossible, to organize the germinating mountain of work and the murky sea of her jumbled thoughts at the same time.

Scanning her messages, she noted Dawn Farley and Rob Lyons were stopping by to pick up the documents for their honeymoon cruise on the *Sunset Dawn*. They were convinced finding a cruise ship with the same name as the bride-to-be was a good omen. *A good omen*. Heaving a sigh, Mindy smiled.

"Poor, starry-eyed kids," she muttered while checking her email. "They're such a cute young couple, innocent, sweet and so much in love. I hope to God their lives together will be better than mine and Edward's." A sneer twitched at Mindy's lip. "Of course *that* wouldn't be much of a stretch."

An email from the Pavchek sisters said they'd be in to pick up documents for their all-inclusive Jamaica vacation. Mindy chuckled as she eyed their paperwork. Vera and Alma Pavchek were the wildest, gaudiest pair of wrinkled old spinsters. But, God bless 'em, the cheeky sisters really knew how to relish life. The sad part was that the old gals' love lives were packed with more vitality than Mindy could even imagine. Love life? Hah! What love life?

The years with Edward had been a waste. Like a big black hole full of misery, angst and struggle for acceptance and affection.

As she sipped from her mug of strong coffee, Mindy recalled the Saturday night nearly twelve years earlier when she'd received a call from a real estate agent whose buyer wanted to make an offer on one of her listings. That was the night she met Edward von Grettle. In her mid-twenties, Mindy was fresh, young, attractive and naïvely idealistic. She couldn't help rolling her eyes, giving in to a gargantuan sigh at the biting memory.

At a fit, well-proportioned weight, she was slender and a real go-getter. Diamond Real Estate's top listing sales person for the region four months in a row.

"Ah, but that wasn't my only youthful claim to fame." Mindy chuckled as she flipped through her files. Back then, much to her chagrin, she was also probably the last twenty-something virgin in all of Chicagoland.

"What was that, Mindy?"

Snagged out of her musings, Mindy glanced up to see Yolanda Gladstone, one of the other travel agents, smiling at her. "Nothing." Mindy returned the woman's smile. "Just talking to myself as usual." She sniffed the air and her eyes grew wide. "I smell chocolate."

"Triple chocolate brownies," Yolanda offered proudly.

Even with yesterday's binge setback behind her, like a true addict, Mindy felt the familiar, lip-licking tug of desire take hold deep in her gut.

Offering a wicked smile, the plump, eye-catching Yolanda wagged her finger. "I know that look. Hands off, Mindy. These are for Felix Garcia. He's coming in to book another trip this afternoon."

"I see," Mindy said with a knowing grin. Yolanda had been doing her best to seize Felix's attention by wearing more provocative clothes and plying the man with home-baked goodies.

As she plopped into her desk chair, Yolanda nodded. "He's going to ask me out this time. I just know it. I could tell by the tentative tone of his voice when he called me to tell me he was stopping by today. Plus Leo said he could feel it in his bones."

"Oh, well then it *has* to be." Mindy offered a warm smile. It's not that she actually put any stock in her boss's inexhaustible, supposedly psychic predictions, but she truly hoped Yolanda and Felix would finally get together. She was a darling and Felix seemed like a truly nice, albeit terribly shy, guy.

Why the hell couldn't Mindy have fallen in love with someone like the sweet, bashful Felix instead of Edward?

Standing about an inch taller than Mindy's five-feet-nine-inches, Edward von Grettle wasn't what most women would have considered a knockout. He had a trim build, dark brown hair and black eyes—wild eyes, always darting this way and that, so as not to miss any action. It was his dynamic personality that initially attracted Mindy. Proud, charming, aggressive, flirtatious. He had an unmistakable air of power about him that she found impressive and exciting.

Little did she know he'd eventually use that power to keep her subjugated.

She breathed a sigh at the stinging memory. What a naïve young woman she'd been.

Edward had wined and dined her, pressing her until she finally agreed to marry him. She'd offered herself chaste and eager to experience the fabulous exploding-rocket magic of passionate physical union for the first time on their wedding night. Almost immediately after their aisle-walk, Mindy's life mutated into a hapless existence that finally left her emotionally bankrupt and void of any love for her husband.

Exploding-rocket magic my ass. Mindy downed another sip of coffee. The only explosion she'd experienced during that night of cherry-popping sex was the thunderous collapse of her naïve, romantic expectations. Unlike romance novels and movies, real-life sex was something rushed, coarse, brutal and ugly.

Edward's incessant badgering about her giving up the real estate career she loved and had worked so hard to build began on the honeymoon. After all, he couldn't have anyone think he wasn't able to properly provide for his wife, could he?

Caving in to the first of his selfish demands, Mindy unknowingly set her husband's warped blueprint for their marriage into motion. It took years for her to realize what Edward *really* feared was the all-too-real possibility that his wife might defame him by proving herself to be the real estate star in the family.

By the time Mindy comprehended the situation, she'd already been sucked down into the dismal bog of Edward's distorted vision and felt trapped.

The wording on the travel documents in her hands blurred and Mindy's gaze narrowed as she remembered Edward's asinine series of edicts. He'd demanded she refrain from any enhancement that might even remotely suggest she was something more than a living, breathing asexual lump of nothingness. No makeup, no form-fitting clothes, no shorts, and no glimpses of her ample cleavage. From then on Edward was the only one who would see her curves.

She was not to visit him at his office—he didn't want the other salespeople to think he was henpecked. His shirts and boxer shorts were to be starched and ironed. The sheets were to be washed and ironed twice a week. The house had to be beyond spotless and impeccably organized to please his manic neat-freak tendencies.

"Prissy, compulsive, controlling bastard," Mindy found herself mumbling under her breath as she double-checked the Pavcheks' travel documents.

Mindy's real epiphany came one evening when she'd accidentally overcooked Edward's steak. It was cooked just past the point of being bloody enough to moo an *ouch* when pricked with his fork. The man's diatribe was deafening. Within minutes his verbal tirade was coupled with physical abuse. All because his goddamn steak wasn't rare enough.

For some unfathomable, godforsaken reason, the previously plucky Mindy knuckled under rather than grabbing what was left of her self-esteem, shoving it into a suitcase and hustling like hell to get away from the bastard.

God, she'd been such a doormat.

Clueless back then as to how to prevent her spunky personality from vanishing, she'd turned to the only thing that gave her any solace. Food. With the velvety smooth tranquilizing effects of chocolate foremost on her list of densely caloric sedatives.

Forty-five cocoa-buttery pounds heavier and counting at their first wedding anniversary, Mindy was subject to Edward's incessant ragging about her weight. Cruel, stabbing comments that cut her right to the core and had her clawing the walls until she could sedate herself with another dose of chocolate.

Mindy's lips quirked into a half smile, recalling that a couple of years later, Edward had stopped having sex with her.

Hallelujah! She toasted the air with her coffee mug. Actually, Edward had shunned her sexually except when he came home drunk. It was difficult to judge his sobriety by his sexual performance, which varied little. Mindy would squeeze her eyes tight, clutching the bedding while Edward popped that swollen little thumb-sized doohickey of his out of his pants to impose his customary two minutes of brusque, selfish needs on her.

She was left bruised, red and swollen with no pleasure to compensate for the pain he'd inflicted with slaps, pinches and punches.

Pompous little prick. Mindy huffed a grim laugh as she slammed a desk drawer. Wham, bam, without the thank you ma'am. Lord, if she could only go back in time knowing then what she did now.

The fatter Mindy got the less Edward touched her—sexually *or* abusively—which was the only benefit of watching herself transform into a shapeless blob. When Edward started sleeping in his downstairs study, telling Mindy that being in the same bed with all those disgusting rolls of fat made him gag, Mindy sent up a jubilant prayer of thanksgiving to the benevolent god of chocolate.

On the weekends Edward was seldom home before four in the morning, which suited her just fine. Since the average real estate deal is rarely finalized between midnight and dawn, Mindy figured it was a safe bet that lover-boy was out screwing around. Why on earth any woman would actually *want* to purposely engage in sex with Edward was light-years beyond her comprehension.

"Thumbkin," Mindy said, looking up from her paperwork and giggling as she wiggled her thumb, recalling her secret nickname for that annoying little member between Edward's legs. She couldn't even refer to it as a cock. His itty-bitty dick wasn't deserving of the term.

Upon reaching a whopping three hundred pounds something finally snapped—besides the pine legs of a kitchen chair during dinner one night. A bloated, lethargic caricature of her former self, Mindy was desperate to recapture her sanity.

She'd enjoyed her years working in real estate, except for having to deal with overly aggressive, cutthroat agents. While the money was good, it was the feeling of satisfaction, of knowing she'd helped pair people with their ideal homes, that motivated her.

But Mindy didn't want to work in the same industry as Edward. She needed to take her life in an entirely new direction. Travel! She'd always had a desire to see the world. As a travel agent, she could help people plan and book their vacations and business trips, as well as visit destinations herself. While the money may not be as lucrative as real estate, the sense of job satisfaction and happiness would match what she'd experienced selling homes.

Guffawing when she announced she was enrolling in school to become a travel agent, Edward offered his *good wishes*. "Who the fuck do you think is going to make any travel arrangements with a whale like you?" he'd graciously asked. "Hey, if they've got a chair wide enough to accommodate your big fat ass, then go ahead and knock your socks off, Moby Dick."

Ah yes, the man had certainly had a way with words.

It was a Tuesday night, Mindy remembered as she scooted to the coffeepot for a refill. Computer training night at the Persimmon School of Travel. The computers were down and the class had been rescheduled. Arriving home about two hours earlier than usual, she heard what sounded like the television coming from her bedroom. She couldn't imagine why Edward was up there watching TV instead of downstairs in his study.

Huffing and puffing the way she always did lumbering up that long flight of stairs, Mindy realized it wasn't the television, but Edward's voice she heard. Edward's and someone else's. A woman's.

Reaching the doorway to her bedroom, she saw them. Some toothpick with chili-pepper-red hair halfway down her spiny back was straddling Edward. And they were fucking.

Her heart vaulting into her throat, Mindy froze. "Edward, what the hell is going on?" Her booming voice trembled with a complexity of emotions.

Jerking around to face Mindy, the anorexic redhead fell from Edward as he scrambled to sit up. Mindy immediately recognized Britney Priest, who worked in the same office as Edward, from her top sales associate photos in the newspaper. Her reputation throughout the real estate industry as a barracuda, cutthroat, aggressive, morally and ethically bereft, was unequaled.

"What the fuck does it look like, you fat, dumb bitch?" Edward said, clearly startled and pissed off by Mindy's unexpected intrusion. "I thought you were supposed to be at school. What are you doing, spying on me?" Snorting, he took a swig from the half-empty Jack Daniel's bottle on the nightstand.

"Shit. Who the hell is *that*?" the redheaded twig asked, giving Mindy an incredulous once-over. "Christ, don't tell me *that's* your wife?"

Sitting there, entwined in the brand new set of three-hundred-eighty-thread-count Egyptian cotton eyelet-trimmed sheets Mindy had just put on her bed that morning, Britney didn't even having the decency to cover up her perky little bee-sting breasts. Mindy knew she'd never be able to look at another set of Egyptian cotton sheets again, much less sleep on them, without envisioning the bee-stung twig.

Edward's head bobbed. "Yeah, that's the little warthog, er, I mean, little woman," he snickered. "In the flesh. They must have sent her home because they can't afford to have any more chairs fractured by her fat ass." Clearly amused by his malicious quips, Edward reveled in base laughter.

Eyeing Mindy as if she were a circus elephant, Britney said, "I know you said she was a whale, Edward, but...holy shit."

With Edward keeping Mindy all but cloistered, the women had never met. After her snarky comment, the naked twig had the further indecency to erupt with laughter. Edward immediately followed suit.

"What did I tell you, baby? It's like living with Moby fucking Dick for chrissakes." Edward pulled Britney back to his side, offering her a swill of Jack Daniel's, which she eagerly sucked back. "Here, Mindy," he said, defiantly fondling one of Britney's mini-tits as an aghast Mindy stood paralyzed in the doorway. "Is this what you came to see? Well, get an eyeful and then get the fuck out of here, you fat, disgusting warthog. You're cramping my style." He and Britney broke into maniacal laughter.

Mindy feared her shattered ego would join in a suicide mission with her pummeled heart and burst right through her chest.

Her vision blurring with tears, Mindy turned and was about to trudge downstairs with the intention of drowning her sorrow in a couple of Whoppers, fries, onion rings and a chocolate shake or two. But this time a tiny voice buried somewhere deep inside stopped her.

Nope, uh-uh...don't even think about it. I'm not the one in the wrong here. I will not allow him to do this to me!

Ten long years of pent-up fear, hurt, anger and frustration churned in her gut and hammered at her temples. Suddenly Mindy heard herself shouting with authority and conviction.

"*I'm* not the one who's going *anywhere*, you goddamned, miserable piss-poor excuse for a man. I want you packed and out of this house in ten minutes, you bastard. You and your little slut girlfriend."

Bolting out of the bed, Edward stood there with all his flaccid, masculine glory dangling between his skinny bird legs. Thumbkin had shrunk to the size of a Spanish peanut.

"Who the fuck do you think you're talking to, huh?" he roared. "Have you forgotten that *I'm* the one who says what goes around here?" He jabbed the air with a pointed finger. "Not you, you lard-assed, mealy-mouthed idiot. Go stick your fat face in a pig trough and drown yourself."

Bringing her full girth into the room, Mindy stood arms akimbo at the foot of the bed. "Your grisly reign as Attila the Hun, head-honcho and chief decision maker has just crashed to a halt, Edward. I'm divorcing you."

He just stood there, his mouth hanging open as he glared at her.

She glanced at her watch. "Tick tock, Edward. Now you've only got *eight* minutes. If you're not out of here I'll call the police first, then contact the press. Let's see how the conservative president of Henshaw Real Estate might feel about the smarmy extra-marital affair of his branch manager and his little hot-shot saleswoman plastered all over social media and the newspapers."

Flashing a victorious smile, Mindy held her head high as she jabbed the air with an outstretched finger. "And don't think for a minute I won't do it. Any pride I once had is long gone, thanks to you. I've got nothing to lose—except for you, you rotten, stinking, vile, amoral sonuvabitch."

Reclaiming the reins to her life, Mindy felt exhilarated.

Hearing Britney mutter something under her breath, Mindy turned her vengeance on the twig. "As for you," she warned, glaring at the woman. "Unless you want your name plastered all over along with that no good, fucking dickhead of a husband of mine, you'd better get your bony ass out of my bed and cover those puny pencil-eraser breasts before I come over there, grab you by that hennaed mop on your head and drop-kick your skinny ass down the stairs."

Yes! God that felt good! Mindy felt twenty pounds lighter and less encumbered than she had in years.

An eye-popping, drop-jawed expression across her reddened face, Britney let out a shriek. "Edward, are you just going to stand there and let that walking tub of lard talk to me like that?"

Clearly flabbergasted and motionless, Edward glanced at Britney. "Just get your clothes on and get out of here." He scrambled into his pants. "I'll meet you back at your place." Heaving an audible sigh of frustration, Britney complied, whispering *fat bitch* to Mindy as she slid past her, ran down the stairs and slammed the front door behind her.

Galloping down the stairs a moment later, Edward promised, "You'll pay for this, Mindora. Mark my words, you'll be sorry."

Mindy plodded down the stairs behind him. "Hah. That's a laugh." She panted breathlessly as she tried in vain to keep pace with him. "Believe me, Edward, there's *nothing* in the world you could do to make my life any more miserable than you already have this past decade. You've pushed me around for the last time, buster."

Stopping dead in his tracks, Edward turned to face Mindy. His fist raised, jaw twitching and eyes blazing, he stepped toward her, causing her to catch her breath. Awaiting the worst, Mindy stood her ground with her chin—both of them—held high. This was it. Edward was going to kill her. She'd be a tsking, laughable finale to the evening news on TV.

And on the lighter side—after a fatal jab to the stomach, a morbidly obese woman exploded all over the walls and floor of her suburban Chicago townhouse tonight. An overwhelming odor of chocolate emanated from the remains. Reportedly busy celebrating his good fortune by screwing his red-haired, teeny-breasted toothpick of a slut, the deceased's husband couldn't be reached for comment.

As Mindy bravely locked gazes with Edward, she silently prayed she'd fall on top of him and crush him to death after he struck the fatal blow.

To her amazement, Edward pulled back and turned away, mumbling a string of creative expletives under his breath. In a matter of minutes he'd stuffed the clothes from the bureau in his study into a suitcase, all the while fuming and ranting. Snatching Edward's perfectly starched and pressed dress shirts from his closet, Mindy hurled them to the floor and kicked them toward him. Then she stomped all over them for good measure. It was the most exercise she'd gotten in months and it felt sensational.

"Here," she blurted, "bring these to your skinny little playmate and tell Brit the Bitch that the laundress job is all hers from now on." Mindy beamed with triumph as she spoke.

Instead of heading for food once Edward was out the door, Mindy sat down and designed a positive plan of action for herself. Bound and determined to drag herself out of the chocolate-coated pits of despair that had become her daily existence, she made a commitment to herself that there would be no more bingeing.

"And," Mindy said at the recollection, "I kept that promise for more than a year and a half—until yesterday's chocolate fiasco."

"Ms. von Grettle? Excuse me..."

Mindy's attention snapped back to the present as she focused on Rob Lyons and Dawn Farley standing at her desk.

"Sorry to bother you," Rob said. "We're here to pick up the travel documents for our honeymoon cruise."

"Oh," Mindy chuckled, "you're not bothering me a bit. Sorry, my head must have been up in the clouds somewhere." She waved her hand skyward, offering a cordial smile. "Preferably first class on a plane, heading for someplace exotic."

They were so young and adorable. So innocent looking.

Including a gift-filled tote bag with their documents, Mindy sent the young lovers on their way. Her eyes brimmed with tears as the young couple bounced hand-in-hand out of the agency.

God, she felt old.

She glanced at her watch. Eleven already. Three hours had passed since she arrived and she'd accomplished nothing other than to answer a few phone calls, wallow in raw memories and steep in the depths of self-pity. Stupid and unproductive.

Drawing a resolute breath, she slapped her hand on the desktop. "Enough already!" It was high time she got her shit together and moved on with her life. Turning to face her computer monitor, she proceeded to check her active client files.

"I see the job's got you talking to yourself. It happens to the best of us sooner or later."

Mindy glanced up at Leo Parker, owner of the agency, who'd propped his ample butt on the edge of her desk.

"It's not the job, Leo. It's just my life." Flicking her hand in a dismissive fashion, Mindy tossed off a nonchalant laugh. "No big deal. Edward's wake just opened some old wounds I thought had healed eons ago."

"It's a damn shame he couldn't have seen you looking the way you do now." Leo placed his hand over hers as he spoke. "You've evolved into a positively ravishing creature since that day you came in here to sign up for my travel course. Look at you."

He appraised her with an approving nod. "Mindy, darling, you're utterly delicious. Spectacular. Breathtaking. Enchanting." Through broad gestures, Leo tossed each word into the air with drama and gusto. "An absolute vision of loveliness."

Scrunching her features into a twisted smile, Mindy patted her boss's chubby fingers and smiled. "Oh Leo, I love you. Now if only I could find a man who felt the same way about me, had all your wonderful qualities and, oh yeah," she laughed, "wasn't gay, I'd be all set." Winking, she squeezed his hand.

"It's gonna happen for you, Mindy. Just last night I had another one of my psychic flashes about you," he confided, leaning toward her.

Resting her elbow on the desk, Mindy cupped her chin with her hand and groaned. "Leo, Leo, Leo. You and your psychic flashes. What *am* I going to do with you?"

"No, really, Mindy, I swear to God." Leo crossed his heart. "Come on, you know how perceptive my premonitions are, especially when they involve my very best friends." Closing his eyes, fingers poised at his temples, he said, "There's a hot, sexy man on the horizon." He paused, peeking at her through one eye. "Yes, he's straight." Winking, he closed his eyes again. "I see splendid things happening for you two...romance...love...travel..."

"Please, spare me, Leo. How many times have you supposedly had the identical vision of a great romantic breakthrough coming my way since I started working here? Ten, twelve, eighty times?"

Mindy peeked under her desk. "Nope, no gorgeous hunks under here." Craning her neck, she scanned the office. "And the office is definitely hunkless, except for you, of course, Leo dear." She patted his knee. "Hmm..." She tapped her finger against her cheek. "Where *could* that mystical, sexy dream-man be hiding?"

"Such a comedienne." Leo folded his arms across his chest. "What you fail to understand, smarty pants, is that the repetitive value of this premonition only substantiates it all the more. Each time I get one of my flashes about you, it's stronger. And last night was the most powerful of all. I had dreams about it all night."

"I told you to lay off those pepperoni pizzas, Leo."

"You know," he wagged his finger, "ESP is a very real phenomenon. Ever since I was a little boy living in that squalid apartment on Clark Street, right upstairs from Sally Filbert's Lounge—"

Dropping her head into her hands, Mindy uttered a pained groan. "I've heard this story a gazillion times, remember? I know it by heart, Leo. Every time old Leopold senior went to the tavern to slosh down a few brews he brought his kid into the bar so the too-artsy little boy could rub shoulders with some *manly men.*" Mindy hung invisible quotation marks in the air. "And learn how to become more of a *real* man."

"Mmmm, I still remember some of those big brawny shoulders too." Leo jiggled his eyebrows.

Smirking, Mindy ignored Leo's interruption and continued. "All the drunken beer-bellied old geezers would humor the cute little kid by having him read their palms. The end."

"Ugh, that sounded so vile." Leo tsked. "How can you take my dramatic, colorful, soulful slice of life and make it sound so lackluster and mundane?"

"Okay, how's this?" Mindy offered. "Each evening the manly, macho patrons of Sally Filbert's Lounge zealously awaited the arrival of Leopold senior's cherubic little blond-banged clairvoyant boy Little Leo. Tethered in ropes of cigarette smoke, the brawny men sat mesmerized as the towheaded wonder-boy gazed at their rough-hewn palms, revealing tantalizing tidbits of their future." Mindy grinned. "Better?"

"Now *that's* more like it." Leo nodded as Mindy collapsed in laughter. Feigning hurt feelings, he pouted. "Sure, go ahead and laugh. You'll see. Sally Filbert's regulars were scoffers too until my predictions started coming true. Then they came back, begging for more. Of course, I made them pay." He hopped down from Mindy's desk.

"So you were an entrepreneur at the tender age of ten, huh?"

"Actually, I was a kept man."

"At ten?" She raised her eyebrows with interest.

"Uh-huh. They *kept me* in bar snacks like pizza, pepperoni sticks, beef jerky, cheese-curls and best of all, they let me suck," he paused, clearly doing his damnedest to increase the drama, "the foamy heads off their beer glasses," Leo finally finished, chuckling at the memory. "It was my first decadent foray into gluttony."

"Tell you what," Mindy suggested. "If your prediction comes true and I find myself swept into the powerful, waiting arms of an irresistible *straight*," she wagged a finger for emphasis, "manly man, I promise to ply you with bar snacks and let you suck...the foam from my beer."

Leo flashed a boyish smile. "Deal," he said, heading back to his office.

Mindy loved Leo. The gregarious, good-hearted man had befriended her at the lowest point in her life. It was Leo who'd repeatedly injected her with confidence and positive motivation. As her body whittled down in size he'd employed his snappy, classy sense of style to teach Mindy how to dress to her best advantage. To showcase the emerging womanly attributes so long hidden beneath mounds of fat.

Best of all, it was Leo who brought sunshine and laughter back into Mindy's life, and who let her cry on his shoulder when she needed to. This funny, warm, nurturing man had become her closest confidant and best friend.

"So Leo sees a sexy hunk coming into my life, hmm?" Mindy mused, sorting through her mountain of paperwork. Steepling her fingers, she looked skyward and whispered, "From his lips to God's ears."

Chapter 3

A WEEK AFTER Mindy attended Edward's wake, she and Leo lunched at Chowder Bay, the trendy new seafood house just down the road from Persimmon Travel.

Scanning the expansive menu, Mindy said, "Okay, help me out here, Leo. In my continuing quest to become more cosmopolitan," she raised her eyebrows and smiled at him, "I've decided to start ordering a glass of wine with lunch instead of the usual iced tea or diet soda. Since I know next to nothing about wine, as my mentor, it's your job to tell me what goes best with salmon."

Regarding Mindy over the rim of his reading glasses, Leo smiled.

"Well, at the wine tasting I took you to a couple weeks ago, they said not to worry about the old red wine with red meat and white wine with fish or chicken rule. Since salmon's a hearty, flavorful fish, you're safe with anything from an earthy cabernet to champagne. Personally, I prefer a good Riesling with salmon. The spicy sweetness offsets salmon's sturdy flavor quite well. After a steady diet of diet cola," Leo laughed, "I have a feeling you'd probably prefer a wine that's not too dry."

"Okay then, wet wine it is." Mindy gave a resolute nod. "I can't believe I'm in my mid-thirties and just now learning about wine."

"That's no surprise. That overbearing, meathead of an ex-husband of yours," Leo injected an insincere smile before adding, "God rest his soul, did his best to keep you sheltered from anything culturally stimulating."

"Tell me about it." Mindy trilled a sigh. "How about we leave the objectionable topic of my dead ex out of our pleasant lunchtime conversation, okay?"

"Done." He offered a warm smile.

"Things were really hopping this morning," Mindy told him, glad to change the subject. "We're booking a lot of Mexico and the Caribbean."

Rubbing his hands with glee, Leo said, "Love it, love it, love it. Ka-ching!" He grinned as he mimed pressing a key on a cash register. "Hey, speaking of money, did I tell you my filthy-rich cousin Jasper called me this morning?"

At the mention of one of her least favorite people, a mirthless smile crossed Mindy's features. "Big Jazz?" Leo nodded and Mindy shuddered. "Please, God, tell me he's not coming up from Texas for another visit."

"I'm afraid so. He wants to sell off his investment properties in the Chicago area because he's—get this, Mindy—going to Russia on business. And he'll probably be there a good five—that's right, I said *five*—years." Leo tapped out a little dance of joy under the table as he snapped his fingers. "Halleluiah!"

"No kidding?" Mindy's face brightened. "Well, pardner," she said in her best Texas twang, "that there's the best dang news I've heard all day." She and Leo broke into laughter.

Wagging his finger, he warned, "I'd watch out if I were you, Min. You know how Big Jazz lusts after you. If you're not careful, he may just hijack you to Russia."

"Oh jeez, Leo. You're going to spoil my appetite."

"What can I say?" Leo shrugged. "You know damn well I'm not kidding. He's hot for you, Min. All you'd have to do is crook your little finger and you could become the fourth Mrs. Jasper Wilson. Just think of all those millions. You'd be living in the lap of luxury. And all it would cost you is a paltry ten percent of Big Jazz's net worth for my services as your matchmaker." Leo grinned. "You've got to admit Jasper's not too hard on the eyes either."

"I don't care how good looking he is. I'd sooner give up chocolate than spend a single night in the lap of that manhandling, overblown, macho, bigoted, racist, pushy side of Texas beef," Mindy made clear.

"Ouch." Leo winced.

Their conversation was put on hold as a striking young man approached the table. "Hi, my name is Christopher and I'll be your server this afternoon. Have you decided yet?"

"Yes, I'll have the fresh grilled salmon fillet," Mindy started, "with the mango teriyaki relish. And steamed vegetables, no oil or butter, in place of the fried rice. Oh, and a glass of your house Riesling," she added confidently. Leo ordered the peel and eat garlic shrimp with a side order of zucchini-crab cakes with pineapple-horseradish sauce, a cup of Chowder Bay's signature New England-style seafood chowder and a glass of Riesling.

Appreciatively eyeing the handsome young server with the wavy jet-black hair and blue eyes as he departed with their order, Leo mused, "Did you see that cute, tight little ass of his? And those teal-blue eyes? They're about the same shade as your suit." Turning back to Mindy, he pounded the table. "Why the hell didn't you stop me from ordering those fattening crab cakes and chowder?"

Pinching the small roll at his middle, Leo sat back in his chair, expelling a sigh of exasperation. "Look at me. How am I ever going to get in shape to attract a luscious sweet thing like that if I keep eating this way?" Crossing his arms over his chest, he grumbled. "Hey, diet buddy, you're supposed to keep me on the right track, remember?"

"Now Leo, you know you hate it when I police you." With a kind smile, Mindy reached across the table and touched his arm.

"Did you really want me to say something in front of that cute, hunky waiter you were drooling over and embarrass you?"

Absently fiddling with the bottle of chipotle pepper sauce on the table, Leo groaned. "No. You're right. I would have bit your head off afterward. I'm disgusting. I'm beyond help. I haven't even worked out in nearly two weeks."

Expelling a sigh of self-loathing, he said, "Look at you. Look how steely your willpower is. You're such an inspiration Mindy. Damn, if I only had one ounce of your determination and resolve." Shaking his head, he flicked his hand through the air. "Aw, what's the use?"

Mindy's cheeks heated with guilt. She hadn't fessed up to Leo about her post funeral home chocolate orgy the week before and was hoping she wouldn't have to.

"You're being way too hard on yourself, Leo. You look wonderful and you've come such a long way. Twenty pounds! You've only got another fifteen or twenty to go. You've just hit a sticky spot, a plateau, that's all. You'll get over it soon enough."

"You think?" Leo scrutinized his midsection.

"Absolutely. Don't forget if it weren't for you, I'd probably still be," Mindy paused, looked to either side, moved in closer to Leo and whispered, "three hundred pounds." She sat back against her chair and smiled at her friend.

A youthful forty-two, Leo was a nice-looking man. Not handsome in the classic sense but certainly attractive. His effusive personality made him even more so. About five-ten and pudgy, he had taffy-blond hair, deceptively innocent hazel eyes and a ruddy complexion. Ties were his fashion-passion, today's bearing little blue and green fish swimming against a murky tan background in honor of their trek to the new seafood house.

Mindy's attention was drawn to the hostess, jiggling her pint-sized fanny down the aisle as she ushered a beefy man, mopping sweat from his forehead, past their table. His girth was so vast, his hips brushed against their table and the table across from them at the same time.

Mindy and Leo shot each other wide-eyed looks.

"Come on, tell me the truth, Mindy," Leo pleaded. "Do I look that bad?" He bit his bottom lip. "Don't pull any punches, I can take it."

Mindy turned to Leo, aghast. "Good Lord, Leo, that poor man is huge," she whispered. "You look a thousand times thinner than him. Sheesh, talk about a distorted body image." She shook her head in disbelief.

"Besides," she went on, "men have it so much easier than women. Heavy guys are universally thought of as big, cute, cuddly teddy bears while overweight women get all those adorable little terms of endearment tacked on like porker, whale butt and lard ass."

"I read that in parts of Europe and the Middle East," Leo said, "men prefer their women zaftig—like you." He molded a curvy figure in the air.

"That's nice," Mindy said, "but here in the U. S., men want women who can double for one of these." Fingering the blade of her butter knife, Mindy smirked.

"Don't kid yourself, Mindy. Men want their *men* to look like that too. You have no idea how hard it is to be a soft, middle-aged gay man trying to compete with all those buff young boys out there." He slapped the table. "There's the answer to all of our relationship problems. We need to relocate to the Middle East where we can both be worshipped as goddesses."

Mindy fell into easy laughter. "Sounds like a great plan. We can get jobs operating camel tours in Egypt."

"All kidding aside," Leo said, "I've got to lose the rest of this weight before I get seriously depressed."

"But you're only talking fifteen measly pounds, Leo. You need to ease up on yourself. After all, we're only human. Everybody backslides now and then."

"No, not everyone. You haven't," Leo pointed out. "You're obviously much stronger than I am, that's all. I'm nothing but a weak-willed, fat-gram-sucking cow."

Groaning, Mindy rested her elbows on the table, propping her head in her hands. "Aw jeez, Leo." She took in a deep breath and sighed. "Now I'm going to have to tell you. Damn it."

"Tell me what?" Leo slanted Mindy a curious look as she sat there suddenly silent. "Come on, you're scaring me. What happened?"

"Get ready, because *Miss Perfect* has a juicy little chocolate-covered confession for you."

Leo gasped. "You mean..."

"Yup. I melted right off my pillar of dieting virtue into a shameful puddle of chocolate transgression." With an utter lack of enthusiasm Mindy spilled her guts about her spontaneous bakery binge after leaving the funeral home.

After finishing the main course, she and Leo were served coffee and the fresh fruit mélange desserts they'd ordered. As the server departed Mindy noted, "I really liked the Riesling, Leo. Good choice. It was—"

Mindy caught a glimpse of a familiar man walking toward their table, led by the fanny-jiggling hostess and accompanied by two other men. He was one of those men with real presence. A head turner. He looked like he could be a male model, or maybe an actor. Yes, that's probably why he looked so familiar, because there sure as hell wasn't anyone in her life who looked even half as delicious as this guy.

"Yes, go on," Leo encouraged. "The Riesling was..."

Mindy snapped her attention back to the conversation. "I liked the wine because it was..." Her gaze shifted again to the guy strutting down the aisle. The man was tantalizing, a tall, broad-shouldered, mouthwatering specimen of manhood. He was nattily attired in a nutmeg brown suit that complemented his dark hair.

Covertly ogling him over the rim of her coffee cup as he neared, the realization hit Mindy. The guy with the chocolate drop eyes! Britney Priest's...*friend*. What was his name? Arness? Adamson? Amberson? Archer? Yes, that was it. Mr. Archer.

"From the funeral home," Mindy said absently.

"You liked the Riesling because it was from the funeral home? Mindy girl, you're losing me."

Mindy felt certain he wouldn't recognize her, which was just as well, considering his dubious connection with Britney. As he strode down the aisle between tables he talked on a phone. Narrowing her gaze, Mindy's lip curled into a sneer as she was reminded of Edward. Like him, no doubt Mr. Archer was one of those self-important business tycoon types with no time for anything but work. Except, of course, for the occasional roll in the hay with some willing little bimbo like Britney Priest.

As the hostess passed their table with the three men in tow, Leo was saying something or other to Mindy, but all she could hear was the pulse-pounding roar in her ears. Angry for reacting like a silly schoolgirl and letting her hormones go haywire, she swallowed hard, trying to dislodge her heart from her throat and guide it back to her chest.

She was doing okay until the man stopped right in front of her, gifting her with a gleaming, drop-dead gorgeous smile.

"It's you," he said, slipping his phone into an inside pocket of his jacket. "I knew I recognized you." With a few words he motioned to his companions that he'd meet them at their table.

When he turned back to Mindy she noticed his eyes were specked with amber and they twinkled when he smiled.

Acknowledging Mindy's wordless stare, he said, "Oh I'm sorry, you must not remember me. We met at Edward von Grettle's wake last week." He paused and smiled. "Let me rephrase that. We were in the process of meeting when you had to leave rather abruptly." With a purposeful clearing of his throat, he laughed, revealing wonderful laugh lines around his striking eyes.

Not remember him? Was he nuts? How could she possibly forget a walking, talking, breathing icon of glorious masculinity with glistening chocolate chip eyes?

Striving to maintain her cool, Mindy returned his smile. "Yes," she said, with as much nonchalance as she could manage, considering her raging hormone attack. Extending her hand, she cleared her throat. "Of course I remember you."

His large hand dwarfed hers and she loved how diminutive it made her feel. What she didn't love was how damned flustered she felt as his magnificent, towering six-foot-whatever frame loomed over her. Something had suddenly made her hot all over. Mindy doubted it was the Riesling.

If all that weren't bad enough, her olfactory receptors caught the gentle traces of his hypnotic, woodsy scent. She couldn't help drawing in a prolonged sniff. He smelled the way he looked. Good enough to lick.

For God's sake, get a grip, Mindora von G. Remember—this man has probably slept with the enemy!

Mindy's heart pounded so fiercely she felt as if the beat was broadcasting over the restaurant's sound system. "I don't want to keep you from your lunch," she managed to say. "So, uh...nice seeing you again." Dragging her attention back to her coffee, she swallowed hard, doing her best to appear casual and thoroughly disinterested.

Mr. Chocolate Chip Eyes hesitated a moment before heaving a shrug and turning to join his lunch companions.

To Mindy's horror, Leo jumped to his feet, yanked on the sleeve of the man's jacket and offered an outstretched hand as he motioned for him to be seated.

"Don't be silly, Mindy," Leo said through his broad salesman's smile. "I'm sure the gentleman has time to join us for a quick cup of coffee." Mindy opened her mouth to protest, but Leo was too fast for her. "Don't you?" he said to the living, breathing Adonis.

Pumping Leo's extended hand, Mr. Archer flashed another of his dazzling smiles and nodded. "Sure. I've got time for a quick cup."

"Excellent," Leo said, his cherubic face captured by a devilish grin that Mindy wished she could scrape off. "Christopher," he called to their server as the young man zoomed by their table with another table's order. "Another cup of coffee here please."

Retrieving a business card from his pocket, Leo turned his attention to their table guest as Mr. Archer took a seat opposite Mindy. "I'm Leo Parker. I own Persimmon Travel, half a mile down the road. This is my vice-president, the best travel counselor in the Midwest, Mindy von Grettle."

Whipping his head toward Mindy, the clearly flabbergasted man arched his eyebrows. "von Grettle? Edward von Grettle's ex-wife?" Mindy nodded with a slow blink. "But you can't be. I mean, I heard you were..." Clearly struggling to mask his expression of bewilderment as he gave Mindy an appreciative once-over, he took in a deep breath, expelling it slowly.

A knowing smile crossed Mindy's lips as she drummed her fingers on the table. "A whale? Is that the word you were searching for?" She batted her lashes.

Wincing, he scanned the floor, perhaps searching for a hole big enough to crawl into. "Whew, nothing like getting off to a bad start, I always say. I'm Archer. Archer Priest." Never taking his eyes off Mindy, his voice was unmistakably hesitant.

Her eyes wide as saucers, Mindy rose halfway out of her chair. "Priest!" she blurted. Aware she'd drawn attention with her outburst she quickly took her seat again, modifying her voice. "You're Britney's ex-husband?"

Grimacing, Archer shrugged his broad shoulders. "I'm afraid it's even worse than that. I'm her brother." He offered a weak smile while Mindy rolled her eyes skyward and folded her arms beneath her breasts. She had no doubt her narrow-eyed glare was sharp enough to razor Archer Priest's suit to ribbons.

After a moment of awkward silence, Leo spooned some fruit into his mouth. "You know, this berry mélange is really tasty. Have you tried any yet, Mindy?" Focusing his wide-eyed gaze on her, Leo cringed when he received only a scowl in reply.

"Now I know why my sister stormed off the way she did when I asked her about you at the funeral home," Archer said. "I brought you up again later that afternoon and all she would say is, 'Don't you *ever* ask me about that...well...expletive deleted, but I'm sure you get the picture."

"Oh I get the picture all right." Mindy's voice was devoid of warmth. "Better not keep your lunch companions waiting, Mr. Priest." She shuddered as the repugnant name seeped past her lips.

"I've got a few more minutes," Archer said through a lazy smile as he folded his strapping arms across his chest, settling his back against the chair.

Flashing a look of incredulity, Mindy said, "Well, *I* don't. Come on, Leo, we have to get back to the office. I've got a one-fifteen appointment coming in." Pushing back her chair, Mindy deliberately avoided making further eye contact with Archer, focusing instead on brushing nonexistent crumbs from her suit.

"No you don't," Leo corrected. "I distinctly remember you telling me that appointment was pushed back to two o'clock." He leaned toward Archer and whispered, "Great girl, but she has a terrible memory." Turning back to Mindy, Leo ignored her threatening glare. "Don't worry, Mindy, we've got plenty of time to sit and get acquainted with Mr. Priest."

Leo offered a beguiling smile while Mindy's anger manifested into a swift kick to Leo's shin under the table.

"Ow!" Leo growled, reaching down to rub his shin.

"Oh, I'm so sorry, Leo, was that your leg?" Mindy said in all innocence.

Archer stood up. "Actually, I really should get over to my table. I think I've kept my associates waiting long enough." He extended his hand to Leo. "It was a pleasure meeting you, Leo," he said as Leo pumped his hand with a firm, enthusiastic salesman's grip.

Placing his hand over Mindy's, Archer said, "I'm glad we finally had a chance to meet, Mindy. Maybe we could have a cup of coffee or a drink sometime and get better acquainted."

She answered his ludicrous suggestion with an unwavering, steely glare.

"You know," he said with an inviting smile, "you just might find out I'm not the demon you apparently think I am."

"I'm sorry, Mr. Priest," Mindy ground out the name she loathed between clenched teeth. "But I really don't think—"

"Great idea, Archer," Leo blurted, effectively cutting her off. "I keep telling Mindy she needs to get out of the office more. She's such a workaholic."

Leo grinned and Mindy wondered if he was aware how close she was to stabbing him with her dessert fork at that moment.

"Go ahead and give him one of your business cards, Mindy."

Mindy narrowed her eyes. "I don't have any with me, Leo," she lied, hoping her threatening posture and expression sent an unmistakable message to her meddlesome boss.

Licking his lips, Leo broke into a volley of staccato laughter, his telltale nervous trademark, surely knowing he'd be in for one hell of a browbeating later.

"No problem, I just remembered I already gave Archer one of my cards. He can reach you at the same number." He rose from the table. Finding the tall Archer's shoulder out of range, Leo gave him a friendly pat on the arm. "Feel free to stop by the travel agency any time you're in the area, Archer. I'll make sure somebody can cover for Mindy while you two go out for a couple cappuccinos or something."

"Sounds good, Leo. I'll take you up on your offer...if it's okay with Mindy."

Mindy shot Archer a frigid glance. "No, it most certainly—"

Stepping in front of Mindy before she could finish, Leo said, "Are you kidding? Mindy would be delighted, wouldn't you, Mindy?" Without daring to glimpse Mindy's way, or risk giving her an opportunity to answer, Leo blurted without pausing, "We'll see you soon then, Archer?"

"You bet." Giving Leo a wink and a hefty pat on the back, Archer strode off to meet his lunch companions.

"Enjoy your lunch," Leo called after him. "The zucchini-crab cakes with pineapple-horseradish sauce are superb."

"Don't bother giving my regards to your sister," Mindy added beneath her breath, purposely too soft for Archer to hear.

"Nice guy, huh?" Leo said, watching Archer depart. "Nice ass too. Bet you any money he lifts weights. I could feel those powerful triceps right through his suit coat." Turning back toward their table, a grinning Leo held a fist up and flexed his biceps.

One look at Mindy's icepick glare wiped the grin right off Leo's face. He took his seat and swallowed hard as the sound of Mindy's fingernails rapped out his death knell on the wood tabletop.

Loosening the tie at his throat, Leo jutted out his chin and ran his fingers beneath his collar to loosen it. Mindy watched as he tried in vain to recapture his lighthearted grin. He cleared his throat. "How tall would you say he is? Six-four, six-five? Nice dark, expressive eyes too, huh?"

Mindy reached over and grabbed his arm, digging her nails into his wrist. "Don't you even think about playing matchmaker, Leo. You hear?"

"Ow, Mindy! You need to file those things down, they're like claws."

"All the better to scratch your eyes out with," she seethed. "Leo, how *could* you? You knew I didn't want to have anything to do with him. I couldn't have made it any clearer unless I'd stood on top of the table and screamed it at the top of my lungs." Releasing the death grip on Leo's wrist, Mindy raked her fingers through her hair. She picked up the dessert fork, waving it toward him.

"I swear, Leo, I could kill you. Just slap you right up on top of this table, eviscerate you with the tines of this little fork, then gleefully feed all the bloody bits into that fish tank over there." Leo opened his mouth but Mindy kept right on going. "This man is Britney Priest's brother. Her *brother*! Doesn't that mean anything to you, you feeble-brained dunderhead? Archer Priest's sister is the skinny slut who—"

"Will there be anything else for you today?" Christopher asked, springing to the table.

"No!" Mindy barked and the young man flinched.

"Don't mind her, Christopher." Leo offered the server a friendly smile. "She's suffering from a severe reaction to omega-3 fatty acids. We'll just take the check, thanks."

Maintaining her irked expression, Mindy waited for the buoyant Christopher to give Leo the check and bounce out of earshot. Snapping her fingers to draw Leo's attention away from Christopher's tight little ass and back to her, she continued her tirade, struggling to keep her volume down.

"Archer Priest's sister is the emaciated tramp I found screwing my husband. In my own house. In my own bed, Leo. Edward's widow." She reached across the table, knocking on his head. "Hello? Remember? Why on earth would I want to have *anything* to do with that vicious, vulgar woman's brother?"

"Oh, maybe the way I caught you drooling over him just before you found out who he is," Leo offered, leaning back in his chair, folding his arms and looking entirely too self-satisfied.

Mindy gasped. "I was *not* drooling!"

"Are you kidding? The spittle's still running down your chin," Leo noted, laughing as Mindy instinctively wiped her chin before realizing what she was doing. "It's terribly unfair to judge this poor guy and write him off just because his sister is an immoral reprobate."

He leaned in toward Mindy, motioning for her to come closer. "Remember my psychic premonition? He's the one, Mindy." Leo nodded with confident assurance. "I knew it as soon as I shook his hand. He's the man you've been waiting for."

"What?! Bullshit!" Nearly leaping from her chair, Mindy grabbed her purse and glared down at Leo. "That's the most ridiculous, preposterous thing I've ever heard. I'll wait for you in the car." She marched toward the restaurant's exit.

Royally pissed off with Leo for his meddling, buttinski performance, Mindy was even angrier with herself for being so damned attracted to *the enemy's* brother.

Just thinking about Archer brought goose bumps to her arms, which she briskly rubbed. But no amount of rubbing could change the fact that her panties had soaked just from being in close proximity to the guy. The impressive bulk of Archer's body made her want to reach out and touch him in ways that sent shivers straight through to her most intimate parts just thinking about it.

With that thought, she slapped the heel of her hand against her forehead. "Jeez, what the hell is wrong with you? Snap out of it, will you, Mindora?" she chastised aloud in the parking lot, drawing attention from passersby and not even giving a damn. "Get it through that thick noggin of yours that Archer Priest is off limits and part of the enemy camp."

Evidently, Mindy's traitorous libido had its own agenda. The lusty image flashing through her mind just before Leo reached the car was of Brit the Bitch's brother sweeping her into his strong arms and divesting her of her clothing. He was licking, nibbling and making her melt. Nice and slow...like a bar of fine chocolate.

Chapter 4

B Y THE TIME Mindy got home from work, the wind howled as a blizzard whipped at the snow, depositing it in deep banks. The short but blinding drive from the office had been stressful, to say the least. Poor Cadbury came back into the house looking like a snow-packed doggy snowman after she'd let him out to do his business. One of these days she'd move to a place where the winter climate didn't coat her lungs with ice crystals when she breathed.

Still reeling from the unexpected run-in with Archer Priest during lunch, Mindy merely picked at her dinner, a rarity for her. In fact, she could barely even remember what she'd eaten because she'd been so focused on the lust surging through her veins. Of all the luscious men in the world she could be attracted to, why did it have to be Brit the Bitch's brother?

Dressed in fleecy layers to fight off the chill, she curled up in an oversized chair in the living room, a soft blanket tucked from her neck to beneath her big fluffy slippers. A steamy mug of diet hot cocoa, topped with an ample plop of fat-free whipped cream, rested on the end table next to her.

It was the perfect opportunity to escape into a romance novel, something she hadn't done in too long. This one was a medieval fantasy, complete with brave knights, fair maidens, dragons and ogres. It was also hot and spicy. She'd never read an erotic romance before, but when Leo gave it to her he assured her it was a good way to learn what she'd been missing all those years that she'd been stuck with Thumbkin. He said it was part of her ongoing process in becoming more knowledgeable and sophisticated.

She pushed thoughts of Leo to the back of her mind. It was going to take time before she could look at him again without wanting to rip his impish face off for playing matchmaker for her and Archer. What in the hell was he thinking?

"It would be nice to have a knight in shining armor of my own," she mused, reading the enticing back cover blurb while sipping her cocoa. "It sounds like a hot, sexy read," she told Cadbury, who'd snuggled up close to her, "but that isn't real life. Ideal men only exist in fairytales and preposterous romance novels. And they don't come equipped with malicious, bitchy sisters either." Cad's soft acknowledging bark proved even canines knew the score.

The wind's menacing, low whistle caught her attention. She had to relax, had to suspend her conscious thoughts for a while. More than anything, she had to get her mind off Archer Priest. There simply wasn't any valid reason to dwell on fantasies involving him. Why torture herself with tantalizing images of something she could never have?

"A little escapism is good," she told herself. "Getting lost in an outlandish romance novel full of sex and mystical creatures is exactly what I need. Plus I'll be learning something in the process."

Mindy focused on the bawdy story of the medieval damsel in distress and her bold, sexy knight. She immediately found herself relating to the heroine, who was Rubenesque instead of a scrawny size zero. What's more, the hunky hero loved her full, ripe curves, Practically worshiped them.

"Now that's my kind of story!"

Her eyes widened in stark, speechless wonderment as she read of such things as colossal cocks, spurting cum, dripping pussies, pulsing clits, creaming cunts and all-encompassing head-to-toe shuddering orgasms. She found some of it embarrassing. Some of it odd. And all of it exceedingly explicit.

The people in this novel did incredible things she'd never even heard of, much less had personal experience with. Like multiple orgasms. During sex. With a man's fingers, tongue, teeth or cock causing the orgasms, instead of a vibrator. She had no idea if such awe-inspiring things were possible, but she was riveted from page one.

Oh the sensuous things she read about asses and their little rosebud holes and what could be done with them. And oral sex. And chainmail and bondage. It was enough to have her panting and squirming in her chair.

Her passionate reaction had her feeling sort of uncomfortable, maybe a little guilty...but deliciously so. It was a for her. Mindy decided to just let herself enjoy this wondrous new experience minus all the unnecessary self-incrimination.

By two in the morning, she'd finished the book that had caused her to slip her hand beneath the blanket and inside her sweatpants to pleasure herself more than once. She'd climaxed more while reading the book than she had in a *long* time.

She never would have believed it if someone told her she could get that turned on simply by reading a romance novel. But oh, what a book it was! Bold and kinky, it fueled Mindy's deeply buried fantasies.

It was hard to imagine going back to the almost chaste romance novels she'd read in the past. Stories featuring itty-bitty, virtuous, virginal heroines with nary a flaw...aside from the fact they were often too stupid to live.

As she read the sample chapter at the back of the book, highlighting the author's next medieval-themed spicy romance, Mindy vowed to purchase the book, wondering what her life might be like if she'd lived in those times. Yawning as she read, Mindy's eyelids became heavy and she nodded off...

As she spotted the figure in the distance, swiftly riding toward her, the sunlight glinted brightly from the form and Lady Mindora felt her loins tighten. Only the shining armor of her true love, the brave Sir Archer, shone with such radiant magnificence!

Her valiant knight was coming to rescue her from Edward-the-tiny-cocked, the fierce ogre who kept her locked away in his terrible sex chamber filled with impotent implements that failed to satisfy her carnal cravings.

"Ah yes, bold knight," she whispered as the figure on horseback drew closer. "Ride quickly. Come liberate me from my torment, my living hell of orgasm-less existence. Then hold me in your strong arms and fuck me as no man ever has ever fucked me before."

Lady Mindora wrestled against the heavy chains that bound her to the drab gray stone wall to no avail. As her knight approached the ogre's castle she lost sight of him, for the chains prevented her from going to the window. She sent up a prayer that her intrepid rescuer be spared any harm.

Harshly raised voices rang out in anger, then the sickening sound of flesh hitting flesh. Finally, the sharp clang of metal against metal.

"Forsooth, protect my brave knight! Provide him the strength he needs to overpower the cold, callous Edward-the-tiny-cocked," she cried out as the ghastly noises continued for a seeming eternity.

The clamor finally terminated with a shocked gasp and cry of pain. But whose? Lady Mindora heard footfalls shuffling up the great stone steps and over to the ogre's sex chamber. The heavy wooden door banged open and before her stood her tall, handsome knight, bloodied and panting. His armor was mightily dented but, merrily, he was victorious!

"My fair Lady Mindora." Sir Archer removed his helmet. "I have slain the ogre, Edward-the-tiny-cocked, and have come to free you from your chains. Then I shall take you in my powerful arms and fill your silken coin purse with my massive iron-hard schlong."

Lady Mindora swooned. "Nay, brave, handsome knight, I cannot wait to feel your magnificent maypole thrusting high and hard inside me. Take me now, whilst I am still in chains. Rip through my garments with your sword and have your way with me now, I beg of you."

Sir Archer's already huge boner increased threefold, the amazing force of it punching through his raiments. Ah, how proud and high his enormous meat rod stood, bobbing and waving its lusty intention in the fair Lady Mindora's direction. Verily, her lady garden was afire with desire. She hungered, besotted so terribly it made her pretty little pink clit quiver.

Wielding his heavy sword with finesse, Sir Archer slit through the bodice laces of his beloved's blue woolen gown. Her colossal aching jugs burst forth, bobbling in place, with eager nipples boldly stabbing high in the air, enthusiastic for his rousing touch.

Verily, Sir Archer's ramrod surged by another inch just then. His sword continued to rip through her gown, down, down, down until the glistening curls atop Lady Mindora's ravenous sausage wallet was exposed.

With a mere glance at the love juices coursing down her pale thighs, his already remarkable length was augmented by another inch.

Only the ragged remnants of Lady Mindora's clothes hung from her shackled arms and her voluptuous form now. The heavy chains were draped in crisscross fashion across her snowy boobage. The harsh metal abraded her jutting, dusky pink nipples in a most scintillating manner each time she moved.

And so, move she did, back and forth. Forth and back. Hither and yon.

Removal of a knight's armor was no quick, easy task. Sir Archer went about it as swiftly as possible, grimacing at the throbbing ache taunting his ready family jewels.

"Nay," Lady Mindora said. "Worry not about your armor, Sir Archer. Take me now. Let me feel the hard steel of your mighty breastplate against my Rubenesque softness."

Sir Archer hesitated not. He crushed her full, supple curves hard against the cold steel covering his chest. Her nipples beaded even harder against the chilly surface and the impassioned Lady Mindora moaned with pleasure at the erotic sensation.

Her eyelids fluttering shut, Lady Mindora contemplated what it might feel like to have her sensitive tatas scraped by the chainmail Sir Archer wore beneath his armor. Ahhh yes, such sweet torture.

"I have changed my mind," she announced. "Strip yourself of your armor, but let your chainmail tunic remain intact." Her lady parts wept freely at the thought.

"The chainmail is rough, coarse and unduly harsh, Lady Mindora. I fear it will pinch and scratch the tiny, tender pink buds of your magnificent knockers and cause them pain." He kissed each delicate, beading nipple, nipping them with his teeth.

Lady Mindora licked her lips. Pinching, scratching, scraping...an exquisite combination of pain and pleasure.

"You waste time talking, Sir Archer. I bid you make haste and do as I ask."

Stripping the breastplate from his well-muscled torso, he replied, "Your wish is my command." Clasping his hands behind her back, he crushed her voluminous ivory tits against his chainmailed chest. Peering at the sight of delicate flesh mashed to metal, Sir Archer's gargantuan pork sword twitched.

"My gonads are heavy and my custard launcher demands to be appeased."

"Indubitably, brave knight." Lady Mindora squashed herself hard to his chest, scraping her hooters across the woven metal, delighting in the agonizingly delicious sensation. When she'd finally had enough, she pulled back far enough for Sir Archer to see evidence of the abrasion, dappling her creamy melons.

"Before we have finished, you shall bathe my tortured bazooms with hot, soothing ribbons of your love juice."

Forsooth, Sir Archer's breathing became labored and he did grow yet another inch.

"Now, my valiant knight," Lady Mindora cried out. "Take me now. Savagely bang, boink, shag, and screw my dripping penis fly trap without mercy. Look deep into my eyes with your molten, chocolate chip eyes as you spear me with that hot, hard python."

Flummoxed, Sir Archer paused a moment. "What are chocolate chips, my lady?"

"I know not," Lady Mindora answered. "I fear they have not yet been invented. But I deem that one day my entire world shall revolve around them."

With Lady Mindora's arms and legs spread far apart in their shackles, Sir Archer had easy access to her lustrous, wet meat curtains. Grasping her jiggly twins, he supported himself as he plunged his mighty purple-headed soldier into her, groaning as he filled her slick, silky bearded oyster completely.

Lady Mindora's abundant bazongas bounced against the big palms of his hands as the randy knight shoved himself high into her unquenchable cooch. As he rammed her, Sir Archer captured one expectant nipple in his mouth, torturing it exquisitely as she begged for more.

"Indeed, I relish taking you, fair damsel, in this crude, wicked manner—shackled in chains and helpless. Fortified by the lush spectacle of my fair lady, moaning and writhing against her chains, my knight's pole of pleasure is indisputably more solid and extended than ever before. Perhaps, before we have finished, my lady will present me with the tight little rosebud nestled at her ass so I may bone that too."

"Your words are like music to my ears, but I wish you now to dispense with your incessant babbling and fixate on your jamming the clam, Sir Archer."

No matter how hard and fast he shoved into her, Lady Mindora begged for more. Higher, harder, faster. Sir Archer happily obliged, unrelentingly assaulting her with his friendly weapon, bringing them both to the brink of nirvana.

But lamentably, escape into paradise was not to be, for in the next moment, Britney-of-red-cunt, the evil, malevolent witch and widow of Edward-the-tiny-cocked, barged into the chamber, wholly unexpected, catching the sex-dazed knight unawares.

Using her shoulder as a battering ram, Britney-of-red-cunt crashed into Sir Archer, pushing him out the chamber window, cackling at him as he fell.

The fair Lady Mindora shrieked in horror as the beady-eyed witch turned toward her, licking her lips in a wild, lusty fashion.

What fuckery was this?!

"Methinks 'tis time for me to finish what your knight has begun, Lady Mindora. Whisking away her skirts, Britney-of-red-cunt uncovered an enormous wooden dildo strapped to her hips and muff. It was certain she deemed to plunge the monstrous contrivance into Lady Mindora's cream pie.

"I shall fuck you over good," Britney-of-red-cunt threatened, "afore wielding my trusty dildo to beat you senseless before I hurl you atop my dead husband, Edward-the-tiny-cocked.

"No. No! Noooooo!" Lady Mindora wailed, but her brave knight had fallen to his death and there was no one left to save her.

"Ta-da! My gay blade and I shall save you, Lady Mindora," Leo-the-meddlesome announced as he pranced into the room, ladylike dagger in hand.

"Not if I de-cock you first, you meddling matchmaker," Britney-of-red-cunt warned, snatching the dagger from Leo-the-meddlesome's hand, brandishing it toward his boom stick.

"Oh...in that case, exit, stage right." With unmatched swiftness, Leo-the-meddlesome was out the door. "See ya, Mindy," he called as his feet pattered down the castle's stone steps.

"Leo, you miserable, meddling, trouble-making coward, you come back here!" Lady Mindora cried as Britney-of-red-cunt closed in on her with a sickening cackle and malicious look in her eye.

Forsooth, Lady Mindora was surely sunk.

Mindy

GASPING, MINDY AWOKE from her wild and crazy dream. "Oh brother! I can't even escape Archer in my dreams," she groused. Cocking her head to the side, she half-frowned and half-smiled, recalling the gratuitous erotic elements of her dream.

"Chainmail, huh? Ouch." Crossing her arms protectively over her breasts, Mindy retrieved the romance novel from the chair and gazed at the explicit cover, showing a half-dressed damsel and her sexy knight, who were clearly ready to do some serious bone jumping.

"Nothing quite as wickedly silly and kinky as Lady Mindora and Sir Archer, though." Mindy laughed. Amazing, one read-through of her first hot and spicy romance novel and her libido had turned wild and wanton

"Lady Mindora," she tsked, "you are one very naughty girl."

Chapter 5

EVERY MORNING for several days Mindy found a little peace offering from Leo, tied with satin ribbon, on her desk. Low-fat granola bars, fat-free brownie cookies, sugar-free chocolate bars, tiny handcrafted items... Each surprise was accompanied by a spicy-hot romance novel.

He'd attached note cards to each book saying things like, *Read this—this could be you...Love, Leo*. A little smiley-face doodle always adjoined his name.

This morning it was a tiny potpourri sachet, embroidered with the words, *Best Friends are Forever*. The romance novel was titled *Beloved Enemy*, and the note card read, *Days have gone by and I've run out of gift ideas. I think I've groveled enough. Read this book over the weekend, there'll be a quiz on Monday...Love, Leo*.

A smile spread across Mindy's face.

Crossing the deep persimmon-colored carpeting in Leo's office, Mindy pulled him out of his chair, grabbing him into a hug.

"Come here, you relentless old meddler. How can I possibly stay mad at someone as crazy and wonderful as you?"

Leo's face lit up with a boyish grin as he motioned for Mindy to sit. "That's exactly the point I've been trying to make. How about a cup of coffee?" He ambled over to his espresso maker after Mindy nodded. "Espresso or cappuccino?"

"Espresso's fine." Mindy snuggled into one of the upholstered chairs, waving the romance paperback in his direction. "*Beloved Enemy*? How long did it take you to dig this up?"

"I just walked into the bookstore and, *voila*, there it was, calling my name," Leo claimed. "Don't forget there'll be a quiz on Monday, so you better read it."

"Yes sir, Mr. Parker, sir." Saluting, she rose from her chair and joined Leo at the espresso maker, draping her arm around his shoulder. "I'm sorry about giving you the cold shoulder lately. I know you meant well, Leo, but that whole Priest thing is still such a sore spot with me."

"I know, sweetie, I know." Leo ground the Italian roast coffee beans to a fine powder. "Mmm, smells good, doesn't it?"

Closing her eyes and breathing in a deep whiff, Mindy nodded. "Heavenly."

"Heard anything from Archer yet?" he asked over his shoulder.

"No, and I don't expect to. He was only being nice because you all but hog-tied the poor man and bullied him into a corner." Mindy chuckled, walking to the far side of Leo's office, checking out the newest cruise brochures.

"Oooh, that sounds kinky. I'll have to remember that." He winked.

"Let's face it, Leo." Mindy did a slow pirouette. "I'm not exactly Archer Priest's type. I mean, did you get a good look at the guy?"

Pursing his lips, Leo fluttered his hand across his heart. "Oh honey, did I ever." He rolled his eyes for effect.

"You nut." Mindy whapped his arm. "I'm serious. Do you think somebody who looks like a movie idol would want to be seen with a plump plain Jane like me?"

A look of genuine astonishment flashed across Leo's features as he bubbled forth with laughter. "Plump plain Jane?" He slapped his hand to his mouth, giggling.

Mindy's eyes widened. "Well I'm happy you find my lackluster appearance so amusing, Leo."

"Lackluster?" Wiping a tear from his eye, Leo propped an arm over Mindy's shoulder. "My God, Mindy, how many times do I have to tell you you're a knockout now? You're a beautiful, breathtaking woman."

Steam hissed from the espresso maker and Leo tended to his preparation, shaving a curl from the peel of one of the fresh lemons he kept in the small refrigerator in his office.

"Believe me, darling, your plump plain Jane days are long gone. Frankly, as far as I'm concerned, you look like a goddess at any weight." He paused to offer Mindy an engaging grin. "So case closed. I don't want to hear any more self put-downs from you, okay? Biscotti?"

"No way. They've got a zillion fat grams."

"These are low fat," Leo promised.

Mindy took one, crunching into the hazelnut biscotti as she sank into her chair. One sip from the molten brew had her expressing an extended *ahhhh* of satisfaction.

"Look at you." Leo gestured. "Curves in all the right places, flawless skin, the biggest deep blue eyes I've ever seen—well, except for that cute little server at Chowder Bay. Mmmm...what was his name again? Oh yeah, Christopher. Be still my heart." His eyelids fluttered closed.

Mindy laughed. "Cradle robber," she said, and Leo snickered.

"Where was I?" he said. "Of course. Your physical attributes. Thick, gorgeous honey-blonde hair, peaches-and-cream complexion, big, beautiful, squeezable breasts. What's not to love?" He gave a nonchalant shrug.

Mindy nearly choked on her espresso. "Leo!" She tugged the cardigan of her heather-gray sweater-set across her chest. "What a thing to say." She took another sip of her brew, cupped her hand over her mouth and laughed. "And anyway, how would *you* know they're beautiful? I don't recall flashing them for you."

"Don't argue semantics with me, young lady. I may be gay, but I'm not blind to feminine charms. And believe me, sister, you've got plenty." He gave a wolf whistle. "You've got the body of a fifties movie queen, darling. A calendar girl. It's time you realized it and stopped trying to conceal it."

Mindy felt her cheeks flush. "Thank you. I appreciate that, Leo. Maybe if I lived in the fifties I'd feel better about myself. But in this day and age, when skeletal is all the rage..." She left the rest unsaid. Why bother dwelling on the fact that she'd never be able to fit society's standards?

"If I may be so bold as to bring up Archer's name again." Leo sported a sly grin. "I noticed him surreptitiously checking out your cleavage at the restaurant."

"You big liar. He was not." Cocking her head, a smile teased at her lips. "Did he, really?"

"May God strip me of my psychic powers forever if I'm lying." He crossed his finger over his heart.

"Psychic, shmychic," Mindy grumbled through laughter before taking another sip of espresso.

Leo moved his hand through the air following invisible curves. "Yup, Archer zeroed right in on those big bazooms of yours." He crunched into his second biscotti, offering another to Mindy, which she declined.

"Gee, Leo, could you be any cruder?"

With a dismissive wave, Leo assured, "Oh sure, lots."

"Anyway, so what if Archer *was* eyeing my," Mindy cleared her throat, "attributes. Big deal. If he's anything like his sister, which is a darned good bet, sex is foremost on the man's brain. Doesn't make a darned bit of difference anyway though, Leo, because that's one man I have absolutely no intention of seeing again. Ever."

"Whatever you say, Mindy darling." With an impassive shrug, Leo drained the last bit of powerful brew from the demitasse cup.

"That seemed a tad too effortless." Mindy eyed her boss through narrowed slits. "It's not like you to give up so easily." Pressing the tip of her finger into the biscotti crumbs on her plate, she licked her finger, uttering a satisfied purr.

"What can I say, Mindy? When you're right, you're right." Leo held his cup aloft. "Want another?"

"No thanks, I'm still working on this one. So, you're just going to let it drop, huh?"

"Hmm? Drop? Let what drop?" Leo offered an innocent smile in response to Mindy's doubtful look. "Oh you mean Archer? Sure. He's a closed subject as far as I'm concerned. You know how I hate to butt my two cents in where they're not wanted."

"This is *me*, Leo, remember? Why do I have a sinking feeling you've got something up your sleeve where Archer's concerned? To which I'd say without hesitation...don't even think about it."

Crossing his arms over his chest, Leo rested against the back of his chair. "I thought you didn't want to talk about Archer."

Mindy glanced up from her espresso. "I don't, that's just the point."

"You could have fooled me."

Clearing her throat, Mindy suggested, "Let's get off the topic of Archer and move on to your favorite subject."

"Which is?"

"You, of course," she teased.

"Funny. Very funny. But true," Leo agreed with a shrug. "Go ahead, mesmerize me." Leaning forward in his chair, he propped his elbow on the desk, resting his chin on his fist.

"It looks like you've lost some weight over the last couple weeks. Lookin' good, boss."

Leo bounced from his chair, proudly sticking his thumbs in the waistband of his pants as he pulled it outward. "Four more pounds." He looked like an excited little boy and Mindy couldn't help smile. "That leaves about eleven pounds to go. Look, I can stick both thumbs in and there's still room. Went down another notch on my belt too. Not too shabby, huh?"

"I'm proud of you, Leo. Keep up the good work."

"How about you and the chocolate monster? You still doing okay?"

"Yup, fortunately binge free." Mindy nodded. "But," a slow, desirous smile spread across her lips, "I still allow myself a little morsel of chocolate each weekend. All in all, I'm doing fine. I'm pretty happy with myself right now. It does take a while for the body image to catch up. I need to remind myself every so often that I'm not that three-hundred-pound plain Jane anymore."

"Atta girl, Min." Leo nodded vigorously. "Now you're talking."

Noticing one of the travel agents settling in at her desk, Mindy said, "I thought this was Carol's day off."

"It was. I, uh," Leo cleared his throat, "I asked her to come in today and take tomorrow off instead."

"Oh. Any particular reason? Seems like a pretty slow day to bring in extra help."

"I just had a feeling we might need Carol this afternoon," Leo said with an odd giggle as he picked up his ringing desk phone. "Yes, sure, Linda, give me five minutes, then send him back to my office."

Looking at Mindy, Leo took a deep breath as he nervously fiddled with his jade-green butterfly-print tie. Then he giggled again.

Mindy suddenly felt a knot twisting deep in her gut. "Leo...?"

"Okay, Mindy, don't panic on me now. Archer Priest is here to see you." Leo raised his hand as soon as Mindy's jaw dropped. She rose from her chair. "Sit down," he said in an authoritative voice.

"Closed subject, huh? I should have known better. You lied to me, Leo."

"I prefer to think of it as gently elasticizing the truth."

"No...I will *not* allow you to do this to me." Mindy gave a determined shake of her head as she wagged a chastising finger at Leo. "I'm getting out of here *now*." As she took a step toward the door, Leo jumped up from his chair to block the doorway.

"Will you puhleeze stop acting like a stubborn child and sit down? Look, it's not going to kill you just to hear what the man has to say, is it?"

"Since he's going to be here in a couple of minutes, I don't seem to have any choice, do I?"

The picture of innocence, Leo smiled and shrugged in response.

Placing her hand to her throat, Mindy sat back into the chair, swallowing hard. "All right. But I'll only give him one minute. Then I'm making an excuse to leave." She jabbed a threatening finger at Leo. "And you damn well better back me up. Do you hear me, Leo Parker?"

Nodding heartily, Leo waved his hand in an indifferent manner. "Sure, no problem. I'll go along with whatever you say." Planting his fingers under his chin, he studied Mindy briefly as he took his seat.

"Flip your marcasite pendant around, it's backward. Okay, now hike your skirt up a notch and stick your chest out a bit. God, I hope you're not wearing grandma underwear. You're not, are you, Min?"

Mindy felt a tingle of panic thinking about her sturdy, white cotton underwear. The old-fashioned utility kind. The kind her grandma probably wore. But that was ridiculous. After all, Archer would never know if she was wearing industrial-strength underwear or a lacy bra and thong, because he was most definitely not getting a peek.

Leo's face fell. "Crap, you are. I can tell by that clueless doe look on your face. Honey, you've got to learn that you can't feel sexy on the outside unless you're wearing something naughty inside. Mark your calendar. We're going shopping at triple L tomorrow."

"Triple what?"

"L...as in Lacy and Luscious Lingerie." He put a finger to his lips as Mindy opened her mouth to protest.

"Shhh, Archer's coming around the corner. It's time to shine. Let's see that winning smile of yours, Min."

Leo rose to greet Archer Priest as he entered his office. "Archer, great to see you again," he said flashing his best salesman's smile.

"Leo, Mindy." Archer returned the smile, nodding at each of them. "I was hoping to take you up on your offer to steal away your best travel counselor for an hour or two."

Archer gazed down at Mindy with those striking brown eyes. He was dressed in a deep blue-gray suit, pale gray shirt, and his tie was printed with tiny wine bottles in shades of blue, gray, cream and maroon. It was a tie worthy of Leo's collection.

"Sorry it's such short notice, but I just flew in from a week-long business trip to California," Archer explained. "Came right from the airport, actually." Smiling at Mindy, he said, "I thought it might be nice to have lunch together. How about it, Mindy?" His inviting voice was as smooth and soft as silk.

With a jubilant look, Leo shot to his feet. "Oh she'd be—" He stopped in mid-sentence, fiddled with his tie-tack and glanced at Mindy who flashed him a warning look. "Uh Mindy, what's your schedule like this afternoon?" he said in a restrained manner entirely unlike him. "Think you can swing it?"

Mindy flashed Leo a smile. She knew how hard it was for him to choke back an exuberant positive reply on her behalf. Taking a moment to enjoy the clean, woodsy fragrance subtly wafting through Leo's office since Archer entered it, Mindy heaved a sigh.

She wished he wasn't Britney's brother and she could say yes. After one glance into those big, chocolate drop eyes of his, Mindy's heart hammered.

"Yes," she flat-out amazed herself by saying. "Lunch today would be lovely, Archer."

"Great!" Leo said. It was amazing he could speak, considering his shit-eating grin. Briskly rubbing his hands together, he scooted past Archer to the door of his office. Pausing just outside, he popped his head back through the doorway.

"Oh, and Mindy, Carol will be here all afternoon, so you can take the rest of the afternoon off." He winked with a devilish grin before flying down the corridor and leaving Mindy with her mouth hanging open.

Chapter 6

A RCHER ESCORTED Mindy to a gleaming black stretch-limousine. The uniformed driver stood at attention as he held the door open for the couple. Mindy was duly impressed. While Archer spoke to the driver, she sank back into the soft, cushy maroon leather and took a deep breath.

Careful... Don't get carried away, Mindora von G. Remember, this guy's Britney's brother.

A moment later Archer gracefully slid across the smooth leather seat, flashing Mindy a mesmerizing smile as his imposing presence filled her senses.

"Your boss seems like a great guy," Archer noted.

"He is." *Except when he's busy sticking his nose in my business and trying to set me up with the henna-haired fornicator's brother.* "Leo's a terrific boss and a great friend."

"Friend? So there's nothing else...I mean, I'm not intruding on a more...serious relationship between you two?"

Archer's question caught Mindy by surprise. "Me and Leo? Oh good heavens no." Placing her hand at the base of her throat, she laughed. "Leo is...uh, well, he's just a very close friend."

Archer eased into a relaxed smile. "I'm glad. That's the impression I got, but I just wanted to confirm."

Mindy chuckled softly. "Although Leo does have a rather annoying penchant for meddling."

"Well, I'm glad he intervened on my behalf. Otherwise, I have a sneaking suspicion you and I wouldn't be together right now."

Archer's smile was so mesmerizing, Mindy found it difficult to concentrate on what he was saying. A blush filtered across her cheeks. "You're probably right, because—"

Archer placed his hand over Mindy's, causing her to completely lose her train of thought. Her mind became oatmeal. All she could focus on was the delicious, tingling current that began at Archer's touch, zigzagging an agreeable course as it sent a shiver jogging up and down her spine and ended with a significant zing in the center of her clit. She found herself shuddering. In a good way.

"Looks like I owe Leo a debt of gratitude." Archer brushed his thumb across her fingers.

Alarmed by her sudden inability to register a logical thought, Mindy closed her eyes, sucked in a deep breath and slipped her hand from Archer's. Finally regaining some semblance of normal brain matter, she opened her eyes and noticed the driver had turned onto the tollway.

Clearing her throat, she asked, "So where are we going for lunch?"

"Well," Archer stretched his long legs out onto the limo's spacious floor, "since you have the rest of this beautiful winter day free, I thought a little picnic lunch in the city might be nice."

Mindy's eyebrows lifted in surprise. "A picnic?" Archer nodded as a broad smile overtook his features. She had to hand it to him for innovation. The last thing she'd expected was to spend the afternoon freezing her ass off, chowing down on cold fried chicken and coleslaw on some brittle, frozen patch of grass. In Chicago. In January.

"Gee, that, um, sounds nice, Archer. Really...nice." Mindy slanted him a dubious look and smiled. Apparently Britney Priest wasn't the only family member with a few screws loose. Thanks to Leo, Mindy didn't have an easy out if she needed it. She was stuck with Archer Priest for the afternoon.

Mindy gave Archer another furtive glance. He may be screwy and he may be a Priest but, damn, she couldn't deny he was one spectacular-looking hunk of man. The kind of guy who could almost make her believe in real life romance novel heroes.

Oops. Wrong thing to think about. Mindy was immediately inundated with kinky images of Sir Archer and Lady Mindora, hard at play. Her nipples grew hard and tight as she recalled the carnal scene. Thank God she had a coat on over her sweater-set. There'd be no way to hide her telltale arousal.

Comfortably immersed in light small talk during the forty-five-minute ride, Mindy found herself so captivated by their effortless, flowing conversation that she hadn't paid any attention to the passing scenery. When the driver stopped and opened the door, Mindy was surprised to find they were parked in front of an imposing lakefront high-rise. The sort of place she'd only seen in high-end real estate listings when she was in the business.

As Archer exited the vehicle, she had a difficult time imagining them spreading a blanket there on the concrete, digging in to a tub of potato salad while passersby ogled them.

"This is where we're having our picnic?" She stepped out of the limo as he guided her.

"Yup." Archer gave her a twinkle-eyed smile. "Chilly?"

To the bone. "Nope, not a bit. The lake air is refreshing. Exhilarating. Don't you think?" She succumbed to a bone-deep shudder.

The bright January sun offered minimal warmth in contrast to the glacial Lake Michigan breeze. Mindy offered a clenched-teeth grin to keep them from chattering as she stood in the brisk, biting wind.

"I'll have you all warm and toasty in a few minutes." Archer offered his arm and they entered the large gilded door held open by a doorman. Mindy bit back a smile as she pictured several appealing methods Archer could use to raise her temperature. Chainmail anyone?

The building's lobby had more marble, gold and crystal than she'd seen since her last travel-agent-tour of one of the new luxury cruise ships. Sedate yet stunning. Dazzling without being garish.

"Is this where you work?" she asked as they stepped into an oiled walnut-paneled elevator.

"I conduct business here when I'm in the city." Archer whisked a security key card across a pad at the elevator's control panel. "It's a good centralized location."

"Complete with picnic tables on the roof?" Mindy noted as he pressed the button for the top floor.

"Something like that." The sound of Archer's laughter was rich, deep and easy.

After a rapid transport to the highest floor, the elevator doors parted. Mindy fully expected to step into a hallway or vestibule but they entered directly into what looked like somebody's home instead. She swallowed a gasp as she took in her surroundings. With its sleek, clean lines and artful yet minimalist décor, the place looked like something out of a swanky architectural magazine.

The first thing she noticed was a still-life painting of a wine bottle and two filled glasses flanked by a wedge of ripe cheese, some crackers and a small bunch of grapes. Painted in the realism style, the perfectly executed scene looked so authentic, so much like a photograph, it made her mouth water.

Her gaze skittered from left to right, observing an abundance of beige marble, onyx black touches, bold artwork, a massive see-through fireplace and a full wall of floor-to-ceiling windows affording a breathtaking view of the cityscape and Lake Michigan. Sophisticated and contemporary, the open floor plan was somehow warm and inviting at the same time.

"Wow...what is this place? It looks like a penthouse suite."

"Bingo." Archer offered a grin. "It's my home away from home."

Mindy fought to keep her jaw from dropping. "You live here?"

"Sometimes. It's my city retreat. My main house is in the country. This place is good for entertaining out-of-town clients and conducting business meetings. Whenever I need a city fix I come here and get my fill."

Mindy slanted him a skeptical look. "I thought you said we were going on a picnic. You never said anything about bringing me up to your apartment. Why, Mr. Priest...did you bring me here to see your etchings?" she asked with a coy smile.

Flashing a devilish grin, Archer flexed his forefinger. "Follow me." They walked through the length of the vast apartment to a set of massive sliding glass doors leading to the rooftop. "Your picnic as promised, milady." Bowing, he extended his hand, ushering Mindy through the door he'd slid open.

His *milady* remark had her ill-disciplined mind skating toward thoughts of him as Sir Archer in her dream again.

Expecting to be chilled to the bone, Mindy found herself perfectly toasty and comfortable. A quick glance at the mostly glass structure surrounding the large area explained the pleasant temperature. This outside room was far from a typical rooftop patio. It was a beautifully appointed extension of the apartment with furniture, artwork, lighting and plenty of green, leafy plants.

"I had this section of the roof enclosed so I can use it all year round." Archer gestured toward a table and chairs. "But we still get the great views."

Mindy smiled as she noted the white linen tablecloth and napkins, gold-edged white china, crystal goblets and gold flatware. A bowl of fresh fruit sat at the center of the table, flanked by white pillar candles in crystal holders, which Archer lit. A large wicker picnic basket rested at the edge of the table.

He slid a panel in the wall and pushed one of the many buttons there. Sensuous sounds of jazz instrumentals cosseted them, adding to an already perfect atmosphere.

Properly impressed, Mindy arched an eyebrow. "You think of everything, Archer."

"I do my best." He graced her with a smooth, sexy smile that made her feel she was way out of her league. "If you get chilly, there are small blankets there." He pointed to what looked like a curtained bed with decorative pillows and several chenille throws.

"I'm fine. It's surprisingly comfortable. And beautiful," Mindy told him, having a difficult time looking away from the fanciful bed. It reminded her of something out of the Arabian Nights. She imagined a handsome, smooth operator like Archer was used to the women he brought up here gracefully sliding from chair to bed and spreading wide for him.

"Thanks." Opening the wicker basket, he retrieved two bottles of red wine. Expertly removing the corks, he smiled. "Here's something guaranteed to warm your innards, Mindy, even if you decide to explore the uncovered portion of the rooftop." He poured them each a glass of the smoky, blood-red wine. "I hope you like cabernet."

Cabernet...cabernet... What the heck was it she'd read about cabernet? "I do, very much. It's the one red wine that's perfectly compatible with chocolate." Quite proud of herself for retrieving that cosmopolitan tidbit from her memory banks, Mindy gave an urbane smile.

"I'm impressed." Archer nodded, studying her with interest. "Not too many people know that."

Maintaining her cultured expression, Mindy tittered a laugh. "As a diehard chocoholic, I've made it my mission to know everything possible relating to the confection." With a furtive glance she held the glass under her nose and breathed deeply, hoping she correctly remembered what she'd been taught at the wine tasting class she and Leo attended.

"Mmmm, great nose," she murmured, taking in the heady fragrance, striving to appear polished and sophisticated. After clinking glasses, she took a sip and closed her eyes. She held the wine in her mouth, swishing it around for a few seconds before swallowing, just as she'd learned.

"Mmmm," she murmured again, adeptly avoiding a shudder as she swallowed the unpleasant liquid.

As the cabernet accosted her uneducated palette, Mindy's eyes flew open in shocked disgust. Pasting a delighted expression across her face, all she tasted was a non-sweet, grapey-mushroomy fluid she was none too thrilled about. She couldn't imagine why anyone would want to spoil the taste of chocolate by washing it down with this stuff.

To Mindy's chagrin, an emerging head-to-toe shudder emerged. Hopefully, Archer would just think she was chilly.

He clinked glasses with her and took a sip. Mindy watched for his reaction. Maybe the stuff was spoiled. Archer's pleased expression as he swallowed said otherwise.

"This one has a nice oakiness," he noted.

Oakiness. Yeah, the taste could definitely be described as wet wood. "Just what I was about to say," she cooed. "I also taste currants and detect a slight undertone of spice. It has a deep, rich earthiness," she added, mimicking the comments she'd heard at the wine tasting.

Gazing up at Archer, Mindy offered a gracious smile. "This is a wonderful cabernet, Archer," she flat out lied.

He nodded approvingly. "It appears you know how to recognize and appreciate a good wine, Mindy. That's something we have in common."

Mindy smiled, almost chuckled. Since Archer had bought every bogus word, she felt pretty confident. Bluffing her way through a wine tasting was a cinch. A snap. Piece of cake. Any buffoon could do it. Puffed with her stellar performance, she couldn't resist showing off more of her phony wine acumen.

"I usually prefer dry wines with red meat and wet wines with white meat." Tossing the comment off with a blasé smile, Mindy was taken aback when Archer nearly choked on his wine. "Are you all right?"

"Yeah, sure," he said through his coughs. "Just went down the wrong way. So...you drink a lot of wet wines, do you?" The corners of Archer's mouth twitched.

"Yes. Like Riesling with salmon. The wine's subtle wetness pairs beautifully with the flavorful fish, don't you agree?"

Archer stared at her blankly for a moment. "Absolutely," he said finally, covering his mouth to cough again.

Oh this was fun! Mindy was impressing the socks off him with her faux wine expertise.

A pleased expression crossing his features, Archer studied Mindy for a moment before reaching into the wicker basket. "Sounds like you've been a wine lover for some time."

Full of bravado, she gave a flick of her wrist. "Oh, eons." She huffed a blasé chuckle.

"How about champagne? Like it?" Archer brought out a couple small covered plates from the basket. Unwrapping a perfectly ripened wedge of French brie, he placed it on the table along with some sesame seed water crackers and two tiny pearl-handled knives.

"Of course," Mindy answered, sipping from her cabernet. This time she willed herself not to shudder as the putrid liquid went down.

"Nothing like a fine glass of champagne to compliment a great dinner," Archer said. Reaching into the basket again, he withdrew a plate of assorted pâté slices and another with cloves of roasted garlic and scalloped pats of butter. "What's your favorite brand?"

Mindy whipped her head toward Archer. "Of champagne?" He nodded. "Oh, uh..." Never having ingested anything more costly than a two-dollar bottle of sparkling wine, she was at a loss.

"Gee, isn't that funny." She took another sip of wine, smiling at him over the rim of her glass, stalling for time. "I can't seem to remember. The name's right on the tip of my tongue. It's one of those expensive French ones."

"You mean somewhere in the six to eight-dollar range?" Archer asked, sporting a curious expression.

"Right." Mindy cleared her throat and flashed a tentative smile. "They're so much tastier than the two to four-dollar variety."

Archer's lip twitched. "Without a doubt." He dug into the basket again, depositing two tiny silver boxes of Belgian chocolates on the table, immediately capturing Mindy's attention.

She couldn't help grinning. Cold fried chicken, potato salad and coleslaw indeed. This guy really knew how to put on a picnic. He'd succeeded in completely bowling her over.

"Archer, this is all amazing, but I don't understand. In Leo's office I thought you said you just came from the airport."

"I did."

"How did you manage to pull all this together so fast?"

The smile he offered was hot, sexy and seductive. It warmed her in places the cabernet didn't reach.

"I was thinking about you during the plane ride back from California." His voice was even sexier than his smile. "I called you at the travel agency but you were on another call. So I spoke to Leo. He told me you were free this afternoon and I could stop by."

Mindy cocked her head, wondering if she'd heard him correctly. "You talked to Leo? This morning?" Archer nodded. "You mean, before your flight left from California?"

"No, from the plane." Archer smiled and sipped some wine.

Bewildered, Mindy spun her body toward him. "You called me while in flight?"

"I told you I was thinking about you." Archer's chuckle was husky. "Since you kept popping into my thoughts during my business trip, I hoped I'd be able to see you when I got back." His eyes sparkling with amusement, Archer reached over to lift Mindy's chin, which had apparently been hanging open for a while.

"After I talked to Leo and ironed everything out with him, I called Williams, my limo driver. I had him gather what I needed for our picnic lunch and...*voila*." Archer gestured toward the linen-covered table spread with gourmet edibles.

Shaking her head in amazement, Mindy placed her wineglass on the table, stroking its stem. "So *that's* why Leo called Carol to switch her day off and come in today, instead. Why that meddling..." Mindy gave in to an exasperated sigh.

"Don't be too hard on Leo." Archer chuckled. "He's a good guy."

"For a busybody." Hiding her emerging smile, Mindy took a leisurely sip of cabernet. It tasted somewhat less offensive now. She slanted Archer an inquisitive glance. "Just what exactly did Leo say to you?"

With an uncertain squint, Archer admitted, "He clued me in on the fact that you're not too crazy about me being Britney's brother. But, believe it or not, I already got that message from you the other day at Chowder Bay."

Mindy felt the color rise in her cheeks. "I'm sorry. I didn't mean to be rude. It's just that...well..." After another fortifying sip of wine, which tasted better all the time, she glanced up into Archer's eyes.

"How much do you know about the situation with me, Edward, and your sister?"

Expelling a deep breath, and looking rather uncomfortable, Archer shifted in his seat. "The condensed version. As told and interpreted by Britney Priest von Grettle. Let's just say it wasn't a very pretty tale and you definitely weren't the heroine." He offered an apologetic smile.

"I can only imagine what she must have told you about me." She drained her glass and Archer poured them each another.

"I think it's safe to say Britney's account is somewhat biased." He laughed. "I can tell you one thing though—she certainly didn't describe you looking like this." He motioned from Mindy's head to her toes with an appreciative smile. "That's why I was so flabbergasted when you told me your name at the restaurant. I'd expected Mindy von Grettle to be—" He stopped short.

With a nonchalant wave, Mindy said, "Yeah, I know. I'm sure your dear sister had no trouble finding a wealth of graphic terms when it came to describing her dead husband's ex-wife." She expelled a tuneful sigh.

Archer stumbled for words. "I'm afraid she didn't speak of you in the most glowing of terms."

Mindy hiked her shoulder in a resigned shrug. "I'm well aware your sister thought I was a whale. I *was* awfully big back then. Edward's wake was the first time Britney had seen me since I lost the weight."

Archer looked Mindy up and down again, furrowing his brow. "How much weight did—" He held up his hand and groaned. "Sorry, that was rude. Never mind."

"No, it's okay." Topping a cracker with a dab of brie, Mindy hesitantly admitted, "Over a hundred pounds."

"*What?*" Archer's eyes shot wide. "No way."

"Yup. During those ten horrible years with Edward, I used food to drown my sorrows. Not the proudest time of my life."

"You're incredibly beautiful. Gorgeous. I-I can't imagine you looking any other way. You're...well, you're just not the fat type, Mindy." He gave an embarrassed chuckle. "I hope you know what I'm trying to say."

Astonished, Mindy still wasn't used to her slender identity. Glancing down at herself, she smiled when she saw her arms drawn tight around her middle, intent on hiding those old phantom rolls of fat. As she relaxed her posture, a tingly rush of excitement danced through her system.

Holy shit. Archer thinks I'm gorgeous!

She gulped down a mouthful of wine.

"Thank you for the lovely compliment. I've come a long way the last couple of years." Mindy felt all warm and cozy inside, from the cabernet, no doubt. Or maybe it was sitting so close to Archer that caused her insides to heat.

After giving her another appreciative once-over, Archer sipped from his wine. He held his wineglass aloft by the stem, twirling it slowly as he studied it. "Nice full body... Mmm, and just look at those great legs."

Preoccupied with positioning a slice of pate on her cracker, Mindy stopped cold. She wasn't expecting, or prepared for, such personal compliments. Feeling uncomfortable, she hiked her skirt down, scooted her feet out of sight under her chair, and crossed her ankles.

"Um...thank you?"

After a quick glance her way Archer broke into easy laughter.

Mindy frowned. "What's so funny?"

"The wine, Mindy." His warm smile quickly put her at ease. "I'm talking about the wine." He held his glass high and twirled it.

"See the way it coats the glass and runs down the sides? Those are the legs. This wine's got great legs."

Finally recalling the phrases from her wine class, Mindy buried her face in her hands. "I could just die." Peeking at him through spread fingers, she said, "You must think I'm an idiot."

"Not at all. With legs like those, it's a natural mistake for you to make." After gingerly peeking beneath the table, he winked at her. "And this time I'm definitely referring to yours."

Mindy held her glass aloft, studying the deep red contents and taking a sip. Nibbling her bottom lip, she sheepishly glanced up at him. "Archer...I've got a confession to make."

"Really?" His twinkly-eyed smile telegraphed his amusement. "And just what might that be, Ms. von Grettle?"

"I'm a fake. You probably couldn't tell, but to be honest, I know next to nothing about wine."

Archer's smile spread. "Is that so?"

"I'm afraid so." Mindy heaved a sigh. "I heard the tidbit about cabernet being compatible with chocolate on one of those food shows on TV."

"I see."

"And you know those comments about the currants, oak, spice, and earthiness?" He nodded and Mindy swallowed hard. "I, uh, I was trying to be cosmopolitan." She offered a meager smile. "I heard all that at the wine tasting class Leo took me to. I really *do* like this wine though." Mindy held her glass high and grinned. "I didn't at first but, you know," she hiccupped, "oops, excuse me...this wine is really pretty damn good once you get used to it."

After licking her lips, she drained her glass and glanced up at Archer with a bright smile before hiccupping again. "More please."

"Are you sure? You might want to slow down, pace yourself a bit, since you're not used to wine."

"Me? Nah, not necessary." She made a raspberry sound while waving his comment off. "I barely feel a thing. I'm really liking this cabernet stuff, Archer." Grinning, she held out her glass, repeating, "More please."

"You must enjoy it because it's a dry wine versus a wet wine," he said as he refilled her wineglass from the second bottle.

"That must be it." She sipped and hiccupped again. "Did we finish that whole thing already?" she asked, pointing to the empty wine bottle.

"We did." Archer scooted his chair closer, wrapping his arm around Mindy's shoulder. "You know, your *wet wine* comment kind of clued me in early on."

"Really? But, I thought Leo said..." Huh...she couldn't remember what the heck Leo said. Her thinking felt all fuzzy for some reason.

"Wines are either dry or sweet. That's where you got mixed up." Archer gave her shoulder a reassuring squeeze.

"Huh...and here I thought I was being so smooth."

"Don't feel bad. You did some pretty good bluffing for a novice." Archer lifted her chin with his knuckle. "Unfortunately, I had to take some points off your score for the champagne comments."

"Oops...guess I should have stopped while I was ahead."

"Yup." Archer nodded.

"It sounds like you're quite a wine connoisseur," Mindy observed, sipping from her glass. And why wouldn't he be? She imagined most guys who had a personal limo driver, lived in a penthouse in the city, and had a house in the country probably knew a thing or two about fine wine.

"Pick up the wine bottle and take a look at it."

She did, taking a moment to focus because things were a bit blurry. With a gasp she read the words on the label. "Archer's Cellars!" She angled him a cautious smile. "This Archer is *you*?"

He fished through his pocket and retrieved a small black case engraved in gold with the words *Archer's Cellars*. He opened it and handed her one of the business cards.

Squinting to read it, she mumbled the words to herself until she came to the part that read, *Archer Priest, Proprietor and Winemaker*. "Oh my gosh, it *is* you!"

"In the flesh."

"Well that's just great. As if I didn't feel like enough of a moron already." Taking another sip of cabernet, she shook her head. "That'll teach you not to put on airs, Mindora von G." She punctuated her thought with another hiccup.

Archer offered an uncertain look. "*Mindora von G?*"

Frowning, Mindy locked her gaze on Archer. He looked sort of wavy so she blinked a few times. "Did I say that out loud?" Archer nodded with a bemused smile. "Well, just pretend I didn't." She hiccupped and giggled. "Gee, you know, I think this wine's starting to affect me. Or is it effect me? I get those mixed up. One's with an A, one's with an E? One two three...a-b-c. That's a grammar rule rhyme I just made up, Archer. I can't let it affect me while it effects me." Finding her nonsensical words downright hilarious, Mindy laughed. "Oh I crack myself up."

"You should think about taking your show on the road." His hand to his forehead, Archer laughed. "Listen, Mindy, since you're not used to drinking wine it's probably best to take it slow."

"No, no, no, if it's my show, I don't want to take it slow. See? Another Mindy rhyme!"

"I had no idea you were so talented. Leo failed to mention that."

"I'll have to talk to Leo." She reached out to finger Archer's tie. "So that's why your tie is printed with little wine bottles all over, huh?" He nodded. "Veeeery clever. But I thought wine only came from California or France or other far-off places. I never heard of vineyards in Chicago." Her fingers tiptoed from the tie's knot down to its pointed tip, lingering there. She was tempted to explore farther down.

"I have grapes shipped in from Oregon's wine country and from the Napa Valley and Monterey in California, in sealed, refrigerated trucks. My other sources include orchards in Michigan, Wisconsin, Illinois, California and Washington State for the fruit wines."

"Fruit wines? Oh I like the sound of that."

"Apple, peach, strawberry, cherry...I've experimented with quite a variety of fruits. They're very popular with customers. Even won a few awards here and there." He smiled proudly as he postured, blowing on his fingernails and polishing them against his lapel.

Thinking Archer was a real cutie pie, Mindy studied his business card again, doing her best to focus in on the small print. "Nasterbon, Illinois. So your winery," she glanced at the card again, "Archer's Cellars, is in Deledan County, right outside Chicago. Are you in one of those corporate parks?"

"Hell no." Archer gave a noticeable shudder. "It's in the older area, near the historic district. Lots of tree-shaded streets and beautiful old homes with character."

"What kind of building is it—where you make the wine, I mean?" Mindy found this all absolutely fascinating. She found *him* absolutely fascinating. And she *really* liked the way his excellent, wonderful, amazing wine made her feel.

"The winery's located in one of those gingerbready Victorian mansions. It's been rehabbed and updated, but still maintains its old-world charm. I'm pretty proud of the place. Did a lot of the rehab work myself."

"I love those old Victorians, especially when they're cared for and restored. I get sad when I see nineteenth-century buildings being demolished to make way for modern sprawl, like shopping malls or parking garages. It's like losing a valuable piece of history."

"I feel the same way," Archer agreed. "I'm all for growth, technology and advancement, but not at the cost of razing those intricate painted ladies. When I found this property several years ago I knew it was perfect."

"Does the winery take up the entire house?"

"No, I live on the second floor, the offices and retail shop are on the first floor and the winery itself, with all the barrels and vats, is underground. We offer wine tastings for a nominal fee and conduct tours of the winery on weekends. I'd love to give you a personal tour of the winery sometime, Mindy. Would you like that?"

Struggling with her inner *but-he's-Britney's-brother* conflict, Mindy furrowed her brow and studied the tabletop as she flicked at a tiny sesame seed. Logic and common sense told her she absolutely should not see him again. However, due in part to her ingestion of Archer's unbelievably outstanding wine, common sense seemed to have taken flight.

"Yes. I'd like that very much, Archer," she said, already fighting back remorse. She couldn't help herself from agreeing, dammit. She had to see him again.

Archer broke into a satisfied smile. "That's great. We'll even conduct our own private wine tasting session. I think you'll find it all very interesting."

"Well, as you witnessed earlier," Mindy laughed, "I believe I could stand a little wine education." Weaving slightly from left to right, she narrowed one eye to focus better on Archer.

"In that case, I'm your man."

"Mmmm, in *any* case, you're my man." Resting her chin on her hand, Mindy gazed at Archer, taking in each chiseled angle and sinfully sexy curve of his handsome face. Eyes suddenly wide, she froze, silently praying she hadn't just verbalized her innermost thoughts.

Observing the surprised curve of Archer's eyebrow, she groaned. "Oh boy. Please tell me I did *not* just say that out loud." She sucked back another gulp of wine.

"Say what? I didn't hear anything," he answered in gallant fashion, making her feel a smidgen better. "We were talking about wine, weren't we?"

"Yes." Mindy nodded, hoping she could avoid making any more of an ass of herself than she already had. "Good idea. Let's talk about the wine. Please."

"We'll turn you into a wine expert in no time." Archer kept his gaze locked on hers. "I don't think I've ever seen eyes quite that color. They're almost sapphire." He smoothed a cluster of curls from Mindy's face. Leaning closer, he whispered, "Beautiful. Like two exquisite, radiant jewels."

A delicious prickle feathered through her clit and she leaned in closer too. "Thank you, Archer." She breathed in his clean, masculine scent as he neared. With the warm sensation of his breath on her cheek, a sigh escaped her lips. Fully aware of the impending kiss, she forced herself to break eye contact and back away.

"Leo says they're Prussian blue." She rolled her eyes and shook her head because it sounded like such a brainless thing to say. But Archer made her nervous, dammit. And all red-hot and juicy with excitement. The only time she'd felt like this before was the first time she had her Duo-Head Maximum Power Thruster vibrator in her hand and pleasured herself senseless.

That sort of feeling was most definitely *not* supposed to be happening in connection with Britney Priest's brother. Lost in thought, Mindy tapped her wineglass, inviting another pour.

The corners of Archer's eyes crinkled as he smiled. He straightened and filled their glasses. "Prussian blue...I like that. Let's toast to Leo." He lifted his glass, clinking it against Mindy's.

She gazed suspiciously at her wine. "You didn't slip anything in here, did you?" she slurred. "Like an aphrodisiac."

"No, why? Do you feel especially amorous?" Archer's voice was deeper and smokier than the wine.

"Nope." She hiccupped. "I'm frigid."

Archer burst out laughing. "What?"

"It's true." Mindy shrugged. "That's what Edward always told me." She glugged from her glass.

"Edward was an idiot," Archer stated flatly. Smoothing one knuckle across her cheek, he gazed into her eyes. "All I have to do is look at you, sweetheart, to know you're not frigid. A little tipsy but certainly not frigid."

"Oh, it's true. I don't like sex. Well," she shrugged, dissolving into a drawn-out giggle, "unless I'm having it by myself." She blinked a few times. Good grief, did she just...? Yes. Yes she did. "Oops...that's another thing I didn't say out loud."

"I didn't hear a thing."

Studying his incredible chocolate drop eyes, Mindy sighed... They glistened the way semisweet chocolate does when it's melted and stirred. Deep and dark with a rich, sparkling luster.

"Chocolate?"

"My thoughts exactly," Mindy said dreamily.

Archer slanted her a puzzled look as he held a little box of Belgian chocolates under her nose. "What?"

Snapping herself back to reality, Mindy felt the color rise in her cheeks for the umpteenth time that afternoon as she looked down at the box Archer held in his hand. "Oh, you mean *these*." She helped herself to a piece as she gulped down more wine, smiling in surprise. "Well what do you know? Cabernet really does go well with chocolate."

"Why do I feel like I'm missing something here?"

"Don't mind me. I was just thinking about something else for a minute." A husky chuckle tripped past her lips.

"Like what?"

She wagged her finger at Archer. "Never mind. It's private."

"I bet you were thinking the same thing I was." Archer brushed his lips across her ear.

"I doubt that." Mindy laughed. "Unless you're gay." She gave him a pointed look. "You're not, are you?"

"Not by a long shot."

"Good because I was thinking what it would feel like to have a magnificent hunk of man like you take me in his big strong arms and kiss me until my eyeballs jiggled." She giggled, then hiccupped. "Is that what you were thinking, Archer?"

"Goddamn, Mindy von Grettle, you're killing me."

Yanking her close, Archer crushed her against his chest, kissing the bejeezus out of her. It was a kiss just like the ones she'd read about in those hot, steamy books Leo had given her, when tongues lashed and tangled and danced and the woman's pussy got all juicy and her bosom heaved until she screamed *Fuck me!* over and over again.

Yeah...just like that.

When she felt her eyeballs jiggle Mindy moaned a sigh into Archer's mouth. Oh this was no good. No good at all. She popped one eye open and glanced at her wineglass. It was the wine! Archer's magical seductive wine was making her feel like this. She had to get rid of it. With that thought in mind, Mindy abruptly broke the kiss, drained her glass, cleared her throat and licked her lips with a smack. "Whew! All gone," she announced with grin.

"Oh boy," Archer said.

"You know, Archer...I'm not used to having so much wine all at once. I feel kind of...shmooshy." Mindy let out an extended giggle. "Shmoooooshy." Another giggle, punctuated by a hiccup.

"Just what I need. A smooshy giggler with—"

Reaching over, Mindy squeezed on either side of Archer's mouth, giving him an exaggerated kissy face.

"Shmooooshy," she told him, still positioning his lips. "You forgot the H. Go ahead...say it again."

"A shmooshy giggler with the hiccups," Archer said while Mindy kept his lips in position. Once she let go, giving him an a-okay for his effort, Archer laughed. He set Mindy's empty glass on the table. "You've got quite a wine blush there, Mindy. You downed that cabernet pretty fast. I think somebody might be inebriated...and in danger of not feeling too well later."

"Just a smidgen smashed, perhaps." Mindy held her thumb and finger an inch apart...at least she tried to. "Can you hear my voice? It sounds thick. Thick and slow and shmooshy." *Giggle.* "What's a wine blush?"

"A lot of fair-skinned people like you get all red in the face when they drink wine."

"Oh," she said with disappointment. "And here I thought I was blushing because you were about to make my eyeballs jiggle again." Mindy surrendered to another fit of giggles. Jutting her neck forward, she tapped her lips, pursing them. "Kiss me again. Let's see what else you can do with that tangly tongue of yours."

"Oh honey, you have no idea." He kissed the tip of her nose. "But I'm not in the habit of taking advantage of intoxicated women."

"The logical Mindora von G agrees with you but the shmooshy Mindy says *kiss me, baby.*" She grabbed Archer's hand, holding it up to hers, comparing the size difference. "Nice, big strong hands," she noted. "Let's put one here," she planted one of his hands behind her waist, "and the other one here." She positioned it on her shoulder, closed her eyes and puckered again.

"You are magnificent, Mindy," Archer whispered before brushing a chaste kiss across her lips. "Common sense tells me getting mixed up with my sister's husband's ex may not be the wisest idea, but damn, you're just too spectacular to pass up." Archer sifted his fingers through her hair. "God, you're breathtaking."

"Well?" Mindy said, peeking at him through one eye.

"Well, what?"

She opened both eyes and shot him an impatient look. "Well, are you just going to sit there endlessly blabbing like you did in my medieval dream," she made a yakking motion with her hand, "or are going to kiss me again?"

"Oh sweetheart," Archer caressed her with his eyes, "if you only knew how much I want to do that, and more, but you're not in any condition right now."

Outraged, Mindy jumped to her feet, teetering as she threw her arms out to the side. "What's wrong with my condition? Do you think I'm fat? Is that why you don't want to kiss me?"

"No, Mindy, I—"

Mindy shuffled backward, losing her balance and falling onto the curtained bed.

"Oh!" When she realized where she was she gave a lazy smile, offering Archer a come-hither look and wiggling her fingers at in invitation. "Archerrrrr," she called in a singsong voice. "I have an idea..."

Archer slanted her a cautious look. "Mindy..." he warned. "Careful, sweetheart...you're playing with fire."

"You have a whole winery full of wine to put the fire out." With a smile both deliberate and sultry, her gaze dropped to the front of his slacks. She licked her lips. "Come on, Archer, let's play." She ran her hands down her sides and belly before stretching and purring like a kitten. "We'll play sheik and captive slave girl."

Eyes widening, Archer's chest expanded with a cavernous breath. "Damn, Mindy, I'm not made of iron," he said in a low, sexy rumble while unknotting his tie. He yanked it from his neck and accepted Mindy's enticing summons.

Chapter 7

Archer

ARCHER WATCHED the tantalizing rise and fall of Mindy's full breasts. The feral part of him ached with the need to tear the sweater from her chest, rip her bra off and see for himself if she looked half as good as he imagined.

He had a hunch she looked even better...and now he was a mere few inches from finding out. He'd start by suckling her breasts, rasping his tongue over her beaded nipples, taking them in his teeth and biting, driving her insane with sweet torture.

But gentlemen didn't take advantage of their inebriated guests. Regardless of how goddamn fucking gorgeous or enticing they were.

And he was a gentleman.

He had to remember that.

Squirming on the bed, Mindy wrapped her arms around his neck and tugged. Christ. She was warm and wiggly and, sonuvabitch, he really needed to see what was under that butter-soft sweater. Those ripe breasts of hers were close. So close. Groaning, Archer's balls tightened and his cock began a steady, insistent throb.

Since he'd first seen her at the funeral parlor he'd dreamed of taking her, thrusting himself into her depths. Then at the restaurant, when she gave him that high and mighty act, it was all he could do not to drag her into the parking lot, slam her sweet ass on the trunk of his car and fuck her senseless.

He never expected their lunch date to take such a sensual turn but, hot damn, Mindora von G, even sloshed, with all her silly pie-eyed giggles, hiccups, and ridiculous nonsense rhymes, was one smokin' hot chili pepper—and he was on the verge of losing control. Thoughts of fucking the luscious blonde had his primal urges surging to the surface.

Because of Mindy, he'd spent an inordinate amount of time circling his fingers tight around his cock and stroking himself to completion. Fuck. She'd managed to reduce him to the level of a horny, testosterone-driven teenager, for chrissakes.

And now here she was, all soft, sweet and compliant.

His gaze fell on her fingers, beckoning him, inviting, luring, as she whispered his name.

Thoroughly intoxicated and horny as hell, Mindy presented herself to him, enticing him to sample her lush, womanly attributes. Aw, fucking hell...what warm-blooded man could possibly turn down such captivating temptation? Not him. Not Archer Priest.

But he had to. He must. No way could he take advantage of a trusting innocent.

"Arrrcherrrrr..." she cooed at him, looking all adorably fuckable there on his rooftop bed. "I need you, Archer. Show me. Please...prove to me Edward-the-tiny-cocked was wrong and I'm not frigid."

Lord have mercy...

Frigid. Shit. He'd bet Mindy von Grettle was the hottest damn tamale he'd ever encountered. She may have started their lunch date like a prim, proper schoolmarm, all tight, stiff and unyielding, but it didn't take much for him to realize that wasn't the real Mindy. No, the real Mindy was a lush, sensual creature. Sex starved and needy, in the best possible way. She was a woman who'd been deprived of her true sexual nature by that pea-brained idiot she'd married.

What was it she just called him? *Edward-the-tiny-cocked.* Yeah, that's it. Archer felt a grin tickle his lips.

All Mindy needed was the right man to help her embrace her wanton, uninhibited side.

"Kiss me, my handsome Arabian sheik. Make me quiver all over." She made a little mewling sound Archer felt clear to his balls.

Oh yeah...he could be that man. Absolutely.

His control dangling by a thread, Archer yanked Mindy tight against him. He groaned in impassioned torment as the hard peaks of her nipples met his chest. His fingers crept dangerously close to one of her magnificent tits. Temptation tore at his insides as his hand stilled, suspended in midair, a mere inch from the soft swell mashed against his chest. Her body heat radiated, warming his skin, inviting him to squeeze.

Allowing only his thumb to graze the curve of her breast, Archer's hand slid leisurely down her rib cage, making itself at home there.

One glimpse of her expectant expression had him keyed up. Her full lips and parted mouth begged to be tasted. Like a starving man, his tongue lunged hungrily. He tasted her deeply, possessively. She was so luscious, warm, passionate. Getting lost in the intoxicating depths of their kiss fueled his desire to the point that his cock demanded satisfaction, appeasement.

He hadn't had near enough wine to feel the effects himself but, just the same, he felt as if his world was spinning as she eagerly explored his mouth with her tongue. Her nails dug into his shoulders as a low, needy sound escaped her, making him shudder with anticipation.

"Is this really happening?" Mindy whispered when they came up for air.

"It's either happening or I'm having the best damn dream of my life," Archer assured, his lips nuzzling into her hair. It smelled of sun-kissed honeysuckle.

"A dream...yes." A slow chuckle bubbled up from Mindy's throat. "This is too wonderful to be real."

Tugging the neckline of her sweater aside, Archer trailed a wet path of kisses down her long throat, then sucked at the soft spot just above her collarbone. She was so fucking irresistible, he licked her neck and face in one lavish swoop.

"My God, you're delicious, Mindy." He wanted to lick every inch of her, starting with that tantalizing pair of tits and tonguing his way down to her juicy pussy. With mouthwatering images of that carnal feast in mind he growled and kissed her again, slow and sensual.

"Mmmm..." She stared up at him with half-veiled eyes, letting out a little moan, which was all it took for Archer's cock to get downright adamant. "You taste like chocolate and cabernet, combined with an alluring taste that's all your own," Mindy half purred, half slurred. As her fingers tripped through his hair, she maintained firm breast to chest contact.

She was driving him insane.

Snaking one hand beneath her sweater, Archer sucked in a deep breath as he connected with the soft, hot flesh of her belly. Her quivering purr of encouragement persuaded him to keep investigating.

He'd prided himself in mastering his emotions, in sustaining control in all situations. But those sweet, needy whimpers of hers threatened to completely undo him. They snagged something deep in his center, and he could almost hear it when he realized his command had snapped.

On a mission, his hand traversed up from her belly. He heard Mindy's breath catch when he cuddled her lush breast in his palm. At the single pass of his thumb, her already hard nipple beaded more, bunching into a tight little bud. He pinched it, rolled it then squeezed the fullness of her breast.

She was incredibly soft—even if her heavy-duty cotton bra was stiff and forbidding.

Her pleasure evident, Mindy arched into his touch, her lips parting in a silent plea.

Smoothing his hand down the side of her breast, Archer molded the curves of her ribs, waist and hip. Her body heat nearly singed his fingers as his hand cupped her mound. The blissful sound she made in response to his touch was like music to his ears.

His hand continued traveling, reaching the bottom of Mindy's skirt. Archer slid his hand up her thigh, gliding over her pussy. Pressing his thumb against the fabric at the crease, Archer smiled, almost chuckled. Alas, her bra seemed to be part of a matched industrial set. His hot tamale was wearing a pair of sturdy cotton good-girl panties.

Still, his fingers found the slit beneath the material that held the promise of a sweet, hot fuck. He could feel the dampness evidencing her desire right through her panties. His frigid little Mindy was already so wet for him. So ready.

"It feels heavenly to have a man touch me, Archer. To have *you* touch me. You're so gentle, so caring. No one's ever touched me like that before."

Archer gazed down at her blissful, imploring expression and stiffened at the look of unchecked trust in her eyes. He groaned. What in the hell was he doing? Since when had he become a testosterone-driven animal who preyed upon intoxicated women?

Assembling every ounce of willpower he possessed, he pulled away, slipping one hand from beneath her skirt and the other from under her sweater. Then he peeled her arms from around his neck, watching as Mindy gazed up at him through clouded eyes that asked why.

"I'm sorry, Mindy. I never should have taken advantage of you like that."

Beaming a joyful smile, she assured him, "That's okay, I liked it. A lot. Go ahead, take advantage of me some more." The hiccup that followed told Archer she was still plenty tipsy.

Heaving a monumental sigh, he struggled to maintain his resolve. "No, not like this, Mindy. Your thoughts are foggy from all that wine now and," he gave a little laugh, "I have a sneaking suspicion you might not feel the same way once the effects of the alcohol wear off. Believe me," Archer shifted uncomfortably, "this is a lot harder for me than it is for you."

Mindy rolled onto her side, bending an elbow and propping her head on her hand. "From now on, Archer, whenever I have cabernet with my chocolate, I'll think of you. And this wonderful picnic. And your delicious kisses." She patted the mattress next to her. "Come here, Archer," she summoned, her big blue eyes looking up at him, calling to him like a siren.

Archer's civilized side was losing the battle. "Only if you sit up first." He knew damn well if he got down on that bed next to her he'd have his cock buried in her so fast it would make her head spin.

Instead of rising, she placed her hand on his chest, purring as she kneaded the flesh of his pecs. He groaned from somewhere deep inside, afraid to open his mouth, knowing the only thing that would come out would be a primitive growl.

Unbuttoning the first few buttons of his shirt, Mindy scooted her hand inside, exploring his chest. "It never happens like this in real life, Archer," she noted, smoothing her fingers over his nipple, causing it to constrict at her touch. "Just in fairytales and romance novels. That's why I'm sure I'm dreaming. Whatever happens, promise you won't wake me up, okay?"

She held his gaze and time stood still.

Taking a moment to breathe, Archer brushed the damp, blonde curls from Mindy's forehead and smiled. "You make me absolutely crazy. Baby, I want you so much I can hardly stand it." He couldn't resist sliding his hand down her arm and over her breast.

"Really? Huh...maybe Leo was right after all." She covered his hand with hers, holding it firm against her with a satisfied sigh.

"Leo?" Of all the things he might have expected to hear at that moment, her boss' name wasn't one of them. "Pray tell, what does your boss have to do with what's going on here, hmm?"

"He keeps telling me sex could be different." When Archer slanted her a questioning look, she added, "Different than it was with Edward."

He watched the wine blush drain from her cheeks.

"He was my first," she confessed. "And...my only. I was a virgin when I married him. After our wedding night all I knew about sex is that it was something ugly and abusive." She drew in a deep breath, breathing out a sigh. "I never wanted to have sex again after what that man did to me."

"Aw, sweetheart, I'm so sorry." Archer scooped her into his arms, cradling her close. "I always thought the guy was a first-class jackass."

At the same time he comforted her, warning bells clanged inside his head. That tidbit of information Mindy shared was enough to have him running for the hills. The last thing he wanted was to get mixed up with a woman he'd have to handle with kid gloves when what he wanted was to pound into her until she saw stars.

He didn't want to get tangled with someone who'd been sexually abused. He didn't want to be the savior to a woman looking for sexual healing. And he sure as hell didn't want to do any of that with the ex-wife of his sister's dead husband.

Shit.

Shit, damn, piss, motherfucking shit.

"I just wanted you to know all that before anything happened between us," Mindy told him. "It's only fair. Don't worry, Archer, I'll understand perfectly if you'd rather just take me back to my office now and not see me again."

There it was. She'd given him a perfect out.

If he had any brains he'd take it.

Yeah, she was beautiful, funny, spunky, and sexy as hell, but there were plenty of other women out there just as good as Mindy von Grettle. He rested a lingering gaze on her.

No there weren't.

"Well," he found himself saying, "I guess it's going to be up to me to show you that sex with the right person can be something beautiful. Extraordinary." He got up and drew the curtains around the bed, affording them privacy from any voyeurs with telescopes.

She gave him a smile so sweet it made his cock jerk. "If anyone can, Archer, I think it's you. Show me," Mindy urged, shrugging out of her cardigan then grasping the hem of the sweater beneath. "Please..." She began lifting her sweater.

Stop," Archer said, "don't go any further."

Mindy froze.

"Allow me the pleasure." He pushed her hands away, replacing them with his. He felt Mindy shiver as he lifted her sweater, his fingers brushing over her breasts as he drew the garment up and over her head. She sat there in her white cotton bra with her curlicue blonde hair all disheveled, looking up at him with such a tentative, cautious expression it almost broke his heart.

"You're beautiful, Mindy. Exquisite," he whispered, watching her expression and posture relax. Hadn't that asshole ex of hers ever bothered to tell her that?

Mindy reciprocated by unfastening the rest of the buttons on Archer's shirt, offering a delighted sound as she smoothed her hand across his chest. "Look at all those beautiful muscles. Even better than my dreams."

"So you've been dreaming about me, hmm?" He gave a devilish grin.

Mindy nodded, her attention still at his chest as she explored. "Mmm-hmm. And in them you're buck-naked."

"That can definitely be arranged."

"Or wearing chainmail."

Archer didn't respond to that curious bit of information. He brushed his thumb over the unyielding casing covering her breast, groaning as the nipple pebbled, beckoning him to savor it. Mindy's breath grew ragged, which turned Archer on even more. Before he went any further he took a deep breath and gazed hard into her eyes.

"Mindy, if I do anything you don't like all you have to do is tell me to stop, okay? I promise I won't hurt you. Do you trust me?"

Mindy did a long, slow blink. "I do, Archer. Thank you."

His fingers captured the taut bud through the cotton and twisted it, causing Mindy to throw her head back and moan. He repeated the process with the other breast until Mindy was a liquid puddle of moaning ecstasy. Without removing her bra, Archer took a nipple in his teeth, nibbling and tugging, pleased as he heard Mindy's satisfied little murmurs.

She reached for his belt buckle, fumbling until she got it loose. Then her fingers were on his zipper, hesitantly at first and then slowly tugging downward. As if she were a child exploring something magical for the first time, Mindy tentatively cupped his cock through his shorts.

She had his nuts in a knot before he could blink.

He scrambled out of his shoes, socks and slacks, kicking them aside before returning to the pleasurable task of fondling her breast.

When Archer's mouth lifted, leaving the fabric over her nipple wet, Mindy moaned her disappointment. He blew on the wet cotton, watching as the beaded crest beneath hardened even more.

"Take off your skirt for me, Mindy." She quickly complied, stripping to nothing but her durable good-girl bra and panties. Detecting the uncertainty returning to her eyes, Archer told her, "I'm going to take these off now. Okay, sweetheart?"

"Yes..." she breathed. "I-I'm really sorry."

"About what?"

"The grandma underwear."

Archer bit the inside of his cheek to keep from laughing. "It's okay, honey. In an odd way, it's kind of a turn-on."

"Oh good, because I have a whole dresser drawer full."

This time he couldn't conceal his laughter. "Eh...not that much of a turn-on, I'm afraid."

"No problem. I'm going shopping at Lacy and Luscious Lingerie for some sexy undies tomorrow."

"I look forward to seeing what you select." Tempering himself to avoid clawing her cotton undies off like a rabid caveman, Archer tugged off her panties then unfastened her bra. The damn sturdy thing had more hooks than he was used to and it took forever. She must have purchased her undies from Chastity R Us.

A monumental groan rumbled up from his chest once he'd finally unveiled her. Sweet Jesus, she had the dazzling tits, pussy and ass of a porn goddess. It was a wonder he didn't come right there in his shorts.

"You look like a goddess, Mindy," he said, wisely omitting the rest of the depiction that came to mind. "Like Venus." He cupped her breasts in his palms, feeling the heft before giving them a jiggle and watching as they bounced in his hands. Then he flicked each nipple with his fingers before twisting them.

Mindy's head fell back as she moaned out her bliss. The action presented her breasts to him in an irresistible offering. He caught one pert nipple in his teeth, lavishing it with attention while he pinched the other.

"Ohhhh God, Archer. That feels soooo good. I can feel the sensation all the way to my..." She moaned again, squeezing her knees together.

"Your sweet little clit," Archer whispered, leaning Mindy back against the stack of pillows. Wedging his fingers between her thighs, he eased her legs apart, slipped past the glistening wet curls and searched until he found her most sensitive spot. "Just relax now...relax and enjoy."

Gasping, her mouth fell open and she sputtered as his finger stroked the small bud.

"There." She stared up at him with an adorable look of amazement. "That's exactly where I feel it. Oh, stop! Stop, Archer." He stopped immediately. "No...no, don't stop," Mindy pleaded hoarsely, her eyelids heavy.

Archer captured a ripe, wet, reddened nipple in his teeth, teasing it as he swirled his fingertip at her slippery clit. Her juices flowed around his fingers. The way she breathed seemed like she couldn't get enough oxygen into her lungs. With each pass of his finger she trembled. He increased the slick friction, loving the way she gasped and clawed at him, wordlessly beseeching him with her eyes.

Christ, he could see it coming, sense her impending climax. Her body tensed, growing rigid. Then the vibrating began. The quaking seemed to start at her clit and radiate outward in fierce, pulsing waves. Watching her shudder, writhe and moan at his touch had Archer so damned hard his guts clenched.

Holding her close as her body jerked and trembled, he swore to God he'd never seen anything quite so beautiful as Mindy von

Grettle in the throes of orgasm. The best part of all was when his name spilled from her lips, sounding almost like a prayer. Watching her come was a treat he'd never forget.

He may have just proven himself to be a prince, a great guy, a generous, unselfish lover—but his cock was pissed as hell. It felt betrayed, deceived. It insisted on being appeased. Well, that was too damn bad. It was up to him, regardless of his urgency, to exercise patience and restraint.

"That was...oh, Archer, that was..." Mindy was clearly at a loss for words. He noticed her nipples were puckered and darkly flushed. Like a cad, all he could focus on as she spoke was tasting those sweet, hard berries again, licking, nibbling, biting until they were red, raw and swollen.

"I don't even know how to describe it, Archer. Incredible. Sensational. Phenomenal." She scooted up until her head rested on one of the small pillows and then peered at him through a thoroughly satisfied smile. "Do you know what that was?"

"From the ear-to-ear grin on your face I can venture a pretty good guess," Archer laughed, leaning down to give her a kiss.

"My first orgasm."

Archer's eyes widened in surprise. Jesus, she couldn't possibly be *that* inexperienced, could she?

"Maybe I should clarify that." Mindy indulged in a soft laugh. "It was the first I've ever had when I wasn't by myself." Her cheeks colored. He loved the way she blushed so easily. "Thank you, Archer." She pulled him down for another kiss.

Bracing his hands on either side of her head before his lips met hers, he said, "My pleasure, I assure you." And he meant it. Watching her reaction as he brought her to climax was practically a religious experience. Sinking into their kiss, Archer savored her mouth at length. "If you think that was good, just wait until you experience it when I'm inside you."

"I don't think I can, Archer." He felt his face crumple with surprise and disappointment. "*Wait*, I mean," she clarified. "I don't think I can *wait*." Tugging at Archer's shorts, she ordered, "Take them off."

Archer and his impatient cock were more than happy to accommodate her. Once his shorts had been shucked and the biggest erection he could remember sprang free, Mindy's breath caught.

"Oh my..."

"You see? That's what you do to me."

"Definitely no Thumbkin here, I see." She reached out tentatively, feathering a light stroke along his cock with her fingers.

Fighting back the urge to detonate from the mere touch of her fingers on his eager dick, Archer lifted Mindy's face and peered into her eyes. "Did you say *thumbkin*? As in the kids' game—with the fingers?" He wiggled his thumb back and forth, staring at it.

"That's the one." Mindy nodded. "It's what I used to call Edward's petite pecker." She giggled, holding her finger and thumb about two inches apart. "His itsy-bitsy mini-penis. Of course, I never actually called it Thumbkin to his face." She lowered her gaze to study Archer's erection. "I can tell you without doubt that old Thumbkin *never* looked anything like this. Are you sure that'll fit inside me?"

"I've got a crowbar around here somewhere in case we need it," Archer joked. "Actually, I think we'll be a perfect match."

Mindy stretched beneath him, a sublime smile lighting her face as she wrapped her cool, soft hands around his cock and applied pressure. "There's only one way to find out."

Yes! Beading with pre-cum, his cock bobbed with the first exulted movement of a happy dance.

Nudging her thighs apart with his knees, Archer felt a rush of anticipation he hadn't experienced since he was a horny kid. He separated her folds, eyeing the shiny pink treasure awaiting him, and broke into a lusty grin.

"I've been waiting for this moment since I first laid eyes on you, Mindy." He slicked two fingers along her slippery wet slit and licked her juice from his hand, murmuring his delight. She tasted of sex, desire and need. He almost laughed when he gazed down into her eyes, witnessing her shell-shocked expression. Apparently he'd just provided another first.

His hands itching to delve into new and stimulating places, Archer thrust one finger into her hot, wet core. Delighting at Mindy's impassioned pleas as he drew in and out, he added a second finger, spearing her juicy hole and twisting inside the tight channel. Christ, he could hardly wait. That taut pussy of hers would feel like heaven on his cock, clamping him hard as hell while he fucked her breathless.

"I love this, Archer." Mindy's breaths came in short, ragged rasps. "I love your hands on me. In me. My God, you can do magical things with those fingers." Her moan sounded so delicious, he claimed her mouth with his, swallowing the sweet murmurs.

Watching the look of sheer bliss on Mindy's face, Archer continued to finger-fuck her, making sure to abrade her clitoris with his thumb as his fingers thrust. Moaning her pleasure, she arched her tits up at him, presenting them for his pleasure. He took advantage of the offer, licking around the dusky pink areolas and nipping at the stiff little peaks at each center.

Her cheeks flushing, Mindy's heated gaze looked a million miles away. Damn if the woman wasn't on the verge of another orgasm. Already. In all his years, and with all the women he'd known, no one had ever treated him to such a precious, beautiful show of unbridled ecstasy. Mindy von Grettle was one very special woman. And sure as hell not frigid.

He held her close as her soft, lush body succumbed to a furious round of quakes. Her full, sensuous lips went from forming little O's to stretching out in flat lines as she caught her plump bottom lip with her teeth, letting it drag through. Her mouth was as expressive as the rest of her. Archer couldn't help thinking she had a mouth made for fucking.

His dick leapt at the thought of being cushioned between the insides of her sultry cheeks. That's it. He'd go insane if he waited any longer to thrust into her sweet, glistening cunt.

Positioning himself to enter, his cock a mere few inches from her glorious, inviting pussy, Archer winced. "Damn," he muttered, reluctantly rising from the bed.

"What? What's wrong?"

"Condom."

"Oh...I almost forgot," Mindy said. "For a minute there I thought maybe you were going to get that crowbar." She laughed and he followed suit.

Wagging a finger at her, Archer retrieved his slacks. "Don't you move a muscle. This'll only take a minute." Before he could fish the condom from his wallet the phone inside his suit coat pocket rang. It was a rude, unwelcome interruption, one he'd ignore if at all possible, but he'd been waiting for a crucial call.

"Nothing like rotten timing. I'm sorry Mindy. I've got to answer this. I'm expecting an important call from one of my vintners in California."

"I understand perfectly. Don't worry. I'm not going anywhere."

Heaving a sigh of frustration, Archer reached into his jacket, retrieved the ringing phone and answered the call without bothering to look at the display.

Big mistake.

Mindy

———————◆———————

WATCHING ARCHER INTENTLY as he answered his call, Mindy wrapped her arms around herself and smiled, luxuriating in the memory of the superb intimacy they'd just shared. And anticipating what she expected to be the thrill of a lifetime once he finished his call. While Archer was certainly dashing, handsome and unbelievably sexy, with the added plus of a stellar cock, it was definitely more than just physical attraction that had Mindy hooked.

The warm, tender feeling blossoming inside her was due in part to her mild state of intoxication, but it was Archer's caring personality, his intelligence, and his engaging sense of humor that had her enveloped in a state of bliss.

As he listened to his call, Mindy saw his eyebrows knit together in a distinct look of displeasure. She wondered who or what was distorting Archer's handsome features into angular lines of anger.

She longed to reach out and smooth her fingers along his creased forehead and furrowed brow. To kiss away all evidence of his scowl. To guide him into her depths where he could forget his woes and lose himself in pleasure. Mindy had little doubt it would be a deliciously pleasurable experience for them both. She hugged herself tighter and moaned a low chuckle.

"Look, Britney, I told you, I'm busy."

Her eyes flashing wide, Mindy stiffened. Ears fully perked, the last vestiges of her pleasant, fuzzy state of inebriation rapidly dissolved. Until the mention of Britney's name, it was as if she'd been encased in a bubble of idyllic fantasy. Hearing the woman's name spill from Archer's lips pricked the bubble, deflating it. She sat up, draping her legs over the edge of the bed and clutching a pillow against her naked self with one arm.

"I'm..." Archer looked at Mindy, offering an apologetic smile. "I'm with a very important client right now. I'll call you later." Heaving a sigh, he ended the call and returned the phone to his jacket pocket. "Obviously not the vintner from California."

"Obviously." Mindy met his apologetic smile with a steely glare.

"My apologies. I know how you feel about Britney." Archer sat next to Mindy, brushing his lips across her temple and smoothing the hair from her face. "Believe me, the last thing in the world I wanted or expected, now of all times, was an intrusion by my lamebrained sister." He covered her hand with his, stroking his thumb over her knuckles.

Sister. Mindy blinked long and slow. *His* sister. Slipping her hand from beneath Archer's, she heaved a sigh at the unpleasant reminder.

"Mindy..."

"That's the problem, Archer." She gazed into his captivating chocolate chip eyes and had to turn away because she couldn't think straight when he looked at her like that. "Britney will always be your sister. She'd always be between us. Always interfering and causing trouble."

Damn, it just wasn't fair. Here she was on the verge of discovering something special, something downright breathtaking with this incredible man. His electrifying touch had already carried her to heights never before imagined. And now she longed to go the distance—to experience the ultimate in pleasure as he held her in his arms, looking into her eyes as he thrust into her.

But that could never happen. Not with Britney Priest's brother. Ever.

"Mindy, listen, it doesn't have to be—"

"Yes it does." Shoving her fingers through her haphazard curls, Mindy sighed. "I'm sorry. I can't deal with this." Retrieving her bra and panties, she slipped them on. "I have to leave."

"Let's talk about this for a while, okay? Look, just because she's my sister doesn't mean we can't still—"

"Think about it, Archer." Mindy reached for the rest of her clothes, methodically putting them on and avoiding his gaze. "That woman would do everything she could to make us miserable. To split us up. The last person she wants to see in a romantic relationship with her brother is her dead husband's ex."

"Mindy, please...don't do this."

After slipping into her shoes, Mindy absently began packing the leftovers into the picnic basket. She had no idea why in the hell she was doing it, but something told her if she didn't busy herself the dam would break, and she'd start bawling and make an even worse mess of things.

"Thank you, Archer. Lunch..." she cleared her throat, "everything...was wonderful." She chanced a quick glance his way. He was still naked. His cock was sizeable even when no longer erect. The guy fucking looked like Adonis for heaven's sake.

And God how she wanted him.

The pained look of confusion on his face tempted her to draw him into a hug. But that would definitely lead to another erotic encounter. And she simply couldn't get any further involved with Britney's brother.

"I'd appreciate it if you'd call your chauffeur, Archer. I'd like to go back to the office now."

"You can't go, Mindy. I won't let you. Not like this. Not after what we just shared. Come on, dammit, you can't stand there and tell me you don't want me just as much as I want you."

Mindy gave Archer a blank, no-nonsense stare. "Either you call your driver or I'm hailing a cab."

Chapter 8

IN LESS THAN five minutes, Mindy and Archer were in the lobby and Williams had pulled up with the limo. She needed to be alone with her own thoughts and told Archer she preferred to ride alone, but he'd insisted on coming. Since it was his limo, she didn't have much choice.

"What else can I say, Mindy?" Archer offered after they were seated. "God knows I certainly didn't plan to have Britney call at that particular moment. It's not as if my sister and I are close. On the contrary, Britney and I have been butting heads since we were kids."

Britney this. Britney that. Britney, Britney, Britney... That's what a relationship with Archer would be like. Constant reminders of Brit the Bitch. Ugh!

"So what was that, your sister's daily butt-head call?" Mindy asked. Archer gave a feeble laugh, which Mindy met with an icy glare and stony silence.

"She was calling to place the personalized wine order for Henshaw, the real estate office she works for."

"Yes, I remember Henshaw," Mindy said with a droll tone. "My ex used to work there too. That's where the lovebirds met."

Archer winced. "Sorry, I forgot. Anyway, I do Henshaw's client gifts, personalizing the wine labels with their names and the addresses of their new homes." He paused, obviously waiting for Mindy to say something, but she remained silent. "That's the reason Brit called. It was just lousy timing, that's all."

Turning to face him, she spoke quietly. "Actually it was perfect timing, Archer. Like a harbinger of unpleasant things to come.

Britney ruined our wonderful afternoon, what we had already experienced, as well as what we were about to experience. Don't you understand? Your sister would always be looming there between us."

To Mindy's chagrin, as she gazed at Archer her thoughts shifted to sensuous images. His hard, hot, sweaty body covering hers as he drove that amazing cock into her. Her screaming out in ecstasy. The two of them collapsing into a sated heap. She folded her arms across her breasts, furious with her corruptible libido for being so damned hormone driven.

"You can't think that way. I don't want to lose you just when I found you, Mindy. Please don't be bullheaded about this." Catching the icy glare she sent his way, he huffed. "Come on...I've apologized a dozen times. Give me a break. What more do you want from me?"

"How about poisoning your sister?" She silently chastised herself after the spiteful words spilled out. Great. Now she sounded more like a bitch than Britney. "Sorry, I didn't mean that...at least not entirely." She shrugged and Archer nodded in understanding.

"What you can do though, is agree never to call me again." She transferred her gaze to the passing scenery and heard Archer suck in a sharp breath.

"You don't mean that."

"Yes...I do."

"Hey, I'm really trying to be a nice guy here. Don't you think you're being a touch unreasonable about this?"

"Yes, absolutely," she readily agreed. "After all, it isn't your fault your sister is an immoral, malevolent witch. But the fact that she is will never change. I was an idiot to think I could be with you and not get smacked with the ugly reminder that you're her brother. I can't help it if just the thought of that viper makes my skin crawl."

Mindy shuddered. "Unfortunately, you'd be a constant reminder of her."

A devilish smile curled Archer's lips. "If you let me," he promised in a husky tone as he stroked her knee, "I guarantee I'd make you forget that my sister, and that drip of a husband you shared, ever existed." He leaned over to kiss Mindy only to have his lips met by her purse.

Lowering her purse, Mindy peeled his fingers from her knee. "Just like a man. You think you can solve everything with sex."

"I'll admit it can be a good starting point." Archer winked.

"Ugh!" Exasperated, Mindy scowled. "Look, I'm sorry. Really. But if I were ever inclined to have sex with a man again, it wouldn't be—*couldn't* be—Britney Priest's brother."

"Obstinate, unreasonable..." Archer growled some curse beneath his breath. "Dammit, Mindy, what happened between you and my nitwit sister has nothing to do with you and me. I had no part in that whole ugly mess. And as far as sex goes, it appears you could use some tutoring, because you seem to know as much about that as you do about wine."

Breathing in an audible exclamation, Mindy pounded a fist into the plush leather seat. "Excuse me? I'll thank you to keep your opinions about my sexual aptitude or lack thereof to yourself, Mr. Priest. Rest assured, your tutelage is neither required nor needed."

"Aw, damn. I didn't mean that. It was just the anger talking. I'm sorry, Mindy."

"Ha!"

"Oh for heaven's sake, Min, you're acting like a child."

Drop-jawed, Mindy rolled her eyes. "A child?" she blurted. The heat she felt creeping across her cheeks had nothing to do with wine or her overactive libido.

"That's what I said." Shifting in his seat, Archer turned toward her, crossing his arms over his chest, mimicking her posture. "It's completely unfair and irrational to blame me just because my sister happens to be your least favorite person on the planet. It's childish to treat me like I'm a fiend because I'm the woman's brother."

"*Britney Priest's* brother." Mindy shuddered as she emphatically enunciated the words. "As soon as I realized who you were, I said to myself, Mindora von G—"

"*Mindora von G*?" Archer slanted Mindy an incredulous look.

Nodding, Mindy continued. "I said, do not, in any way, shape or form, get involved with that witch's brother. But my buddy Leo had to go and play matchmaker. I just knew it would turn out like this." She expelled a sigh of exasperation and sank deeper into the seat.

"When you said it earlier, I thought I misheard you." Archer huffed a disbelieving laugh.

"Misheard what?" Mindy's eyebrows pinched together. "What are you talking about?"

"Your name." He chuckled. "Sounds like Endora, from Bewitched, but with an M."

"And you point is?" She stared him down. "Mindora was my grandmother's name and I love it."

"Yeah but then you go tacking on the *von G*," he used air quotes, "referring to yourself like you're royalty or something. It's—"

"*We* are not amused," Mindy countered.

Archer opened his mouth and shut it again. "Aw," he gave a dismissive wave, "forget it," he muttered. "Never mind."

Sitting tall, Mindy balled a fist, planting it on her hip as her chin jutted high. "No, please go on. By making fun of my name like an adolescent fifth grader you've just revealed a whole new side of yourself, Archer. This is quite fascinating."

"Hold on, I was not ridiculing your name. I was making fun of how you refer to yourself in the third person. And you," he pointed at her, "are purposely trying to start an argument so I won't call you anymore."

"Excuse me, I'm not the one who ridiculed your name, you—"

"Okay, I know, I know. Guilty as charged." Archer's head bobbed. "I apologize, You just had me so riled up with your stubborn stance about us not seeing each other because I have the misfortune of being Britney's brother that I'll admit I may have become somewhat, uh..."

"Oh let me help, please—childish? Juvenile? Immature? You know, anyone who has a last name for a first name shouldn't throw rocks at a glass house...*Archer*." Flashing a smug smile, she turned away.

"You really screwed up that cliché," he shot back at her. "It's *People who live in glass houses shouldn't throw stones*."

"You can stop mansplaining. I know the cliché. I simply misused it because I'm perturbed."

"And speaking of childish, Archer is my mother's maiden name and it suits me just fine, thank you very much." He crossed his arms over his chest, glaring at her. "But *Archer* does not go around speaking about *himself* in the third person."

Wagging a finger under his nose, Mindy narrowed her eyes. "After that juvenile display, don't you ever call *me* childish again, Archer Priest."

"Can I help it if you drive me to distraction?" Archer growled in return. "Tell me, why stop at the abbreviation?"

"What are you talking about now?" a clueless Mindy asked.

"I'm talking about the von G. Why not von Grettle? Remind you too much of Hansel?" Archer snickered.

"Ha-ha, very funny." Mindy's eye twitched. "I don't use von Grettle because I'm not particularly fond of my full last name, that's why."

"Didn't you have the opportunity to change it back to your maiden name during the divorce?"

"Yes but I don't like my maiden name either."

"What is it?"

"After the way you cruelly mocked my first name? Ha!" Mindy shot Archer a disbelieving look. "Uh-uh. No way am I telling you. I have no desire to be the continued butt of your juvenile humor."

"Hand to God," Archer made the gesture, "I promise not to make fun. Come on, what's your maiden name? Now I'm really curious."

Mindy looked left, right, then left again before all but whispering the name.

"What? I didn't hear you."

"Klopenshaw, okay? It's Klopenshaw! There, are you happy?"

It took all of two seconds before Archer's handsome face crumpled and he burst out laughing, repeating the name Mindy had always hated.

"'Oh, you can trust me, Mindy,'" she mimicked him, making a face. "Yeah, bullshit. See? I knew you'd laugh."

"If you recall, I never said I wouldn't laugh, I merely stated I wouldn't make fun. And I haven't...Mindora Klopenshaw von Grettle." Again, his features collapsed together and he was caught up in laughter.

When his laughter subsided they rode together in silence until Archer closed his eyes and groaned. "You know, we're getting way off the track here, Mindy. Both of us. Let's put our serious adult faces back on and get back to the issue at hand—the fact that I'm Britney's brother. I honestly don't see what the big deal is. We were getting along just fine before Brit called, weren't we?"

"If your definition of *just fine* includes the fact that you tried to get me drunk so you could take advantage of me." Mindy knew they'd crossed the point of no return. She had to make sure it stayed that way by keeping Archer angry. Putting an end to their short, promising relationship was unfortunate, but necessary. She believed it was better they parted as adversaries rather than forlorn almost-lovers.

"*What?*" Archer's eyes bugged, his voice coming out in a disbelieving growl. His jaw jutted and his face took on an incredulous expression. Scooting forward in his seat, he nearly squawked, "Get you drunk? That's the most inane, ridiculous thing I've ever heard." He spilled forth with an explosion of sardonic laughter.

Mindy's lips curled into a one-sided smile. "You were all over me like a lovesick octopus as soon as I became slightly inebriated."

"*Slightly?* Hah! There's a good one."

Gasping with indignation, Mindy told him, "Thank God your sister *did* call. Heaven only knows what devious plans you would have put into motion next."

Scraping his fingers through his hair with a clearly frustrated lament, Archer sank back against the seat. "You're unbelievably exasperating."

Lifting her chin with a haughty air, Mindy turned away from him to look out the window.

"Hey lady, if you remember correctly, you weren't exactly pushing me away. You were begging for more, Miss Goody Two-shoes."

Snapping her head toward Archer, Mindy smacked the leather seat with her hand. "*That* is only because I was under the influence of your putrid-tasting wine. The wine you kept pouring in my glass long after you shouldn't have."

"Yeah, it was so putrid you did everything but squeeze the damn wineglass to get the last drop. If you recall, you kept demanding more."

Mindy gawked at him. "I can't believe I ever agreed to have lunch with you, Mr. Chivalry. Believe me, Archer, I would have found your charms perfectly and utterly resistible if you hadn't plied me with all that second-rate wine of yours." Hot with anger now, Mindy reached up and turned on the limo's air conditioning, eagerly welcoming the cool stream of air on her blazing cheeks.

"If it makes you feel better to fool yourself, go right ahead." Archer's expression twisted. "It's not my fault you chose to guzzle down a bottle of fine cabernet like a dehydrated sailor."

"Guzzle?" Mindy clapped her hand against her chest. Briskly fanning the coolness from the air conditioning vent toward her face, she added, "I knew I should have trusted my first instinct about you."

"Oh?" Archer slid across the seat, positioning himself close to the door of the limo, as far away from her as possible. Leaning against the door, he folded his arms across his chest and crossed a leg over his knee.

His closed-off body language strongly suggested to Mindy that she'd successfully rankled him to the nth degree. She reminded herself it was just as well.

"Your first instinct?" Archer continued. "What exactly is that supposed to mean?"

"It means you're a product of the *Priest* gene pool." With a disgusted sneer, Mindy voiced his last name as if speaking of something related to the cockroach family. "I really shouldn't have expected anything more from the brother of that amoral bitch."

A distinctly distasteful smile spreading across his features, Archer bobbed his head, muttering something under his breath. When he turned toward Mindy his eyes looked a whole lot more like scalding coffee than chocolate chips.

"I'm well aware of my sister's propensity toward making herself sound blameless, Mindy, even when all evidence points to her as the culprit. So at first, when I heard Britney's version of what happened between you and Edward, I naturally discounted it. But now, after getting to know you better..." Archer rubbed his hand across his jaw, and raised his eyebrows as he gave Mindy an icy once-over. "I'm not so sure."

"Oooh! Of all the nerve." Punching her fist against the cushy leather seat resulted in a marshmallowy whoosh, not exactly the resounding effect Mindy was aiming for. "You can sit there and say that after all the pain and humiliation that remorseless, husband-stealing sister of yours put me through?" She plowed the fingers of both hands through her hair, growling in frustration.

"Your sister...the woman I caught screwing *my* husband, in *my* house, in *my* bed. That, Mr. Priest, is hitting below the belt." Mindy was appalled to find her chin trembling and tears accumulating in the corners of her eyes. Gathering her purse from the floor, she grabbed a tissue and dabbed at them. Damn, the last thing she wanted to do now was cry. She needed to keep Archer pissed off, not sympathetic.

His face softening, Archer hung his head, whispering an expletive under his breath. "That was cruel and insensitive. I never should have said it. I apologize, Mindy. I," he breathed a heavy sigh, "I let my anger get the better of me and went right for your sore spot." Sliding closer to her, Archer clasped Mindy's shoulder. "Please don't cry, Mindy."

Determined to control her tears, Mindy took in a wavering breath and said nothing.

Smoothing his hand over her shoulder and down her arm, Archer went on. "My angelic sister neglected to mention the part about you catching her and Edward in your bed when she related her version. She just said you were," he hesitated, "a fat, bitchy shrew who henpecked poor Edward and made his life miserable."

Mindy turned her watery gaze toward Archer and he winced, evidently seeing the pain etched across her features. "My sister told me when she and Edward fell in love, he asked you for a divorce. You flew into a jealous rage and kicked him out of the house."

"My God," Mindy whispered. Squeezing her eyelids shut, she sank back against the soft leather seat and massaged her temples. In a moment her lashes fluttered open. "If that's what you believed about me, why on earth did you ask me out?"

"I didn't say I believed it." Smiling warmly, Archer took the tissue from Mindy's fingers and dabbed at the single, fat tear trickling down her cheek. "Don't forget, not only do I know my sister all too well, I also had the express displeasure of knowing Edward. The guy was an asshole. A first-class scumbag. You want to know why I asked you out?"

He moved closer to Mindy, capturing her hand in his. "Because you're beautiful, captivating, funny and sexy...and maybe a wee bit stubborn." He kissed her hand. "And I wanted to get to know you better. Much better." He kissed each of her fingertips.

Chaotic desire stirred deep within her belly but while Mindy found Archer's words and the ardent look in his eyes deliciously enticing, she closed her heart to his appeal. Reluctantly retrieving her hand from his grip, she pulled away and breathed a sigh.

Afraid to meet his gaze, Mindy turned to the window and spoke softly. "I wish it could be different but it would never work, Archer. Today was a mistake. Look at the way we've been at each other's throats ever since Britney called. That's just a minuscule sampling of what would happen if we continued seeing each other."

She risked a peek at him, wincing when she saw his steely expression and the rigid lines of his jawbone flexing. Placing a hand on his arm, Mindy said, "I'm not saying it's your fault, Archer. It's mine. I never should have let Leo talk me into spending time with you. Just do us both a favor and forget about calling me again...please. Believe me, it's for the best."

"Sonuvabitch," Archer hissed. Yanking his arm from Mindy's touch, he pounded his fist against the armrest. "Talk about tunnel vision. There's just no getting through to you, is there?" He gestured wildly as he spoke. "You don't want me to call you again? Okay, Mindy, if that's the way you want it, that's fine with me. I'm certainly not going to put myself through this kind of shit again."

"Fine." Mindy folded her arms across her chest, once again shifting to face her window.

"Fine!" Crossing his arms, Archer sloped his large frame toward his window.

For the next few minutes the air between them prickled with stinging silence. Finally, after what seemed an eternity, the limo came to a stop in front of Persimmon Travel. Scrambling to gather her coat and purse, Mindy raced to get out of the vehicle as fast as she could but Archer beat her to it.

As he held the door open for her, she was struck again by how devastatingly handsome he was, even when he was seething with anger. God, how she wished he wasn't Britney's brother.

Emerging from the limo, Mindy extended her hand and looked up into those incredible eyes for the last time. They reminded her of simmering pools of chocolate now. As he glared down at her, Mindy's resolve began to melt. The man was so magnificent. So delicious. So extraordinary.

So irrevocably related to the undisputed queen of bitchery.

"Goodbye, Archer," she said as coolly as she could manage as the heat of unrequited passion raged through her veins.

Towering over her, ignoring her proffered hand, Archer nearly bore a hole through her skull with the blistering intensity of his gaze. Hard lines of anger and frustration marred his handsome features. This was all her fault. She'd done this to him. On purpose.

"Maybe the next time you think of the name Priest, you'll think of this." Grabbing her roughly, forcefully by her shoulders, Archer yanked Mindy into a kiss, bursting with such force and fire it literally made her knees buckle.

Completely taken aback, she dropped her coat and purse on the ground. Archer's kiss was so passionate, so furious, she felt downright scorched. Releasing her just as abruptly as he'd grabbed her, Archer was back inside the limo in an instant. Immediately, it disappeared into dense traffic.

Stunned beyond measure, Mindy touched her fingers to her swollen lips. She stood in the middle of the parking lot for the next few minutes staring in the direction of the departed limo. The piercing memory of Archer's kiss rocked her world.

She was so disconcerted she didn't even realize it had started to rain. Once she finally had her wits about her again, Mindy gathered her coat and purse from the ground and dragged herself into the agency.

Chapter 9

"YOU LOOK LIKE hell. Like a drowned rat."

"Thank you very much." Mindy sneered at Leo as she walked past his office, swiping wet locks of hair from her face.

"What are you doing back here? I gave you the rest of the day off."

Rising from his chair, Leo followed Mindy. She slammed her purse into the bottom drawer of her desk, then opened the drawer and slammed it again, harder.

"Uh-oh, doesn't look good. What happened, Min?"

Mindy probed the contents of another desk drawer. "I've got to find something first." After tearing through the rest of the drawers she growled in exasperation. Raking her fingers through rain-soaked curls, she walked past the desks of the other travel agents, her eyes in stealthy search-mode.

"Where the hell is some goddamned chocolate when I need it?" she barked.

Giving her a quick once-over, Leo crooked his finger. "My office. Now." Grumbling, Mindy complied.

Once in his office, he motioned for her to sit. Reaching into the middle drawer of his desk, he retrieved a chocolate bar and waved it toward her with a devilish smile. "Lookee what I have."

Mindy's eyes bugged as she leaped from her chair and grabbed for the bar. "Chocolate!" Even to her own ears she sounded like a wild crack-head, desperate for a fix.

"Uh-uh-uh." Leo jerked the candy away from her reach. "Not until you tell me what provoked you into this savage state of chocolate fixation."

"You!" Mindy wagged an accusatory finger. "If you hadn't been so damned determined to play matchmaker none of this would have happened."

"None of what? You're not making any sense." His eyebrows knitting in concern, Leo leaned forward. "My God," he whispered. "Archer didn't hurt you, honey, did he?"

"He most certainly did." Glaring at Leo, Mindy narrowed her eyes. "That bastard kissed me!" She yanked the chocolate from his grasp, tearing ferociously at the wrapping. Stuffing a third of the bar into her mouth, Mindy's eyes drifted closed and she moaned a conciliatory sigh. Ready to sink her teeth into it again, the ear-popping sound of Leo slapping the top of his desk with such force it made his pencil holder rattle stopped her cold.

A furious scowl across his face, Leo grabbed the desk phone, punching in numbers. "I'm calling the cops. I want that lowlife, rotten sonuvabitch thrown in the slammer. The nerve of that guy, disgracing your delicate honor by kissing you." He glanced up at Mindy as he held the receiver to his ear, clearly trying to cover his smirk with the mouthpiece.

"Oh for heaven's sake, give me that phone." Snatching the receiver from Leo's hand, Mindy returned it to its cradle. "You are positively incorrigible." Unable to disguise a smile, she jammed another third of the chocolate bar into her mouth. Approving purrs of satisfaction escaped from her throat as the confection calmed and coated her psyche. There was no better tranquilizer.

"He kissed you." With a slow, side-to-side shake of his head, Leo said, "Mindy von Grettle, aren't you ashamed of yourself? All this fuss just because Archer gave you a little kiss." He sank back in his chair.

Mindy jammed the last third of the bar into her mouth as her eyes brimmed with tears. The sedative effect of the chocolate wasn't strong enough to blot out the memory of that haunting kiss.

"Oh Leo," she blurted, her mouth full of chocolate and tears streaming down her cheeks. "It wasn't a *little* kiss. It was an *adios* kiss. A *sayonara* kiss. A don't-call-us-we'll-call-you goodbye forever kiss."

"Archer dumped you? Why, the man's obviously a nincompoop, a moron, a-a dimwitted ignoramus!" Leo closed the door to his office and drew the blinds. Drawing a handful of tissues from the dispenser on his desk, he took a seat in the chair next to Mindy and put his arm around her. "Go ahead, tell Uncle Leo all about it." He patted Mindy's back as she buried her face into his shoulder and let the waterworks flow.

After a couple minutes Mindy blotted her eyes and blew her nose with the tissues Leo held out to her. "He didn't dump me. I dumped him." She offered a pained smile and shrugged.

Leo lurched back, shooting Mindy a look of incredulity. "You dumped that tall, dark, handsome incredible monument to manhood?" He hit his forehead with the palm of his hand, mumbling something inaudible. "I don't get it. Why?"

"Because after Archer's private chauffeur drove us to his lakefront penthouse and we had a gourmet picnic lunch on the enclosed rooftop terrace with wine from the winery he owns, Archer—"

"Whoa, whoa...hold on a minute. Archer's a walking wet dream *and* he's rich too?" Leo fanned himself. "Be still my heart!"

"Oh for heaven's sake, Leo," she growled, "I practically threw myself at the man. Attacked him like a sex-starved maniac."

"Well," Leo gave a nonchalant nod, "seeing as how you *are* a sex-starved maniac it's perfectly understandable why you jumped his bones."

"Very funny, Leo. You're making jokes while I'm baring my wretched soul to you. I need more chocolate."

"It's time for talk now, more chocolate later. And I'm *not* joking. How long has it been? Two years? Three?" He smiled kindly. "Mindy, darling, you really need to get laid."

"I was doing my best. I was just about to when his spawn-of-Satan sister called his phone."

"Yeah, and?"

Mindy offered Leo an incredulous look. "And nothing, of course. We argued and I told Archer never to call me again. When he dropped me off, he..."

Her bottom lip trembling, Mindy's face contorted as she struggled to keep from blubbering. "He grabbed me and kissed me like I've never been kissed before in my entire life. Then he just merrily slid back in the limo and rode right out of my life. *Forever.*" The last word came out on a tortured, extended sob as she gestured dramatically.

"Mindy, Mindy, Mindy." Leo rubbed her back. "You poor little darling."

"Oh Leo, I'm so confused. He was so wonderful and we got along great. And now the man thinks I'm a drunken sex maniac, a lunatic, and a bitch and...and he hates me."

"Don't be silly. Why would he hate you?"

"Well..." Cocking her head, Mindy curled her lip.

"Mindy...?"

"I might have accidentally on purpose said some nasty, spiteful, awful things to him after he got off the phone with Britney." She gnawed the tip of her finger. "It may have come across that I was being a teensy bit childish." She lifted one shoulder in a shrug.

"I'm sure Archer doesn't hate you." He wiped the smudged mascara from under Mindy's eyes. "He probably just thinks you're a sex-starved bitchy lunatic." He chuckled then gave her a sideways glance. "You got drunk, huh?"

"Maybe just a smidgen." Mindy shrugged. "More than a smidgen," she admitted. "I had a few glasses of cabernet from his winery, mostly on an empty stomach."

"Oh boy. Tell me you didn't get giggly when the man was getting amorous."

"Okay...I won't tell you," Mindy said in a small voice.

Leo's head lolled on the back of his chair as he groaned a sigh. "Okay, no problem. All you have to do is give Archer a call and apologize. Invite him out to lunch or dinner to make up for it. Simple."

As Leo's remarks fully registered she gasped. "Leo, are you insane? I can't call him."

"Sure you can." Leo dragged the telephone toward him, holding the receiver to his ear. "It's easy. *Hello, Archer? It's me, Mindy. I'm sorry for being such an ass. Let's do dinner tomorrow.* See?" He thrust the receiver toward Mindy who looked at it like it was a two-headed rodent. "Look, I'll even punch in the numbers for you. You *do* want to see him again, don't you?"

"More than anything." She shoved Leo's hand and the receiver away. "And that's exactly why I can't call him. Ever!"

Leo hit the heel of his hand against his temple as if to shake things loose. "I must be losing my mind because that didn't make a single bit of sense." He folded his arms across his chest, shooting Mindy a challenging gaze. "Come again?"

Hopping out of her chair, Mindy paced. "Archer's the first man who's made me feel really alive since I hit puberty." She paused in her pacing. "The man has magic fingers, Leo," she said just above a whisper.

Eyeing her cautiously, Leo nodded. "That part I understand. What I don't understand is why you seem to think there's a gargantuan problem."

Uttering a piqued growl, Mindy explained, "The man is Britney Priest's brother, remember?"

"And what? He should be crucified for that?"

"If we were in a relationship, I'd be running into that bony bitch sister of his on a regular basis. Every time I saw her I'd want to rip her ugly face off, stomp on it and choke the living shit out of her." Mindy grasped the invisible neck before her, wringing her hands around it with unbridled glee. "That could possibly be construed as a problem as far as her brother is concerned, don't you think?"

Leo chuckled. "Into every relationship a little rain must fall."

"Listen, Confucius—"

"Darling, do you know how many people go through their whole lives searching in vain for their soul mate?" Leo wrapped his arm around her shoulder and squeezed. "And here you've had the good fortune to find your soul mate—before you get all saggy, bent and wrinkled. Are you really prepared to throw this golden opportunity for love and happiness away?"

Mindy's shoulders slumped and she hesitated a moment before speaking. The last thing she wanted to think about was a future that could never be. "Soul mate? Aren't you jumping the gun? Archer and I only had one date." Shrugging loose from Leo's arm, she resumed her pacing.

"You drive me crazy, you know that?" Leo shook an accusatory finger. "Remember my psychic flashes? I predicted Archer was the one, didn't I?"

Mindy slapped her hand against her forehead. "Oh puhleeze. Don't tell me you're going to start *that* crap again. Give it up, will ya, Leo?" Circling around to the front of his desk, she scanned the surface. "Enough talking. Got any more chocolate?"

Leo reached in his drawer and pulled out a bright yellow bag of Toll House chocolate chips. Mindy held out her hand, staring as

Leo poured the first few semisweet morsels into her palm. Her eyes became all watery again and she sniveled.

Then she whimpered.

Slanting her a puzzled look, Leo stopped pouring. "*Now* what's the matter? You're looking at the chocolate chips as if they were poison."

Chin quivering, a fat tear rolled down Mindy's cheek as she looked up at her boss and back at the chips. "I'll never be able to look at these again without thinking of Archer Priest's eyes."

⸻ ◉ ⸻

Mindy

⸻ ◉ ⸻

"GOOD BOY. YOU'VE DONE your business outside. I've got you all set with fresh water, half a bowl of dog chow, your favorite yellow duck squeak toy and a brand new rawhide bone," Mindy told Cadbury. "Everything you need to keep you happy, occupied and out of my hair for at least the next hour." Patting his head as he settled in the midst of his treats, she left the room.

Once in her bedroom, she closed the door and tossed the plain, brown-paper-wrapped box that had arrived in the mail on the bed. On the way to the bathroom, she stripped out of her clothes, letting them fall to the floor in haphazard fashion.

Closing the tub's stopper, she turned on the water, nice and warm, spilling three capfuls of her favorite lavender bubble bath into the churning stream. Then she lit the dozen candles she'd placed around the tub and lit a stick of lavender-scented incense. Surveying her handiwork with a slow smile, she returned to her bed and tore open the package.

"Wild and Wanton Underwater Wonder," she read aloud from the package that held her brand new waterproof vibrator. She'd found it online at the same sex toy store where she'd purchased her Duo-Head Maximum Power Thruster vibrator, which, unfortunately, wasn't recommended for water submersion.

She'd resisted as long as she could, but after that lollapalooza orgasm Archer had treated her to during their picnic lunch, Mindy simply hadn't been able to get enough of a punch from her trusty old Duo-Head. Where that clever device used to rock her whole body and have her quivering like a bowl of jelly in two minutes flat, it just wasn't the same anymore.

Not when the memory of Archer's magic fingers kept lurching into her brain.

But the neon green Wild and Wanton Underwater Wonder would fix that. It would succeed in obliterating all thoughts of Archer Priest from her mind. Satisfaction guaranteed, the package stated.

"The most powerful, jarring vibrator you've ever used, or your money back," she read.

The added bonus of using a vibrator in the bathtub made it extra erotic. By the time she was finished fucking herself senseless with this marvelous tool, Archer would be nothing but a distant memory, swirling down the drain along with the used bathwater.

Padding back into the bathroom, WWUW in hand, Mindy sucked in an exhilarated breath. God, she was becoming a fiendish orgasm addict. Titillating her clit had become almost as important as soothing her wounded psyche with chocolate.

She gave a satisfied *ahhhh* as she slipped into the water and settled beneath the fragrant bubbles. Her new vibrator had multiple options, some labeled with cautionary advisories to avoid too powerful an orgasm. The thought made her chuckle. It was kind of like those commercials for peppy pecker pills that warned men to seek medical attention if they maintained an erection for more than four hours.

Studying the WWUW, Mindy wondered why they chose to make the vibrator in that particular shade of light glowy green. It made her think of aliens.

Aliens.

Oh yeah...she could have some fun with that. Giving a husky chuckle at the thought, she rested her head against the small bath pillow, turned on her new sex toy, and got busy with the pleasurable task of satisfying herself...

Mindy von Lustful relaxed in her lavender-scented bath, plucking her pretty pink nipples until they were rigid and she felt the delicious ache, clear to her shiny pink clit. The fingers of one hand snaked down her silky soft flesh until they came into direct contact with her submerged lotus flower. Snaking her finger inside the petals, she tiptoed through the twolips and diddled at the center to her heart's content.

Alas, if only she had a big, brawny, colossal-cocked man at her disposal. One with a powerful five-speed stick shift, who could piston into her glove box and send her over the moon with a mind-blowing, teeth-rattling orgasm. It had been far too long since her last, full service lube job.

Fully expecting to arrive at the annual intergalactic Council of Chicago Kinkiness convention, otherwise known as COCK, the lieutenant found he had instead been transported down from his spaceship to the bathroom of a lip-lickingly luscious Earth woman with hair of spun gold.

One look at the living, breathing goddess told him this was a detour he would not regret.

Filled with lusty longing, his large love-lollipop lengthened considerably upon glimpsing the naked, too-beautiful-for-words woman of faultless Rubenesque proportions as she luxuriated in her bath. Her tits floating atop the water reminded him of magnificent warheads and he wanted nothing more than to detonate them with a wicked twist of his teeth.

Her face was flawless, and he could tell her little bow mouth would provide scintillating, sweet suckage for his sizeable swizzle stick. The goddess's little pink tongue peeked out, sliding across her lip as she lay in her bath, eyes closed and moaning as she diddled herself.

Indeed, she was in need of an able male as much as he needed a fuck-ready female.

With a single wave of his hand, he removed his invisibility shield and smiled down at the bubble-covered beauty.

"Good evening, my tantalizing temptress. My name is Lieutenant Largo Lovethruster from the planet Dickprobe. May I join you in your bath, you incredibly gorgeous specimen of womanhood?" He stood before her with his divining rod fully erect and bobbing in anticipation of their flesh-to-flesh joining.

The Earth woman appeared to be more pleased than startled at his sudden appearance. A ravenous look of hunger was evident in her hypnotic Prussian-blue eyes.

"I come expertly equipped," he assured, "with a dynamic ding-a-ling guaranteed to satisfy your creamy cock cave. I shall provide you with the most powerful, jarring climax you have ever experienced, or your money back."

Mindy von Lustful took a moment to drink in Largo Lovethruster's family jewels with her eyes before speaking in a breathy voice. "How could I possibly pass up an offer like that?"

Other than being bright neon green from head to toe, and having a set of gills, Largo was a vision of anatomic perfection. Her love purse drooled in response. The expectation of being filled with heavy alien coin was most pleasing.

"Sure, big boy," she said in a sultry tone. "I invite you to poke me with that great big neon pickle of yours. Come on in, the water's fine."

As he got into the bathtub with her, Mindy von Lustful's gaze zeroed in on the latitude and longitude of Lovethruster's love lance. Lordy, Largo was large. Having him light her lamp would be a luscious experience.

"That's one mighty fine set of missiles mounted on your chest, Mindy von Lustful," Largo said, just before taking the tip of one in his mouth and nibbling, driving her insane with pleasure. The alien certainly knew how to handle the equipment.

"I've been told they make great pool toys," Mindy von Lustful breathed, clasping her missiles and mashing them hard against Largo's lips. "Listen, handsome, I'm eager to get down to the business of fucking, so how about taking that monstrous gherkin of yours and diddling my little bean, Largo? After that, I'll let you drill my ditch."

He diddled her bean with such intensity, Mindy von Lustful's eyeballs crossed and she yelped. That was nothing compared to when his ding-a-ling got to doing the dance. Diving in the dark. Digging and driving, deep, deeper. Damn!

Mindy's eyes popped open wide and her alien fantasy went *poof* as her neon green Wild and Wanton Underwater Wonder lived up to its cautionary claims, edging Mindy toward a new precipice. One so jarring and forceful it almost frightened her.

If she'd been smart, she would have tossed the perilous plastic vibrator out of the tub right then and there. But she held on tight, with one part lodged inside her and the other part positioned at her clit as she tortured herself sweetly.

The vibrations were so powerful she thought she might take off, shooting out of the tub and crashing through the ceiling, heading for the stars...or Largo Lovethruster's planet, Dickprobe.

Most disconcerting of all, and the reason Mindy just couldn't bring herself to let go, is that, as her body trembled and shuddered, her senses were overcome with thoughts of Archer. Sexy, sultry images, memories of his taste, his smell, his eyes, his voice as he whispered her name.

Her head inadvertently slipping under the water while she cried out Archer's name as she came in great, undulating waves of pain-tinged pleasure, Mindy was certain she was killing herself. Good God...what a way to go!

Local travel agent Mindy von Grettle was found dead in her bathtub last night. From the shit-eating grin on her face, the cause of death appears to be clitoris electrocution, caused by a malfunctioning waterproof vibrator. News at eleven.

Chapter 10

THE BRUSQUE late February elements filled the travel agency with people eager to escape the harsh winds and bone-chilling cold. Thankful to have something to occupy her thoughts so completely, Mindy threw herself into her work.

Even Leo was too busy to harp on Mindy about Archer, thank God.

"Whew." Mindy wiped her brow as she collapsed against the back of her chair and spun around. "That makes eight all-inclusive Jamaica packages, four Grand Cayman packages, half a dozen Puerto Vallarta packages and a handful of Caribbean cruises just since nine o'clock this morning."

"Carol, Yolanda and I have been booking like crazy too," Leo said. "As soon as the temperatures dropped, I knew those phones would be ringing off the hook." Rubbing his hands together briskly, Leo looked like a kid on his birthday. "God, I love the travel business. Bring on the blustery cold weather, I always say." He reveled in a wicked laugh.

"I never knew anybody who loved their work as much as you do, Leo." Mindy laughed.

Peeking at her computer screen, Leo drew in a deep breath, expelling it with a satisfied *ahhhh*. "I get goose bumps looking at all those pretty little dollar signs." Glancing at the wall clock, he grabbed Mindy's coat and tossed it at her. "Here, put this on and go warm up my car." He tossed his keys on her desk. "It's almost one-thirty and we haven't even had time to stop for lunch. Let's grab a bite somewhere."

"Sounds great, I'm famished." Mindy scrambled to her feet. "Do we have enough staff to cover?"

"Yeah, I'm letting Yolanda go early because she and Felix Garcia have another hot date tonight." Leo beamed a satisfied grinned. "God, I love it when my psychic flashes are right. Anyway, Tracy and Bob will be here in a few minutes for the next shift, so we're covered. I'll be outside in a couple minutes, Mindy. I just have a quick call to make."

The car was just getting warm inside as Leo scooted behind the wheel.

"This icy weather always makes me homesick for my Grandma Gert's hearty German cooking," he said, pulling out of the parking spot. "I heard about a German restaurant not too far from here called Bavaria Haus. Supposed to be very good. Real authentic. Want to give it a try?"

"Sure, I'm game." Shivering, Mindy tugged at her coat so it overlapped in front of her. "I need something hearty to warm my innards."

"Once we drink a couple steins of good German beer you won't be thinking anymore about the cold," Leo assured her.

"Beer?" Mindy stuck out her tongue and shuddered. "Hate it. Never drink the stuff."

"Rich, nutty, amber brew with a creamy head on top. Ahhhh..." Leo said with a fond smile. "My favorite's Winterfest Marzen from Munich. I guarantee you'll love it. It's not that pale, namby-pamby American stuff they try to pass off as beer. This has real gusto with a rich, full-bodied maltiness, a lightly hoppy background and bittersweet, but clean-tasting palate."

Mindy couldn't help chuckling. Leo talked about beer with the same knowledge and reverence that she did chocolate. "Sounds very...gusto-y."

"Speaking as your mentor, appreciating a good brew is the next lesson in your quest to become more cosmopolitan."

Cringing, Mindy recalled the fool she'd made of herself in front of Archer with her dopey *wet wine* remark. She slanted Leo an uncertain look. "Well, since I'm sadly in need of all the mentoring I can get, I suppose I should broaden my cosmopolitan horizons to include," she shuddered, "beer."

"Good girl. Now you're talking. The trick is to take it easy. Once you get used to it, beer goes down real smooth and before you know it, bam, you're plotched and accompanying the oompah band as they play 'Roll out the Barrel.'" Hoisting an invisible beer stein, Leo kept time with the polka music he hummed.

By the time they reached Bavaria Haus it was after two. Given the in-between hour, there were few people in the restaurant. The cute little place was a gem. The décor was storybook German and the staff wore old-world costumes. Male servers were garbed in fanciful lederhosen, knee socks and little hats sporting a stubby feather, while female servers wore peasant-style dresses with aprons and long blonde braids.

Mindy immediately liked owners Rolf and Marta Haggenmacher, a brother and sister team who'd moved to the U.S. from Germany recently. With their pale blond hair, light blue eyes and rosy cheeks, they were a robust, attractive pair who looked as if they could have stepped off an inviting *Come Visit Germany* travel poster.

Friendly and jovial salt-of-the-earth types, they treated Leo and Mindy like old friends, plying them with free steins of beer and slabs of flaky apple strudel. Mindy feared she must have gained a good fifty pounds over lunch.

Once the other customers left, Rolf and Marta pulled up a couple of chairs, joining them. During their conversation, they told them they had four other siblings, each sharing in the ownership of Bavaria Haus, even though two of them still lived in Germany. Mindy wondered if the other four had the same picture-postcard good looks as Rolf and Marta. There were definitely some fine genes running through that family.

The brother and sister were single, which had Mindy's increasingly naughty thoughts stirring. She wondered what it might be like to have a big, blond barbarian type like Rolf carry her off and have his way with her. The man was a giant, gorgeous block of nonstop muscle, oozing with sex appeal and broken-English charm.

Leo practiced his fractured German and the owners practiced their fractured English. They even broke into song several times, treating Mindy to one of the most enjoyable, laugh-filled afternoons she'd had in ages.

"What a terrific lunch," Mindy said as they left the restaurant. "Good food and sensational company. Believe it or not, I even liked the beer. I had a great time, Leo."

"It *was* fun. Weren't the owners adorable? Did you get a load of the muscles on Rolf?" Leo jiggled his eyebrows.

"I'd have to be blind not to. The man is definitely eye candy," Mindy agreed. "A real hottie."

"My thoughts exactly." Elbowing her, Leo confided, "Rolf wants to get together with me next week over a couple of beers."

"Rolf's gay?" Mindy caught the lusty look in his eyes and smiled. "I never would have guessed. And here I thought he was giving *me* the eye. Shows you how perceptive *I* am." She laughed.

"I could tell he definitely likes you. As a friend. But the big guy has the hots for me," Leo informed her with a devilish grin. "I guess it's like you said, Mindy, those Europeans like their partners zaftig." He clapped his hips.

"Aside from being gorgeous, he seems really nice, Leo. Fun-loving and genuine. I can really picture you guys togeth—" Mindy stopped short. "Eh, what I meant to say—"

Leo gave her a hearty slap on the back and laughed. "I know what you meant."

With their arms wrapped around each other's backs, they walked toward the restaurant's parking lot.

Sticking out his belly, Leo puffed his cheeks. "Boy, am I stuffed. How about you?"

"Are you kidding? It's going to take me a month to work off all that food, not to mention the beer." She clapped her hands over her belly, jiggling it Santa Claus style. "Not only am I stuffed, I think I'm borderline sloshed too." She giggled.

Wagging his finger, Leo chastised, "I warned you to take it easy on the beer. That good German stuff is almost as smooth and creamy as a milkshake. It creeps up on you real fast, kid. Especially if you're an inexperienced drinker."

"Yeah, yeah, okay, *Dad*." Mindy waved his concern away. "Good grief, if this is the way they eat and drink every day in Germany it's a miracle everybody there doesn't weigh four hundred pounds and walk around in a perpetual state of insobriety."

"We deserve a good, brawny, ethnic meal like that every so often, instead of always worrying about our diets." Leo took in a long deep breath through his nostrils and breathed it out in a loud, satisfied *ahhhh*.

Once they reached the parking lot, he was about to unlock his car as he turned back to Mindy with a thoughtful expression. "You know, I feel like walking for a while, how about you?"

"At this point," Mindy groaned, "I think that's my only alternative. If I tried to sit in the car now, I'd probably get wedged in the seat. Plus, I think I need to walk off the effects of all that beer. My head feels a bit woozy."

"Remember one of your first lessons, Mindy? Cosmopolitan people avoid getting soused at all costs."

"Leo, I am *not* soused." Her vexed expression morphed into a grin. "Maybe just a little bombed. It's only the second time in all my life." The first time turned out to be a disaster but she certainly didn't want to think about that fiasco with Archer Priest now. Taking in a deep, cleansing breath, she looped her arm through Leo's. "Enough lecturing. Let's get walking."

After visiting a few shops, Leo turned a corner, heading away from the main street.

"Maybe we should head back," Mindy suggested. "I'm starting to get chilly again."

"Uh...I thought we'd take the long way back to the car," Leo said. "Remember, we want to stay fit." He briskly jogged in place. "If we're going to eat big we've got to pay the price, right?" Mindy nodded. Already out of breath, Leo ceased his jogging.

"You're right, Leo. Let's go."

"Looks like there are more shops just down the street," he noted. After walking half a block, Leo stopped in front of a restored Victorian mansion. Standing arms akimbo, he looked up at it, beaming a wide grin. "Well, I'll be darned. Look what we have here, Mindy."

Turning absently to the beautiful structure, Mindy read the sign. Her jaw dropped. "Archer's Cellars!" She nailed her boss with an accusatory glare. "Leo Parker, you planned this whole thing."

Feigning wide-eyed innocence, Leo clapped a hand to his chest, gasping in disbelief. "Me? Why, Mindy, this is sheer coincidence. A random twist of fate. A fluke. You know I would never do something like that. I swear I wouldn't."

"Yeah right." She narrowed her eyes.

"You hurt me, Mindy." Leo stabbed an imaginary knife into his heart. "You really hurt me, you know that?" He gave her his best hangdog expression and turned away.

"I'd sure as hell like to." Balancing her weight on one hip, Mindy bobbed her head rapidly. "Don't give me that *poor me* song and dance of yours, Leo. I don't buy it for a minute. I'm going back to the car." Mindy swirled around and Leo grabbed her coat sleeve.

"Aren't you even a little bit curious?" He held his thumb and forefinger together.

"Don't even think about it, Leo. I am *not* going in there." She yanked her sleeve from his grasp. "No way, no how. No, *nein*, nix. Got it?" She started walking.

Leo grabbed her sleeve again, yanking her back. "But he's not even in there, Mindy. Archer's away on a business trip."

Mindy slowly crossed her arms over her chest. "And just how would you happen to know anything about Archer's whereabouts, hmm?" She peered at him through narrowed slits. "Seeing as how you swore to me you didn't purposely plan this *accidental* stop at Archer's winery."

Shrugging, Leo smiled sheepishly. "Okay, so shoot me."

"Don't be so cavalier, buster. If I had a gun, you can bet I'd be using it right now." Mindy punctuated her sentence by jabbing a finger in Leo's gut and pulling the imaginary trigger.

"Ow." Wincing, he fell into his nervous staccato laughter. "So I made a little call to see if Archer would be here today, that's all. What's wrong with that?"

"*Gee, what say we go for a little walk after lunch?*" Mindy said, mimicking Leo's voice.

Leo pouted and Mindy mumbled an expletive under her breath.

"Uh-uh-uh, Mindy," Leo tsked, "cosmopolitan people never resort to that base sort of language."

Mindy slapped the palm of her hand against her forehead. "You're standing there making droll remarks while I'm struggling to keep from committing homicide. What the hell's the matter with you, Leo?"

"I can't help it." Looking like a little lost puppy, he added, "I'm pixilated."

Caught off guard by Leo's ridiculous remark, a smile teased at Mindy's lips. Determined not to let him get off so easily, she spun on her heel and started to walk away again, biting the inside of her cheek to keep from laughing. Damn him, he always knew how to make her laugh. Well, this was one argument he wouldn't win.

Close on Mindy's heels, Leo pleaded, "Aw, come on, Mindy, I *know* you're anxious to see the winery. This is the perfect time. You can't tell me you're not dying to get a glimpse."

She made the mistake of hesitating for an instant and Leo went in for the kill. Draping his arm around her shoulder and resting his forehead on hers, he spoke in a soft, soothing voice. "What can one little peek hurt? We'll just zip around real fast. And then we'll leave. Just tip-toe right out." He did a finger-walk through the air. "Trust me, Archer will never even know you were here."

Mindy nibbled her bottom lip. "You're absolutely positive he's out of town? I mean, that wasn't another one of your *elasticizing the truth* things, was it? Because if we go in there and I find out you were lying, Leo..."

Flinching at Mindy's ominous expression, Leo solemnly crossed his heart. "This time, I promise. I'm telling the truth. I swear, Mindy. On my Grandma Gert's life."

Shifting her weight to one hip, Mindy heaved a tuneful sigh. "Your Grandma Gert's been dead for years, Leo."

Gushing nervous, staccato laughter, Leo said, "Of course she has. I just forgot for a minute, that's all. What I meant to say was,

I swear on my Grandma Gert's grave." He crossed his heart again, clearly doing his best to look like a choirboy.

Speaking in low, conspiratorial tones, he leaned close. "Just before we left the office, I called and talked to a woman who said Archer was out of town until tomorrow." Raising his eyebrows, he nodded, as if that sealed the deal.

Mindy threw her hands into the air. "Lord knows why I should believe you...but I do." She clenched Leo's sleeve and yanked him close. "Just five minutes, though, that's all. Deal?"

"Deal." Leo beamed a satisfied look, expelling the breath he'd been holding while Mindy made up her mind.

Leo

ENTERING THE RETAIL area of Archer's Cellars was like taking a step back in time. As soon as they crossed the threshold, Leo knew he'd made the right decision in bringing Mindy here. She and Archer were meant to be together. No doubt about it. He'd made it his personal mission to see that it happened.

It was his sacred duty. After all, that's what best friends and mentors are for.

He and Mindy whispered to each other, awed by the finite detail that had gone into the renovation and décor of the shop. In the vestibule was a little marble-topped table that held a large thermal carafe of warm, spiced red wine and small, disposable tasting cups. Leo poured a sample for each of them. After sipping, they marveled at how flavorful and delicious the spiced brew was.

To the left was a large shop area with gift packages and baskets of all shapes and sizes, along with plenty of paraphernalia for the wine lover. Shelves were stocked with locally made flavored oils, mustards, honey, preserves and a select assortment of gourmet edibles.

The large room to the right was set up as a tasting room with mahogany-paneled walls lined with racks of wine, available for purchase. Rich, dark wood was everywhere, from the lustrous floors and baseboards, to the crown molding and ornate ceiling trim. The entryway to each room boasted an ornately scrolled and carved mahogany arch. Everything about Archer's Cellars exuded class, style and good taste.

"I had no idea it would be so beautiful," Mindy noted. "This place is exquisite."

"Didn't I tell you the man has good taste? Like I told you before, Mindy, Archer is definitely the man for you. I feel it in my—"

"Stop right there," Mindy warned. "Don't start in on me again with that nonsense." She grabbed Leo's sleeve, digging in deep enough to pinch a fold of skin and give it a good twist.

"Jesus, Mindy." Leo rubbed his arm. "A couple of German beers and you turn into a Nazi. Come on, let's taste some wines. Look, it's only five bucks to sample six of their wines. What a deal!"

Mindy tugged at the back of Leo's coat before he could walk into the tasting room. "First of all," she whispered, "our deal was only five minutes. We've already been here longer than that. Second, how do you expect me to drink six wine samples after I had all that beer and not fall flat on my face? Are you purposely trying to get me drunk?"

"Of course not. Don't be ridiculous." While Leo certainly didn't want to get her drunk, he figured getting Mindy *mildly mellow* on the beer and wine might work to his advantage. If he could just get her relaxed, loosened up and pliable enough, he'd have a far better chance to talk to her about her future with Archer. The girl obviously needed his informed guidance in that area because, Lord knows, she'd certainly made a mess of things on her own.

Leo gestured around them. "Look, Mindy, it's their dead time. There's not a soul here to see you. Only the saleswoman behind the counter. Archer's gone anyway, so why don't you just relax and sample a few of the wines. Just take a sip or two of each. It won't take us long at all. After all, we've driven all this way and—"

"Oh all right already, you can stop all your coaxing and cajoling." Mindy chuckled. "I guess there's no harm in having a few quick samples."

"Good!" The back slap Leo gave Mindy was so exuberant, it nearly sent her flying across the tasting room. It would be perfect. She'd have a little wine, look longingly at her surroundings, sigh a bit and start pining for Archer. Then, on the drive home, as he had her captive in the car, Leo would convince her, once and for all, that the two lovebirds were destined to be together, Britney or no Britney.

Piece of cake.

"Good afternoon, folks, I'm Agatha. Is there anything I can help you with?" The sixty-ish, salt-and-pepper-haired woman sported a friendly, welcoming smile.

"Yes." Leo gave an enthusiastic nod. "We'd like to sample some wines."

"Does it take long?" Mindy asked nervously.

"Well, that's up to you." Agatha chuckled. "It's five dollars for six samples of wine and you can take as much or as little time as you like. We have a selection of traditional, earthy reds, including cabernets, merlots and pinot noirs, or a sampler of our sweeter wines."

"The sweet ones," Mindy said without hesitation. "I'd like to do this as quickly as possible, please. I have to get back to work soon."

Agatha nodded. "Of course."

"No you don't," Leo said. He *oophed* as Mindy elbowed him in the gut.

"Pay the lady, Leo."

He fished the bills from his wallet and passed them to Agatha.

"These are the selections we're offering today," she said, pouring samples of deep, dark wine for Mindy and Leo. "This first is our marionberry wine, made from Oregon berries. It's a silver-medal winner. The flavor is similar to blackberries and not as tart as raspberries. If you take in a deep sniff, you can smell the lush ripe fruit. Wonderful, isn't it?"

"Oh, this *is* good," Mindy and Leo chorused.

Agatha poured the other five samples, setting them on the counter in front of them.

Pointing to each as she spoke, Agatha explained, "This is strawberry. Door County cherry. Our award-winning apple-pear. Our Winterfest Riesling. And finally, there's apricot, a gold-medal winner. If you look at the paper placemat under the samples, each wine is described in detail."

She placed a basket of crackers and a platter of cheese cubes in front of them. "These will help to cleanse the palate between tastes. Just help yourselves and enjoy. If there's anything you need, or if you have any questions, I'll just be in the next room." With that, Agatha scooted around the corner.

"Boy she certainly gave us our money's worth," Leo said. "Look at the size of these samples." Tasting the pale golden Riesling, he murmured his satisfaction. "Ah, this you have to taste. I know that boy must have some German in him somewhere to make a Riesling this good."

"Mmmm, it's delicious," Mindy agreed, pouring the entire sample down her throat in two gulps. "They're all really delicious, especially the apricot, that's my favorite. Come on, Leo, drink faster. We've been here long enough."

"Whoa, slow down, Mindy." Leo savored a cube of Muenster cheese. Fine wine, good cheese, atmospheric surroundings...he was in no hurry to leave. "That's not how you're supposed to drink wine. You're supposed to savor it. Sip it slowly. If you guzzle, it'll hit you hard, just like that." He snapped his fingers. "Especially on top of all that beer you just had." He wagged a finger at her.

"Nag, nag, nag. What are you, my father or my boss?" Mindy laughed. "Besides, most of it was just fruit wine, Leo. It's not strong at all. I can hardly even taste any alcohol in it." She gulped back another sample.

"Oh, listen to Miss Urbane here. Of course it doesn't taste strong, it's not supposed to, you ninny. That's why it can creep up on you so fast." Leo licked his lips after sipping the Door County cherry sample. Noticing Mindy getting mellower with each sip, he indulged in a rascally smile. It was time. Time to sneak the topic of Archer Priest into the conversation.

"Obviously, Archer is an even more amazing man than I gave him credit for," Leo said. "He's a master at his craft. You know, you could do much worse than Arch—"

"Okay, that does it. We're outta here." Ignoring Leo's warning, Mindy quickly downed the last of her samples. "Come on, let's go." She grasped Leo's arm and yanked.

Damn. He'd obviously moved too fast. He had to take things slower, wait until she was more calm and relaxed before he broached the subject again.

"Hey, I still have three samples left," he told her. "I'm not going anywhere until all of my wine is finished."

"Ooh Leo Parker, you are so exasperating. I knew you'd do something like this once you got me in here." Mindy's incensed glare made him flinch. "What's next on your agenda, finding something to keep me here overnight?"

Pushing him aside, Mindy methodically wolfed down the rest of Leo's samples as he watched, aghast.

"There. All of your wine is finished. Now we can go, because you're clean out of excuses." Turning on her heel, with Leo in tow, Mindy marched toward the door, stopping a few feet from it.

"Ooooh...gee..." She placed her hand to her head and teetered. "I feel kind of funny. Hey...Leo...did it get really hot in here all of a sudden or is it just me?"

Leo indulged in an exasperated sigh. He didn't want her *this* relaxed. "It's you, you little idiot. I warned you this would happen. But would you listen? No." He clutched Mindy's arm to help steady her, hoping once he got her outside, the cold air would help sober her up fast.

Agatha turned the corner and smiled. "Come again soon." One glance at Mindy had her eyebrows knitting. "Oh dear, the young lady doesn't look well. Are you all right, dear?" Crossing the room, she took Mindy by the elbow.

"I...I..." Mindy continued to waver, clearly trying to get her wits about her. "I'm not sure." Her words were followed by a meager giggle as one knee buckled beneath her. "I think I had just a smidgen too much fruit."

Leo and Agatha supported Mindy to keep her from falling.

"She's all right," Leo said. "She just drank too much wine too fast. If it's all right with you, I think she just needs to rest here for a little while."

"Certainly." Agatha motioned toward the nearby staircase. "She's less likely to fall if we prop her there than if we put her in a chair."

"Good idea, thanks," Leo said. "Mindy, honey, I'm afraid you're blotto. Come on, you need to sit down for a few minutes." He and Agatha guided Mindy to the stairs leading to the second floor, perching her on a step where she could lean against the wall.

"Is that better, dear?" Agatha asked.

Mindy answered by slapping her hand against the stair she sat on. "Booful stairs. Jus booful." She belted out a string of giggles.

"Uh-oh." Agatha winked at Leo. "She's a giggler."

"Is she ever." Leo rolled his eyes. "She's not an experienced drinker. Goes right to her head. She figured because it was fruit wine it didn't have much alcohol and she drank it too fast."

"I understand. It happens frequently." Agatha smiled, shaking her head sympathetically. "I'll get a pot of coffee brewing. I'll be back in a few minutes."

"Oh you're a doll," Leo said. "Thanks, Agatha." Turning to Mindy, he looked at her wilted posture and tsked. "You're not going to be sick, are you, Min?" She shrugged and offered a giggle in response.

Leo gently smoothed the blonde strands from her eyes. The poor kid had come so far from when he first met her. Tethered to that chauvinistic lout, Mindy was sweet, kind, accommodating and a real people-pleaser.

She was also a fashion disaster and meek and mousy as hell. But Leo saw there was more beyond the tense, timid, insecure woman who'd decided to become a travel agent. Once he'd glimpsed the bright spirit inside struggling to break free, he made it his personal mission to help Mindy von Grettle blossom—to reach her full potential.

Eager to spread her wings and fly, under Leo's tutelage she quickly bloomed into a confident, radiant woman.

A woman who, unfortunately, hadn't yet learned how to pace herself or hold her liquor.

"You look a little green around the gills, honey," he told her.

"Uh-oh." Mindy hiccupped. "I think I'm soused, Leo."

"Yeah, big time, I'm afraid. Here, you better put your head between your knees, just in case, until Agatha gets back with the coffee."

Readily obliging, Mindy slumped like a rag doll into position, her arms dangling. Leo couldn't help chuckling at the sight. Sure, he'd been trying to get her more relaxed and carefree, to let go of her inhibitions, but this was far looser than he had in mind.

"Leeeeooooo?" Mindy called from between her legs in a singsong voice.

"Yes, sweetie, I'm right here." Bent over and doing his best not to laugh out loud at poor Mindy, he patted her back gently.

"Where's the oompah band?"

"The what, darling?"

"The oompah band," Mindy repeated, her head still between her knees. "I feel like singing some polka songs."

"Oh boy... Not here, honey. Wait 'til we get back to the car and I promise you can sing to your heart's content."

The bell on the front door jangled. Still bent over, Leo turned to see an attractive, slender redhead enter the winery. She looked curiously at Leo and the woman on the steps with her head between her knees, before walking across the floor and heading to the back room, where Agatha had gone.

Leo thought for a moment. That face. He knew that face.

With the horror of wide-eyed recognition, he snapped bolt upright.

"Oh dear God no. Tell me this isn't happening," he muttered beneath his breath. Glancing down at Mindy, he cringed. "Mindy, honey, come on, get up. We've got to get out of here. *Now*."

He tugged, but Mindy was like dead weight. "Shit. Oh shit, oh shit, oh shit." Leo sent a beseeching look skyward. "God," he pleaded, "don't you do this to me."

"Roll out the barrel. Boom!" Mindy sang out exuberantly.

"Shhh, shhh, shhh." Leo winced as he lifted Mindy's head, covering her mouth with his hand. "Mindy, come on. You've got to cooperate so I can get you out of here before Britney gets back in here and recognizes you."

Mindy frowned. "I don't like Britney."

"Yes, I know. That's why I need to get you out of here." He tugged, but it was like pulling greased jelly.

"So we can go someplace where we can sing?" Mindy asked.

Leo rolled his eyes, brushing his forehead with his sleeve to mop the nervous perspiration gathering there. "Yes, yes, exactly. So we can sing."

"Good. Because I like to sing," Mindy said through a thoroughly smashed smirk. "We'll have a barrel of fun. Boom, boom, boom!" Swinging her fist in the air to keep time with her music, Mindy dropped her head back between her knees.

Before Leo could escape with Mindy, Agatha returned with a mug of black coffee and the redhead a few steps behind. "I heard what happened," the redhead said to Leo. "Is your friend okay?"

"Sure," Leo answered Britney Priest von Grettle, Mindy's sworn arch enemy. He bit the inside of his cheek, struggling not to erupt in nervous giggles. "She's just a little, uh—"

"Oompah, oompah, oompah-pah!" Mindy sang out, still swinging her fist.

"Plastered?" Britney offered with a knowing grin. "Is that the word you're looking for?"

Leo nodded and they both laughed. He thanked his lucky stars that she hadn't recognized him.

He decided Britney didn't really seem so bad. In fact, she seemed reasonable...perhaps even good-natured. A sense of assurance took hold. Yes, this might just work after all. Maybe he could actually get Mindy out of there without Britney ever realizing. If he could just keep Mindy's head covered...

"Poor thing." Agatha chuckled. "Something tells me she's not going to feel much like singing when she wakes up with a whopping hangover tomorrow morning. Here, let's get her to drink some of this coffee. It'll help to sober her up."

Agatha sat on the step below Mindy, placing her hand on Mindy's head. "Come on, dear, sit up and have some coffee. You'll feel better."

"No!" Leo blurted, making Agatha jump, nearly spilling the mug of hot coffee. "I, uh, I just remembered that Min—I mean, *Mimi*..." Smiling broadly, Leo patted Mindy's head. "Mimi here has a severe allergic reaction to caffeine."

Slowly raising her head, Mindy sang out. "Everybody sing! Roll out the barrel—" Leo quickly pushed her head back between her knees, causing both Agatha and Britney to eye him dubiously.

Through nervous blips of laughter, Leo explained, "She needs to keep her head down or she'll throw up all over. Trust me, I know. Seen it happen dozens of times. Nasty." He shuddered. "Projectile vomiting."

Mindy struggled to bob up again and Leo pressed down harder, resting his elbow on the back of Mindy's head and grinning all the while. "Really," he said, giggling, "trust me." He bobbed his head as the two women stared at him curiously.

Just then, the door opened, and Leo Parker's worst nightmare became a reality.

"Hi, Mom," Archer said as he dropped his bags and scooped Agatha into a hug. "The meeting ran shorter than expected, so I'm back a day early. Hey, Britney," he addressed the attractive redhead. "Thanks again for picking me up at the airport on such short notice. I gave Williams the day off," he explained to Agatha.

"Perfect. The boyfriend...the boyfriend's sister...and the boyfriend's mother," Leo mumbled, shaking his head slowly from side to side. "We'll never make it out alive, kid," he whispered to Mindy, still keeping her head down with his elbow.

"Oompah-pah," she replied.

As Britney shot Leo a narrow-eyed, inquisitive look, Leo cringed. "Lord," he murmured, "you may as well go ahead and take me now, 'cause Mindy's going to eviscerate me for this."

Chapter 11

Archer

ARCHER COCKED his head at the sound of the familiar voice. "Leo?"

"I'm afraid so," Leo admitted.

"Hey," Archer smiled, "I didn't expect to see you here. What's going on?" He nodded in the direction of the woman on the steps. "Somebody sick?"

Offering a meager smile, Leo draped his overcoat across the woman's head, resting his elbow on top while supporting his head in his hand. "Eh...something like that."

At the sound of girly giggling Archer walked closer to the staircase, lifting Leo's coat and bending down to gaze at the woman with her head between her knees.

"Mindy?" he said incredulously, as he watched her golden locks bouncing in time with a string of giggles. He'd know that head of disheveled blonde and that distinct giggle anywhere.

"Mindy? *Mindy!*" Britney shrieked, balling her hands and firmly planting them against her hips. Turning her wrath on Leo, she transmitted a narrow-eyed glare. "*Mimi*, huh?"

"Mindy?" Agatha asked Britney.

"Edward's bitch of an ex-wife," Britney spat.

"Oh dear," Agatha said.

"Oh God," Leo muttered, removing his elbow from the back of Mindy's head and burying his face in his hands. "Please tell me this isn't happening."

Popping her head up, Mindy held her outstretched palm high in the air, moving it in a wide, exaggerated half-circle. "Hiya,

Archer," she said exuberantly. Focusing on Britney with a pouty scowl, she folded her arms across her chest and tucked in her chin. "Hello, Britney," she said an octave lower, with all the distaste she could evidently muster in her wobbly condition.

Expelling a pained groan, Leo shook his head, mumbling to himself.

"Archer, you *know* this woman?" Britney demanded.

Glancing at the obviously inebriated Mindy, Archer sucked in a deep breath before turning to Leo, who threw his hands into the air with a defeated shrug.

"Answer me, Archer." Britney's grating voice was insistent.

Huffing a resigned laugh, Archer replied, "Yes, Britney. I know Mindy."

His sister's jaw dropped, rendering her momentarily speechless. Archer was always thankful for those rare, precious times. Returning his attention to Mindy as she veered back and forth on the step, he broke into full laughter.

"Mindy von Grettle, I do believe you're plastered. Again."

"Maybe jes a lil' teensy bit," Mindy slurred, holding her thumb and forefinger an inch apart. "Hey, I know." She grinned, patting the step she sat on. "Let's all sit down here together and sing polka songs!"

"Jesus H. Christ." Britney threw her hands into the air, letting them fall, slapping at her sides. "I don't fucking believe this."

"Britney!" Agatha reprimanded. "Language." Britney just rolled her eyes.

While the awkward situation was unsettling, Archer also found it highly amusing. "Mindy, maybe this isn't the best time to—"

"Roll out the barrel, we'll have a barrel of—"

Leo clapped his hand over Mindy's mouth as she belted out her refrain. "Ixnay, Indymay," he said out of the corner of his mouth.

Mindy peeled Leo's hand from her face. "I like your fruit wine, Archer. Tastes just like liquid jam." She smacked her lips. "Lots better than that crappy cabernet you gave me. Yeeeeuuuuuk!" Pinching her nose, Mindy stuck out her tongue and shuddered for added emphasis.

"Spoken like a true wine aficionado." Archer chuckled.

"A true sophisticate." Leo nodded.

"And your store is real nice." Clearly on a roll, Mindy continued. "Really, really, really nice. But you oughtta do something about that furnace 'cause, boy, is it ever hot in here!" With that, Mindy abruptly stood up on the stair, fanning her hand in front of her face. In a few seconds her eyes grew wide and she went chalk-white. As her knees buckled, Archer grabbed her in his arms, catching her before she collapsed.

"Mindy," Archer whispered as he looked down at the beautiful, unconscious woman resting limply in his arms.

"What are you looking so worried about?" Britney snapped. "Haven't you ever seen a drunk pass out before?" Archer shot his sister a warning glare. Tapping her foot rapidly against the wood floor, she crossed her arms over her chest. "How about telling me just what the fuck is going on here, Archer? How do you and that bitch know each other?"

Agatha clasped her daughter's arm. "I'm warning you, young lady, watch your language. For heaven's sake, Britney, now's not the time for an inquisition."

"But Mother..." Britney protested, waving an urgent finger in Mindy's direction.

"But nothing," Agatha admonished. "Archer, why don't you bring the poor girl upstairs to your apartment where she can get some rest? Dampen a wash cloth with cold water and dab it around her face until she comes around, dear."

"Poor girl, my ass," Britney mumbled, then held her hands up in surrender as Agatha shot her daughter a threatening look.

"Good idea, Mom," Archer said. Of all the damn times for his cock to make itself known, this had to be about the worst. But that didn't keep it from happening as he held Mindy's lush body close. He just prayed her coat hung low enough to cover his burgeoning erection.

He gazed down at her face again. So sweet. So angelic. So utterly intoxicated. She smelled like sweet fruit wine, and he wanted to lick the taste from her lips. Suck her tongue into his mouth. Strip her naked and find out how she tasted everywhere else...

Archer groaned. How the hell he could get so turned on holding a drunken, passed out woman in his arms, while his mother, sister and the woman's boss were a mere few feet away, was beyond him. Clearly, lust and desire knew nothing of logic or timing.

Turning to Leo, Agatha touched his shoulder. "She, um, she's not really allergic to caffeine, is she, dear?" Leo shook his head from side to side, adding an apologetic shrug. Offering a warm smile, Agatha said, "Well then why don't you and I fix Mindy a nice, fresh mug of coffee and a little something bland to eat? I think it'll make her feel better."

"Sure, thanks." Leo mopped the sweat from his brow with the sleeve of his coat.

Agatha looped her arm through his. "I think you could use a little something to make yourself feel better too." She winked and Leo nodded thankfully as they strode out of the room. "Britney," Agatha called as she rounded the corner, "you stay down here and mind the store until I return."

Already halfway up the stairs behind Archer and Mindy, Britney whined, "But Mom—"

"Britney!" Agatha countered with some vehemence.

Britney stamped her foot, grumbling curses as she headed back down, taking her position behind the tasting counter.

Once upstairs in his apartment, Archer gingerly deposited Mindy across his bed, stripping her winter coat off and willing himself not to go any further. He ran a clean washcloth under cold water in the bathroom, wringing it out before gently dabbing Mindy's forehead.

Sitting on the edge of the bed beside her, he said, "Hey, sweetheart, open your eyelids so I can see those Prussian blue eyes of yours." He continued to blot the cool cloth around her face, smiling as she began to come around. "Feeling better?" he asked as Mindy's eyelashes fluttered.

Eyes fully open, she took a moment to focus. Beaming a joyful smile, she threw her arms around Archer's neck. "Mmmm...nice dream," she murmured, licking her lips. "I always have the nicest dreams about you."

The involuntary gesture sent an aching jolt to Archer's libido. "Nope." Chuckling, he smoothed a few errant locks of hair from her face. "This is no dream, sweetheart, this is real life." He traced her features with his fingertips, groaning as his cock continued to stiffen.

Her eyelids fluttering closed again, Mindy sighed, smiling dreamily. "I don't think so. The only time I see you anymore, Archer, is in my dreams or fantasies."

"Aw, honey..."

She let out a breathy little sigh and opened her eyes. Frowning, she tugged at his tie. "Except you don't wear a suit and tie in my dreams. We're both naked. Sometimes you're a green alien named Largo."

"Is that so?"

"Yup, and we're making love. For hours and hours and hours..." A breathy little sigh escaped her lips an instant before she spouted forth with a giggle.

If her words hadn't gotten to him, their huskiness would have. Archer shifted positions to accommodate his throbbing hard-on. Vivid images of the two of them happily fucking raced across his mind.

"You're driving me crazy, Mindy." He traced his fingers along the collar and shoulder of her soft, silk blouse. When he found his thumb trailing toward the inviting swell of her breast, Archer swore under his breath, fighting to restrain himself.

"I've missed you so much," he whispered, his hands ghosting over the curves of her breasts.

She clutched his hand, bringing it down to connect, molding it to her shape. The nipple beneath his palm pebbled immediately. God, how he wanted to paint her nipples with his cum.

"Kiss me, Archer. Just like you did the last time." He dragged the fingers of one hand over his chest, clutching his shirt just over his heart. Her eyes fluttered closed on a soft moan. "Except don't get all angry and leave me this time."

The pained little catch in her voice was like a fist to his gut.

"Stay with me, Archer. Please. Make love to me." She gazed up at him, her tongue peeking out and sliding slowly across her lips.

If ever there was an irresistible erotic come-on, this was definitely it.

Goddamn, he wasn't a saint. Succumbing to primal urges, Archer grabbed her so hard she gasped. Crushing her breasts against his chest, he captured her mouth, plundering the sweet depths with his tongue. She tasted of fruit, wine, and pure, unadulterated Mindy.

"Ohhhhh..." she breathed in such a way that had Archer going nearly insane with lust. The sound tightened the skin of his cock until it stung.

"I have to feel you, Archer. Deep inside...here..."

She reached down and touched herself. He gazed at her fingers stroking the cloth of her skirt, lingering, skating left and right over her mound.

"Please..." Her voice was a soulful entreaty.

Somehow she found the strength to yank him down hard atop her, wrapping her legs around him and arching her hips as she kissed him like there was no tomorrow. Wedging a hand between them, she cupped his erection. His demanding cock was ready to detonate on the spot.

Biting back a low growl, he unbuckled his belt and unzipped his pants as she squirmed beneath him. Watching her touch herself was the last straw. This time he remembered the condom. Untangling himself from Mindy long enough to retrieve one from his nightstand drawer, he tore the packet open with his teeth and sheathed himself. He hiked her skirt up and, like a man possessed, all but ripped off her panties.

"I'm so hot, Archer. So wet...I need you..."

"Oh baby, I've been waiting so long to do this." Eyeing her glistening pussy, Archer positioned himself for entry, guiding her hips with shaking hands. He paused and smiled.

"I can't resist...I've got to taste you first." Head lowered, he spread her labia and breathed in her musky fragrance, her scent inundating his senses. "The sweet smell of sex," he said hoarsely, just before licking her dewy pink box in a long, purposeful lap.

Mindy gasped and trembled. A cry tore from her throat as she dug her fingers into his shoulders. "My God, Archer. What are you doing? And whatever it is, please do it again."

"I'm eating you." He swirled the tip of his tongue at her clit, savoring the wet, hard berry. "Sampling your delicious private stock." Delving deep inside, he fucked her intimate flesh with his tongue.

"I can't stand it. Archer. I want you so much it's making me tremble."

He looked up at her, the desire in her gaze making his gut clench in raw pleasure as she clawed at him like a bold, glorious wild animal.

Archer got back in position fast, anticipating the satisfying flush of wet heat gloving him as he sank into her silky depths, experiencing nirvana as his cock grazed her womb. His erection nudged her pussy and she spread her legs wide.

"Mindy...sweetheart..."

She locked her ankles behind his ass, the silky softness of her thighs clasping his hips.

And then she gushed a boozy little hiccup.

Shit.

And then she giggled.

Double shit.

He waited a moment, hoping he hadn't heard right.

Giggle, hiccup, giggle.

Sonuvabitch.

The next thing he knew she'd be belting out polka songs in time with his thrusts.

Archer filled his lungs with air, closed his eyes and released the breath with an extended whoosh. The groan that followed was so pained, tortured and bloodcurdling it sounded like something out of an anime cartoon.

Employing every last ounce of his tapering control, Archer tore himself from Mindy's impassioned clutches and sat back on his heels. Blood screamed in his veins, through his cock. He felt about to expire from a severe case of unrequited lust.

"Archer...? What's wrong? Don't you want to make love to me anymore?"

Hiccup. Giggle.

He looked down at her sweet, waiting pussy again, wanting nothing more than to thrust into it, high, hard and deep, over and over until his cum burst white hot and he roared out his satisfaction. Closing his eyes for a moment to muster additional strength, he took another deep breath and pulled Mindy's panties back up over the too-inviting, juicy little sanctuary he longed to plunder.

"Seems like we've been through this scenario before," Archer told her, dragging her skirt back in place.

"Huh?" Mindy gazed up at him with a bewildered expression. She gave a bright smile, puckered her lips, made a series of air smooches at him and then giggled again. "Kiss me, Archer. Kiss me. Eat me. Fuck me." *Hiccup.*

"Believe me." Archer laughed softly. "I'd like nothing better than to make love to you right now, Mindy. I want to shove inside you and make us both go up in flames. But not when you're sloshed. If you still feel the same way when you're sober I promise I'll ravage you in a flash."

He planted a soft kiss on her forehead and another on her lips. "I don't want to be accused of taking advantage of your condition again." He dotted the tip of her nose with his finger.

"Oh I would never do that."

"Yeah, famous last words." Archer stripped the sadly unused condom from his cock, depositing it in the trash with a regretful sigh.

"But Archer..." Mindy luxuriated in a languorous groan as she stretched against the bedding. "This is soooo romantic. So perfect.

Just you and me and this nice big, comfy bed." She crooked her finger in invitation and he clamped it in his hand.

"Eh...not exactly. I can think of more conducive romantic settings than here with my mother and Leo in one room and my sister—your arch enemy—in another." Archer laughed at the irony of it all. "On top of that, I know from past experience you're going to hate yourself, and me too, probably, once you come out of this warm, fuzzy alcohol haze and realize what you said."

"Oh no, I could never hate you, Archer. I love you."

Archer drew in a sharp breath. "Sweetheart, you don't know what you're saying. That's just the wine talking."

"I like wine talk." Mindy gazed longingly into his eyes and gave a wicked smile. "Like twin glistening, passion-filled, chocolate drops..."

Archer skewed his features. "You're not making any sense."

"Your eyes," she explained. "They're like shimmering chocolate chips." Bolting up, she plastered herself against Archer, locking her lips with his.

It wasn't long before he found himself lost in desire again. Putting up a not-too-valiant struggle, he finally allowed himself to be tugged on top of Mindy as she rested against the pillows.

She paused in her kiss long enough to moan as she licked his jaw, his neck, under his chin. Archer fastened his mouth on hers, mesmerized by the liquid stroke of her tongue as they engaged in a languid, oral dance.

A chorus of throat clearing interrupted the kiss as Agatha and Leo entered the room. Displaying embarrassed smiles, they bore trays with coffee, cheese, crackers and fresh fruit.

"Mom!" Archer squawked as he pried himself from Mindy's arms and shot to his feet.

"Mom?" Mindy echoed quizzically.

Archer cleared his throat. "I was just—" He stopped short, following his mother's and Leo's gaze to his unzipped trousers...which had fallen to his knees. "Oh shit." He yanked up his pants, thankful as hell he still had his shorts on. "This isn't what it looks like," he claimed, turning his back to them while he zipped, buckled and tucked. "Really, I can explain."

"Oh boy," Leo muttered.

"There's no need to explain." Agatha held up her hand to signal a stop to her son's sputtering account. "I'm not blind, Archer. I see exactly what's happening here. You were clearly taking advantage of this poor young woman's intoxicated condition. Archer Priest, you should be ashamed of yourself."

"Wait. No." Shaking his head fervently, he claimed, "It wasn't like that." He looked back at Mindy who looked all sweet, innocent and wide-eyed, blinking up at him as if she hadn't a clue in the world why his pants had just been around his knees. "You know, this is the second time in just over a month that I've been wrongfully accused of taking advantage of—"

"*Mom*!?" Mindy blurted again, shaking her head as if to clear the cobwebs. She propped herself up on her elbows as the full realization of the events seemed to come into clarity. "Oh my God." She looked straight at Agatha. "You...you're..."

"Yes dear, I'm Agatha Priest. Archer's mother. Um...apparently you and my son already know each other. Quite well, it seems." She offered a polite smile as she deposited the tray she carried on Archer's nightstand.

Mindy slowly rose to a full sitting position, scooting to the edge of the bed, one hand on her head and the other on her stomach. She looked pretty dazed and wobbly so Archer did the gentlemanly thing, sitting next to her and wrapping an arm around her to steady her. She eased into him, resting her head against his chest. He put his other arm around her, patting her back in a chaste, soothing fashion.

"Come on, Mom," he said, "it's not what you think. Mindy just thought I was a dream, that's all."

"Oh I could die...I could just die," Mindy lamented. Focusing her attention back to Archer, whose arms were still around her, she glared up at him with an outraged expression. "What do you think you're doing? Stop manhandling me."

"Manhandling?" Archer carped, refusing to release his grip.

"That's what it looks like to me," Agatha noted.

"Thank you, Mrs. Priest." Mindy tried to shrug Archer off.

"You're welcome. Call me Agatha, dear."

"I may as well give up." Archer huffed a humorless laugh. "The man's always the guilty one."

"You got that right," Leo agreed.

"You!" Mindy shot an accusatory glare at Leo. Finger outstretched, she charged, "This is all your fault, Leo."

"Mindy, I swear...I had no idea." Leo crossed his heart before pressing his steepled fingers to his lips.

"If there was any manhandling going on here, Mom," Archer said, "it was on Ms. von Grettle's part, not mine. I was only doing my best to oblige her drunken desires."

"What!" Mindy sucked in a breath of indignation. "Oh! Get off me, right now, you...you..."

"Dreamboat?" Archer teased. "Fantasy man? Alien lover?"

"You egotistical, grape-stomping baboon!" Shoving Archer away with a mighty thrust, Mindy bolted to her feet. "What is it with you, anyway, Archer? Aren't you capable of making time with a girl without getting her drunk first?"

Slapping his hand to his chest, Archer's neck and chin jutted out in astonishment. "Excuse me? You were well on your way to a state of intoxicated delirium long before I got here from the airport. It's not my fault if you're a lush."

Mindy breathed in an audible exclamation. "Archer Priest, how can you say such a thing? I don't even drink."

"Ouch." Leo winced. "I'm afraid that one's not going to hold water, Min."

Mindy blinked. Apparently recalling the beer and wine she'd imbibed earlier, she rolled her eyes and corrected herself. "What I mean is...I very rarely drink."

Archer smirked. "Hmmm, let's see... At Chowder Bay, you were sucking down a glass of Riesling. At our picnic lunch you knocked back a bottle of cabernet. God only knows what you guzzled this afternoon to get you this loaded. In fact, the only place I didn't see you with a drink in your hand or intoxicated was at the funeral home. That's three out of four, Mindy. For someone who's trying so hard to paint herself as a near teetotaler, the odds are against you."

"Archer Aloysius Priest!" Agatha admonished her son. "What *is* the matter with you?"

"Aloysius?" Mindy said incredulously.

Archer groaned as Mindy clapped her hand over her mouth, giggling. "Gee, thanks, Mom." He rolled his eyes.

"I thought I raised my son to be a gentleman," Agatha went on. "Apologize to the young lady at once."

"Mom, you don't understand." Archer hit the wall with his fist and growled. "It's not my fault. There's just something about Mindy that brings out the worst in me." He glanced at Mindy who stood there, her chin elevated in defiance, looking like a deliciously wicked temptress. "Dammit, she drives me crazy. I mean look at her." He gestured toward Mindy who glared at him in return.

Fists firmly planted on her hips, Agatha slanted her son a warning look. "Archer..."

"Okay!" Archer plowed his fingers through his hair, growling a sigh. "I apologize for implying that you're a wino, Mindy." He looked back at his mother. "Satisfied?"

"The only reason you're apologizing is because your mother made you," Mindy accused.

Letting out a cry of vexation, Archer paced back and forth. "There, you see?" he said to Agatha, as he held his outstretched fingers toward Mindy. "That's exactly what I'm trying to tell you. She's impossible. Exasperating! She comes here uninvited, gets plotched on wine, which was by no means force fed—unless, of course, you're using a new technique on the customers, Mother..."

Agatha's hand flew to her chest as she gasped. "Of course not."

"And yet somehow," Archer continued, "*I'm* the one to blame. And, dammit, I wasn't even here until just a short time ago! Does that make any sense? Huh? Does it?"

"I can vouch for Mindy," Leo said, before Mindy or Agatha had a chance to retort. "She's not an experienced drinker, Archer. It was my bright idea to come to your winery and sample those wines, not Mindy's. I had to practically drag the woman in here kicking and screaming for God's sake." His nervous laughter ensued.

"We'd already had a few mugs of beer over at Bavaria Haus..." Leo held up his hands in a gesture of surrender. "Again, at my suggestion. I should have had more sense than to insist Mindy drink wine on top of that."

"Leo Parker, I most certainly do not need you, of all people, defending me," Mindy snapped. "If it wasn't for you, I wouldn't even be in this mess, would I?"

"If you'd been paying attention, you'd realize that's exactly the point I was trying to make, Mindy," Leo said.

Mindy fidgeted with her hair, smoothing it in place. "Oh, let's have a little lunch, Mindy. Oh gee, Mindy, look, here's Archer's

Cellars, what a surprise. Archer won't be here—I promise. *Trust me*, you said. Hah!"

She dropped her head into her hands, talking through spread fingers. "I swear, Leo, sometimes I could just strangle you. In fact, after this fiasco, I just might."

"It seems your employee struggles with a Jekyll and Hyde complex, Leo," Archer noted. "She changes personalities faster than you can flick a light switch."

"It does seem that way sometimes, doesn't it?" Leo chuckled.

"Leo!" Mindy chastised. "Whose side are you on?"

"Think of me like Switzerland, Mindy," Leo informed her. "Neutral. Totally neutral."

The sound of rapid footsteps on the stairs was followed by Britney's pinched face, peeking through the doorway.

"What the hell is going on up here? Control yourself and stop screaming like a drunken banshee, Mindy. This is a place of business. There are customers downstairs."

Clearly horrified, Mindy looked from Britney to Leo to Agatha and finally to Archer. Her eyes brimmed with tears. "I-I'm sorry. I'm so embarrassed. Please forgive me." She cradled stomach. "Please, can someone show me to the bathroom? I'm going to be sick."

Brushing Archer's helping hand from Mindy's arm, Agatha stepped between them. "I think you've helped the young lady quite enough for now, Archer. Come along, dear." She led Mindy from the room.

As soon as Agatha was out of sight, Britney pinned Archer with a caustic gaze. "Okay, big brother, Mama's not here to protect you now. I want an explanation." Indignant, she flipped her long red locks from her shoulder. Folding her spindly arms across her chest, she demanded, "What's going on between you and that fat pig?"

It was a damn good thing he wasn't a violent man, because Archer would have enjoyed nothing more at the moment than to haul off and give his acerbic sister a solid punch in the nose.

Through clenched teeth, he said, "Don't ever call Mindy a fat pig again, Britney. Do you hear me? Ever! Or you'll have me to answer to. Is that clear?"

Mocking her brother, Britney dangled her hands in a jittery fashion. "Oooh, look at me, I'm shaking. I'm so scared." Rolling her eyes, she barked a laugh. "Good Lord, Archer, don't tell me you're fucking that porker."

Seething, Archer moved toward his sister. Leo quickly stepped between them. Addressing Britney, he grinned, reminding her, "Excuse me, but didn't I hear you say you had some customers downstairs? Maybe it would be a good idea for you to see how they're doing."

"I couldn't care less. After all, this isn't my winery, it's *his*." Britney said the word as if Archer were nothing more than a bug underfoot as she pointed a bony finger. "I am *not* moving from this spot until I get some answers." Britney gave Leo a loathsome once-over. "You're the bitch's faggot boss, aren't you?"

"Britney!" Archer belted out. "Jesus..." Clapping a hand over his eyes, he shook his head back and forth.

Shoulders back and head held high, Leo took in a slow breath, undoubtedly struggling to maintain his composure and keep his temper in check.

"Now I understand why Mindy got sick right after you came into the room." Curling his lip, Leo returned Britney's distasteful once-over. "She clearly wasn't exaggerating when she described what you're like."

"Oh yeah?" Britney advanced toward Leo with a menacing look. "Well, let me show you exactly what I'm made of, you fuckin' queer."

Leo's eyebrows raised in response. It was his only visible reaction.

"Oh no you don't." Archer grasped his sister's arm, holding firm as she tried in vain to tug free. "Goddammit, Britney, get a grip, will you?"

He shifted his gaze to Leo. "I'm sorry you had to get in the middle of this. I'm going to take Big Mouth here," he shot Britney a lethal look, "downstairs so we can talk. Do me a favor and take care of Mindy for me, okay?"

Chapter 12

Archer

"WILL YOU FUCKIN' let go of my arm," Britney insisted as Archer all but dragged her down the stairs.

"Keep quiet, you foul-mouthed little troublemaker," Archer warned. "I don't want the customers to hear you." It was increasingly difficult for him to remain calm and level-headed with all the raw emotion simmering inside his brain. At the bottom of the stairs, he loosened his grip and Britney yanked her arm away.

"Ow, you big ox..." She rubbed her arm. "I'm going to be black and blue. You know how easily I bruise." Archer aimed a narrow-eyed glare her way. "Anyway, there's nothing to worry about. There aren't any customers here. I just said that for Mindy's benefit."

"What?" Throwing his hands into the air, Archer mumbled a string of curses beneath his breath. "You know, Britney, you are really one fine piece of work."

"Thank you." She fluffed her hair.

He shot his sister a noxious look. "It wasn't a compliment."

Arching one penciled eyebrow and offering a calculated sneer, Britney slid past Archer to retrieve her coat and purse from the back room. When she returned, she draped her things over the banister and faced Archer, arms crossed over her chest.

"So, are you going to tell me about you and whatzerface or not?"

"Not if I can help it." He'd had thousands of run-ins with his mouthy sister over the years but this one...this one was different. "It's none of your business, Brit."

"It most certainly is." Britney stamped her high-heeled foot against the floor. "How can you say that? She's the bitch who made Edward's life a living hell for ten years. She's the last person on earth I want to see you tied up with." She stamped her foot again. "I swear, Archer, sometimes you're such an idiot."

Archer cringed as he studied the spot on the floor where Britney had twice punctuated her point with the metal-tipped heel of her shoe. "God damn, Britney, do you have any idea how many back-breaking hours I put into finishing this hardwood floor?"

"Don't try to change the subject, creep."

"I really don't want to get into this with you, Britney. But," Archer pointed an implicating finger, "since you're being so damned obstinate about it, are you forgetting I knew that rotten sonuvabitch you were married to?"

His hand shot up to silence his sister's impending protest. "Before you say another word, remember *I'm* the one you called, bawling your eyes out, when you first discovered Edward von Grettle, your wonderful, perfect new husband, was sleeping through the entire roster of female real estate agents in the Chicago area. You were nearly hysterical, remember?"

"Yeah but—"

"I remember," Archer continued, "when that bastard pummeled you so badly you were covered with black and blue marks, had a fat lip and your eye swollen shut. You had to practically tie me down to prevent me from killing that scumbag myself. Any of that sound familiar?" The recollection of seeing his sister in that condition and realizing her husband was responsible was still an all too lucid memory.

As far as Archer was concerned, any man who laid a hand on a woman in violence ought to have his balls squashed in a vice. From the little Mindy had said during their lunch together, Archer suspected Edward had used her as a battering bag too. The thought was bloodcurdling.

"Rat bastard, woman-beating sonuvabitch," he muttered.

Heaving a shrug, Britney sighed. "Yes, I remember."

His sister's words snapped him back to the present. "I still can't come to terms with the fact that you actually chose to go back to that sub-human piece of shit after what he did to you, Brit. So don't even try talking to me about how Mindy made *his* life miserable, okay? I rather doubt that's an accurate accounting."

Wearing a guilty pout, Britney gave her brother a hesitant hug. "All right, yes, everything you said is true. And you were wonderful about it when I needed help. But don't you see, Archer? That's all beside the point. We're not talking about me. We're talking about the bitch upstairs," Britney jerked her head with disdain toward the second floor.

"Give it up already, Britney. What happened between you and Mindy is done and over. That scum-sucker husband, the only element you two had in common, is dead and buried. Can't you just leave it at that?"

Britney poked her brother hard in the gut with her finger.

Archer winced. "Ow. Shit. What the hell was that for?"

"Because you don't understand that I have your best interest at heart, Archer. If only you could have seen Mindy nearly two years ago." Britney made a wide circle with her hands and bloated out her cheeks. "She was huge, Archer. *Huge.* A whale. A pig. A fucking warthog. For fuck's sake, how the hell could you possibly be attracted to something like that?"

"Damn." Archer pounded his fist against the wall, hard enough to rattle the framed pictures, causing Britney to flinch. "I don't give a damn what Mindy looked like two months ago, two years ago or twenty years ago. It doesn't make any difference to me. Period. That asshole husband of hers obviously drove Mindy to overeat."

"Yeah, to eat herself into wearing a circus tent," Britney elucidated. "Looks like she's a wino too."

"That's definitely a case of the pot calling the kettle black. If memory serves, sister dear, you were mighty dependent on the old vino, as well as your close pals, Jack Daniels and Johnnie Walker, during your marriage to that rotten SOB."

"*That*," she complained with another sharp poke to Archer's gut, "was a low blow."

"Damn." He clapped his hand to his belly. "That finger of yours should be licensed as a deadly weapon." Lifting an eyebrow, Archer nodded with a devilish smile. "You know, you alone sucked back most of the winery's profits last year."

Gasping, Britney stamped her heel against the floor again, making Archer wince. "Are you implying I'm an alcoholic?"

Sporting a smirk, Archer folded his arms across his chest and leaned back against the mahogany paneling. "Now that you mention it, your insides have been in contact with so much alcohol I think I'm gonna start calling you Pickles." He cracked a laugh.

Britney sneered. "Your questionable charisma and cloying sense of humor might work on desperate bimbos like Mindy, but as your sister, I'm above falling for your boyish charms. So put a lid on it."

Archer began to pace. "Why do you detest Mindy so much anyway? What did she ever do to you personally?"

"She has this nasty habit of breathing," Britney oozed.

"Real mature, Britney," Archer huffed. "The way I hear it, Mindy caught you and Edward screwing in her own bed." He abruptly stopped pacing, turning on his heel to face his sister. "How come you conveniently failed to mention that interesting nugget when you first told me about you, Edward and Mindy? In your version, *you* were the poor, innocent, virtuous woman."

"So what?" Shrugging, Britney gave a disinterested wave. "Mindy deserved everything that happened to her because she let herself grow into a fat disgusting pig. She couldn't honestly expect Edward to still find her attractive at that horrendous weight. I mean, seriously. Come on, Archer, of course Edward was going to seek satisfaction elsewhere. What man wouldn't?"

"And my sweet, accommodating little sister was more than willing to oblige Edward in his quest, right?"

"Jesus H. Christ, what's the big deal? It's not like I committed a crime because I had sex with a married man. These aren't the dark ages, you know?" She fluffed her hair. "Let's just say I was there to give the poor, sex-starved man a little sympathy and understanding when he needed it most."

"Don't you think Mindy was just as devastated to find you humping her husband as you were to find Edward humping that twenty-something bimbo from your office? Remember how you felt when you walked in on that, Brit?"

"Of course I was devastated. I mean, look at me, Arch." She brushed her hands up and down her slender frame. "I can think of at least a dozen guys who'd give their eye teeth to spend just one night with me. There wasn't a single goddamned reason in hell why Edward should have had to go elsewhere with *me* in his bed."

"Maybe so, Ego Queen, but apparently your dearly beloved husband felt otherwise. After all, Britney, the man had a heart attack and croaked while boffing some sexy little piece of jailbait, didn't he?"

Britney threw her arms skyward and growled. "What the hell do you want me to say? Okay, yes, it's true. Edward was a philandering piece-of-shit-bastard-fuck and the longer we were married the more I grew to detest him. And I'm fucking glad he's dead. It's like a blessed reprieve. There, is that what you were waiting to hear?"

Britney's face contorted with a mixture of rage and hurt as she wiped away the tears trickling down her flushed cheeks.

"Yeah, I guess so," Archer said softly, his posture deflating. "But somehow it doesn't give me the satisfaction I'd hoped for." He smiled sympathetically as he drew his sister into a hug. "I'm sorry. I didn't mean to make you cry." He held her at arm's length. "So tell me, doesn't any of that stuff we just talked about make you feel just a little bit of sympathy for Mindy and what she went through with that jerk?"

Shedding Archer's hands from her shoulders, Britney looked at her brother as if he were an imbecile. "Of course not. What does one thing have to do with the other? Like I said before, Mindy von Grettle was a fat pig who got exactly what she deserved. Boy, men can be so dense." She laughed incredulously.

"How could you even attempt to make a comparison between her circumstance and mine? Get real, nutsoid." Tapping her finger against his temple, she grabbed her coat and purse and headed for the door. "That's it, I'm outta here." With that, she made a rapid exit, slamming the door behind her.

"I may as well just give up," Archer muttered to himself. It was about time he faced facts. His sister was hopeless. Her thought patterns were skewed. She was never going to get it.

The door opened again and a party of five strolled into the winery, telling Archer they were there for a wine tasting. Archer led them into the tasting room while Mindy came down the stairs with Leo and Archer's mother.

As he poured wine samples, giving the tasters his usual spiel, he overheard Mindy making her umpteenth apology to his mother and thanking her for her kindness.

Well hell. There was obviously something seriously wrong with him because just the sound of Mindy's voice had Archer's cock jerking to life in his pants. If he didn't know better he'd say he'd been bewitched by the loony blonde.

She and Leo headed toward the exit. Archer glanced up in time to see Mindy pause, casting a brief, regretful look toward him. While focusing on Mindy he overfilled the small glass and quickly attended to the spill, watching out of the corner of his eye as Mindy walked out the door.

Following Mindy, Leo paused, nodding in Archer's direction with a sympathetic look.

Archer returned the nod, thinking it was for the best that Mindy was walking out of his life. The last thing he wanted or needed was a schizophrenic dame screwing with his mind—or his libido. There was a pleasant calmness and sanity when Mindy wasn't around. That's the way his life should be. Calm. Sane. Mindy-less.

Continuing to dispense wine samples as he made polite conversation with customers, all Archer's tortured, hapless brain could think about was sampling Mindy von Grettle's lush, succulent curves.

Crap. He was losing his damn mind. There was no other explanation.

After the last customer of the day left the winery and his mother had gone home, Archer locked up and headed upstairs to his apartment, glad to finally be alone with his thoughts.

It had been one hell of a day. The last thing he'd expected, after his unforeseen flight back from California that afternoon, was to find Mindy von Grettle at his winery. Especially after what transpired the day of their ill-fated picnic. Archer had written her off that day. As far as he was concerned the nutty-as-a-fruitcake dame was out of his life forever.

"So long. See ya around, baby," he muttered with an adieu salute as he fished his keys, wallet and change out of his pockets, tossing them onto the hall table in the foyer. No matter how fascinating or desirable she might be, he wasn't a masochist. And subjecting himself to another bout of her twisted female logic could only be a painful experience.

At least, that's how he'd felt until he saw her slouched on the steps with her head between her knees, belting out polka songs. Raking his hand through his hair, Archer laughed at the recollection.

Not only was today's encounter with Mindy less than idyllic, again, but to make things even worse, he had to contend with his self-serving, addle-brained sister. Oh but that wasn't the end of it. Nope. His mother practically forced him to sit through a probing, accusatory third degree so intense it would have driven a lesser man to drink.

With that thought in mind, a chuckle surfaced as Archer glanced toward the glass of deep, heady cabernet he'd set on his nightstand. Heaving a sigh, he took a purposeful sip of the earthy liquid.

A slow smile stretched across his weary features as he sat on his bed, removing his shoes and socks. The memory of Mindy lying passed out, right on this very spot across his bed, all soft, curvy and luscious-looking, had his cock stiffening. It was like God was playing some cruel joke when he made that woman so damned beautiful yet screwy as a loon.

The thought of Mindy's breasts heaving as she lay semiconscious certainly didn't do anything to thwart his burgeoning arousal. When the inebriated temptress threw her arms around his neck, yanking him into that succulent kiss, Archer was a goner. The urge to tear off her clothes and savor every square inch of her curves was nearly overwhelming.

"That would have given Leo and my mother an eyeful." Archer cringed at the thought. He'd have to remember to keep his door locked in the future.

The term *dizzy blonde* crept to the forefront of his thoughts, although it wasn't entirely apropos where Mindy was concerned. While she could be batty and unpredictable, she was also intelligent, fun-loving and had a great sense of humor. Her curvaceous shape and angelic face made her the epitome of many a man's fantasies. Archer's fantasies to be sure.

If only that vexing stubborn streak of hers didn't surface every time they were together. That irritating warped thinking of Mindy's drove him to distraction until it felt like a tight band was clamped around his head, squeezing like he was an orange on the verge of being juiced.

Muttering beneath his breath, Archer snatched the tie from around his neck and whipped it across the room.

"The woman's impossible," he groused, unbuckling his belt and unzipping his fly. Kicking his pants off, he continued, "Stubborn, bullheaded, incorrigible, inconsistent..."

A slow, lingering smile crossed his lips as he unbuttoned his shirt, remembering holding her in his arms earlier and tonguing her juicy little pussy. Sucking in a breath, he closed his eyes. Once he opened them again he gazed down, shaking his head in frustration as his cock saluted the ceiling.

Archer grasped it tight, massaging his dick hard, with slow, even strokes, watching it expand in his hand. Christ, he wanted to be inside her so bad he could fucking taste it.

He let the shower run hot enough to burn all thoughts of Mindy from his mind, to dampen his raging libido, but his strategy backfired. Stepping into the misty spray only reminded him all the more of the hot silky flesh between her thighs. The inviting warmth of her eager mouth and tongue.

Archer slid his hands up and down his engorged cock, squeezing as he imagined her knees parting, presenting him with her glistening slit, all pink, rosy, and ready for him. She'd beg him, and he'd take her with one swift merciless stroke, pounding his cock deep, gliding in and out of her cream slicked pussy.

She'd be wet and writhing beneath him as her cunt convulsed wildly around his cock. Punishing Mindy for her rebellious ways, he'd give it to her harder, faster, deeper, until she was breathless and panting. When she'd open that pretty mouth of hers, all indignant and ready to tell him off, he'd drive all defiant thought from her mind with another jackhammer thrust.

Pumping his dick furiously, Archer envisioned the blissful look of longing in her big blue eyes. Her pouty lips forming his name while her nails raked his back.

He'd tame her wayward ways by keeping her caught up in a frenzy of one shattering orgasm after another.

He'd watch the erotic slip and slide of his cock as he hammered into her, burying himself balls deep into her soaked satin heat. She'd gaze up at him in wonder as his fingers dug hard into her full, luscious ass cheeks, possessing her, making her his. Her sweet body would quiver, shudder. His name would escape her throat in a tortured cry as her back arched and her slick walls vibrated around him.

Archer growled out as his cum thundered up from his balls down the length of his cock and spurted in hot ribbons against the dripping shower wall.

"Mindora von G," he ground out, "you drive me crazy—in more ways than one."

Chapter 13

"THIS WAS ABSOLUTELY the worst, most heinous, humiliating afternoon of my entire life." Mindy scrunched down in the passenger seat of Leo's car, burying her head in her hands. "I will never forgive you for this, Leo. *Ever*!"

"How many times do I have to tell you I didn't know he'd be there?" Leo countered, slamming his hand against the steering wheel. "Mindy, I swear on all that's holy I had no idea. I swear on my Grandma Gert's grave—"

Mindy threw her hands up and growled. "Here we go again with the grandmother's grave. You probably never even had a Grandma Gert. She's probably just another of your ten million elasticized truths." She sank farther down in the seat, folding her arms across her chest.

"Now that's cruel." Leo looked pained. "When you say things like that it's like a knife right through my heart."

Shifting to a more upright position, Mindy shot Leo a noxious glare. "Believe me, Leo, if I had a knife on me that's right where I'd plant it." She wiped the angry spittle from her chin. "Then I'd twist it this way," she relished in a dramatic gesture, "and back again." She smiled for the first time since they'd gotten in the car.

Cringing, Leo observed, "You're becoming a bitter woman, Mindy. It's very unbecoming." Reaching into the backseat, he snagged a facial tissue from a box, handing it to her. "Here. I think you're starting to foam at the mouth."

"Is it any wonder? I've morphed into a foaming-at-the-mouth, polka-singing, hormone-driven, murderous, slutty drunk thanks to you."

"And bitter. Don't forget bitter," Leo offered, wagging a finger as Mindy did her best to bore a hole through his head with her heated glare. "But you can't blame me for the hormone-driven or slutty part. After all, it's your fault not mine that you've got the hots for Archer Priest."

Leo gave her one of those all-knowing, tongue-in-cheek smiles, infuriating her even more. Because he was right. But she'd be damned if she'd admit it to him. "It's your fault I got smashed and threw myself at Archer like a wild nymphomaniac, Leo." She slapped her hands over her face, groaning. "And then the man's mother comes into the room while I'm clawing at her son. God help me, I've never been so mortified in all my life."

"I have to admit that was pretty funny." Leo chuckled. "But not as funny as seeing Archer with his pants around his knees."

"*Funny?*" Bellowing the word, Mindy whipped her head in Leo's direction, transmitting a lethal look. He gripped the steering wheel tighter and winced.

Slipping into his goosey, machine-gun laughter, he said, "Now, Mindy, I can fully understand why you're so upset but you have to believe me when I tell you I was absolutely clueless about Archer, or his mother or sister, showing up at the winery. You know I would never purposefully do anything to cause you that kind of grief."

"If all that weren't enough," Mindy persevered, "now my head's throbbing so bad that only smashing it against a brick wall could feel worse."

"Welcome to the world of hangovers, darling." Leo reached over and rubbed her back. Ten minutes later as they sat waiting for a freight train to pass and watching a flurry of fat snowflakes falling, he said, "If it's any consolation, I don't think Agatha thought poorly of you. She seemed very nice. I'm sure she understood."

"Understood that the woman who was once married to her daughter's dead husband is a drunken slut who's now trying to snare her son?" Mindy expelled a pained whimper. "Perfect first impression." She turned toward the window, gnawing on a fingertip as she absently watched the snow accumulate. "If Archer thought I was an idiot before, I can only imagine what he must think of me now."

"Not that you give a damn, of course," Leo said.

"We have nothing in common, except for the fact that we both have the misfortune of knowing his sister. There have never been two people less compatible. Then there's that giant ego of his." Mindy shuddered. "To be honest, I don't give a damn what Archer Priest thinks of me."

"You don't, huh?"

Mindy didn't like the meddlesome tone of his voice. "Leo, I want you to make me a promise."

"Shoot."

"Don't tempt me." She fought to hide a smile. "After today, you'll never mention Archer's name to me again. You owe me that much. Promise?"

"Sure." As he pulled into Persimmon's parking lot, Leo offered an innocent shrug. "As a matter of fact, I've been giving it a lot of thought during our drive back from the winery. I think you're absolutely right. I realize now you're not Archer's type at all. Not even remotely."

"I'm not?"

"Good heavens no." With a flick of the wrist, Leo went on, "What can I say? You were right and I was wrong. It's as simple as that. From now on, the subject of Archer Priest is a dead issue. Guaranteed."

"Oh...well, good. That settles that." Mindy gave a triumphant nod as a sick feeling gnawed at her insides.

Leo put the car in park and unfastened his seatbelt. Before he could get out, Mindy grabbed the sleeve of his jacket, bunching it in her hand.

"I'm going to have to get the steamer out to get rid of those wrinkles," he groused. He looked her in the eyes, heaving a tuneful sigh. "Okay, what's the matter?" Her jaw hanging open for a moment, poised to speak, Mindy heaved a sigh of her own and clamped her mouth shut. "Well?" Leo pointedly looked down to where Mindy was still clutching his sleeve.

"Nothing." Mindy released her grip. "Never mind."

"Good, then let's go before this snow gets any worse." Leo opened the car door, only to have Mindy grab his arm again. Expelling an impatient groan, he said, "Do you have any idea how much this suit you're destroying costs?"

Mindy turned her attention to her nails as she polished them against her coat. "I was just wondering what you meant when you said I wasn't Archer's type." Shrugging, she chanced a brief glance at him. "Why? What makes you so sure we wouldn't be right for each other? Not that it matters, of course. I couldn't care less. I'm just curious."

"Right. Just curious." Leo offered a matter-of-fact nod. "Where do I begin?" Slapping a hand to his cheek, he adopted a contemplative expression. "There are tons of reasons why you wouldn't work as a couple. Archer's too slick and aggressive for you for one thing. He'd be better off with a woman who's unbridled, carefree, adventurous, fun. You're more the cozy, housewifey, hands-in-the-mixing-bowl, milk and cookies type."

Mindy's jaw dropped in amazement.

"A well-traveled, cosmopolitan man like Archer Priest needs a worldly, sophisticated woman. One who can keep pace with him mentally as well as physically."

"But I—"

"He needs a chic woman," Leo continued, "who'd be comfortable mixing and mingling in the same whirlwind social circle. Besides, Mindy, Archer is brash, egotistical, arrogant and...well, he can be just plain obnoxious."

"Well, I wouldn't go so far as to say that he's—"

"He's an ass. No doubt about it." Reaching over, Leo patted her shoulder. "Remember the way he took advantage of your inebriated condition and pawed at you this afternoon? He behaved like an animal. You're definitely better off without him."

Mindy's shoulders slumped.

"After the abominable, shameful way Archer treated you today, I can see why you have no use for him, Min. He lacks patience, sympathy or understanding. Thank God you found out what a jerk he really is. The last thing I want is for you to be stuck with another Edward von Grettle. Now come on, let's get out of this car before these old bones of mine stiffen up in this cold."

Again Leo started to open the car door and again Mindy jerked at his sleeve. Expelling a sigh of exasperation, he plopped down hard against the back of the seat, telegraphing an impatient gaze in Mindy's direction.

"This is getting real tiresome, Mindy. Can we please go inside?"

"Actually, I-I think of myself as being rather carefree and adventurous," she said thoughtfully, tracing her finger over the gear-shift. "Even unbridled occasionally." She glimpsed a quick, docile peek at Leo. "Lord knows, Archer's nothing at all like Edward. Don't you think you're being too harsh, Leo?"

This time, Leo swung the car door fully open and exited, with Mindy following suit, clutching her coat closed against the whipping wind and snow. Slipping into his overcoat, he quickened his pace.

"It's just like you said, Mindy, he's a Priest, tainted with the same genes as that bitchy little sister of his. It's better you wash your hands of him now. He's no good. Besides, he'd just be a constant, thorny reminder of Britney."

Mindy sprinted alongside Leo's bold strides to keep up, mindful of not slipping on the icy patches and falling on her ass. She'd already had more than enough humiliation for one day.

"Okay, I know I made that wisecrack about the Priest gene pool but I was just being stubborn. And stupid. You basically told me so, remember?"

"Bah..." Leo waved his hand, walking even faster. "I should learn to keep my mouth shut and quit interfering."

Mindy took two steps to every one of his so she could keep up. "He's not like Britney at all. Archer's kind, caring, sweet and funny. As far as what happened today, um, it's possible I may have overreacted. Just a bit."

"You don't have to come into the office, Mindy. You can go home. We're covered here. You're going to need to take some aspirin and put an ice-bag on your head."

Ignoring Leo's suggestion, Mindy trotted alongside him, slipping and belting out a loud *Woooooo!* as she skidded along the pavement, smack dab into Leo just before they reached the travel agency's door. Clutching wildly at him, she hung on for dear life only to knock Leo off kilter and send them both careening to the ground.

"You did that on purpose," Leo accused.

Gazing down at her boss beneath her, Mindy gasped. "Don't be ridiculous." She scrambled off him into a sitting position.

"First you destroy my designer suit and now you break my ass." He sat up, winced and reached behind himself, rubbing.

"People like us with plenty of padding don't break our asses when we fall," Mindy noted. "It's one of the advantages of being zaftig. You know," she went on, spitting snowflakes out of her mouth as Leo got up and pulled her up after him, "it wasn't Archer's fault that I got smashed at his winery."

"I don't want to discuss Archer anymore, Mindy. I just want to go inside and get far away from you. Besides, after all that wine you're in no condition to deal with clients. You'll probably end up booking trips to Vienna when they ask for Venice. Go home."

Leo swung the door open and entered with Mindy at his heels. She trailed along as he went about his business, greeting the evening staff and the customers they were attending.

"Sure, Archer and I tend to get on each other's nerves but, when you come right down to it, I think we could really be great together. As a matter of fact, I-I think I'm very much Archer Priest's type." Mindy planted her fists on her hips, nodding with conviction and sending a fluff of snow falling from her hair.

Shrugging out of his overcoat and hanging it on the clothes tree at the back of his office, Leo spun toward Mindy, displaying a jubilant ear-to-ear grin.

"Aha! I knew it!" Slapping the top of his desk with pencil-cup-rattling vigor, he jabbed a triumphant finger at her. "That's what I've been trying to tell you all along but you just wouldn't listen to me. *Of course*, you and Archer Priest are made for each other." He threw his arms into the air, forming a victory vee.

Mindy stood agape.

Leo clapped his hands together, rubbing briskly. "Ah, there's nothing like the feeling of adrenaline coursing through your veins when you know you're right. I love it!" He engaged in a euphoric little jig.

Vehemently wagging a threatening finger, Mindy said, "Leo Parker, you conniving phony, you stop that ridiculous victory dance right now, do you hear me?" She pounded her fist against his desk. "I trusted you and you tricked me. How could you do that?"

"Oh Lord, it was pitifully easy." Leo smirked.

"Very funny." Mindy scowled.

"Leo's my name and strategy's my game." Tipping an invisible hat, he folded his torso into a little bow.

"Strategy? Try *manipulation.*"

"Potato, potahto." Buffing his fingernails against his lapel, Leo shrugged. "Call it whatever you want. It worked, didn't it? Deedle-dee-deedle-dee-dee," he sang as he hoofed another jig.

"I'm glad you think this is all such a big joke, Leo."

"Oh, stop being so melodramatic." Laughing, he came around to the front of his desk, pulling a reluctant Mindy into a hug. "You have to admit, I really had you going there for a while, didn't I?"

After a moment of silence, her glare dwindled, her lips twitched and finally curled into a smile. "All right, I admit it. You got me good, you pixilated old buzzard." She laughed. "I'm crazy about Archer Priest. Absolutely head over heels. Every time I see him all I can think about is tearing his clothes off and jumping his gorgeous bones." She thought for a moment.

"What if I'm terrible in bed? The only experience I've had is with Edward. What if he was right and I turn out to be frigid?"

Throwing his head back, Leo laughed. "After what I witnessed this afternoon in Archer's bedroom, I can assure you, frigidity is something you needn't worry about, darling. You're a hot-blooded woman, Min.

"Besides," he continued, "you've been devouring all those spicy hot romance books, and getting up close and personal with your new arsenal of sex toys as you fantasize." With a knowing smile, he added, "About Archer."

"I've made such a mess of things though." Mindy leapt up from her chair and paced, wringing her hands. "Tell me, Leo, what should I do?"

"Ahhh...that's music to my ears." Beaming a smile, Leo exuberantly rubbed his hands together. "I thought you'd never ask.

Don't worry, Uncle Leo's got an excellent idea up his..." He looked down and brushed the arm of his suit coat. "Wrinkled sleeve."

"Such as?"

"Such as getting rid of your nemesis."

"Britney?" Stopping her pacing abruptly, Mindy turned to Leo and blinked. "You mean...as in murder?"

Leo engaged in devilish laughter. "Nothing quite that extreme. You'll see. Trust me, Mindy...*trust me.*"

"Famous last words," Mindy offered with a cautious smile. "Something tells me I'm going to regret this."

Chapter 14

"HAIL, HAIL, THE gang's all here. Break out the band 'cause Big Jazz's back in town. Yeehaaa!"

Mindy cringed at the sound of the booming Texas drawl coming from the front of the travel agency. It belonged to Leo's cousin, Jasper Wilson, otherwise known as *Big Jazz*.

"Oh God," Leo said, dropping his head into his hands. "It's Jasper."

"There's still time to escape out the back door if we hurry," Mindy offered, only half joking.

"Hey, cousin, where ya hidin'?" Big Jazz's boisterous voice grew closer.

"Not a good idea," Leo said. "Especially seeing as how Jasper is a key player in my dastardly plan to get rid of Archer's sister."

Mindy vaulted out of her chair. "*What?*"

"Don't plan on going *anywhere* until he leaves because I'll need you in here with me," Leo instructed. "Okay?"

"Now you just hold it right there, Leo, I—"

"Shhh." He tapped his forefinger against his lips. "He might hear you. Look, I know how you feel about Jasper. And Lord knows I don't blame you. But just go along with me and put up with him this one last time. Remember, he's moving to Russia so you won't have to see him again for years."

"God willing." Mindy rolled her eyes.

Leo tiptoed to the door of his office, stealthily peeking out. "He'll be here in a few minutes," he whispered. "He's schmoozing and flirting along the way and the girls are giggling and eating it up."

"How can they fall for that chauvinist crap of his?"

"Gee," Leo said, laughing, his gaze still directed at Big Jazz. "Do you suppose it could have anything to do with the fact that Jasper's filthy rich, powerful, tall and ruggedly handsome?" He slipped his head back into his office.

"Rich and handsome or not, the guy's still a jerk, a bigot, and a racist." Big Jazz reminded her of a taller, handsomer version of Leo. Same hazel eyes, same shock of taffy-blonde hair, same engaging smile. But that's where the similarities ended. While Leo effervesced with charm, charisma and a winning personality, Big Jazz had all the appeal of a rain-soaked swatch of cowhide.

"And for God's sake, don't say or do anything to piss him off," Leo pleaded. Clearly anticipating Mindy's retort, he held his hands up in defense. "He's part of my plan to get rid of Britney, remember? We need to keep Jasper in good spirits."

Mindy sighed. "You conveniently neglected to mention that the scheme you're brewing involves me and that insufferable asshole cousin of yours."

Wincing, Leo pushed at the air with his hands in a shushing motion as he scooted back to his desk. "Don't worry, Mindy, my plan is foolproof...well, pretty much." Leo offered an ambiguous smile.

"Well lookee here," Big Jazz blared as he came around the corner and poked his head into Leo's office. "Cousin Leo's got a *bony-fide* angel in his office."

"Oh gawd," Mindy mumbled, closing her eyes.

"Lil' lady, you come right on over here and let Big Jazz get a good look at you."

Doing her best not to sneer, Mindy offered Big Jazz a reluctant smile as she extended her hand. "Nice to see you again, Jasper."

"*Big Jazz.*" He nodded and winked. Rather than shake Mindy's proffered hand, the strapping six-foot-six Texan drew his hand from his side as if it were a six-shooter and pointed it toward her. "Hey now, Big Jazz never shakes hands with a lovely lady when he can give her a big ol' Texas-style hug instead."

"Oh, but Big Jazz, I—"

Flashing a gleaming white-toothed smile, he grabbed Mindy into a hug, squeezing the breath from her lungs. Holding her at arm's length a moment later, he lifted her into the air as if she were a rag doll and swung her around.

"Now, ain't you just the purdiest little thing I ever did see?" Still holding Mindy high, he gave her an appraising once-over and whistled. "Why Mindy darlin' you're just a wispy little bit of a thing now."

"Jasper..."

"Uh-uh." Big Jazz shook his head and tsked.

"*Big Jazz*," Mindy corrected, flashing the best apologetic smile she could muster under the circumstances. "Please put me down." Like a true Texas gentleman, Big Jazz obliged and tipped his Stetson, revealing a thick head of hair.

Cringing when she looked down at the wrinkled mess that was once her favorite black silk blouse, Mindy mumbled something inaudible as she smoothed and tugged at the fabric.

Leo walked around to the front of his desk, hand extended. "Hey, Jasper, er, Big Jazz, great to see you."

"Cousin Leo, you old hound dog." Bypassing Leo's hand, Big Jazz pulled him into a bear hug. Once he let him go, he gave Leo a friendly whack on the back so powerful it sent him careening halfway across the room. "How the hell are ya, boy?"

"Whew. Still alive, I think." Leo gave a tentative laugh as he tugged at his collar and adjusted his tie.

"I see you're wearin' that classy tie I sent you last Christmas, cousin."

Fingering the gaudy lasso and cowboy boot-covered monstrosity, Leo forced a smile. "One of my absolute favorites. Can't wear it often enough, can I, Mindy?"

"He practically sleeps in it," Mindy confirmed.

"I wore it in honor of your visit today." Leo nodded convincingly.

"Glad you like it, 'cause I got another real humdinger for you out in my suitcase."

Leo's shoulders slumped. "Gee, Jasper, you shouldn't have...really."

"Aw, nothin's too good for my favorite cousin—even if he is a Yankee." Guffawing with big *haw-haw-haws*, Big Jazz walloped Leo with a playful punch in the arm.

By the look on Leo's face Mindy figured it had rendered Leo's arm all but useless for the next hour.

"I've decided the time's come for me to steal away this purdy little secretary of yours, cousin." Big Jazz raised an eyebrow, motioning toward Mindy. "And convince her to become the next missus."

"I am *not* Leo's secretary, Big Jazz. I'm his vice-president."

"Aw, well sure you are, honey." Big Jazz directed an exaggerated, conspiratorial wink toward Leo and laughed.

"Well, I *am*." Huffing an exasperated sigh, Mindy planted her fists on her hips. "And, for the hundredth time, I am not interested in becoming the fourth Mrs. Big Jazz Wilson, thank you very much."

"Hot diggity, she's a lively one, Cousin Leo." Big Jazz laughed and scooped Mindy into another airborne hug. "That's how I like my women. Good and feisty." Standing with her locked in his arms, her toes dangling, Big Jazz rocked from side to side. "You know, Cousin Leo, sweet pea here and me could make beautiful music together."

Her face buried in the fringe across the chest of Big Jazz's doe-skin-tan suede jacket, Mindy cried a muffled, "Ooooh!" She pushed with all her might until she finally escaped his firm clench. After taking a deep breath she tunneled her fingers through her disheveled hair.

"Why do you insist on talking about me as if I weren't even in the room?" she asked the towering Texan.

"She always this hot-tempered?" Big Jazz asked Leo, bypassing her direct question.

Mindy threw her hands into the air. "That's it, I give up." Turning to leave Leo's office, she was blocked by Big Jazz's massive frame in the doorway. He may as well have been a brick wall. Glancing up into his handsome, grinning face, she sneered before plopping down into a chair, burying her face in her hands and groaning.

"*Mindy...*" Leo said in a warning tone out of the corner of his mouth. He tugged at his collar and plastered a cheerless smile across his face.

Transmitting a narrow-eyed glare at her boss, Mindy slowly rose from her chair, sidled over to him and discreetly crunched her heel into the toe of his shoe. Smiling for Big Jazz's benefit, she grabbed Leo's sleeve and yanked him close.

"Jesus, you're killing me," Leo whispered through a grimace, struggling to maintain his smile.

"Don't you *Mindy* me, Leo," she whispered, mocking his warning tone. "There is no way on earth I'd ever consider marrying that walking, talking side of Texas beef. Plan or no plan. You got that?"

"I told you to trust me on this, didn't I?" Leo muttered through clenched teeth. "Don't worry, marrying him isn't part of the plan."

Turning his attention to his cousin, Leo turned on his best salesman's smile. "Don't mind Mindy, Big Jazz. She's just overtired.

We've been swamped. Everybody wants to get away from Chicago's winter freeze and Mindy's been putting in too many hours at the office."

"Well that explains it," Big Jazz said with a thoughtful look. "Sweet little thing like that shouldn't be out here in the corporate world tryin' to bust her butt." He turned to Mindy and doffed his Stetson. "Pardon the profanity, ma'am." Mindy rolled her eyes and huffed. "Why, our little Mindy here should be at home takin' care of womanly things like birthin' babies and seein' after her man's needs."

"*Leo...*" Mindy drew his name out through clenched teeth.

Giving her an acknowledging nod, Leo led his cousin to a chair. "Come on, have a seat, big fella. I'll fix us a cup of espresso while we catch up on things."

"Sure." Big Jazz wedged his large frame into one of the armchairs. Studying the subtle peach, ivory and gray tones of Leo's office, he turned to Mindy and smiled. "This here stuff is all new since I was here last. Bet you picked out all this cute, fluffy, flowery stuff all by yourself, didn't you, honey?" He smoothed his hand over the persimmon print fabric Leo had taken weeks to select for the upholstery in his office. "I can always tell a woman's touch." He winked.

"Not me." Mindy extended her arm toward Leo. "Leo's the one who picked out—"

"The designer," Leo blurted, nearly spilling the coffee beans as he slid into a rapid burst of jittery laughter. "I picked out the interior designer for the redecorating project." He tugged at his collar as if it were strangling him. "She was a real doll. You know," he laughed again, "thirty-six, twenty-four, thirty-six." Winking, Leo waved his hands along invisible curves in the air, ignoring the sound of Mindy's gasp.

"Gotcha, cousin." Big Jazz winked back. "Tell ya what, let's make that coffee a little more interesting with some of this." He slid a cowhide-covered silver flask from inside his jacket. "Nothin' goes better with coffee than a little bourbon I always say." He flashed a grin.

"I've got work to do." Mindy rose from her chair. "I'm leaving."

"*Sit down,*" Leo commanded, flashing a friendly smile when Big Jazz eyed him curiously. Glaring at Leo, Mindy expelled the breath she'd been holding and returned to her seat. "She looks peaked," Leo explained to Big Jazz. "She needs to rest—*until I tell her it's okay to leave.*" Leo pinned Mindy with a no-nonsense glare.

"Nothin' wrong with bein' a little firm, Cousin Leo. Sometimes that's all the little ladies understand." Grasping the brim of his hat, Big Jazz tipped it toward Mindy. "No offense meant, ma'am."

Folding her arms across her chest, Mindy projected a malicious sneer. She imagined whipping that damned Stetson across the room like a boomerang so it would take out Big Jazz first and then knock the crap out of Leo before it returned to her. The satisfying image brought a smile to her lips.

Leo stopped grinding the coffee beans long enough to jump in before Mindy had a chance to say anything. "So how's Aunt Ruthie and Uncle Joe?"

"Mama and Daddy are doing real good. Got their fiftieth wedding anniversary comin' up, so I thought I'd send them on a little boat trip. You can help me put somethin' nice together for 'em, can't you, Cousin Leo?"

"A cruise? Absolutely. We'll get right on it. What did you have in mind? Caribbean, Hawaii, Mexico, Alaska, Europe?"

"Yeah, that sounds real good."

"Which one?"

"All of 'em. I want to send Mama and Daddy on one of them 'round-the-world boat trips."

"Excellent." Leo rubbed his hands together briskly.

Mindy could swear she saw neon-green dollar signs flash across Leo's hazel eyes as she imagined hearing his thoughts scream, *ka-ching!*

After Big Jazz's third cup of espresso-laced bourbon he leaned forward, resting his elbows on his knees. Half-closed eyelids framed the fervor in his eyes as he languished in a long, lusty appraisal of Mindy's physical attributes. Before she realized it, he'd reached over and clasped Mindy's hand in his own, studying her fingers and gently stroking her skin.

"Soft as a baby's behind." He lifted her hand to his lips, kissing it. "Mindy, honey, I don't know if Cousin Leo mentioned it or not, but I'm movin' to the USSR on business. I'd be right pleased if you'd join me."

Mindy squirmed uncomfortably in her seat. "First of all," she said, "it's no longer the USSR, it's just plain Russia. Second—"

"We'd have to get hitched, of course," Big Jazz continued as if Mindy hadn't spoken. "Them there commies don't take none too well to livin' in sin from what I hear." Patting Mindy's hand, he smiled and winked.

Her eyes wide with astonishment, Mindy made a move to extricate her hand from his, but he was too fast. "Russia hasn't been a communist country for some time, Big Jazz," she informed him.

Before Mindy could protest, he slipped his arms around her, scooped her from her chair and planted her on his lap. "I love you, Mindy darlin', sure as I'm sittin' here, I do. You and me'll make some mighty fine-looking babies together, yes siree." He leaned his head down and nuzzled Mindy's neck.

"Oh for—" Mindy grumbled a few choice expletives under her breath as she toiled in vain to escape his grasp. "Let go of me, you big ox!"

With a firm hold on Mindy, Big Jazz laughed and turned to Leo. "Cousin Leo, I'll never be able to understand why you didn't snap up this feisty little firebrand all for yourself when you had the chance."

A reddened hue swept over Leo's cheeks as he laughed nervously. "I uh...I guess Mindy's just not my type."

"A little too ballsy for ya, huh, cousin?"

"Interesting phraseology, Jasper." Leo tugged at his collar for the umpteenth time and chuckled.

Mindy felt sure he was wondering what his macho, good ol' boy homophobe cousin would do if he ever found out Leo was gay.

"Actually, she's not quite *ballsy* enough for me," Leo offered. "But let's get back to the subject at hand. You and Mindy."

Mindy shot Leo a laser-sharp glower, intense enough to bisect a slab of granite in two seconds flat. "Leo, you son of a bitch—"

Puckering his lips, Big Jazz jutted his chin out to Mindy, who was still scrambling to get away from his hold. "How's about planting your betrothed with a little kiss right here." He tapped his lips. "To seal the deal, honey?" He made a series of annoying smooching sounds.

Mindy would have clobbered him upside the head if her hands were free. Seething, she looked up at her captor. "Jasper Wilson, not only would I not go to Russia with you, I wouldn't even let you walk me across the street. And as far as getting *hitched*...hah! I wouldn't marry you if you were the last—"

Slamming his hand against his desktop with a resounding wallop, causing Mindy and Big Jazz to whisk their heads in his direction, Leo jumped up from his chair. "Mindy, you're such a kidder." His laughter sounded peculiar. "What Mindy's trying to say, Jasper, is that she'd love to go with you more than anything."

Mindy gasped.

"But she can't," Leo finished.

"Can't? Why not?" Furrowing his brow, Big Jazz glanced from Leo to Mindy and back again.

"Because...because it's our busy season," Mindy blurted.

"Heck, is that all?" Big Jazz guffawed. "Cousin Leo, if you're worried about missin' out on some revenue 'cause of losin' Mindy, you just tell me how much you want. I'll scrawl you out a check for whatever you need to cover what she'd be bringin' in for the next five years. Now, we got a deal?"

"Five years' worth, huh?" Leo rubbed his chin in contemplation.

"*Leo!*" Mindy bellowed as Big Jazz squeezed her close.

"Gee, Jasper," Leo said, "as tempting and generous as your offer is, and as much as I'd *love* to accept it..." He slanted Mindy a questioning look and she shot back a toxic glare. He heaved a great sigh and continued, "I'm afraid it's just not possible for Mindy to go."

"Because?" Big Jazz looked mighty perturbed.

"Because eh..." Leo licked his lips nervously. "Because she's pregnant."

"*Pregnant!*" Mindy and Big Jazz shrieked in unison as the tall Texan shot up from his chair, dumping Mindy on the floor in the process.

"Ow." Mindy rubbed her butt as Leo and Big Jazz helped her to her feet.

"But she ain't even married."

"Well," Leo cleared his throat, "yes, she is actually."

"I am?" Mindy angled Leo a puzzled expression. Prompted by his coaxing look, Mindy said, "I mean, I am." She smiled up at Big Jazz. "I'm married."

Folding his arms across his chest, Big Jazz slanted Leo and Mindy a dubious look. "Since when?"

"June," Leo said, just as Mindy said, "Last month."

Knitting his eyebrows together, Big Jazz barked, "Well, which is it?"

"Uh..." Leo and Mindy chorused as Leo stirred his little cup of espresso with a tiny silver spoon. The only sounds in the room for what seemed like a small eternity after that were his and Mindy's thundering heartbeats and the incessant clinking of the spoon against the cup.

"Well," Leo finally offered, "they were secretly married in June and they just made it public a month ago." He wiped his sleeve across his forehead. "Isn't that right, Mindy?"

"Right. We had to keep it a secret because of, uh..." Mindy threw a desperate glance at Leo.

"Because her husband was an illegal immigrant at the time," Leo offered quickly.

"Huh?" Big Jazz removed his Stetson and scratched his head as Mindy shot Leo an incredulous look. "Mindy married a *foreigner*?" He said the word with distinct distaste.

"It's a long story." Leo waved his hand and shook his head. "Very dull. Believe me, Jasper, you wouldn't be interested."

Big Jazz straightened to his full height and threw his shoulders back. Cocking his head in a menacing fashion, he asked, "Just who is this foreign guy? What's his name?"

"Rolf. Rolf, uh, Schwarzenegger," Leo said, offering an apologetic shrug to Mindy. Rolling her eyes, Mindy groaned and slapped her hand to her forehead.

"*Schwarzenegger*? You mean like the foreign movie actor who went and got himself elected mayor?"

"He was governor, actually. Yes, exactly," Leo answered Big Jazz through nervous bursts of laughter. He fished out his wallet, flipping to a photograph of Rolf that he removed. "Mindy and Rolf had to keep their marriage a secret until Rolf became a citizen so it wouldn't reflect poorly on his cousin...Arnold."

Mindy eyed Leo who had dissolved into manic, staccato laughter as he handed the photo to Big Jazz.

"You know how the media loves to get its hands on a juicy story like that," Leo added.

Peeking over Big Jazz's arm, Mindy eyed the photograph of Rolf, the handsome co-owner of Bavaria Haus and Leo's lover since they'd met two weeks ago—the last time she saw Archer. The thought of Archer had her indulging in a wistful sigh as she glanced at the wall clock.

Actually, it had been two weeks, one day, four hours and seventeen minutes since she left his winery. Not that she was keeping count or anything. Mindy hadn't heard a peep from him since. Well, no wonder.

When Big Jazz turned Rolf's photo over, Mindy saw the inscription and cringed.

"To Leo—with love and affection—Rolf," Big Jazz read aloud. With a look of revulsion he looked up at Leo. "*Love and affection*?"

Leo winced. "Oh yeah, I forgot about that."

"Austrian men are more inclined to openly express emotion than American men," Mindy explained, swallowing hard. "Rolf loves Leo like a brother, because Leo's the one who introduced us and helped Rolf become an American citizen." Mindy blinked. Hell, she was becoming as inventive as Leo.

"Yeah, that's it." Leo nodded enthusiastically. "Like a brother."

Big Jazz's broad shoulders slumped. "Well, shoot. I'm downright brokenhearted." He looked to Mindy who offered a gleeful shrug. A moment later he clapped his hands and broke into a broad grin. "Well this is cause for a celebration. If you got yourself any plans for tonight, cancel 'em, 'cause Big Jazz's taking y'all out to dinner. I want to meet the lucky son-of-a-gun who stole away my Mindy and shake his hand."

"No!" Mindy and Leo blurted as their faces drained of color.

"Rolf's sick," Leo offered at the same time Mindy said, "Rolf's working late." Exchanging horrified expressions, they expelled pained groans.

Scowling, Big Jazz crossed his arms over his expansive chest as his gaze flew back and forth. "There's somethin' cockeyed goin' on here and I don't mind tellin' you I'm startin' to get a might ticked off. Now I don't know if this is supposed to be some sort of Yankee humor you two are pullin', but Big Jazz ain't laughin.'"

After a moment of utter stillness, Leo's telltale laughter shattered the quiet. "You're right, Jasper, Mindy and I were just joshing. Guess some jokes just get lost in translation from North to South, huh?" Cringing against the ferocity of his cousin's scowl, Leo tugged at the loosened knot of his tie. He gave Big Jazz a hearty slap on the back. "Of course, we'll all have dinner with you tonight, Jasper."

Her face contorting in alarm, Mindy screeched, "*Leo!*" Leo responded with a sick smile and a not-too-confident thumbs up sign.

"That's more like it." Big Jazz gave Leo a solid crack on the back that all but brought Leo to his knees. "Now all I got to figure out is, with my darlin' little Mindy here married and about to become a mama," he looked at Mindy who beamed a smile as she pooched out her belly and patted it, "what am I gonna do for fun out there in the USSR all by my lonesome?"

"I'm mighty glad you asked that question, Jasper." Leo gave his cousin a sturdy whack on the back that didn't even cause Big Jazz to budge.

"Why's that?"

"Because, cousin o' mine, I happen to know of a hot little flame-haired filly who'd make your spurs spin and your Stetson steam, that's why."

Mindy's ears perked.

Rubbing his hands together, Big Jazz flashed a smile as he took a seat again. "Always did have a thing for redheads. I'm all ears, cousin."

Planting her hands on her hips, Mindy smiled down at Big Jazz. "Well, I'm awfully glad to see you were able to get over your broken heart so fast."

"Aw, honey," Big Jazz patted his chest with one hand and Mindy's ass with the other, "you know you'll always be number one with me."

He tossed a charming wink before turning back to Leo. "Now let's hear all about this little redheaded filly of yours, cousin."

Chapter 15

Leo

"MY COUSIN'S sending his limo to Mindy's place about seven o'clock," Leo said, absently gnawing on a knuckle. "I wish we had more time to practice." He groaned and sagged at the feel of strong, capable hands kneading his neck and shoulder muscles. "It's really important that we're convincing."

"It will be fine, *Liebling*." Rolf nipped Leo's earlobe with his teeth, causing Leo to suck in a sharp breath. "I will make you proud in front of Big Wilson." Turning Leo to face him, Rolf offered a confident grin and an exuberant thumbs-up sign.

"Big Jazz," Leo corrected. He wanted to believe Rolf, he really did, but he had the sinking feeling they were dead meat. "Yeah...it'll be a cinch," he muttered. "No problem. Piece of cake."

"*Ja. Apfelkuchen*." Rolf grinned and nodded.

"Eh...right." Leo groaned. "Okay, let's go over it again, Rolf." He could feel the tension releasing in his shoulders. Rolf's attention to his tight muscles was working. The big brawny blond was a master at massage...among other things.

A prickle of desire inched up his spine. Being with the big German was like Oktoberfest—vigorous, heady, wild, fun and exhausting as hell.

"Okay now...who are you?" Leo prompted, trying to ignore the way Rolf's inviting scent filled his nostrils. There wasn't any time to play. It was imperative they spend every moment possible preparing for the dinner with Jasper.

Clearing his throat, Rolf stopped the massage and hopped off the bed, standing in front of Leo and straightening his broad shoulders.

Bad position. Very bad. Because it meant Leo had no choice but to look at Rolf's Conan-the-Barbarian body. All those bronzed, well-defined muscles...the barely there sprinkling of pale blond across his chest that trailed down his abs and led to his...

Damn.

Rolf licked his lips and cleared his throat again, reminding Leo of a nervous, overgrown kid preparing to give a school recital. All he needed was a little bow tie.

"I am Mindy's loving husband, who just became an American citizen, and we are going to have a little baby. I am also Arnold Schwarzenegger's cousin." Furrowing his brow, Rolf rubbed his jaw. "*Ja*, that part could be a problem, Leo. Schwarzenegger is Austrian and I'm German," he said proudly, puffing out his chest.

"Yeah, and?" His gaze glued to those broad, expanding pecs of Rolf's, Leo's mouth went dry.

Rolf looked at him as if he had two heads "The accent and the mannerisms are completely different."

"They are?" Leo said incredulously. He wondered what was different. Maybe it was a slight inflection when pronouncing *ja*, or perhaps it was the manner in which they held their steins when they were tossing back beer. "No kidding?"

Rolf's frown deepened. "*Ja*."

Leo focused on the sound of the word and shrugged. Damned if he could tell the difference. Rolf sounded just like Schwarzenegger to him, although he certainly wasn't about to insult Rolf by mentioning that little fact.

"I am not sure I can be a convincingable Austrian. I am worried Big Jasper might get suspended."

"You mean suspicious." Leo did his best not to laugh at Rolf's genuine look of concern and butchering of the English language. "Believe me, Rolf, you don't have to worry about convincing my cousin. Anything that's not a Texas drawl sounds foreign to him."

"I am excited to meet him. I hear many stories from the time I am a child about cowboys and Texas."

"I'm afraid Jasper's no cowboy. He's a racist, a bigot and a horny sexist in a big ol' Stetson." Leo sighed. "And he's just going to think of you as a kraut-head." He offered an apologetic shrug.

"Since he is half German on his mama's side, that makes Big Wilson half a head of fermented cabbage too, *ja*?" Rolf asked, apparently in all seriousness.

Leo chuckled. It never ceased to amaze him how this big, gorgeous, sexy towhead could keep him in stitches. Yup, Rolf Haggenmacher was a prime example of German ingenuity at its best.

"I'm afraid it doesn't work that way, Rolf. Big Jazz thinks of himself as one hundred percent pure Texan. Period. That means, one," Leo counted off on his fingers, "anybody outside the Texas border is a foreigner. Two, anybody from across the ocean is the enemy and, three, anybody who's a homosexual is from another planet. And should be sent back as soon as possible. Preferably in tiny pieces."

Wincing, Leo made a motion as if breaking matchsticks.

A mask of solemnity pinching his features, Rolf harrumphed. "*Ja*, I understand this type of man. We have them in Germany too." He crossed muscled arms over his chest, and Leo's gaze locked on to his huge biceps and the magnificent pecs they bordered.

"Good," he said, tearing his gaze away. "So for God's sake, Rolf, whatever you do," Leo steepled his fingers and looked skyward, "don't say or do anything that might lead Jasper to believe that we're anything less than shining icons of macho virility and heterosexual manhood."

Rolf looked clueless. "This means?"

Leo couldn't help breathing an exasperated sigh. "That we're straight," he clarified. "You know, heterosexual. *Nein* gay. *Nicht* queers. Not fairies. I don't want Jasper thinking we're a couple of pansies. Get it?"

"*Ja*. Don't worry, *liebling*," Rolf said earnestly in his thick, melodic accent as he returned to the bed, scooping Leo into a hug and kissing the top of his head.

"Big Jasper will never suspect you and I are queer pansy fairies from outer space. You can count on me to protect your proud, macho, manly, very unwomanly image."

Leo just gazed at Rolf silently for a moment. "Great," he said finally, with a resigned smile. "That makes me feel a whole lot better," he lied.

"We will belly up to the bar, pardner," Rolf boasted in what Leo imagined was his idea of a Texas drawl. "Listen and listen up tight," Rolf added, sounding like a gay, German John Wayne. "I'll be back," he added, and then broke into a grin. "That was my Schwarzenegger imitation. What do you think?"

Leo thought it sounded exactly like Rolf's regular voice. "Superb," he said. "For a moment I thought Arnold had come into the room."

"Good." Rolf nodded happily. "Then I will use that voice tonight for Big Jasper so he will think I'm from Austria."

Leo sighed. Dead meat. Definitely.

Rolf brushed his hands together, beaming a satisfied grin. "All done," he announced. "*Das is gut*. Now we have vigorful man-to-man togetherness before we go to dinner, *ja*?"

"Vigorous," Leo corrected absently, wondering if he should call the whole damn dinner with Jasper off, claiming a sudden three-way case of stomach flu. Jasper would no doubt be pissed, and damned suspicious. Leo supposed he could always come clean and just tell his cousin the truth.

After all, there's no way he, Rolf and Mindy were going to pull off this charade. While Jasper might not be the brightest crayon in the box, he'd see right through it.

But, dammit, he owed it to Mindy to try. He *had* to make this work somehow. Had to make Jasper believe Rolf and Mindy were happy honeymooners and expectant parents. It was the only way Leo could think of to keep his amorous cousin's mind off Mindy, and set his plan of getting rid of Britney in action.

His thoughts a mile away, Leo started at the feeling of Rolf's fingers expertly massaging up and down his spine.

"This is hard" Rolf said.

"My spine?"

"You make a good joke." Rolf's genuine laughter rang through the room. "No, *Liebling,* I mean this is hard to be close to your big, strong, muscle-bound, burly body without enjoying being with you in a strong, masculine way."

Since he worked out periodically, Leo wasn't exactly cushy, but he knew he sure as hell wasn't muscle-bound, much less burly.

"You really know how to lay it on thick, don't you, Rolf?" Leo gave him a playful whack on the back.

Returning the whack, which almost sent Leo sailing across the bed, Rolf smiled broadly. "*Ja,* I like to lay thick with you. But Big Wilson will never know we lay like pansies."

That had Leo collapsing in laughter...tinged with an ample touch of dread. He winced from the powerful collision of Rolf's big paw with his back.

"This is getting ridiculous." Leo flexed his biceps, which were puny next to Rolf's. "I've got to get back to the gym and build myself up."

"You look just fine to me." Rolf yanked Leo into an affectionate squeeze, wrapping his arm around his shoulder. "You are very perfect to my eyes. Your body feels good in my hands, and you have good heart, *Liebling*. You are everything I could ever want in a lover man."

"Oh my darling boy," Leo breathed. "Where have you been all my life?" He still couldn't believe he was lucky enough to have a man as sensational as Rolf in his life.

"Did you forget, Leo? I was in Germany. Remember?"

Chuckling at Rolf's literal response to his question, Leo felt his insides light up with a buoyant sensation he'd never experienced with another man. Joy. True, unbridled and complete. He never would have believed it, but in the short time he'd known Rolf Haggenmacher, Leo had fallen in love with him. Deeply.

"Maybe now we have time to be sex together, *ja*? I will make you too happy and tired to be nervous about Big Jasper."

Before he could say, *sounds good to me*, Leo found himself being tossed onto the center of the bed as if he weighed no more than a slab of *Wiener Schnitzel*. Oh yeah, there was definitely something to be said for having Conan as your lover.

"Your ass is like a big, full moon," Rolf said, and Leo knew it was meant to be a compliment. God, those hands of his were magic.

The short time they spent before getting ready for their dinner with Jasper had Leo wanting to crawl the walls from an overdose of sheer bliss.

"I like to hear the cloud nine sounds you make when I make you happy," Rolf said. "Ahhh, *Liebling*, what a wonderful fucker you are."

Leo bit the inside of his cheek to keep from laughing. Rolf was killing him in more ways than one.

"I never be so happy being with anyone else, Leo."

"Same here, Rolf. You're amazing."

Finally, that perfect moment of otherworldly existence where pain commingled with pleasure in an almost unbearable rush of ecstasy gripped Leo.

"*Ach, du lieber*!" Rolf belted out at the same time Leo yelled, "Holy shit!" the instant before they collapsed together into a well-sated heap.

———◉———

Mindy

———◉———

THE DOORBELL RANG AND Cadbury raced to the door, barking. "That's my good little guard dog." Mindy laughed as she reached down to pet Cad who gratefully lapped up the attention. She opened the door to find a mesmerizing, blond mountain of a man flashing a gleaming white-toothed smile down at her. "Hi, Rolf, nice to see you again. Come on in."

"*Guten Abend*...good evening, Mindy," Rolf said in his considerable accent, nodding a polite half-bow. "Do I look good enough to be your husband?" Holding his arms out to the sides, he turned left and right.

Taking in the striking German's smart, charcoal-gray suit, crisp French-cuffed white shirt and conservative tie, Mindy eased into a smile and nodded. The guy was a knockout, a certified heart-stopping hunk.

"Oh yeah. You look just fine, Rolf. Amazing, in fact."

"Good. My sister Marta picked out this suit. She said it made me look like a sexy American husband." He smiled proudly. "You look very amazing too, in your fancy dress, Mindy. Zaftig."

Mindy felt herself blush as she smoothed the skirt of her little black dress. "Black hides a multitude of sins," she said. She glanced to the left and right of Rolf. "I thought you and Leo were coming together."

"I'm here." Leo stepped out from behind the big German, wiggling his fingers in a wave. "He's deliciously big, isn't he? Makes me feel like I'm thin." He brushed his hand along the arm of Rolf's jacket and Mindy caught the look of affection that passed between them.

"Cadbury, stop that," she said, noticing her curious little dog spent more time sniffing this stranger than most. "Shame on you. That's not very polite."

Contentedly planting himself next to Rolf's leg, Cadbury cocked his head and looked up adoringly as he licked his chops.

Rolf laughed as he splayed his huge hands, turning them to and fro. "It must be the sauerbraten I was preparing this afternoon. The ginger smell stays on the skin for a long time."

"Eau de Kraut," Leo offered. "It's my favorite new scent."

Rolf laughed. It was one of those laughs that began at the eyes and lit up his face. "Leo is so funny. He always makes me laugh."

Mindy looked at Leo, who stood there looking as sweet and innocent as a cherub. "Oh he's a riot, all right," she said with a smirk. "Rolf, are you sure you don't mind going along with this ridiculous charade tonight? I feel terrible that you got roped into this."

"Mind?" Leo said. "Of course he doesn't mind. Do you, Rolf?"

Rolf draped his arm around Leo's shoulder. "Of course not, *Liebling*. I would do anything to make you happy."

"What does *Liebling* mean?" Mindy asked.

Rolf gazed down at Leo with a lovestruck grin. "It means *darling*."

She smiled when she saw Leo's cheeks flush. It was obvious he'd flipped for Rolf in a big way. They really did seem perfect for each other.

"You do not have to worry about anything tonight, Mindy," Rolf assured. "I will make sure Big Jasper will never guess in a million years that Leo and I are from another planet."

"Oh...well, that's, um...that's good." Mindy shifted a questioning glance toward Leo.

Rolf squeezed Leo's arm in a buddy hug. "Tonight Leo and I are macho, manly men who only like to fuck with women."

"That's great, isn't it, Mindy?" Leo offered with what looked to Mindy like a highly uncertain smile...just before he let forth with a staccato giggle.

That's when Mindy knew for certain they were sunk.

Chapter 16

MELLIFLUOUS SOUNDS of a string quartet floated gently on the air. Silver, fine china and crystal gleamed in the golden flicker of candlelight and the soft glow of the grand chandeliers overhead. The ambience of Montague's, an upscale restaurant in downtown Chicago, was subdued, stylish and elegant.

The foursome was seated in a roomy semicircle booth upholstered with fine-grained black leather so yielding it felt like cashmere. It was by far the ritziest, and no doubt priciest, restaurant in which Mindy had ever dined. That was probably the only advantage to dining out on Big Jazz's tab.

"Give me the biggest, best doggone steak ya got, son, with all the fixin's," Big Jazz addressed the young male server. "And tell the cook I want it well-done."

"I'll advise the chef of your request, sir," the server said.

"Now when I say *well-done*," Big Jazz raised his finger for emphasis, "I mean I wanna see that sucker blacker than a spear-chucker's heinie, ya got that?"

A pained collective groan could be heard around the table. It was all Mindy could do to keep from whapping the big Texan oaf upside the head with her menu and hightail it out of the restaurant.

"Oh dear God," she muttered, massaging her temples, unable to believe she'd just heard him make that atrocious remark. "Please tell me you did *not* just say that." When Jasper didn't respond, she shot him a caustic glare. "Honestly, Jasper, could you possibly be any more embarrassing?"

"Well sure I can, honey," Big Jazz said with a broad, lazy smile. "Just give me a chance. The night's still young and we've got lots of drinks comin' our way."

He winked, no doubt imagining he looked charming as hell. Which he did, but he was still an unrelenting, obnoxious, racist jerk.

"I could die," Mindy said beneath her breath, sinking down in her seat after catching the server's well concealed but clearly repulsed expression. "I could just die."

Lifting an eyebrow, the attractive server, crisply attired in the restaurant's uniform of white shirt and black bowtie, sniffed as he looked down his nose at Big Jazz. "Most definitely," he said with a slight huff.

"And keep those drinks comin' too, all around the table. Big Jazz doesn't want to see any empty glasses in front of his dinner guests, ya hear?"

"I'll alert your cocktail server to your wishes. Will there be anything else...*sir*?" The word clearly stuck in the young man's throat.

"Nope, that'll do it for now. Just keep in mind, boy, that I'm very generous when I get good service and I ain't a happy cowpoke when I don't."

Shifting his jaw from side to side, the server closed his eyes in a long blink. Mindy could only imagine what was going through his mind. One thing she knew for certain—after tonight she'd never be able to step foot in this restaurant again.

"I assure you, I'll do my best to accommodate your needs...sir." With that, the server left the table.

"Kind of a pretty boy, if you know what I mean," Big Jazz said, snickering as he elbowed Leo. "One of them delicate, pansy types." He made a limp-wrist gesture for effect.

Neither Mindy, Leo nor Rolf dared move a muscle. In fact, they didn't even breathe.

Big Jazz swatted the table with an open palm, which succeeded in getting their full attention.

"So yer the foreign fella that stole my sweet little Mindy away from me, huh?" He eyed Rolf up and down. "I was jealous as all get-out when I learned I'd lost Mindy's heart. Especially to a foreigner. You ain't half bad lookin' though. Tell me about yourself, boy." He swigged down half a glass of bourbon, sat back against the cushy, oversized black-leather booth and folded his arms across his chest.

"Yes, Big Jasper—"

"Big Jazz."

"Oh yes, sorry. Big Jazz." Clearing his throat, Rolf sat up straight and placed his arm stiffly around Mindy's shoulder. "My name is Rudolph Schwarzenegger," he announced, sounding like a game show host reading from cue cards. "I am from..." He cleared his throat again, looked left, then right and swallowed hard. "Austria."

When he didn't detect any signs of disbelief emanating from Big Jazz, he continued. "I am Mindy's dreadfully passionate and strongly loving husband, and the papa of the little baby growing inside her *schwanger* stomach."

His eyebrows knitting, Big Jazz said, "Her what?"

"Sorry, it means pregnant. Her pregnant stomach," Rolf explained. "Mindy and I are delighted newlyweds." He mechanically kissed Mindy on the cheek as she bit the inside of it to keep from laughing. Rolf was so buff, so handsome, so endearing...so unbelievably wooden and ill at ease.

"My female wife and I created the baby by having numerous sex together in the regular way." Rolf grinned.

Mindy and Leo groaned.

"I soon ago became an American citizen," Rolf went on, placing his other arm around Leo's shoulder and squeezing. "Thanks to my strong, extremely macho and masculine friend Leo. Go ahead, Leo, make a big muscle for everyone to show them how strong and manly you are."

Clearly proud of his stilted performance, Rolf flashed a bright smile while Mindy and Leo sank lower in their seats.

"Uh-huh," Big Jazz said, nodding with a curious expression. After a contemplative moment, during which he stuffed half a buttered roll into his mouth, and the other three sat on the edge of their seats awaiting his reaction while he chewed, he simply shrugged and turned to Leo.

"So, cousin, when do I get to meet this little filly you want to set me up with?" he asked, stuffing the other half of the roll in his mouth and talking around it.

"Well, Jasper—" Leo began.

Draining his glass of bourbon and swallowing, Big Jazz gave the glass a solid whack against the linen-covered table, making his dining companions as well as those at nearby tables jump. He held the empty glass aloft and snapped his fingers toward a passing cocktail server while giving a shrill whistle. "Hey, there, sweet thing," he yelled. "We need another round of joy juice here, darlin'"

Silence enveloped the room. All eyes were on their table as diners transmitted harsh, disapproving looks, whispering to each other about the uncultured, boisterous lout and his probably equally loutish dinner companions.

"This here sure is a great little beef barn, ain't it?" Big Jazz asked the other three at his table, clearly oblivious to the tension hanging over the room like a shroud.

Mindy wondered if she could possibly be any more mortified.

Once the deafening silence in the dining room subsided, Leo inched forward in his seat, resting his arms and hands on the table.

"Okay, Jasper, here's the deal. You've got a whole bunch of investment properties in the Chicago area that you want to liquidate before you leave the country, right?"

"Yup." Big Jazz nodded.

"Well I just happen to know of a sexy hotshot little Realtor named Britney Priest von Grettle—"

"von Grettle?" Big Jazz cut in. "Hold on there. Didn't that used to be Mindy's name before it was Schwarzenegger?"

"Eh..." Leo waved his hand. "Yeah, yeah, I'll get to that part later. Anyway, Britney's got the knowhow and experience to get the job done for you and maybe..." Leo jiggled his eyebrows. "Just maybe, she'd be willing to perform a few other *services* for someone with all your...uh—"

"Money?" Big Jazz offered, laughing.

"Charm," Mindy said quickly. "Someone with all of your irresistible Texas charm. And sex appeal. Why, money can't even begin to compare to your other attributes, Big Jazz." Nearly choking on the words, Mindy batted her eyelashes while smiling adoringly.

"Aw, you sweet little thing." He flashed Mindy a charismatic smile. "Y'all better be careful or you're gonna make your hubby there jealous."

"You are right, Big Jasper. I am very jealous of your Texas sex charm," Rolf offered.

Big Jazz gave him a dubious look and Mindy sighed.

"Getting back to Britney," Leo said, chomping on a forkful of the salad their server had just set before him. "The only caveat is that—"

Big Jazz screwed his features. "The only what? Skip the ten-dollar words, cousin, and give it to me in plain American English."

"Stipulation," Leo substituted. "The only rule," he amended when he saw his cousin still looked clueless.

"All righty." Big Jazz smiled and nodded. "Rules I understand. Go ahead."

"The only rule is that you can't let Britney know that Mindy and I set this whole thing up. Or that you're my cousin. Or that you even know either one of us. At all." A clipped spurt of staccato laughter tumbled from his throat. "Mmm, great creamy garlic dressing, don't you think?"

Leo turned to Mindy, who figured she probably looked about as green as their salads.

With a sneer, Big Jazz pushed his salad away. "Texans don't eat that little, piddly rabbit food. I don't get it, cousin. Why the big secret?"

"Funny thing." Leo let forth with a volley of telltale laughter then licked his lips nervously. "You see, Britney's the widow of Mindy's ex-husband. Let's just say they're not exactly on the best of terms."

"A little catfighting goin' on, huh? Sounds reasonable enough." Big Jazz nodded. "Why can't I tell her you're my cousin?"

"Eh..." Leo tugged at his collar and looked toward Mindy for help.

"Well, uh..." Unable to come up with a good reason, Mindy just shrugged and sank down a little farther in her seat. At this rate, before long she'd be on the floor.

Clearly picking up on the dilemma at hand, Rolf took a break from wolfing down his salad. Broadcasting a wide smile, he slapped Leo on the back.

"Because Britney and my virile, robust, masculine friend Leo used to be sexual lovers. But she detests him now because she found out he is a wild sex machine who was also sexing many other women every day."

"*Oh God,*" Leo and Mindy said in unison as he choked on his salad and she sprayed a mouthful of Riesling across the table. Receiving dual whacks on the back from Rolf and Big Jazz, Leo fell forward, smacking his forehead onto the rim of his salad plate.

"Ow," Leo said in a small voice.

"Is that all?" Big Jazz asked. "Well, shoot, why didn't you say so in the first place, cousin?" He reached over and jabbed Leo in the arm with what he figured was a playful punch.

"Ow."

"You ol' hound dog. That's perfectly understandable."

Leo shot up in his seat. "It is?" he said in surprise, wiping salad dressing from his forehead and wincing in pain. He shot a caustic look at Rolf who smiled proudly and gave a thumbs-up sign.

Mindy watched Leo shake his head in resignation and sigh. It was obvious the big, dopey, gorgeous, good-hearted German was bound and determined to preserve his lover's *macho image*.

"Why sure," Big Jazz said. "A man can't help givin' in to his natural urges. That'll teach ya to be more careful about gettin' caught next time, cuz." Sporting a conspirator's wink, he gave Leo another enthusiastic slap on the back.

Leo just mouthed a silent *ow* this time.

"Now don't you or Mindy worry none, Cousin Leo. I won't let on to Britney that I know either of you." Big Jazz cocked his head and studied Leo. "You okay, cousin? You're lookin' kinda green around the gills."

"Oh yeah, I'm peachy...just peachy." Gingerly fingering the growing egg on his forehead, Leo grinned.

"Being the strong, sturdy man that he is," Rolf offered, "Leo hardly even feels pain. Isn't that right, my macho buddy?" Rolf gave Leo another hearty slap on the back.

Cringing, Leo uttered something resembling a sad, sick laugh. "Oh yeah. Me strong like bull," he muttered weakly.

While Leo deserved to be thrashed for getting Mindy in this mess, as well as all the others, she had to admit she felt sorry for him. The poor guy would probably be sore for the next two weeks.

The entrees were brought to the table. The server stood with his hands behind his back after placing a charred-beyond-recognition burnt offering in front of Big Jazz.

"The chef would like to know if he has succeeded in achieving the proper shade of ebony for your steak, sir."

A determined look etched across his features, Big Jazz sawed through the big leathery slab and shoved a piece in his mouth. After an inordinate amount of time chewing, he swallowed.

"Mmm-mmm!" Bobbing his head, Big Jazz tossed a wink at the server. "Son, you go tell that cook of yours that he did a right fine job with this here piece of cattle."

"I'm sure he'll be delighted to hear you approve." The server offered a brisk nod before departing.

"Them prissy, fussy little fellas," Big Jazz said, jabbing his fork in the air toward the retreating server, "make the best waiters, don't they? Guess it's either that or bein' a hairdresser, florist, or a dancer." He shrugged. "The little dandies ain't fit for anythin' else, know what I mean?" He stuffed a chunk of burned leather in his mouth and proceeded to give his jaw muscles a workout.

"Yes, Leo and I know what you mean." Rolf nodded vehemently. "Don't we, Leo?"

"Oh yeah, absolutely," Leo agreed.

"*Ja*, because we are such manly men who love to have sex only with women. Like you, Big Jasper, we are not liking the kind of dandy men who act like they are from other planets. We detest them. We spit on them." After making a ptooey gesture, Rolf offered Leo, who sat in horrified, drop-jawed amazement, a confident wink.

Something akin to an ailing groan escaped Mindy's lips. She knew tonight was going to be bad, but not this bad.

"You know, Rolf," Big Jazz said, tsking as he angled his head, "you kraut-heads sure as heck got a funny way of talkin'."

"*Ja*. That's because I am German."

"Austrian," Leo quickly corrected.

"Oh yes, I mean Austrian," Rolf agreed. "Sometimes I even forget where I am from." He broke into nervous laughter. "That is an Austrian joke, Big Jasper. I made it because I am Austrian, not German."

Big Jazz just eyed Rolf for a moment. Mindy could almost see the gears and wheels turning inside his head. Of course, she highly doubted there were any workings whatsoever in that melon that sat atop his broad shoulders.

"You do an awful lot of talkin' about macho this and manly that, Rolf." Big Jazz gestured with his fork in the air. "But here you got the purdiest little thang sittin' right there next to you and you ain't even made a move to plant a smooch on that little lady's kisser yet."

Rolf paled and swallowed hard. Leo buried his head in his hands and Mindy offered up a silent prayer.

"Now," Big Jazz continued, "if that was *my* little filly sittin' next to me, especially if we was still newlyweds like you, you'd better believe I'd be a whole lot more attentive. That's fer dang sure."

"Believe me," Leo said, "Rolf can't keep his hands off Mindy when they're in private. He's, uh...he's just being on his best behavior tonight." With an exaggerated wink, Leo nudged Big Jazz with his elbow.

"That's true," Mindy confirmed. "He's like a sex-crazed animal. Aren't you, Rolf?" She smiled and pinched Rolf's cheek.

"Yes, a crazy sexual animal." Rolf nodded. "I cannot keep my hands off Mindy's zaftig body, even when we are in a restaurant.

Since we were seated, I have been rubbing against her big, beautiful breasts and..." Rolf cleared his throat and swallowed hard. "And my fingers have been very attentive to the wet sex spot between her legs, under the table where you cannot see."

Mindy gasped. "Rolf!" she blurted, knocking her wineglass over as she turned to face her pseudo husband.

"Oh God." Shaking his head, Leo dissolved into sickly, pained laughter. "Oh dear God..."

"Well, hot damn! Score one for the kraut-head!" Big Jazz whacked the table hard as he broke into laughter.

"Man, you foreigners sure are sneaky little rascals, that's fer dang sure. Well, I reckon that'd explain why Mindy's been lookin' kinda funny on and off all night." Big Jazz gave Mindy an appraising once-over and winked.

As sheer, unmitigated horror skewed her features, Mindy whispered, "This isn't happening." Closing her eyes, she massaged her temples and scrunched low in her seat. "Please, God, tell me this is all just a bad dream."

"Aw, a little pleasurin' under the table ain't nothin' to be embarrassed about, Mindy, honey." Big Jazz tossed another charming wink. "After all, he's your husband, ain't he?"

Mindy opened her eyes and glared at Big Jazz. It would be so easy just to whip off her high heel, aim for that smug, good ol' boy puss of his and send her shoe careening across the table.

"Yes," she said instead, aiming a deadly, warning glare at Rolf. "But there are some things ladies and gentlemen simply do not discuss, or allude to, especially when they're at the dinner table—in public." She yearned to escape by seeping into the intricately detailed carpet and becoming *one* with the fibers.

"*Ich bin traurig,*" Rolf said. "I am sorry," he quickly translated, apparently realizing he hadn't spoken in English after Big Jazz gave him a *what-the-hell* look.

"I should not have mentioned our happy secret pleasure under the table. But as a manly animal, who enjoys sex with his female wife, I cannot help myself from bragging." He beamed a bright smile and turned to Mindy. "*Liebling*, my beautiful, zaftig wife, you are always very sexy and desiring to me." Rolf placed his arm around her. "It is so hard to keep my hands from your sex-filled body."

Mindy didn't know whether to laugh or cry. "Yes, yes, I know," she said through a sigh as she patted Rolf's face. It was impossible to be angry with the big lummox. After all, it wasn't his fault Leo had roped him into this disaster. Rolf's earnest attempts to be a convincing, loving, heterosexual husband were really very sweet. Awfully strange, but sweet. It certainly wouldn't be fair to blame poor Rolf if this berserk idea of Leo's flopped.

Leo. Mindy shifted her gaze to him. Suddenly she wasn't feeling quite so sorry for him. In fact, she could easily have him drawn and quartered for putting her through this humiliating charade.

"*Ich liebe dich*," Rolf said to Mindy. "That means I love you," he explained to Big Jazz. "And I love the little baby we have made from having sex so many numerous times together."

"I love you too, Rolf," Mindy said wearily. "Kiss-kiss." Offering a drained smile, she kissed the air between them.

Evidently mistaking that as a cue, Rolf grabbed Mindy and nailed her to the back of the booth with a head-spinning humdinger of a kiss. One of his hands was at Mindy's crotch while the other was clamped to her breast, kneading.

Flabbergasted, she slapped her hands against the back of the booth and shot a frantic, wide-eyed look at Leo—who clearly wasn't going to be of any help because he looked just as stupefied as Mindy.

"Well, hot damn!" Big Jazz smacked the table with his big paw. "Now that's the way it's done in the good old U S of A. Ain't that right, cousin?" He laughed and elbowed Leo.

A disquieting expression across his features, Leo let go with a weak, squeaky laugh. "Darn tootin', Big Jazz," he said with a wink, feebly punching the air with his fist.

Mindy wasn't sure what surprised her more, Rolf's impulsive, speed-of-light move or the fact that he was such a phenomenal kisser. If this wasn't one of the worst moments of her life, she could really get into that succulent kiss of his. But right now she had to get the big, muscle-bound German off her before her lungs collapsed.

Shifting in her seat and pushing against Rolf's massive chest, Mindy's eyes darted from left to right, growing as large as pie tins when she spied an all-too-familiar man coming their way.

No, her thoughts screamed. *Oh God, no! Please God, please don't let that be Archer. I swear, Lord, I promise on Leo's Grandma Gert's grave that I'll denounce chocolate for the next six months if you just let it be someone else...*

No doubt about it. It was Archer Priest all right.

Mindy shoved with all her might but the determined German wouldn't budge. She guessed he had a point to prove to Big Jazz and he was bound and determined to follow through.

Great. Just great.

Making frantic sounds through their kiss, Mindy shifted her eyes to Leo and back to Archer in the hopes that Leo would see him coming and could do something to get Rolf off her. Unfortunately, by the time Leo picked up on Mindy's signals and realized what was happening, Archer and the shapely brunette with him were striding by their table.

"Oh shit," Leo said, leaning his elbow on the table and covering his eyes with his hand.

Oh yeah, that really helped. Mindy's heart sank.

Nonchalantly glancing toward their table as he passed by, Archer caught a glimpse of the kissing couple making a public spectacle of themselves. He did a classic cartoon double take when he realized the woman was Mindy.

While Mindy sank down in the seat to escape detection, the counterfeit smooch ripened into a full-blown lusty exhibition as Rolf, still passionately attached at the mouth—and tongue—sank down right along with her.

Chapter 17

Leo

"WHY? JUST TELL me why you think I'd do something so unbelievably stupid, like arranging for Archer to come to the same restaurant as us last night," Leo said the next afternoon. He'd toiled so hard to set things right for Mindy and Archer and she was being terribly ungrateful.

"Because that's your nature." Lowering the passenger side visor of Leo's Cadillac, Mindy checked herself out in the mirror and groaned

"You sound like a sick cow, Mindy."

"I've never worn so much makeup in my life. I barely even recognize myself. I look like a vampire in this black wig."

"Nonsense. You look amazing. Very...gothic. Now stop griping."

"Of all the restaurants in Chicagoland, you're going to tell me Archer just *happened* to choose the same one?" She slammed the visor back in place. "I don't buy it, Leo. Not for a minute."

"Use your head, Mindy. Why would I go through the trouble of concocting such a brilliant plan only to—"

"Brilliant?" Mindy scoffed. "Leo Parker, you are certifiable, do you know that?"

"It *was* brilliant. It worked, didn't it? Jasper's off your back because he's convinced you're happily married and he's got an appointment to see Britney this afternoon. "Besides," he patted Mindy's hand, "Big Jazz chose the restaurant, not me. It was sheer coincidence that Archer was there."

"Do you think he recognized me?"

Cringing, Leo couldn't avoid spilling forth with a volley of nervous laughter as he remembered watching Archer's classic double take. And the way he'd craned his neck as Mindy and Rolf slid down the seat of the booth in what looked like the heat of passion.

"Eh...I'm afraid so," he admitted. There really wasn't any use lying about it. Half the restaurant was aghast at the tawdry display. Tugging at his shirt collar, Leo stretched his neck.

"Oh Leo..." Mindy's shoulders slumped as she succumbed to an involuntary shudder. "What must he think?"

Leo sure as hell wasn't about to tell poor Mindy the truth. She was too close to killing him in cold blood as it was. "That you're a passionate and desirable young woman who can't keep her suitors at arm's length," he said instead. "I'll bet Archer was jealous as hell when he saw Rolf climbing all over you like that."

"Either that or he thinks I'm a cheap tramp who's into exhibitionism."

Leo figured that was probably closer to the truth. He cocked his head thoughtfully. "That could be a definite turn-on. In fact, I'm betting Archer made good use of a bottle of hand lotion and a box of tissues last night when he was thinking about that hot little scene with you and Rolf."

"Leo, that's terrible." Mindy slapped his arm. "Did you get a load of that sexy brunette draped over Archer's arm?"

"You're exaggerating. She wasn't draped. There wasn't even any bodily contact between them."

"But she *was* sexy."

"Maybe a little," Leo admitted with a hesitant shrug. The woman was a definite knockout. Cover girl material. "Maybe she's a business associate."

"You mean like his chief grape crusher?"

"Grape crusher." Leo laughed. "That's a good one." Beaming a sprightly smile, he glanced toward Mindy, who sported a sullen glare.

"What if they're lovers?"

"I doubt it," he lied, "but that's all the more reason for us to proceed with phase two of our plan so you can snag Archer and reel him in before the grape crusher has a chance to bottle him up all for herself." Leo grinned, quite pleased with his wittiness.

"Very metaphoric." Mindy rolled her eyes. "What's with this *our* plan stuff? This incredibly moronic phase two idea is solely your brainchild, Leo."

"Well, I just hate to hog all the credit. Come on, Min, it's an ingenious plan and you know it." Seizing a quick glance in the rearview mirror, Leo sprouted a wry grin as he fingered the brim of his hat. He was the epitome of style. Class personified. "Just look at us."

"My point exactly. *Look at us*!" She flipped down the visor again and gazed into the mirror. "We look like Boris and Natasha for chrissakes."

Leo chuckled. "Boris and Natasha. I like that. Very funny. I guess it's better than going into Henshaw Realtors looking like Rocky and Bullwinkle, huh?"

"That remains to be seen," Mindy huffed. "I can't believe I'm actually going along with this cockeyed scheme of yours. What if Britney recognizes us?"

"Relax, Mindy. It's not going to happen. With that long black wig and those big dark glasses you're wearing, she'll never suspect a thing. And with my dapper new mustache," Leo patted the fake mustache that was spirit gummed above his upper lip, "snappy fedora, and dark glasses, that little bitch wouldn't recognize me in a million years."

Leo slapped Mindy's hand away before she could gnaw on a fingernail. "You have to remember not to do that," he instructed. "They'll come off."

Mindy glanced at the long crimson fake nails she'd donned to complete her undercover agent look and groaned. She checked herself out in the mirror again. "This red lipstick is so dark it's practically black."

"It's movie-siren crimson. My show business friend told me so."

"He's a female impersonator, Leo. That's what *I* look like. And I still don't see why you insisted on penciling in the fake beauty mark above the corner of my mouth. It looks ridiculous."

"It's a necessary component of the disguise."

"What if Archer comes into the real estate office to visit his sister while we're there? I'd die if he caught us. How would I ever explain something like this in a million years?"

Leo studied Mindy's appearance and shrugged. "Granted, it might be a little difficult to explain, but—"

"A little?"

Leo sighed. "Honestly, Mindy, you're such a worrywart. Even if Archer bumped into you head-on, he'd never know you in that get-up. Trust me."

"Why is it whenever I hear you say those words I shudder right down to my liver, Leo?"

"Because you're being silly. Nobody's going to think we're anything more than an average married couple interested in buying a house." He gave Mindy a sideways glance. "Of course, if you'd rather we didn't go, I can always turn back."

"I really couldn't care less." Mindy stretched her hands in front of her, studying the glossy red talons.

Leo knew he had her. "Okay, let's just call it off then. I'll turn around at the corner and we can head back."

Mindy folded her arms across her chest and stared at Leo a minute, smirking. "Quit trying to bait me, Leo. You know damn well I want to go. I've got to see what transpires between the slut and the cowboy with my own eyes."

"That's my girl." Leo beamed a smile. "We'll only stay long enough to see how everything is progressing with our little matchmaking venture and then we'll skedaddle out of there. It's a cinch. Trust me."

———◉———

Britney

———◉———

"GOTTA GO," BRITNEY Priest von Grettle said into the office telephone. "My one o'clock's here. From what I understand, he's got mega bucks." She cackled at her friend's comment.

"Are you kidding?" Britney replied. "I don't care if the guy's deaf, blind, bald and limbless." She cackled again. "As long as he's got big bucks I'm his girl. Hell, after being tied down to that cheating bastard husband of mine, I damn well deserve to meet someone loaded. Someone who can give me the life I deserve. Furs, diamonds, a mansion with my very own hunky pool boy." Another cackle.

After some final chitchat, Britney planted the receiver in the cradle, stood up and adjusted her skin-hugging navy knit dress. She knew she looked hot because she'd gotten those poisonous glares from the other women in the office when she arrived earlier. The sort of looks that telegraphed envy. Britney looked down at her conspicuous cleavage and smiled.

"God, I love these new tits."

A quick lipstick check and a fluff of her hair and she was off to the lobby to greet her new client.

"Well, lookee here," the big, strapping cowboy said, giving Britney a slow, agreeable once-over as she rounded the corner and introduced herself. "Danged if you ain't just as purdy as my cousin...uh, I mean, my business associate, said you were. Come on over here, little lady and let me get a good look at you."

Britney momentarily found herself at a loss for words, which was rare. The tall, handsome Texan in the costly Stetson, expensive duds and megabucks cowboy boots was magnificent. Not at all what she'd expected.

"Well howdy there, big fella," she cooed, her eyelashes all a-flutter. God damn, this guy was a stud. Her pussy was drooling already. "You're not so hard on the eyes yourself." Planting her hands on her hips, she thrusted her pricey new tits forward. She looked down at the card in her hand. "Jasper Wilson. Who was it that referred you to me, Mr. Wilson?"

The cowboy doffed his Stetson. "My friends call me Big Jazz, ma'am." He winked and Britney's eyes flashed with interest.

From his smooth, confident stance she'd bet he *was* big. All over. Her gaze fell to the bulge at his crotch and the apex of her thighs watered again.

He stroked his jaw and shook his head slowly. "Can't rightly say as how I remember exactly who referred me, ma'am. A man in my powerful position deals with so many important people on a daily basis it's hard to remember one from another. A corporate chairman here, a news anchor there, a Saudi sheik here, a governor there." Big Jazz shrugged. "After a while all them big shots just sorta run together if ya know what I mean, ma'am."

The door behind them opened and a couple came in. After exchanging a few words, the receptionist showed the trench coat-garbed pair to one of the wall-of-windows offices lining the real estate office's interior.

"Of course." Britney nodded, returning her full attention to the Southern-fried prize before her. "I understand completely...Big Jazz." She liked saying his name. It was so...promising. She downright trembled as she allowed her gaze to take in every inch of the to-die-for cowboy. Oh yeah, she'd have this choice cut lassoed, naked and busting her bronco before the night was over.

"Big Jazz?" she said, stepping close and fingering the silver state-of-Texas-shaped slide on his bolo string tie.

He looked down at her with a lazy, liquid smile. "Yes, ma'am?"

"Call me Britney...please."

"Britney," Big Jazz repeated, clasping her hand, bringing it to his lips and kissing her fingers as he gazed into her eyes.

The big gorgeous hunk of Texas beef had her so on edge with expectation, Britney nearly climaxed right there in the middle of Henshaw Real Estate's lobby.

Mindy

"DID YOU SEE THAT?" Leo whispered. "What'd I tell you? She's drooling all over Jasper. She can't wait to fuck him."

Mindy lowered her dark glasses just enough to peer over the frames. "I've gotta hand it to you, Leo," she said softly. "You were right on target with this one." She gazed quickly around the room and breathed in a sharp exclamation. Tugging on the sleeve of Leo's trench coat, she said, "Leo, look. Up there on the shelf."

Leo looked up to see a row of wine bottles from Archer's Cellars. "Good luck...best wishes...much happiness..." he read aloud from the labels. "All the labels are personalized. Must be names of buyers and their new addresses."

"They're sales gifts. Archer told me about it that day we went on the picnic." Mindy hated what happened every time she mentioned or even thought about Archer. Her insides got all primed, hot, wet and ready for a delicious invasion—one that would probably never happen.

Even now as she sat in a public place, looking like a Russian transvestite, her panties got wet and her clit gave a quiver of anticipation. She was hopeless. Her growing arsenal of multi-featured vibrators was getting one hell of a workout lately. She was going broke on batteries.

"Clever idea," Leo said, snapping Mindy back to the present. "I'd like to look into personalized wine bottles for our clients."

"Shhh." Mindy put her finger to her lips. "They're coming this way."

Britney led Big Jazz to the office right next to Leo and Mindy's.

"You just take a seat there, cowboy, and get comfy while I get you that cup of coffee," Britney cooed. "That was four sugars and no cream. Black as—"

"A spear-chucker's heinie," Big Jazz finished.

Britney giggled. "That's such a cute little phrase."

"Not near as cute as you are, lil' lady."

The crude, bigoted pair made Mindy want to gag. "Eeew, they're absolutely made for each other," she whispered.

"Hate to say I told you so." Leo reveled in a smug smile. "Actually, that's not true. I love saying it."

An eager-looking man entered the office and extended his hand to Leo. "I'm Joe Fletcher. I understand you and the missus are in the market for a new house."

Leo cleared his throat. "Yes, we'd like to take a look through some of your listings," he said in an indeterminate accent, his voice a full octave lower than normal.

He ignored Mindy's questioning expression. Leo had conveniently neglected to mention the fact that they'd be using foreign accents.

"Certainly. Just let me get some information from you," the salesman said as he positioned himself behind the computer. "Your name?"

"Eh...Boris," Leo said, and Mindy shot him an astonished look. "Boris and Natasha. Smith." Leo shrugged and Mindy rolled her eyes as the salesman input the information, eyeing them skeptically.

"Do you currently have a house to sell?"

"No," Leo answered. "We just arrived...from Yugoslavia. On the boat."

Looking through the glass wall, Mindy noticed Britney coming back into the next room with Big Jazz's coffee.

"You go now," Mindy said to the salesman, mimicking Leo's deep voice and nondescript accent. "We will look at your books alone for a while." Her voice was bold and authoritative as she pulled the stack of multiple listing books toward her.

With a dubious look, the salesman shrugged and complied, saying he'd check on them later.

"Boris and Natasha?" Mindy whapped Leo's arm as soon as the salesman left the room. "From Yugoslavia?"

Leo shrugged. "It's all I could think of after you mentioned the names in the car. That's why I added the Smith—to make it sound more ordinary."

"Oh yeah," Mindy said, "*that* really worked."

"Shhh, listen, Britney and Jasper are talking."

"So what type of business are you in, Big Jazz?" Britney sat in the chair across from Big Jazz, crossing her legs and allowing her dress to creep up far enough to thoroughly tantalize the horny Texan.

"Whew. Just lookin' at you is makin' my temperature rise, honey." Removing his Stetson, Big Jazz fanned himself. "I work at a little of this and a little of that."

He never took his eyes from Britney's legs. She unfolded them and leisurely crossed them again. Mindy wondered if she was going commando. The disagreeable thought had her features scrunching into a curious frown.

"Oil, elevators, cattle, finance, real estate... You name it, darlin', and I've probably had a stake in it one time or another." Looking slowly from Britney's legs to her plastic breasts to her face, he broadcasted a wide, lazy smile.

Britney sat there giving him the eye as he watched her lick her lips and twist her index finger through her hair.

"Right now, I need to sell off my investment properties here in the Chicago area because I'm movin' to Russia, over there in the USSR for a while on business."

"Russia?" Britney leaned forward. "Ooh, the KGB, cosmonauts, vodka and James Bond. How exciting. I've always wanted to visit Russia."

"James Bond?" Mindy whispered, slanting Leo an incredulous look. "She's not only a slut, she's a dopey slut."

"Who cares," Leo shrugged, "as long as we manage to ship the dopey slut off across the ocean." Nodding, Mindy returned her attention to Britney and Big Jazz.

"You a fan of them double-oh-seven spy movies, darlin'?"

"I've seen every one of them, with each of the Bonds," Britney gushed. "I've watched *From Russia with Love* dozens of times."

"A woman after my own heart," Big Jazz said. "I knew I liked you for more than just that curvy little body of yours. You know, it's gonna be mighty lonely out there in that great big ramblin' palace they're settin' me up in."

"Palace?" The telltale way Britney's ears perked made Mindy feel like she was watching a cartoon. "You're going to be living in a palace?"

"Darn tootin'! One of them rich commie fellas I do business with over there is giftin' me with one of his sprawlin' palaces, complete with servants and all the usual fancy-shmancy stuff that goes along with livin' in a castle."

"Castle..." Britney repeated, her gaze intense.

"I hear tell it looks like somethin' right out of the movies, with all sorts of gold trim, and them pricey antique carpets, and lots of paintin's by famous artists. Ain't many people in the USSR with that kinda money."

"USSR," Mindy whispered to Leo with a roll of the eyes.

"Is that so?" Britney responded with a hungry, almost wild look in her eyes. She sat forward, clearly doing her damnedest to look seductive and alluring. "Will, uh, your wife be making the move to the USSR with you?"

Mindy giggled at that.

"No, ma'am. I'm not married. I'm sorry to say it's just gonna be me all by my lonesome."

Britney glanced at her watch and licked her lips. "What do you say we finish this fascinating discussion over drinks and dinner, Big Jazz?" She touched his knee as she rose from her chair.

"I'd like to hear everything about you and your trip. And that fabulous Russian palace. Then we can iron out all the details on the marketing of your investment properties. When we're finished we can head on back to my place for a little," she raised an eyebrow, "*dessert*, if you like." Her voice was low and husky as she issued an unmistakable invitation with her eyes.

Big Jazz rose from his chair. "Why I'd like that right fine, ma'am." As he tipped his Stetson, his gaze trailed over Britney's body. "It'd be my honor and privilege to sample some of your...dessert." He winked.

"Yes!" Leo yanked his fist down through the air toward his chest. His boisterous exclamation was so loud, Britney and Big Jazz turned to see what was going on. Pulling his fedora down over his eyes, Leo lifted the collar of his trench coat, cupping it around his face.

"Careful, you big lunkhead," Mindy whispered. "You almost gave us away."

"Sorry, I couldn't help it. Did you hear that, Min? Britney's panting over Jasper and his millions and he's hot for that much-used little body of hers. Don'tcha just love it?"

Mindy couldn't help feeling enthused. "If this harebrained scheme of yours actually works, Leo, I promise to cancel all the contracts I put out on your life."

"You better hold me back, Mindy, because I swear to God, I could just jump up and do the dance of joy right here and now." His body twitched and his toes started tapping.

Mindy's hand flew to Leo's shoulder to keep him from rising. "Are you insane? Sit still until they're out of here." Mindy watched as Big Jazz offered his arm and Britney wrapped herself around it with a syrupy smile.

As they ambled out of the office, Britney glanced Mindy's way.

"Yikes! Duck, Leo, they're leaving and she's looking at us." She and Leo buried their faces in a pair of multiple listing books as Big Jazz and Britney strolled past the office they sat in.

When the sound of their voices diminished, Mindy peeked up to see them walk out the door and into his big stretch limo in the parking lot.

"Okay, we're clear," Leo said. "Let's blow this place." He and Mindy scrambled to get out of their chairs. "But first..." A grinning Leo proceeded to indulge in a joyful little jig, only to have Joe

Fletcher, who must have been keeping an eagle-eye on his prospective new clients, interrupt.

"Would that merry little step indicate you may have found a house to your liking, Mr. Smith?" The grinning salesman stood with his arm resting on the doorjamb, blocking their immediate exit.

"Uh, no, not yet," a startled Leo said in his deep accent. "I was...eh...just performing the traditional Yugoslavian house hunting dance to increase our chances of finding the right house."

Dropping her head, Mindy groaned.

"I see." Joe eyed the pair doubtfully. "Well if you'll allow me to get some additional information from you, I'm certain I can help you narrow your search. Before you know it you and Mrs. Smith will be doing a Yugoslavian celebration dance. If there is such a thing." He cleared his throat and smiled.

Uttering a gasp, Mindy yanked frantically at the elbow of Leo's trench coat. She motioned to the door at the reception area with her thumb. Leo looked up to see Archer Priest walking into the real estate office.

"Whoa!" Leo said, loud enough to make Joe jump. "We'll be in touch, Joe. Gotta go now." The salesman eyed Leo curiously as his accent slipped and his voice raised an octave.

Placing a large carton on the receptionist's desk, Archer stood there chatting a few minutes. He looked toward Leo and Mindy and waved. Mindy felt her heart lurch out of her throat and vault clear across the floor. She'd just have to come back and find it later because right now she had to get the hell out of there.

Leaning close to Leo, she whispered, "He recognized us. What are we going to do?" She knew she should be running for the back door, but the sight of Archer in tight, faded blue jeans, a gray flannel shirt and black leather jacket was just too delicious a sight to pass up.

She'd never seen him in anything but a suit and tie...well, except for when she'd seen him naked. Not that he didn't look positively scrumptious all dressed up, but there's just something special about a gorgeous hunk of man outfitted in flannel and tight denim.

Joe Fletcher returned Archer's wave. "Hey, Archer, good to see you."

"Stay cool," Leo said out of the side of his mouth. "He wasn't waving at us. We're safe."

As Archer walked toward them, Leo and Mindy clutched each other, jointly uttering a muffled, "Oh shit." Archer extended his hand to the salesman who pumped it enthusiastically.

"I was in the area, so thought I'd drop off this week's wine order myself," Archer said. "Your clients happy with their personalized bottles of wine, Joe?" Glancing at Leo and Mindy, Archer offered a polite nod. Mindy felt her gut clench when he furrowed his brow and eyed the pair a second time as they worked to shield themselves from his curious gaze.

"You bet," Joe assured. "Great success. Oh, sorry, Archer, these are my new clients, Mr. and Mrs. Smith. *Boris and Natasha* Smith," he elucidated with a smile. "Mr. Priest owns the esteemed Archer's Cellars winery in Nasterbon. He supplies us with our most popular personalized gifts for clients. Just like the one you'll receive when we close on your perfect residence." His smile gleamed in true salesman style.

Leo stuck out his hand. "How do you do," he said in his deep, strangled accent, keeping his head low.

"Pleasure...Boris." Archer smiled. "Nice to meet you, uh...Natasha, wasn't it?" He bent to get a better look at the woman with the long black hair, blood-red lips and oversized dark glasses. Mindy raised the collar of her trench coat and dipped her head to avoid his scrutiny.

"Pleasure," she said in her best affected sort-of-Yugoslavian accent. Archer's presence overwhelmed her senses and her libido went into high gear. Heated skin, trickling pussy, on-guard clit... In a mere three or four steps she could press herself against him, breathing in his scent, capturing his mouth with her crimson lips, wildly running her ruby-nailed fingers over his torso and that great ass of his.

It would be so easy. He'd have no idea who she was. She'd just be some anonymous, sex-crazed, Yugoslavian woman who felt compelled to do a little groping, tasting and explicit experimenting with the denim-clad American hunk.

Mindy blinked. *Mindora von G, you are definitely losing it.*

"You just missed your sister by a couple minutes," Joe said.

"That's what I hear." Archer shrugged. "No big deal. I didn't come here to see her anyway." He smiled and extended his hand. "Take care, Joe."

"You too, Archer."

Before turning to leave, Archer said, "Nice meeting you...Boris and Natasha."

Tugging their collars up and hunching, Leo and Mindy mumbled and nodded in return, then breathed audible sighs of relief as Archer finally left the building.

Joe handed Leo and Mindy one of his cards. "Just give me a call any time and I'll be happy to do whatever I can to help you find your dream home."

"Sure thing." Nodding, Leo pumped the salesman's hand. Grabbing Mindy by the wrist, he stealthily crept toward the main door. "I don't see Archer's limo out there, do you?"

Mindy craned her neck, scanning the parking lot. "No."

"Okay, looks like the coast is clear," Leo whispered. "Let's make a run for it." He pushed the door open and the pair raced toward Leo's Cadillac.

"Wow, Leo. That was *way* too close for comfort."

"I know, I know. But we made it." Fishing the keys from his pocket, he pointed and clicked his car's unlocking mechanism. Before they could get in, they heard another car door slam and saw Archer walking toward them.

"Oh God, oh God, oh God." Mindy struggled to open the passenger side door.

"Get in the damn car," Leo said, opening the driver's side door.

Mindy yanked but the door didn't open. "You didn't unlock my side, you big jerk." She banged on the window. By the time Leo unlocked it, it was too late. Archer stood before her, smirking, with his arms folded across his big broad chest.

"Oh shit," she mumbled as she lowered her head, tugging long strands of black hair in front of her face.

Archer looked through the windshield and crooked his finger, motioning for Leo to get out of the car. Once Leo was standing, Archer grinned.

"Well, well, well. Fancy running into you again...Boris and Natasha." He planted his tongue firmly in his cheek as he gave the squirrelly pair a once-over.

Leo cleared his throat. "What can I do for you, Mr. Priest?" He still maintained his deep accent.

Archer shook his head and laughed. "You can tell me what the hell you two characters are up to and what exactly is going on around here, that's what." Plucking something off Leo's overcoat, Archer handed it to him. "Lose something, Boris?"

As Leo looked down at the article Archer handed him, he let loose with a volley of nervous, staccato laughter and Mindy knew they were dead. She glanced over at her partner in crime, cringing when she saw Leo had lost half his fake mustache and Archer had just returned it. Searching in vain for a crack in the asphalt big enough to sink into, Mindy uttered a croaking sound.

"And you." Archer wagged a finger as he stepped close to Mindy.

Cloaking herself against his gaze, she valiantly answered in her deep accent, "Vhat do you vhant, Meester Priest?"

"Playtime's over, Sarah Bernhardt." He snatched the wig from Mindy's head with one hand and removed her dark glasses with the other. Holding the long, dangly black mass at arm's length, Archer laughed. "I just know there has to be a good explanation for this."

With a sheepish grin, Mindy shrugged. "Not necessarily."

"Did you know right away?" Leo peeled off the other half of his mustache then removed his dark glasses and forties-style fedora.

"Not right off the bat," Archer admitted. "But I had a pretty strong hunch something was going on. I don't run into too many people named Boris and Natasha on my journeys."

Cringing, Mindy buried her head in her hands.

"The peach-colored Cadillac with the distinctive vanity plates was a dead giveaway though." Archer sidled up to the front of Leo's car, pointing to the license plate that read PERSIMN. "Not too easy to be incognito riding around in that, Leo."

Mindy shot Leo a lethal look as he hit the palm of his hand against his forehead and groaned.

"*Trust me*, you said," Mindy grumbled to Leo. "I should have known better." She heaved a sigh and grabbed her wig back from Archer's grasp.

"Believe it or not, Archer, there really is a perfectly logical explanation for all of this." Leo nervously licked his lips.

Archer smirked. "Oh, I'm sure there is. I'd love to hear all about it."

"Gee, I wish I had the time to tell you." Leo glanced at his watch. "But I've got the rep from a new cruise line coming in to meet with me so I've got to be off." He flashed a smile, opened his car door and scooted inside.

"Right, I forgot all about that," Mindy said, scrambling to open the passenger side door. The distinct click of the door lock from inside the car made her eyes bug wide. "*Leo?* What the hell do you think you're doing? Let me in." Jiggling the door handle, she knocked against the glass.

Letting his window down just enough to be heard, Leo said, "Mindy, you can't come into the office looking like that. Your hair looks atrocious."

"He's got a point there." Archer chuckled.

Her hand whipping up to her head, Mindy felt all the hair clips she'd used to pin up her hair so the wig would fit smoothly. She bent to see her reflection in the door's window and gasped. Here she was, standing in front of the man of her dreams, looking like a red-lipped, half-crazed, flat-headed transvestite with a smudged fake beauty spot over her lip.

Ripping the clips from her hair, she said, "Leo, you can't just leave me here like this. Open this door and let me in. You can drop me off at home."

"Sorry, sweetie, I just don't have the time." He started the car, allowing it to creep forward.

"Leo, what are you talking about? I only live two miles from here. Besides, my car is back at the office. How am I supposed to get home without my car?"

"I'm sure Archer won't mind dropping you off at home, would you, Archer?"

Mindy's jaw dropped and she resumed her banging on the car window. "Don't you do this to me, Leo Parker. I mean it. I'm warning you, don't even think about it."

Offering a gallant smile and bow, Archer said, "It would be my pleasure to escort this vision of loveliness home, Leo." He glanced at Mindy before bending to the ground to retrieve two more of the clips that had fallen from her hair.

Feeling the heat rise in her cheeks, Mindy ground out an expletive and buried her head in her hands. "This is not happening. This is *not* happening!"

"Good, Archer, then Mindy can fill you in on all the details about our little costumed drama." The Cadillac pulled out a little farther.

"What?! *Leo*!" Mindy screeched. "You sonuvabitch."

Leo shook his head and tsked. "You know, you really should have more respect for your boss, darling. Oh, and don't worry about making it back to the office this afternoon. Just take the rest of the day off." Beaming a bright smile, Leo snapped the brim of his fedora and winked.

"Toodles," he said, waving his fingers through the open window crack before he closed it, heading out of the parking lot.

"Leo, you come back here this instant, do you hear me? *Leo*!" Waving the wig in the air in a sorry attempt to catch Leo's attention as she ran after his car, Mindy stamped her foot, snapping off her high heel in the process.

"Great, just what I needed." She retrieved the two-inch heel from the ground, growling in exasperation as her boss turned out of the parking lot, waved and took off. "Oooh, of all the conniving, low-down, miserable, sneaky, underhanded..."

"Yeah, Leo's definitely a character all right." Archer chuckled.

Enraged enough to spit fire, Mindy turned on her one good heel to face Archer. "I suppose you think this is really funny."

Archer scratched his head. "As a matter of fact..."

"Oh, you men are all alike." Mindy hobbled past him.

"Just where do you think you're going?"

"I'm walking home."

"Looking like that?"

Her curls half hanging and half still clipped to her head, Mindy stopped dead in her tracks. In one hand she held her wig, which was so tangled and bedraggled now it looked more like road-kill, and in the other hand she carried her broken heel and spy-worthy dark glasses. Her shoulders slumped and her head drooped. She looked like hell and she knew it.

"Come on, Mindy," Archer coaxed, "quit being so stubborn. Let me take you home."

Heaving a melodious sigh, Mindy turned back to Archer. "All right, you may drive me home."

"Thank you, your highness." Archer engaged in another courtly bow. "My carriage awaits." He motioned to the little red sports car.

Mindy held her chin proudly as she tottered back toward Archer with as much grace as she could muster under the circumstances.

Chapter 18

A FTER GIVING directions to her townhouse, Mindy discreetly tried to remove the rest of the hair clips from what was now a tangled mass.

"Okay, so what's the story, princess?" Shifting into gear, Archer deftly piloted the snazzy red Porsche out of the parking lot and into traffic.

"Story? What story?" As Mindy endeavored to appear calm and nonchalant, her mind raced. How on earth was she supposed to come up with a plausible explanation? Especially when the only thoughts flitting through her brain at the moment had to do with gleefully pulverizing her boss in some wonderfully gruesome manner.

"The Boris and Natasha story."

"Oh, that."

"Yeah...that."

"I used to watch them on the old Rocky and Bullwinkle cartoon reruns when I was a kid, how about you?" She didn't give Archer a chance to answer. She figured if she babbled enough she might be able to distract him from the incriminating issue at hand. "As a matter of fact, I used to do a mean imitation of Bullwinkle back in the day. Gee, I wonder if I can still do it."

As Mindy opened her mouth to continue, Archer pressed his finger to her lips. "As much as I'd love to hear your Bullwinkle the Moose impersonation, it'll have to wait for another time. You're not getting off that easy, Mindy, so stop trying to change the subject."

He looked down at the glossy smudge of deep red on the finger he'd pressed to her lips and laughed. "Put this on with a trowel, did you?"

Flushing furiously, Mindy retrieved the travel pack of tissues she carried in her purse. Grabbing one, she rubbed at the stain on Archer's finger. "Sorry about that."

"No problem. Don't worry about—" Turning to glance at Mindy, Archer stopped in mid-sentence. Eyes wide, his face contorted and twitched. In the next instant he was engaged in full, snorting laughter.

Alarmed, Mindy bolted upright in the black leather bucket-seat. "What? What are you laughing at?" Wiping the tears from his eyes, Archer pointed to Mindy's hair. She flipped down the visor and gasped when she peered at her reflection. There, embedded right on the top of her honey-blonde crown of tangles, sat two inch-long, fire engine red fingernails.

"Oh my God. I could just die." As she attempted to pick the fake nails from her head, two glossy fingernails from the other hand dropped off and Mindy groaned.

"I guess this is what's known as having a bad hair day, huh?"

Mindy slapped her hands over her face. "Don't look at me. I'm grotesque."

"You are *not* grotesque, Mindy." Reaching over, Archer drew her hands from her face. "You're just a little...a little..." Archer's mouth twitched again.

Mindy wailed a pained groan as she looked down at her palms. Unfortunately, covering her heavily made-up face with her hands only seemed to exacerbate the problem. She didn't even want to look in the mirror again but, of course, she had to.

Taking in the full picture of the disheveled, woefully smudged, dilapidated woman looking back at her, she wished she could die right there on the spot. At least the mortician would have a good laugh when he got a load of her clown face.

She had to give Archer credit. He was doing a commendable job of gallantly fighting back fits of laughter.

"You're just a little tousled," he offered. "And smudged..." The corner of his lip quivered as he clearly struggled not to laugh. "You'll feel better once you scrape all that gunk off your face."

Mindy braved another glance at her reflection. Raccoon eyes stared back at her. She sank down in her seat. "Oh my poor face," she moaned, covering it with her hands again.

"At least it's still there. I had my doubts."

Mindy shook her head as if to clear it. "Archer, you're not making any sense. What are you talking about? Turn left in here, on Walnut." She pointed ahead. "This is my complex. Just keep going straight."

Turning, Archer drove on silently. She studied him—his strong jaw, sensuous lips, classic nose and proud chin. His hard, fit body. She squirmed as her panties dampened. "Um, what did you mean about doubting my face would still be here?"

He gave her a sideways glance. "I'm just surprised to see it's still in place after it nearly got sucked off last night."

Mindy sank down in her seat another notch, bracing for the impending coronary because her heart was pounding so fast it was about to burst. "You saw that, huh?"

"I couldn't help notice that you and your...*friend* were actively engaged in some heavy mouth-to-mouth maneuvers as the two of you slid under the table." Tightening his jaw, Archer glanced accusingly at Mindy.

"Turn right on that next street. Not that I owe you any explanation, mind you, but what you saw wasn't at all what it appeared to be."

"Yeah right." Archer huffed a humorless laugh. "I mean, not that it's any business of mine, of course. It's not like you and I have a commitment or anything." He gave a nonchalant shrug.

"Exactly," Mindy agreed. "In fact, I noticed you and that little brunette seemed to be rather cozy, so let's not point fingers. There," Mindy pointed, "that's my townhouse. You can let me off at the curb."

"So you noticed me and Carla, huh?" Pulling up in front of Mindy's townhouse, Archer put the car in park. "I'm amazed you could notice anything at all while making a spectacle of yourself, getting it on, right in the middle of the restaurant."

Mindy sucked in an audible gasp. "I was most definitely *not* getting it on. And don't try to deflect things, Archer. You were obviously enjoying yourself with *Carla*." Mindy heard herself say the woman's name in a singsong voice that smacked of junior high jealousy. She could have kicked herself for being so transparent.

"Methinks I denote a touch of jealousy, hmmm?"

"Hah." Mindy scoffed. She wanted to wipe that smug look right off his face. "Don't be ridiculous."

"Not that I owe you any explanation either, but Carla Davenport happens to be the head of the Michigan Fruit Growers Advisory Board, Miss Smarty-Pants. She's fifty years old, has six kids and has been married to the same man for thirty years—who, by the way, was in the restroom while I escorted Mrs. Davenport to our table."

Mindy discovered she was more delighted than ashamed at her faulty assumptions.

"And neither of us tried to suck the other's face off even once during the entire evening," Archer added. "Nor did I usher the woman under the table to engage in anything even remotely smacking of carnal playtime."

"Oh." Shrinking from embarrassment, Mindy felt so small she wondered if she could reach up to open the car door. "Sorry." She offered an apologetic shrug. "Uh...I better go in now. Thanks for the ride, Archer. I appreciate it."

"Nope."

"What do you mean, *nope*?"

"I mean I'm coming in, that's what I mean."

"No you're not. Look, Archer, I appreciate the ride and all, but—" As she reached for the door handle, Archer pushed the automatic locks. Breathing out a sigh of exasperation, Mindy searched for the unlocking mechanism on the passenger side, giving up when all she managed to do was raise and lower the window and turn on the heating element in her seat.

"Cute. Very cute. In less than an hour my annoying boss locks me out of his car and you lock me in to yours. That's it. I've had it, Archer. I am *not* amused. Please unlock this door—now!"

"You don't honestly think I'm going to let you get away that easily, do you? Without any explanation after the masquerade you and Leo just pulled? Uh-uh. No such luck, sweetheart."

"I have a huge, fierce dog. A guard dog."

"Is that so?"

"Yup. Absolutely ferocious." Mindy nodded. "And he hates men. He's liable to tear your head off if you come in."

"You don't say."

Mindy wanted to smack that self-assured smile right off his painfully handsome kisser. "Don't make light of this, Archer, I'm serious. I'm sorry but I simply can't take responsibility for what might happen to you if I let you come into the house. You'll just have to drop me off and trust me to explain all of this to you another time." She shrugged and smiled.

Archer stared at her blankly. "I think I'll take my chances with old Rover in there. Now let's go."

"But—"

"Mindy, either you let me in or I'll make you sit here in this locked car until you explain every last detail to me. What's it gonna be?"

Rolling her eyes, she pinned Archer with an icy glare. "It appears I don't have much choice." Grumbling something inaudible, she let her head fall back against the headrest and sighed. "All right, have it your way. You can park over there."

As soon as Mindy opened the door to her townhouse, little Cadbury sprinted toward her, wagging his tail and eagerly leaping up to greet her. After shucking off her trench coat and kicking off her broken high heel, Mindy bent to gather the spirited pup in her arms.

"Hey there, Cadbury, how's my best buddy today?"

The dog slobbered a series of kisses across Mindy's heavily made-up face before he finally took notice of Archer. Cadbury let out a low mini-growl.

"Whoa!" Archer said in mock horror, raising his hands in surrender and backing away. "Please, Mindy, restrain that vicious killer before he tears me to pieces."

Cadbury jumped to the floor, bounded over to Archer, took a few cautious sniffs, then soared into his arms, licking his face from chin to hairline.

Groaning, Mindy slapped her hand against her forehead. "Cadbury, you traitor, how could you do this to me?"

The little dog glanced at his mistress, slanting her one of those adorable, tongue-lolling dog smiles. Then he returned his attention to his new friend, gifting Archer with another generous lick.

When Archer finally stopped laughing, he placed Cadbury on the floor. "So you have this little attack dog trained to kill them with kindness—is that it?" He was barely able to get the last words out before he erupted into laughter once again.

"Just-just-just..." Mindy sputtered in exasperation as she frantically motioned toward the family room off the kitchen.

Archer folded his arms across his chest and smirked. "Yes?"

"Just go sit down in there while I clean some of this gunk off my face. And consider yourself *very* fortunate that Cadbury was in a magnanimous mood this afternoon and spared your life."

"I'll reflect on my good luck as I rub my hands together in anticipation of your explanation...Natasha."

Mindy brushed by Archer, turning her head away to hide her crimson-hot cheeks. "Help yourself to whatever I have in the refrigerator. There's diet pop, low-fat chocolate milk, some orange juice, and a bottle of Baileys."

"Sounds like a great concoction," Archer teased.

"Throw everything but the orange juice in a glass and you'll be in heaven," Mindy offered as she left the room.

"What the hell am I going to do?" she whispered to herself as she sped into the bathroom and snagged a handful of tissues from the container on the quartz counter. "Leo, how could you do this to me?" she muttered while wiping the smudged mascara. Stopping to take a good look at her wretched, makeup-encrusted reflection, Mindy cringed.

"I can't believe Archer saw me looking like this. I swear to God, Leo Parker, I'll get you for this. I'll make you pay for humiliating me in front of the man. Now he thinks I'm a certified nut case." Mindy tried in vain to remove the dark red stain from her lips. She had to stall Archer until she could think up something plausible.

"And don't try to stall, Mindy," Archer's voice called out from the family room. Freezing in place, Mindy's eyes shot open wide. "I'm not leaving until I hear your story," he finished.

"Sheesh, what is this guy, a psychic?" Mindy hissed. "Okay, I can tell him Leo and I were...no, that wouldn't work. Maybe he'd buy it if I said we were...no, Archer's too savvy for that. I could always say..." Heaving a gargantuan sigh, Mindy's scheming came to a screeching halt as the realization and magnitude of her situation took hold.

"There's nothing I can possibly tell this man that he'll believe." She stared at her partially repaired reflection. "Nothing." He'd find out what they were up to and think she was a terrible, conniving, horrid bitch, out to snare him at any cost. Mindy heaved another sigh.

"Maybe that's exactly what I am." She made an attempt to brush out the tangled mass of blonde while fighting back the tears threatening to erupt.

Taking a final look at herself before leaving the bathroom, Mindy decided she looked fairly presentable. She had no choice. She was just going to tell Archer the truth, then have a good cry when he walked out of her life. Forever. She turned to leave then stopped to gaze at the mirror once more.

"Then I'm going to kill myself with a massive chocolate overdose." Throwing back her shoulders, she sucked in a deep breath and opened the door, heading for the family room.

"I guess you weren't kidding when you said you loved chocolate," Archer said, nodding to the wall display as she came around the corner. Looking as if he'd known Archer all his life, Cadbury was sprawled across his lap, blissfully soaking up Archer's attention.

Mindy looked at the chocolate-brown wall decorated with shadowboxes and picture frames holding assorted chocolate memorabilia. Vintage examples of Cadbury chocolate bar wrappers, Toll House chips bags, original labels from old cans and jars of cocoa powder and chocolate Ovaltine, and ads declaring the healthy merits of chocolate from turn-of-the-century magazines were displayed alongside small shadowboxes filled with cocoa beans, Hershey Kisses, mini-boxes from Godiva and other revered chocolate icons.

"What can I say?" Smiling, Mindy shrugged. "I'm an avowed chocolate lover, and this," she gestured, "is my shrine to chocolate."

"I like it. It's very...you. I noticed even your dog is named after a brand of chocolate."

"One of my favorite brands," she confirmed, studying his charming grin, committing it to memory. This was probably the last time she'd ever see him smile at her, because he'd be furious and disgusted after she spilled her guts about the plan to ship his sister to Russia with a rich, horny, bigoted cowboy.

She entertained a fleeting thought of rushing Archer, tackling him to the floor and ripping off his clothes. Then she'd jump his gorgeous bones and fuck him until they both passed out from exhaustion. Yup. That would make an even better mental snapshot than the one she'd taken of his smile.

"Now that's an interesting smile, Mindy." Archer ushered Cadbury from his lap and rose from his chair. He stepped toward her and gazed into her eyes. "What's going through that busy little brain of yours, hmmm? Probably some whopper of a story you're making up."

Mindy felt her cheeks flush. She wanted more than anything to snatch a convincing lie out of the air. Something that might prevent him from turning his back on her in loathing. She breathed a sigh. No, she couldn't be like Leo and get herself all tangled in a never-ending web of deceit. She had to be honest with Archer. He deserved that much.

"Okay, Archer, I'm going to tell you the entire truth about what Leo and I were doing at—"

Archer abruptly cut off her confession with a kiss so powerful it would have flipped Mindy's wig if she were still wearing it. He held her close with one hand while cupping her breast with the other.

Oh, the sweet, luscious sensations coursing through her body as he rubbed his thumb over her nipple. It was enough to make her moan with delight. And indeed she did.

The warmth, the richness, the smooth silky wet taste of him. Delicious. Succulent. Hypnotizing.

In that instant Mindy realized no chocolate could ever compare with the exquisite taste of Archer Priest.

She was just about to wrap herself around his body when he released her lips, held her at arm's length and smiled. It was an entirely different smile this time. Hot, needy, desirous.

"Wow! What was that?" Mindy brought her fingers to her lips.

"Truth serum." Archer winked, his voice reverberating along her nerve endings. "Now you'll have no choice but to tell me the truth about your Boris and Natasha masquerade at the real estate office." He chucked her chin lightly with his knuckle. "After that, you can tell me all about the guy who was sucking your face last night at Montague's."

Swallowing hard, Mindy gazed at Archer. She felt every nerve ending come to life, as if Archer's kiss had watered her soul, making the seeds of love sprout and blossom. With a slow, purposeful lick of her lips, she wrapped her arms around his neck.

"I think I need another dose of truth serum first." Standing on her toes she reached up, brushing her lips across his, but Archer pulled back, keeping her at a distance.

"First you explain, then I'll give you the antidote to the truth serum. It's far more potent, and takes more time to deliver." Jiggling his eyebrows, he gave a devilish smile.

He was so darling, so adorable, so big, hunky, and beautifully muscled. "Did anyone ever tell you that you don't play fair, Mr. Priest?"

"All's fair, etcetera, etcetera." He took Mindy's hand in his, studying it for a moment, smoothing his thumb over her skin.

"You're a very special woman, Mindy. A little crazy, maybe," he chuckled, "but definitely special. And I want to get to know you better." He leaned in close, his lips grazing her temple. "Much better," he whispered as her heart shifted into overdrive.

Archer brushed his lips across hers before plundering her mouth with his tongue.

Moaning, Mindy sank against him, wanting him to sink into her. Hard, fast and relentless. She plastered herself against him, loving the feel of his big denim-clad cock nestled against her belly. "I want to get to know you much better too, Archer."

"Good. You can start by telling me about the guy I saw you with last night." His words snapped her out of her fuzzy, dreamlike state. "Are you in love with him?" His mouth went hard.

Mindy choked on a laugh. "Oh good heavens no. He was just..." Her shoulders slumped. "Oh Archer," she said with a forlorn sigh. "How I wish I didn't have to—"

She stopped abruptly, just short of telling him she wished she didn't have to spoil everything by telling him the truth, the whole truth and nothing but the truth. She couldn't do it. Couldn't come clean. Damn it, she couldn't risk having Archer disappear from her life.

Tracing her jaw with a featherlight touch of his finger, he asked, "Didn't have to what, sweetheart?"

"Nothing. Never mind." Something awful inside told Mindy that if she didn't clutch onto Archer now, she'd never get the chance again. As soon as he learned about her lies, her deceit... With a muffled cry she wrapped her arms around him, resting her head against his chest. "Oh Archer..."

Enclosing Mindy in his arms, he rested his chin on her head. "What's the matter, sweetheart? Guilty conscience?" he said in a light, teasing manner.

Little did he know.

Her thoughts raced. Right now, this very moment, might be the only chance she'd ever have to hook Archer. To fully capture his heart and throw away the key.

Naturally, that meant desperate measures were in order. She needed something foolproof. A surefire plan. A bold, brazen move guaranteed to make Archer Priest so hot and horny he'd forget about Boris and Natasha—and Rolf sucking her face off.

Seduction. Mad, passionate, wild seduction.

Yes. She could do it. She could!

Maybe she wasn't the worldly, sophisticated, sexually competent woman she longed to be. Maybe, in fact, she felt like a bumbling clueless dork when it came to the fine art of sex. However, while she may not have any personal experience as a seductress, she'd read enough of those hot, steamy, spicy romances Leo had given her to come up with a few damn good ideas.

Ooh! She could make it a chocolate-related seduction. Perfect! The one thing she *did* know about was chocolate. Intimately. By adding chocolate to her seduction, she'd have a far better chance of succeeding.

"Mindy?"

An unpleasant sensation curdled at her spine as Archer gazed at her, waiting for her to open her mouth and say something. What if she made a fool of herself and Archer laughed at her feeble, unpracticed attempts at seduction?

Oh for fuck's sake, Mindora von G. At this point you've got nothing to lose. Just fucking do it!

Knees knocking, Mindy felt the stirrings of daring taking hold. Dammit, it was about time she used her womanly wiles on Archer. Even if she wasn't certain she *had* womanly wiles. Both she and Archer were about to find out. Sucking in a deep breath, she sent up a silent prayer.

"Cookies!" she finally blurted, firmly clapping her hands over Archer's groin with perhaps a bit too much enthusiasm.

His cock immediately rose to the occasion.

Clearly startled, her looked down at her hands and back up to her eyes, giving Mindy a dubious look. "Sorry, but the last time I looked I didn't have any cookies squirreled away down there, honey."

A low, lusty, prolonged chuckle rose from deep within Mindy's throat. Pleased with the way it sounded—rather porn-queen-esque, she thought—she did her damnedest to look the part of a seductive temptress too.

Tiptoeing her fingers around the bulge in his jeans, she cooed, "I've been thinking about how your cock reminds me of chocolate chip cookies, Archer."

One of his eyebrows lifted.

Hell. That wasn't exactly what she'd planned to say. Painfully aware the smooth seduction scene in her head wasn't playing out nearly as well as it had in her imagination, Mindy winced.

Snorting a chuckle, Archer told her, "I have to admit...that's definitely a first."

"Trust me, Archer, it's a compliment," she assured, determined to do better. "You do like chocolate chip cookies, don't you?" she cooed.

"Sure, but—"

"How about games?" Her voice dipped low, as sultry as she could make it. "Do you like to play games?"

Now his eyebrow arrowed down. "Mindy, what's this all about?"

It was all about driving him wild with lust, passion and desire. It was about showing Archer what he'd be missing if he walked out on her after learning the truth. It was her last goddamned chance to fuck him clear to the edge of insanity so he'd never want to leave, even after finding out what a terrible person she was.

"We're going to play school," she told him, trailing the fingers of one hand up to his chest and circling over his nipple. "You're the student and I'm the teacher. And today you're going to get a lesson in baking."

"Baking?"

"Mmm-hmm. *Erotic* baking," Mindy clarified, in that same husky, sultry tone. "We're going to make chocolate chip cookies together. In the nude."

"Right now?"

The poor guy looked half turned on and half flummoxed. Mindy almost giggled, but if she wanted her extreme scheme to work, she had to play it smooth and sophisticated.

"Mmm-hmm, right now. You're going to love this very special baking class, Archer." With that, she cupped his three-piece package, giving it a gentle squeeze, loving the pleasured groan rumbling up from his chest as his arm snaked around her. A delicious frisson of sexual heat curled down her spine when she saw the evidence of raw desire in his gaze.

"Well, damn. Home economics never sounded so good," he said.

"Teacher's first rule," Mindy purred, unfastening Archer's jeans, "is for her star pupil to get naked."

Chapter 19

Archer

O NCE MINDY put Cadbury in the laundry room with the door closed, she all but clawed his clothes off. He hadn't detected even a trace of alcohol on her breath. Finally, in a sane, sober, normal state—well, at least sober—she wanted him naked. Bad.

His cock jerked hard in his pants.

Archer enjoyed the eager scrape of her cool fingers against his skin as she undressed him. He had no idea where this sudden urge to whip up a batch of chocolate chip cookies came from. And he thought her comparison of his cock to a cookie was rather odd, to say the least. But he'd learned oddity was pretty much par for the course where Mindy von Grettle was concerned.

Grabbing the elastic of his shorts, she dragged them down over his hips. The best part was when her pretty mouth was perfectly aligned with his liberated cock. She looked at it, then gazed up at his eyes and smiled before returning her attention to her task until he'd stepped out of his shorts and was naked as the day he was born.

"You know," Mindy said, "I just hate to be encumbered with clothes when I'm hard at work teaching students how to bake cookies. You wouldn't mind if your teacher took off her clothes and got comfortable, would you, Archer?"

His cock twitched, drawing both her attention and his. "Clearly, my cock and I would be delighted," he replied, playing along with her sexy game. "Does teacher want some help?"

"No...teacher just wants her student to watch."

Archer had no clue about what was going on, which he actually found stimulating. Intriguing. Maybe this was Mindy's kinky side coming out. His cock tingled at the thought. An instant later, his attention was fully on her as she started singing.

Well, it wasn't actually singing, it was more like a slow and sexy *da-da-da boom da-da-da boom* kind of sound to the tune of some stripper music he vaguely recognized from old movies.

Swaying to the tune as she backed away from him, Mindy tugged her sweater over her head, letting it slip to the floor. With a curious look of determination, she shimmied for him, her full breasts jiggling in the lacey bra cups that barely contained them.

She'd obviously done the triple L shopping she told him about when he caught her in her industrial-strength cotton underwear at their picnic lunch.

Christ almighty, that body of hers was hot.

Next came her jeans. Unclasping them, Mindy brought the zipper down with a torturously slow glide that matched the rhythm of her lusty *da-da-da boom-boom-boom* tune. His eyes popped as she treated him to a full-body shimmy until her jeans slipped down and pooled at her feet, leaving her in a lacy scrap of panties and that wispy little nothing of a bra.

"I'm enjoying this, teacher...very much."

"Good." Mindy's gaze zeroed in on his jutting cock. "Teacher can see you're very alert." Kicking aside her jeans, her hands went to her back, unclasping her bra.

Archer's mouth went dry as her bountiful breasts bounced free.

Sidestepping to the beat of the sexy vocal she'd created, Mindy used her bra like a stripper uses an over-the-elbow glove, sliding it across her breasts, behind her neck and between her thighs. As she whipped it around, her hips got more into the act too, making purposeful thrusts and swirls.

Images of a dark, smoky room with a dimly lit stage came to mind. At the center of the stage was a pole, with a voluptuous, naked blonde named Mindora von G wrapped around it, dancing, enticing, teasing, promising deeply carnal secrets with her eyes. The room was packed with men, drooling, calling out to her, making wolf whistles, but the blonde only had eyes for him.

Jesus, he wanted to fuck her so bad at this moment he could taste it.

By her tentative, somewhat jerky movements, paired with the uncertain look in her eyes, Archer surmised this was probably the first time Mindy had ever done a striptease for a man. The sweet idea touched a soft spot deep in his center. He felt honored to be the first male to witness Mindy in full, deliberate seduction mode.

Archer strongly suspected her seduction was a delay tactic, to make him forget about all the explaining she had to do. Although it wouldn't work, he couldn't think of a better way for her to try, and he certainly wasn't about to spoil her fun. Or his.

Even though Mindy's private dance reminded him of a corny, mid-century B-movie, watching her bump and grind for him was about the sexiest damn thing he'd ever seen. She might be inexperienced, but the woman was a natural-born heart-stopping temptress, just the same.

His gaze took a leisurely up-and-down tour of her body as Mindy turned her backside to him, shimmying out of her panties. Bending over, she clapped one hand to her ass cheek, followed by her other hand to the other side. She squeezed as she peeked back over her shoulder at him and winked.

"Beautiful, baby. Just beautiful," Archer assured her, realizing she needed to hear those words, to be sure he was enjoying her sexy little show. He was more than happy to encourage her scintillating efforts.

Her grand finale was a series of bumps, grinds, shimmies and jazzy steps, ending with her standing with arms stretched high over her head and legs together with one knee bent. She stopped doing her *da-da-da boom* tune and smiled at him.

Archer clapped. "That was so hot, sweetheart. *You* are so hot." He saw her eyes light up at the praise and felt that odd, sweet sensation touch his center again. "It seems baking cookies isn't teacher's only talent."

"Oh! I almost forgot to preheat the oven." Mindy ran into the next room, her lush body parts bouncing and bobbing as she went to the oven and turned it on.

The next thing Archer knew, Mindy had a pot of coffee brewing and he'd been dispatched to an area of the kitchen greasing cookie sheets while Mindy broke eggs into a bowl and beat them.

He wondered if she had any idea how fucking sexy she looked scurrying around the kitchen in the nude, gathering all the ingredients and throwing them together in the bowl.

His favorite part was when her gorgeous tits got dusted with flour and jiggled as she beat the batter. His masturbation fantasies would never be the same after this.

"So why exactly are we in here naked, baking cookies? Did you just get an overwhelming craving or something?"

Mindy stopped what she was doing long enough to peek at his dick and lick her lips. "I guess you could say that." She issued a ravenous smile.

Archer winced when his cock flared out in salute, thumping against one of the lower kitchen cabinets.

"Archie Priest, did teacher see you raise your hand?" Mindy asked.

Playing along, his hand shot up, waving wildly. "Yes, teacher. Me, me!"

"Good boy. Bring the cookie sheets here." Once he did, she dropped globs of dough onto each oiled sheet. "Now, Archie, teacher will explain why your cock is like a chocolate chip cookie," she announced, and he was all ears. He didn't even mind the nickname he'd always hated.

"You see, class," she said, clearly enjoying giving him this lesson in carnal gastronomy, "the chocolate chip cookie starts as a small, limp, doughy blob." She shifted from the cookie sheet to his cock, taking it in her hand and squeezing, kneading.

"Teacher can see that your dough is already far beyond the limp stage, Archie. Anyway, the dough is manipulated with the fingers..." she took her time, fondling his dick until he thought he'd go mad. Just as he felt his balls tighten, she dropped his cock and returned to the cookie sheet.

"After sufficient manipulation, the nicely formed dough is placed on the cookie sheet before going into the oven." She sank her teeth into her bottom lip, giving an impish smile. "Archie, using teacher's example, can you give the class a hands-on demonstration of how to properly manipulate dough with the fingers?" Her gaze clamped on his cock, which immediately bloomed from erect to gargantuan.

Taking himself in hand, Archer kneaded and stroked his cock, loving the way Mindy watched with rapt attention. "How's this, teacher? Am I doing it right? I'm not sure if I am, because it felt much better when teacher's soft, cool fingers were molding my dough."

"You did a fine job, Archie. You get a big gold star for excellence in dough manipulation." Mindy licked her lips. "Have I told you you're my favorite student?"

"Because I have the best and biggest cock, teacher?"

"Exactly," Mindy answered through a bright grin.

"Good," Archer responded, his hand still busy at his cock. "I always wanted to be a teacher's pet."

"Would you like to lick the bowl?" she asked after scraping the last mound of chocolate-flecked dough and plopping it on the pan.

Archer chuckled. He hadn't licked cookie dough from a bowl since he was a kid. "Sure."

Watching Mindy's tits get dusted with flour was quickly demoted to the number two spot as Archer gaped while she buttered her breasts with the small amount of dough left in the bowl.

"Eat me," Mindy said with a twinkle in her eye as she stood before him, thrusting out her cookie-dough-decorated nipples.

Thinking he must have just died and gone to heaven, Archer happily complied, grasping her breasts with his hands, licking, nibbling and scraping them with his teeth. Mindy moaned, shuddering with pleasure at each swipe of his tongue across her pebbled nipples. It was the best damn thing he'd ever tasted. Fucking fantastic.

"You've just earned another gold star, Archie," Mindy said, her voice raspy.

His cock was hot, hard, throbbing and getting impatient as hell. Good God, he wanted nothing more at that moment than to shove into her, high and hard. But Mindy clearly had other ideas once he'd thoroughly emancipated her flesh of all cookie dough residue.

"While baking," she slipped the cookie sheet into the oven, "the cookie slowly expands with just the right amount of heated attention." Her gaze fell to his cock again. "Are you beginning to see the similarities between cocks and chocolate chip cookies, young man?"

Archer eyeballed his raring-to-go dick. "I sure as hell can, teacher. As teacher can see, my dough has already expanded. It's all ready and waiting for the next step. See?" He saw Mindy's cool, calm, teacher-esque composure slip when her eyes locked on his erection, bobbing before her in an anticipatory dance.

Uh-huh. Teacher was just as hungry as he was.

"Absolutely." Mindy's voice was breathy. "I'd say we're looking at a perfect example of a hard and ready cock. And teacher can barely wait for the next step."

She was driving him insane in slow, tiny increments.

Mindy cleared her throat, only to gasp when Archer took her hand and brought it to his cock. The wispy sound of her ragged breath and the vibration he felt as her body trembled made him ache with longing.

"As the intended cookie receiver," Mindy's voice wavered while she stroked his cock with a featherlight touch, "I can hardly wait to get a sample. But patience is needed because when the cookie first comes out of the oven it's so hot it can singe."

"I can definitely relate. My dick's so hot it could singe you right this minute, teacher." Archer wrapped an arm around Mindy, crushing her soft breasts to his chest. "Would teacher like a nice, hot demonstration?"

The oven timer rang.

Sucking in a deep breath, Mindy donned an oven mitt and slipped the tray of cookies from the oven, setting it on a rack to cool.

"What happens now, teacher?" Archer asked, thoroughly enjoying her deliciously naughty, seductive culinary lesson.

"The cookie," she removed her mitt, surprising him by grabbing his cock with her warm hand, "gradually becomes harder until it's firm enough not to crumble." She stroked his length with gentle firmness, whimpering a little moan as her fingers glided back and forth on his engorged flesh.

"There's nothing like hands-on experience in the classroom, teacher," Archer offered. "I'm all for visual aids."

"The best time is when the cookie finally connects with the warm, sultry regions inside the receiver's body..." With a long, slow swipe of her pink tongue across her lips, Mindy got down on her knees, making Archer damn near shudder in response.

"The cookie," she continued, "brings extreme pleasure to the taste buds."

Archer looked down at the prettiest picture he'd ever seen as Mindy took him into her sweet mouth, inch by inch. A groan rumbled up from his chest, loving the way her lips glided over his flesh as she licked and sucked his cock. It was as if his dick was the finest chocolate chip cookie ever created and he was just what she needed to satisfy her cravings.

"Mmm...scrumptious," she mumbled around his cock, grazing it now with her teeth. "Amazing..."

"Aw, Jesus, Mindy..." Archer buried his fingers in her hair, fisting handfuls of gold as her lips, tongue and teeth worked miracles on his cock.

Mindy latched on to one of his ass cheeks with one hand, kneading his flesh, while cupping his balls with the other and massaging the heavy sac with loving attention. Since his cock was too big for her to take all at once, she twirled the tip of her tongue at its crown and then licked her way down its length to the base where she began to nibble.

Nipping his rigid flesh all the way back to the tip again, she took as much of him as possible, fucking him with her pretty mouth until Archer thought he'd go clear out of his mind.

Just when he was on the verge of exploding, Mindy let his cock pop out of her mouth. It bobbed there a moment, desperately needing to be sheathed in her soft, wet heat again.

"Before long," she stilled his cock with her hand, kissing the crown, then flicking her tongue quickly over the tiny hole, "the cookie achieves its maximum potential and purpose. Then, in a sudden burst of melting passion, liquid chocolate bathes the tongue and throat, bringing ultimate satisfaction to both the cookie and the cookie receiver."

The realization that she intended to swallow jarred him.

Before he could string two coherent thoughts together, her luscious mouth covered him again, doing her special magic. After every few strokes she let his cock pop from her mouth and blew on it, as if to cool it off, before closing her lips around him again. He wasn't quite sure why she did that, but he didn't care. The important thing was that his beautiful Mindy was paying homage to him with her mouth.

It didn't take long before Archer felt his balls draw up and tighten. The powerful wave of ecstasy rising within him thundered down the length of his cock, gushing out in hot ribbons against the back of Mindy's throat. After howling out his pleasure and staggering back to support himself against the kitchen counter, Archer looked down to find Mindy gazing up at him, licking his male essence from her lips and projecting an extremely satisfied smile.

Archer clutched her arms, drawing her from her knees to her feet, holding her close. "That was fucking incredible, teacher." He kissed her soundly, tasting himself on her tongue.

When their lips parted, Mindy snatched two warm cookies from the rack, placing one on Archer's tongue and one on her own. Her eyelids fluttered closed and Archer watched Mindy chew.

As the melting chocolate glided down the back of his throat, he figured it must be doing the same for her then because he saw a blissful orgasmic expression as she thoroughly savored her cookie. Archer felt his cock twitch. If he hadn't just come, his dick would be ramrod hard again just from watching that remarkably expressive face of hers.

"And that, my dear student," she opened her eyes after swallowing and licking her lips again, "is why your cock is like a chocolate chip cookie."

"Damn, Mindy. I'll never be able to look at a chocolate chip cookie the same way again."

"Excellent." Mindy nodded. "Then you've learned your lesson well," she announced, shoving another cookie into each of their mouths and pouring them cups of hot coffee.

Mindy

"BY THE WAY, DID YOU happen to notice that no alcohol whatsoever was involved in my chocolate chip cookie lesson?" Mindy asked.

"I did."

"Good. I just wanted to make that point. See? I told you I'm not a lush or a wino. Those times I became inebriated were merely..." she flicked her wrist, "a serious of unfortunate events."

"I stand corrected." Archer made a small bow from the waist. "And you sound just like those children's books," he added with a laugh.

Mindy's expression must have mirrored her confusion.

"Lemony Snicket's *A Series of Unfortunate Events*," Archer explained.

He sipped from his coffee and *ahhhhed,* looking just as happy and satisfied as she felt.

"If you've got any more lessons of culinary carnality like that in mind, teacher," he said, "I just might have to go back to school for another degree or two."

She was amazed at how natural, how easy, how *right* it felt to perform oral sex on Archer. Especially since she'd never done it before. Edward had never asked for it and she certainly wasn't about to offer to suck that anemic little doohickey of his.

She glanced at Archer. They were both still naked, which meant she could drool over his beautiful, beefy body to her heart's content. Nope, there was nothing even remotely anemic about Archer.

Through the intimate mouth-to-cock contact, she could easily feel his shaft react, pulse and twitch in her mouth. It was fascinating to explore the complicated fleshscape with her tongue—all the veins, wrinkles, slopes and the smooth bulb, with its tiny hole at the tip.

She hadn't quite known what to expect as far as the taste of his semen. She'd heard and read differing accounts. Some described the taste of cum as fishy and unpleasant. That's what she was prepared for, just in case. But it wasn't like that at all. It was warm, creamy, mildly salty and not at all unpleasant. She scored a big plus for the hot, spicy romance novels she'd read.

If the rest of the steamy stuff she'd read about was as accurate, she and Archer were in store for some amazing sexual adventures.

That is, if all went well and she didn't lose him.

The periodic cock-blowing part she did really didn't seem to do much of anything for either of them, but she'd included it just to make sure she did the job right. While she hadn't read about actually blowing on a man's cock in any of the sexy romances, Mindy figured it was simply a given and needed to be done.

"So I did okay then?" Mindy asked, suddenly feeling shy as she peered at him over the cup's rim.

Incredulous laughter bubbled from Archer's throat. "Okay? Jesus, Mindy, that was abso-fuckin-lutely fantastic. Phenomenal. Incredible. Definitely the last thing I ever expected when I drove you home."

"Did I get the blowing part right? Was there enough of it?"

Coffee cup poised in midair, Archer sat motionless for a moment, looking at her as if trying to decide what to say. Oh crap. She must have screwed up on the blowing after all and now he didn't want to tell her and hurt her feelings.

Archer set his cup back in its saucer. "The, uh, the blowing was...very nice. Just perfect." He smiled. "I enjoyed the entire experience immensely."

"Oh, that's good." Mindy engaged in a relieved sigh. "I don't really understand why it's called a *blowjob* though. It seems more appropriate to call it a *suckjob*, doesn't it?"

After some hesitation, Archer answered, "I guess it does," looking just a tad uneasy.

"I really liked the way you tasted too. Your semen, I mean." She bit into a cookie, moaning her satisfaction.

Archer gave her another hesitant look. "Well...thank you. I definitely like the way you taste too."

"I read that oral sex is a man's favorite kind of sex." Mindy sipped from her coffee, loving the way the dark brew complemented the chocolate. "Is it your favorite?" She was banking on it because that could mean she'd succeeded in making him forget about Boris and Natasha and face-sucking with Rolf.

Archer chuckled. "You're an interesting woman, Mindy. I don't recall any other woman asking me those questions before. I like sex, period. As for favorite types, ask me again after we've tried them all." He winked.

"That sounds good. I will." Mindy felt a deliciously warm tingle flush at her pussy. The fabulous new experience of giving Archer a blowjob had set her hormones on high. Now she wanted more. Much more.

"You know one of the best things about sex after it's over?" Archer asked.

Leaning forward, Mindy rested her elbow on the table, propping her chin on her hand. "No, what?" Good Lord, he was handsome. She could sit there looking at him, listening to him, studying him for days without getting bored. Especially when he was stark naked and she could get an eyeful of his muscles contracting and expanding as he moved.

"The wonderful clarity that comes after a great climax," he told her. "And before you ask me, because I'm sure that question's next, yes, that *was* a sensational climax. Thank you."

"My pleasure. What do you mean by clarity?"

"Fascinating thing. It's like the brain awakens, opening itself to reveal all the thoughts, musings and ideas previously buried. Know what I mean?"

"Not really." Mindy had a feeling she wasn't going to like where this was leading.

"Like the questions I'd asked you earlier, for instance. You know, the ones about your little masquerade and that muscle-head at the restaurant. The one you sank under the table with. Remember?"

"Oh...uh..."

"So," Archer went on, clearly determined to get answers, "since we're sitting here naked, cozy, and relaxed, why don't we have another cup of coffee and another cookie while we chat about those things?"

Narrowing one eye, Mindy glared at him. "I guess bringing you to orgasm was my big mistake." She heaved a resigned sigh. "Looks like I should have stopped short of letting you climax to avoid giving you," she hung invisible quotes in the air with her fingers, "*clarity.*"

Archer laughed, waving a chastising finger. "You didn't honestly think I was going to forget, did you?"

"Well, *duh*, of course I did!"

"Come on now, sweetheart. Whatever it is can't be that bad. I'm dying to hear all about it."

Mindy's eyes widened. *Not yet. Oh please...not yet.* She couldn't tell Archer about the terrible things she'd done. Not now. Not before they'd even had a chance to make love. Once...just once in his arms was all she asked. One wonderful, magical experience she could lock away in her heart to keep with her forever.

Clutching her coffee cup as the starkness of losing Archer made her eyes sting with unshed tears, Mindy sent up a silent prayer. *Please, let him stay with me...just a little while longer.*

Let's start with why you and Leo were disguised as—"

"Fuck me, Archer," Mindy blurted.

"What?"

"Right now. This minute. I can't wait any longer. I'm serious. I need to feel you deep inside. Your cock. My pussy." Slapping the table, she added, "Let's get it on."

"You're trying to distract me again," Archer accused.

"Is it working?" Mindy asked.

Archer looked down at his cock.

"Oh hell yeah."

Chapter 20

ARCHER GATHERED his clothes, bringing them upstairs to Mindy's bedroom. As she pulled back the bedspread, he fished a row of condoms from his wallet, tossing them on her nightstand.

It felt like Archer had been here with her in her bedroom before. Of course, he hadn't.

How many times, with the help of one of her vibrators, had she engaged in enticing, full-blown fantasies featuring Archer? Too many to count. Rich with the heat of passion, the joy of beauty, and the warmth and assurance of love, Mindy's comprehensive fantasy world was the closest thing to heaven on Earth.

Now she had more than a set of batteries and chunk of plastic. She had the real deal, the authentic flesh and blood original, just a few feet from her bed.

Sinking back against the pillows, she gazed at him as he walked toward her. This might be their one and only experience as lovers. Flooded with joy to have this precious gift of time with the man she wanted, the man she loved, Mindy offered her warmest, most inviting smile.

He climbed into her bed and her heart skipped a beat. "Oh, this is going to be exquisite," she said, allowing her innermost thoughts to pop out of her mouth.

"I'll do my best to make it that way for you, sweetheart. We'll see if you want to give me a gold star once we've finished."

I'll never be able to get enough of you, Archer Priest. Not ever.

Her gaze dropped to his cock. "Look how big you are already."

"That's what you do to me, Mindy."

"I'm glad to hear that. *Very* glad. So which position are we going to try first?"

"Me on top, you beneath me, on your back." He straddled her. "You've had some bad experiences in the past, honey. The first time we make love I want it to be special for you. I want to show you how a man is supposed to treat the woman he loves. So we're going to start slow, with good old-fashioned missionary style sex."

"Missionary style with a Priest!" Mindy couldn't help giggling at the irony. Indulging in a melodic sigh, she added, "You have no idea how much I've wanted to feel you inside me...to experience sex the way it's meant to be, for the first time in my life."

She noticed Archer eyeing her belly in a peculiar manner that made her self-conscious. "What's wrong? What are you looking at?" She sucked in her gut, fighting the urge to cover herself with the sheet. Maybe she had lint in her bellybutton. Maybe her belly fat reminded him of Jell-O. Maybe...

"Nothing. I was just trying to picture you with a staple in your navel."

"Oh...uh...well, I hope that's not some sort of turn-on for you because I'm not into weird piercing stuff, Archer. I mean, I've got pierced ears, but I'm not too keen on body staples. I didn't even know you could do that."

A devilish laugh rumbled up from Archer's chest. "I meant you have a centerfold's body, Min. The curvaceous kind in a magazine or calendar you see tacked up in car mechanic shops, with a center-page staple right about here." He smoothed his hand over her belly then dipped low to kiss her navel. He swirled his tongue around the perimeter and dipped it inside.

Harsh moans slipped from her throat as the warm, wet contact made her shudder. Whoever would have thought a warm lick at her bellybutton could be so sensuous?

"Big breasts, soft belly, round hips." His hands slid across her flesh, molding her curves. When he clutched her butt his eyes darkened. "And the sweetest handful of ass I've ever grabbed. Beautiful, supple and voluptuous. You've got a bad girl body and a good girl past, sweetheart. An irresistible combination. And you're all mine to do with as I please."

Archer's words were like magic, especially considering the horde of body image issues Mindy warred with. Knowing he liked her body, actually loved it, just the way she was, infused her with confidence.

"Go ahead. Be my guest." Arching her back, she thrust her breasts high. "Do with me what you will. I'm yours for the taking." After her unpleasant history with Edward, Mindy never imagined a time when she'd freely and fully surrender herself to a man again. The thought of giving Archer carte blanche over her body was heady and exhilarating.

Gazing at the pink, mushroom-shaped head of his cock, she remembered running her tongue over it earlier, tasting the smooth satiny flesh and his salty essence. It was hard to take her eyes from his sizeable dipstick as he sheathed it with a condom. She'd never experienced anything so big inside her before. Edward's little shelled peanut of a penis simply couldn't compare.

"I almost feel like a virgin again, anticipating that very first time," Mindy confessed, a thrill sweeping through her at the idea. She'd been cheated that first time on her wedding night years ago. Edward's selfishness had blotted out any of the special magic that marked a woman's first sexual encounter.

"I'll do my best to keep that in mind, Mindy. Hopefully I can last long enough to make it good for you. But I've gotta warn you, you're so goddamn hot it won't be easy. Right now there's a wild animal inside me, clawing to get out. It's that part of me that wants to tear into you and fuck you until you're senseless."

The carnal image and pointed words had Mindy's pussy soaking. "There's definite appeal to that scenario," she said, her voice sultry.

A moment later, his hands captured her full attention. They were all over her, as if he was trying to memorize each curve through touch alone.

She reached for his sac, cupping it gently and enjoying the weight of his balls in her hand. "Even your balls are big. I like the way they feel."

"They're very happy right now." He smoothed his hand over Mindy's as she caressed him. She could feel his sac contract slightly at her touch.

A needy whimper escaped her lips.

"I like the sound of those sexy little cries you make when I touch you," he told her. "It lets me know you're just as turned on as I am. That you want to feel my cock driving home, hard and deep. That's what you want, isn't it, baby?"

"More than anything, Archer." Her hand fell away from his balls and she splayed her fingers against his biceps, feeling the muscles bunch and cord with his movement. He was so tall, so big and well-muscled, it made her feel itty-bitty next to him. There was no sensation quite as agreeable and satisfying for a big girl.

He toyed with her nipple, flicking it with his finger and plucking it until it stood high, aching for his mouth, longing to feel his tongue, his teeth.

"When I'm near you, I'm like a crazy man, consumed with lust and desire. All I can think about is rubbing your glorious tits all over me."

Archer cupped her breasts with both hands, gazing at her flesh as if worshipping it. He buried his face between the mounds, cherishing each breast with his mouth as she melted beneath him.

Supporting his arms on either side of her, he dragged his chest over her swollen breasts. Crushing them against his hard pectorals, he swiveled slowly, the crisp curls of his chest hair scraping her nipples. The slight tickling sensation heightened her longing.

Mindy had never felt more desirable. Lifting himself, he caught one nipple between his teeth, nibbling, sucking, driving her mad. Liquid threads of delight shot through her, warming her like a hot toddy on a frosty night.

"I need you, Archer," she said on a sigh. "Deep. All the way inside."

Archer touched her intimately, sweetly. Her clit came alive with sensation at his slow, tender contact. When he sank two fingers deep inside, Mindy gasped.

"And I need you, baby." His eyes locked on hers as her breaths became shallow. "I need to fuck you, hard and long until my cock explodes inside you." While Mindy murmured tiny, nonsensical syllables, he twisted his fingers inside. "I can't believe how tight you are."

Aware of cream drenching her already wet pussy, she whispered, "It's been a very long time. And I've never had anything big enough inside to stretch me before."

"Ah yes..." His eyes half-lidded, a smile quirked at Archer's lips. "Your only other experience was with Thumbkin." A third finger joined the others, and Archer thrust hard, stretching her as he moved in and out. Mindy nearly died of an overdose of pleasure. "I can guarantee you a much fuller experience, I'm just afraid I won't last more than ten seconds in there."

"Then we'll just have to make it the best ten seconds ever." She was squirming now, writhing in anticipation of the big event.

"I'll do my damnedest. I just want to make this good for you, sweetheart."

"Oh it will be. Don't worry. Just do it, okay? Before I go out of my mind from expectation."

Archer withdrew his fingers and Mindy immediately missed the feeling of fullness inside. He spread her thighs wide. Fitting the hard length of his cock directly against her pussy, he stroked it against her slit then nudged his way inside by an inch or so.

"Yes...more, Archer. Give me more..."

He sank deeper and Mindy moaned, clutching the bed sheet.

"Let me know if I'm hurting you," he said through clenched teeth. "Tell me if you need me to stop and I will."

"No, it feels great." Mindy was half-tempted to shout with glee at the welcome invasion of Archer's thick cock. "You're so big you almost fill me up inside."

"I'm taking it as slow as I possibly can. It feels like virgin territory in there." Mindy focused on his eyes when she heard his wicked laugh. "And I'm not even halfway in yet, honey."

"You're kidding?"

Trembling all over as sweat trickled from his forehead, Archer looked pained. "Do I look like I'm kidding?"

Unable to wait, Mindy thrust her hips high, forcing more of Archer's cock into her depths. God, it felt good.

With a primal growl, Archer lifted Mindy's hips from the mattress, filling her so full it stole her breath.

"Sorry, I couldn't help it. You're just so hot and wet in there, Mindy. So tight. Damn, you feel good."

Just this side of pain, she found herself encompassed in a state of bliss so complete she never wanted to move again. But when Archer drew back and plunged into her once more, stretching her, possessing her, Mindy's pleasure meter registered a new high.

His balls slapping her pussy with each downward stroke, he gazed at her like she was a beautiful fairytale princess. At least, that's how he made her feel. She watched her Prince Charming's dark eyes grow even darker until they became pools of molten chocolate.

He felt so good, so right. She dug her fingers into his waist, clawing at him, needing to bring him closer, to touch him, soul to soul. This, *this* is what making love was all about.

Mindy's breath caught as she felt Archer's fingertips trace lightly over her breasts. Her eyes closed on a whimper as he suckled her. Sweet heaven, this was bliss. The sensation was too much, too superb. A tear trickled down her cheek and a moment later Archer stopped thrusting and her breast popped from his mouth.

"Did I hurt you?"

"No...no. I'm okay. It's wonderful, Archer. Extraordinary." How could she possibly put it into words to make him understand? How could she explain the flood of emotion coursing through her right now? It had been so long since she'd been held like this, loved like this. Mindy fought to remember the last time. Hell, she'd *never* been held or loved like this before. Ever. Good God, what she'd been missing!

Guiding her hips with shaking hands, Archer stared at the place where they joined. "I've wanted this for so long," he said hoarsely. "Since that first time I saw you at the funeral home, all dolled up in that little black suit with the naughty bit of red lace peeking out at your cleavage." His gaze was still locked on the connection of cock to pussy as he sank in and drew back.

"Those plump lips of yours were all red and shiny, just begging to be kissed." He paused long enough to feather a kiss across her lips. "I knew then it would be this good with us, Mindy."

"That was my *farewell-you-bastard* outfit," she told him, remembering her finely calculated ensemble. "But now I've come to think of it as my *well-hello-you-gorgeous-hunk* outfit instead." She was about to engage in a little laugh but when Archer thrust hard and high, her voice caught on a lingering moan.

There was nothing quite as superb or gratifying as being made love to by a breathtakingly gorgeous man. A generous, gifted man. Archer's exceptional carnal skills transcended anything Mindy had read about in her steamy romance novels.

Please, Archer, don't ever leave me...

As he pleasured her, she tried to tell him what he was doing to her, how utterly magnificent he made her feel. But his impassioned deeds had rendered her speechless. Awash in love, passion and emotion, Mindy gave herself fully to him, body and soul, as one final, purposeful twist of his hips sent her careening into yet another dimension where pleasure and satisfaction merged, permeating each cell of her being.

The only thing that could possibly make her climax any better happened an instant later, when the sound of Archer roaring out his release, crying out her name, bonded with her own soulful cries.

Tears of joy blurring her vision as Archer's muscled magnificence slumped against her, Mindora von G was a well-fucked, utterly satisfied and thoroughly pleasured woman.

Mindy

"THAT WAS FUCKING AMAZING," Archer said a few minutes later as Mindy cuddled against his chest.

"Your expert workmanship earned you a whopping five gold stars." Mindy drew random patterns on his chest with her finger. "I never dreamed sex could be so beautiful."

"I'm glad you felt that way. I was afraid I'd traumatized you by acting like an animal." Archer chuckled.

"Nope. I liked seeing the fire in your eyes—and that fierce, commanding way you took me, still being mindful enough to make sure the experience was good for me. What a generous, unselfish lover you are." Splaying her fingers on his pecs, she kissed one of his flat, brown nipples.

"And what a hot tamale you are." He kissed her forehead. "So, you're feeling good?"

"Mmmm..." she nodded, "sensational."

"Good...good. Nice and relaxed?"

Mindy stretched. "Extremely."

"Me too. That makes this an ideal time for a little post-coital pillow talk, sweetheart."

Mindy froze.

"Hey, I know," Archer said with mock innocence. "Why don't you start by telling me all about Boris and Natasha? Unless you'd like to start with the scene at the restaurant first."

Mindy's thoughts whirred, like a blender at high speed. There had to be something else she could do to distract Archer. Something that would capture all his attention.

Something extraordinary that would save her sorry ass from having to make explanations.

"As a matter of fact, I had the same thought, Archer. It's definitely time we talk."

Giving a resolute nod, he said, "It's about damn time."

"Right after I introduce you to one of my best friends," Mindy said.

"What?" Archer whipped his head, looking from left to right. "Who?" His expression morphed into a scowl. "Mindy, you're stalling again."

Sucking in a gasp of mock indignation as her hand flew to her throat, Mindy pinned Archer with a wounded glare. "Oh Archer...that was unkind." She sniffed. "And after what we just shared together too. I'm shocked. Shocked and hurt." She forced her bottom lip to tremble.

Archer's face fell. "Aw, I'm sorry, Min. I'm an ass. Just forget what I said. Please, don't cry."

"Well...okay." She batted her eyelashes at Archer, doing her best to look like an angel radiating pure innocence. Smiling sweetly, she raised a finger as she maneuvered to the edge of the mattress. "Just give me a minute." She got up and padded to the bathroom, formulating her idea as she opened the linen closet, clutching the item she prayed would stun Archer's senses.

"Archer Priest," she said, returning to the bed, hands behind her back. "Meet Lieutenant Largo Lovethruster from the planet Dickprobe." She brought her hands to the front and presented her precious neon green vibrator to Archer, who gaped at it as if it were a sewer rat.

"What the hell is that?" he asked, a definite vibe of disgust in his tone.

"I told you. One of my best friends." She flicked one of the switches and Largo came to life. "Largo's one of my favorite vibrators."

"Jesus, you use that thing on yourself? It looks like an alien."

"My thoughts exactly," Mindy agreed as she got in the bed and knee-walked toward Archer. "Thus the name Lieutenant Largo Lovethruster from the planet Dickprobe."

"You give your vibrators names, ranks, and origins?"

"Of course. Doesn't everybody?" Mindy shrugged. "This little green alien is capable of amazing things, Archer."

His lips quirked into a smile. "I hope to hell you're going to show me." His gaze dropped to her pussy and he licked his lips.

"Definitely. I want you flat on your back," Mindy instructed, giving his chest a shove until he fell back. "You can prop your head on a couple of pillows so you can see better."

"Oh, I definitely want to see, all right."

"I'm going to turn this to low first, to let you get used to the sensations. Spread your legs for me, Archer." He did and Mindy got on her knees, positioning herself at the center, hovering just over his cock. "Mmm, look at that. Your cock is already coming around again." She feathered her fingers across it. "Perfect."

"It'll get even bigger once you start working your magic on that little pink clit of yours with the alien."

"That's not exactly what I had in mind," Mindy told him. "Now just relax while I get you and Largo acquainted, up close and personal."

She brought the vibrator to Archer's groin, clicking the lowest setting. Aiming the fork of the unit at the base of his cock, so that a vibrating sphere was on either side of his shaft, she turned it on.

Archer yelped, yelling out an amazingly colorful string of oaths.

"Jesus! Fuck!" He scooted back like a crab into a full sitting position. "What the hell do you think you're doing, Mindy?"

"Haven't you ever been pleasured by a vibrator before?" she asked, wondering if maybe she might be the first woman to ever think of using a vibrator on a man. If this diversion worked as well as she hoped, maybe she'd design and package her own line of vibrators, specifically made for cock stimulation. Maybe with an expanding donut-ring center. She'd make a fortune overnight!

"Of course not. That's for women. You can't use one of those things on a guy's dick."

"Why not?"

"It's...well, it's just not something you do to a guy, that's all."

"You're not chicken, are you, Archer?" she baited him, wondering at the same time if she might be making a terrible mistake. What if vibrating a cock somehow rendered it useless? What if cock-quaking made a guy sterile? What if the poor trembly cock got all shriveled and tiny and it retreated back inside the man's body, never to be seen again...kind of like Edward's Thumbkin?

"No, I'm not chicken, I just—"

"Is there a medical reason why a vibrator shouldn't be applied to a man's cock or balls?" Mindy asked, seeking verification. "I mean, did your peniscologist, or whatever a man's private parts doctor is called, warn you to avoid stimulating your cock with a vibrator?"

Archer burst out laughing. "I can't believe we're having this conversation. It's ridiculous. And, believe me, it's certainly not a conversation I'd have with my doctor. He'd think I was gay for chrissakes."

"So to the best of your knowledge, there's no valid medical reason why I can't vibrate your cock with this, right? Masturbating with a vibrator's not something little boys are cautioned against doing?"

Archer laughed again. "I suppose not. At least I don't remember the subject ever coming up in conversation with my parents over Sunday dinner."

"Good. Get back in position," she ordered. "Time's a-wastin'." She turned the vibrator on again. "How did it feel when I touched it to your cock? Did it hurt?"

"No, it just felt weird," he answered, a resigned look on his face.

"Okay. Weird can be good. Now let yourself relax and enjoy this, Archer." Wrapping one hand around the top of his shaft, she positioned the vibrator low, at the root again. She moved the unit up and down slowly, while pumping his cock with her hand at the same time. "How does that feel?"

"I'm not sure...either really good, or really bad."

Mindy watched Archer's cock bloom. "Your cock definitely thinks it feels good." She removed her hand from his cock and ran the vibrator up and down the full length of his shaft.

Archer groaned.

Mindy smiled.

She turned the power indicator to medium and Archer tensed as she dragged it up his fully erect cock.

"Shit. I'm going to come."

Mindy was delighted that her plan was working, but she didn't want him coming quite so fast. No, that wouldn't do at all. She needed to draw this out, to pleasure him long enough for his mind became a complete blank, forgetting all about Boris and Natasha and the sordid restaurant kiss.

"Not so fast, speedy." She took the vibrator away from his cock. "Would you like to see how I use Largo on myself?"

"Oh yeah. Show me, baby." His passion-fogged gaze zeroed in on her pussy as Mindy aimed the vibrator at her clit.

Under normal circumstances she'd never be able to do this. So bold. So brazen. But these weren't normal circumstances. Emergency measures weren't only necessary, they were mandatory! She had no choice but to sacrifice her timidity for the sake of saving her relationship with Archer.

Swallowing hard, Mindy drew her labia back with the fingers of one hand and pressed one of the green plastic balls between her thighs. As soon as it made contact with her clit, her breath caught and she moaned.

"Now that's what I like to see," Archer said. "That's beautiful. Make yourself come for me, Mindy."

"Just for you, Archer." Mindy turned Largo on high, fixing the side with the plastic spikes against her clitoris. Her eyelids fluttered closed and she almost forgot Archer was there. Except for the decidedly naughty thrill that shot through her, knowing he watched.

"Even your moan is vibrating," Archer noted. "I love it...love watching you, sweetheart."

Mindy's eyes popped open when she felt a delicious mix of pain and pleasure at her breasts. Kneeling before her, Archer pinched and twisted her taut nipples as she vibrated her clit.

"Dear God..." Mindy was on the threshold of paradise. Weaving the fingers of her free hand through Archer's hair, she leaned close to kiss him. His hands never leaving her nipples, he turned her tender kiss into a wild festival of bliss as his tongue fucked her mouth.

The array of erotic sensation was too much for Mindy to bear. As the heavenly pull, pound and throb exploded through her clit, her breath shuddered. Archer captured her orgasmic scream in his mouth, swallowing every last vestige of her trembling cries.

Before Mindy could collapse, he enveloped her in his arms, whispering words of endearment at her ear, kissing her temple, her throat, her shoulder.

"That was so beautiful it was almost a religious experience," he whispered.

As Mindy's pleasured senses tripped through time and space, the nagging reminder that she needed to keep Archer's mind occupied intruded, propelling her back to the present. Doing her best to gather her wits, she cupped Archer's jaw in her hands and smiled.

"Now let me do the same for you," she said. "Together we can discover what it's like to bring a man to climax by vibrating the bejeezus out of his cock." She indulged in a throaty chuckle, at the same time giving Archer's chest a nudge, letting him know she wanted him on his back again.

He complied without argument and Mindy breathed a sigh of relief.

Before she used the vibrator on him, her fingernails lightly scraped the underside of his balls and she felt him shiver. "Archer Priest, I'm going to send you over the edge of sanity," she promised.

"I'm going to make every last nerve ending in your body come alive and vibrate as your body is wracked by endless shudders of ecstasy."

Her own words were making her hot again.

"Do it to me, baby. I'm ready."

Loving the lusty, expectant look in his eyes, Mindy positioned the vibrator at the tip of Archer's cock this time and turned it to medium. His body immediately tensed and she heard him suck in a breath.

"When your hot male essence comes shooting strong and fast out of your cock," she told him, working the vibrator up, down and all around his shaft, "I'm going to seize every last drop of that velvety cum in my mouth and swallow it all down."

Giving Archer her best wicked smile, Mindy flicked Largo to low and positioned her open mouth at the apex of Archer's cock. Then she lightly stroked the vibrator over his scrotum.

That single pass was all it took to trigger his ejaculation, with Archer's hands threaded in her hair, fisting it. He roared out his climax as she drank from his spurting cock.

A serene eternity passed as they lay together in silence, with her head on Archer's chest and his arms around her, lazily caressing her. She loved listening to him breathe, feeling his heartbeat beneath her cheek. It was all so perfect. She could stay like that forever.

"What an amazing woman you are, Mindy. I've never met anyone like you before. You make me feel happy, content, supremely satisfied."

And so blissfully, entirely, wholly stunned that he'd forgotten about pummeling her with annoying questions, Mindy hoped.

"I can't think of a better time for a heart-to-heart talk, sweetheart, can you?" Archer asked.

Her eyes flashed wide. What the hell? Archer had a one-track mind.

Mindy contemplated ignoring him by pretending she was asleep and snoring, instead she manufactured a huge yawn.

"Oh boy. I'm so tired," she claimed through a second yawn. "All that wonderful lovemaking really wore me out. Too sleepy to talk. I think I'll take a nap for a little while." Shutting her eyes tight, she did her damnedest to look like she was asleep.

Archer opened Mindy's eyelid with his fingers. "Wake up, sleeping beauty. It's time to talk."

Heaving a defeated groan, Mindy sat up, with Archer following suit. "In most of the romance novels I've read, the hero likes to roll over and go to sleep after sex. Or maybe have a pizza. He never wants to talk."

"I could definitely go for a pizza." Archer glanced at the clock. "It's just about dinnertime."

"Good. I'll order one." Mindy started scooting off the bed until Archer grabbed her, holding her in place.

"Great. We can talk while we're eating."

"Why don't you just roll over and go to sleep instead?"

"Because I'm not that kind of romance hero. I'm the kind who likes to get all cozy, cuddly and chatty after sex."

"Chatty, huh?" With a dubious look, Mindy offered, "Okay, so tell me all about your childhood. I'm all ears."

"Face it, Mindy." Archer grinned. "I've got you cornered." He wrapped his arms around her waist and held tight. "No more excuses. Time to spill your guts."

Mindy gave him a narrow-eyed glare. "Did you have sex with me just so you could give me the third degree?"

"Absolutely. That was the only reason," he teased, cupping her breast and jiggling it in his palm. "Now let's have it. Why were you and your crazy boss dressed up like a couple of cold war spies at my sister's office?"

Mindy's heart sank. Her time was up. She had to face the music.

Shit!

At least she got to sleep with him one glorious, magical time.

"Okay, Archer, you win. I'll tell you everything. You see, Leo's cousin—"

Her phone rang.

Yes! Saved by the bell!

Chapter 21

MINDY'S DEMEANOR brightened considerably. "Excuse me for a moment, Archer, that might be important." She crawled over him, reaching for her phone on her nightstand to answer the call, happy for anything that would help delay the inevitable. A quick glance at the time told her it was almost five-thirty. She wouldn't normally answer a number she didn't recognize, letting it go straight to voicemail, but...

"Hello?"

"Hello, ma'am, this is Alice with Surveys USA. I'd like to ask you a few questions about your television streaming preferences. Do you have a moment?"

Rescued by a telemarketer? Well, son of a gun. The quivery-voiced woman sounded positively ancient. Mindy pictured a sweet, silver-haired senior citizen, volunteering her time for the arts.

Sending up a silent prayer of thanks, she vowed never to offer curt replies and hang up on telemarketers again. Pregnant with possibilities, her mind raced before she responded.

"Yes, of course," she said. "My goodness, Alice, you sound upset. Is anything wrong?"

"I do? Oh...no, I'm just a little tired, that's all. It's the end of my shift. Sorry. So, how many hours would you say you spend watching TV each day?"

"Oh dear. You mean now? Isn't there anyone else available to handle this?"

There was a brief silence on the other end of the line.

"*Um...is this a bad time for you, dear? I can call back later or tomorrow if that's better.*"

"No, not at all, Alice. I understand. You don't have any choice. Of course I'm available. After all, I'm the vice president, it's part of my job." Shrugging, she glanced at Archer, who eyed her skeptically. A nervous giggle escaped her lips. "Just give me ten to fifteen minutes."

"*The vice president?*" Long pause. "*So...ten to fifteen minutes of television watching each day?*"

Mindy felt guilty for confusing the poor old woman, but she simply couldn't pass up this golden opportunity to escape Archer's persistent questions.

"I believe so. I'll have to find all the paperwork with the stats. It's in Leo's file cabinet. He still hasn't got around to digitalizing his paperwork."

"*Stats? Oh that's not necessary, dear. We're just looking for approximates. What about your favorite streaming station? Do you prefer...*" The woman rattled off a bunch of streaming services.

"That's hard to say without going through Leo's documents. It all depends on the client's preferences. Do your best to hold down the fort, Alice. Just let them know I'm on my way."

Silence ensued. "*Um...what? Let who know?*" The woman sounded flustered. "*Dear, you don't have to come down to our office, all I need is—*"

"Alice?" Guilt gnawed harder at Mindy's gut. Jesus, she was screwing with the mind of someone's sweet old grandma!

"*Yes?*"

"I wanted to let you know I think you're doing a wonderful job."

"*Oh...why, thank you, dear.*"

Mindy said goodbye and ended the call. Taking a deep, cleansing breath, she turned to Archer.

"I'm terribly sorry but there's an emergency at the office. Being vice president, I need to pinch-hit for Leo."

Archer slanted Mindy a wary look. "A *travel* emergency?"

"They happen all the time." She shrugged. "You know, lost luggage, hotel switches...but this one's major. Can I impose on you to drive me to the office? My buddy Leo stranded me, remember?" She gave a little laugh.

Scurrying about, Mindy scrambled into her clothes.

"Sure." Archer got himself dressed. "But what kind of travel emergency—"

Mindy raced out of the bedroom and down the stairs with Archer at her heels. Gathering her purse and keys, she remembered her broken heeled shoe and slipped into a pair of flats from her coat closet.

Just as her hand was about to grab the doorknob, Archer clasped her arm.

"Slow down, madame vice president."

"Archer, I've got to go now. They need me!"

"Your office isn't that far. You told them you'd be there in ten to fifteen minutes. I'll have you there in plenty of time. What's this dire travel emergency?"

"Eh...a VIP client just flew in from Austria. He's there at the office, waiting to go over the travel arrangements we made for him. He's...he's, uh...going to travel across the U.S."

Taking in Archer's disbelieving expression, Mindy swallowed hard. Damn it, if Leo could get away telling those whoppers of his, so could she!

"His name is Rudolph Schwarzenegger. He's a wealthy big shot."

"Schwarzenegger?"

Mindy nodded, placing her fingers to her lips. "One of Arnold's relatives. It's all very hush-hush." Now Archer *really* looked skeptical and Mindy got nervous and licked her lips. She felt one of those awful telltale, nervous staccato giggles of Leo's rising, but suppressed it.

"Leo must have forgotten about this client flying in," Mindy continued. "Evidently, Leo got stuck having cocktails with the rep from the new cruise line and the office can't reach him."

"I see. So...I guess his phone and pager are both dead, hmm?" Archer asked with a know-it-all smirk.

Damn! She'd forgotten about that ancient pager Leo insisted on carrying around with him. Archer must have noticed it, or maybe Leo mentioned it.

"Oh...well, when Leo left your sister's office, he was running late for his appointment with the cruise rep. He rushed back to Persimmon to get the paperwork he needed and...uh, in all the commotion he left his pager." She cleared her throat. "And-and his phone's in his trench coat in his office. Leo's so forgetful."

She smiled brightly, trying her damnedest to look convincing and camouflage her anxiety. By Archer's disbelieving expression, she had a sinking feeling it wasn't working.

"Mr. Schwarzenegger is an elderly gentleman who no doubt feels a little lost here in a foreign country, all by himself. So I really do need to get to the office right away." She hiked a shoulder in an apologetic shrug.

Archer stood silent for a moment in apparent contemplation. After what seemed like forever, he finally said, "Sure, no problem. Under one condition."

Mindy blinked. "Condition?"

With a resolute nod, Archer said, "Yup. I'll be back here at your place tonight at nine o'clock to pick you up. You better be here. No excuses."

"Pick me up? For what?"

"A date. You know, you, me, food, conversation...and *more*." Placing special emphasis on the last word, Archer jiggled his eyebrows in a devilish manner and Mindy felt her heart lurch.

"And tonight, Min..." he said just above a whisper, yanking her close to slide the tip of his tongue back and forth across her lips.

Her heart tap-danced through her chest. "Yes, Archer?" She gazed dreamily into his chocolate chip eyes, anticipating his next remark. "What about tonight?"

She got all girly, batting her lashes at him. It was going to be something stupendously romantic, she could feel it. And she was this-close to melting into a puddle of goo at his feet.

Tilting her chin, he kissed the tip of her nose. "Tonight over dinner, you can give me all those explanations you owe me." Winking, he broadcast a self-satisfied grin.

So much for stupendous romance. He was only interested in that damned explanation. Her visions of another hot, juicy, passionate romp between the sheets thwarted, Mindy's tap-dancing heartbeat slowed to a clumsy box step.

"Sorry. No can do, Archer. I'll probably have to entertain the Austrian this evening."

"At nine o'clock at night?"

"What can I say?" Mindy shrugged. "It's part of my job description."

Archer nailed her with yet another dubious expression. "No problem. We can bring the old geezer along. But he gets dropped off after dinner—and before *dessert*."

Archer flashed a smile and Mindy's heart leapt at the renewed hope. After all, they had all those varieties of sex to explore to see which he liked best. Maybe they could try them all before Archer asked any more questions.

"Now, any more excuses...Natasha?"

Before she knew what was happening, Mindy heard herself let go with one of those hideous nervous giggles of Leo's—the ones she positively loathed.

"Nope. Nine o'clock it is."

Her anticipatory glow faded to black and panic set in when she thought about Archer seeing Leo at the travel agency when he dropped Mindy off in a few minutes.

She had to reach Leo—now!

"Excuse me for a moment while I run to the powder room, Archer." She took the stairs two at a time to retrieve her phone.

Mindy

"YOU CAN COME OUT NOW, Leo, Archer's gone," Mindy said, opening the door to the office supply room where Leo sat hunched behind a pile of boxes.

Leo peeked his head out. "What was that frantic call all about, telling me I had to hide?"

"Archer just dropped me off. I didn't want him to see you. I told him you're with the cruise rep and I have to fill in for you."

"I don't understand. Why would—"

Mindy waved an outstretched finger at him. "You miserable, chicken-hearted, lily-livered, hideous excuse for a human being. You just left me out there in that parking lot with Archer all by myself, looking like a clown!" She whapped her shoulder bag against Leo's side as he rose.

Cringing, Leo rubbed his arm where the weighty purse made impact. "Honestly, I don't know why you're so upset with me, Min. Granted, I may have been a little hasty locking you out of the car this afternoon," he lapsed into a nervous giggle when Mindy glared at him, "but it all worked out for the best. You got to spend the afternoon with Archer, didn't you?"

"Yes..." Mindy couldn't help the wistful sigh that escaped her throat at the thought of the phenomenal sex they'd had.

"Oh my God," Leo gasped. "You did it. You had sex with Archer!"

At a loss for words, Mindy just stared at him with a blank expression.

"Yes! I knew it! That means you're not a semi-virgin anymore. *Finally.* How was it? As good as you thought?"

"Better..." Mindy whispered on a dreamy sigh, before her attention snapped back to the present. "I mean, that's none of your business, Leo."

An elated expression across his features, he rubbed his hands together. "Everything's working out just the way I planned. Oh this is rich. Sensational! Before you know it, Mindy, Britney and Jasper will be on their way to Russia." His arms outstretched, Leo beamed a toothy grin. "See? What did I tell you? No problem. Life is perfect. In fact, I think I feel a dance of joy coming on." He snapped his fingers high in the air.

Mindy gave Leo another solid roundhouse whack with her purse and he winced. "Are you insane, Leo? Is that the problem? I mean, you *must* be crazy if you don't realize that, because of you, any future with the man of my dreams might be kaput."

"Come on, Mindy, stop exaggerating. It's not *that* bad. I mean, really, how bad could it be if you had sex with him, huh? You snagged him, reeled him in. He's hooked." Leo glanced at Mindy, who would have been breathing fire through her nostrils if at all possible.

He quickly averted his gaze. "Okay, judging by the highly unattractive scowl across your face, I guess it *is* that bad. What did you tell Archer about our Boris and Natasha masquerade at Britney's office? I'm sure you came up with something dazzling."

"I told him nothing."

"There, see?" Becoming comfortably animated again, Leo smiled at Mindy. "Archer didn't even ask. He was obviously so mesmerized by your voluptuous body that all he cared about was dancing the mattress jig, stuffing the taco, hiding the hot dog." *Elbow-elbow. Wink-wink.* "So what are you worried about, honey?"

Mindy's laugh was a sick, strangled sound. "Leo, sex or no sex, that man has a mind like a steel trap. The memory of an elephant. Archer's determined to find out every last detail of our escapades. I'd finally decided I had no choice but to tell him the truth—"

"The truth! But Mindy, you can't—"

"Until the phone rang," she continued. "I pretended it was the office saying I had to cover for you." She proceeded to tell Leo the whole Austrian client story she told Archer.

"Brilliant! Good thinking, Mindy. You're getting more like me every day." Laughing, he draped his arm over her shoulder. She promptly removed it.

"Don't add insult to injury, Leo. I figured I could stall for time until you and I could come up with something plausible. At least moderately rational." She slapped her head. "Listen to me. I must be crazy too if I think you, of all people, can come up with something logical and believable."

"Don't worry, we have plenty of time to concoct a convincing story."

"He's picking me up for dinner at nine o'clock tonight."

Leo glanced at his watch. "Oh."

"How can we possibly explain being caught in his sister's office in those ridiculous disguises?"

There was a long pause as Leo sat on one of the boxes and rubbed his chin, while Mindy tapped her toe against the concrete floor.

"I've got it!"

Eyes closing in a long blink, Mindy shook her head. "I'm afraid to ask."

"We'll tell him we were plotting out the script for Persimmon Travel's first mystery dinner! It's a cinch. Remember the one we went to last year at that restaurant downtown?" Mindy nodded. "We'll just say we were doing some live-action script testing. And since the plot involves a Realtor, we decided to act out part of the script at the closest real estate office to see if it was believable."

Beaming a triumphant grin, Leo leapt up and gestured dramatically. "Ta-da!"

Mindy thought for a moment before nodding. "My brain must be fried."

"Huh?"

"Because that doesn't sound half bad, Leo. It's simple and not too elaborate. It-it *almost* sounds credible." She smiled for the first time since she got to the office. "Okay, we'll go with that. Do you think Archer will buy it?"

Draping his arm around her shoulder again and pulling Mindy into a buddy-hug, Leo said, "Are you kidding? Trust me."

Chapter 22

MINDY'S DOORBELL rang at eight forty-five and Cadbury yipped, alerting his mistress to the arrival.

"Archer's early," she said, glancing first at the clock, then down at Cadbury. "What do you think, Cad? Do I look good enough to wow Mr. Priest?" She gave herself a final mirror check and smiled. Her chic black dress was smart, simple and slimming. The few tasteful gold accessories she'd chosen looked just right. Patting her hair, which she'd pulled back in a deliberately messy curly bun, she saw Cadbury slant his head. He seemed to smile as he studied her.

Heading for the front door, Mindy thought about the terribly naughty crotchless panties and lacy, barely there bra she wore beneath her dress. A warm tingle lodged at her pussy as she contemplated an extensive night of sizzling, hot passion.

She had a really positive feeling about tonight. Leo's mystery dinner rehearsal idea was fairly believable. And she'd decided to tell Archer that it was just her overly amorous, dopey, intoxicated cousin he saw kissing her at the restaurant. She grinned at Cadbury and he bellowed a sickly whimper.

"Nope," she patted the little dog, "you don't have to worry, Cad. I think everything's going to work out perfectly for Archer and me. I can feel it in my bones." She sucked in a deep breath and answered the door.

Mindy gasped. "Rolf! What are you doing here?"

"I've come to help you, Mindy." He stepped into her living room. "Hello, my fur-buddy Cadbury." He petted the little dog, who was clearly in heaven, sniffing the restaurant odors clinging to Rolf's body.

"You *what?*"

"*Ja.* I feel so terrible when Leo told me about the bad situation you have with your dreamship."

"My what?"

"Your lover boy." Rolf nodded with a wink. "I fear I did not do a very good job at the restaurant with Big Jasper last night. So I am here to pretend to be your rich Austrian travel client tonight." Holding his shoulders back proudly, he grinned. "Surprise, Mindy!"

Mindy's hand flew to her mouth in horror. "Oh no! No, Rolf, you have to leave."

"But—"

"I'm sorry, I don't mean to be rude. This is a very sweet gesture on your part, and I really appreciate it," she said gently, as she pushed the hulking German out of her house. "But I'd rather be alone with Archer. You can understand that, right?"

Rolf nodded knowingly. "Ahhh, you want to get cozy and have more sex with your dreamship. *Ja,* I understand." He offered a thumbs-up sign.

"*Dreamboat,*" Mindy corrected. "Besides, I told Archer our Austrian client is an elderly man and you're certainly not—" Mindy gasped and clapped her hand against her mouth. "Oh dear God, Rolf, I nearly forgot. Archer saw you putting the moves on me at the restaurant. We have *got* to get you out of here before he sees you." She pushed him again, barely moving him an inch.

"Putting the moves?" Rolf scrunched his handsome features. "This means?"

"You know, the lip-lock, the clench." She rolled her eyes and groaned as Rolf stood there looking gorgeously befuddled. "The passionate kiss you gave me, Rolf, remember?"

"Oh! My macho-man smooch. *Ja,* sure I remember." He broadcast a bright smile. "I did an excellent job of putting the moves on you, *ja,* Mindy? We fooled Big Jasper pretty good. He thinks Leo and I are manly men and that you are I are having much newlywed sex." He broke into a wide-toothed grin, looking for all the world like a big kid.

Sighing, Mindy patted his solid arm and nodded. "Yes, Rolf, you did a fine job. Your performance was so...dramatic...that it flabbergasted not only Big Jazz but Leo and me too." She smiled weakly.

"*Ja,* I can be very dramatic when I need to. Don't worry, if I can fool Big Jasper, I can fool your dreamship too. I have been practicing my Austrian accent."

"Oh good Lord. No, Rolf. Really, it's not necessary. You have to go. Now." Mindy shoved him again, which had about as much effect as trying to topple a brick wall.

"Archer's likely to be here any—" Inhaling an audible gasp, Mindy yanked Rolf into the house and slammed the door. "Damn it!" She hunched down into a squatting position, pulling Rolf down along with her.

Obviously dumbfounded, Rolf said, "What's wrong, Mindy?"

The doorbell rang and Mindy grasped Rolf's arm, digging her nails into the sleeve of his sport coat. "Shhh. He's here," she whispered, placing her finger to her lips. "We need to stay down here, quiet and out of sight."

"Who is here? Big Jasper?"

Mindy gave him a disbelieving look. "Haven't you been listening to anything I said?" she whispered. "Archer's here. He just pulled up. That's him at the door. He can't see you here. I could never explain it if he recognized you from last night. He thinks you and I are—"

The bell rang again, this time followed by a knock. Mindy held her finger to her lips in a shushing motion again. "If we're quiet, maybe he'll just go away."

"Ah, but that would be terrible, Mindy. Then you would miss your dreamship man." Bestowing a kind, gentle smile, Rolf patted her coiffed hair. "Don't worry, little one. Everything will be fine. Trust me." With that, he rose and opened the door before Mindy could stop him.

"No!" she squealed to no avail before coming face to knees with Archer.

Trust me? Trust me! My God, Rolf and Leo really are *made for each other*, Mindy thought as her heart slid down to her toes.

Archer looked astoundingly handsome in his dark suit and tie. "Hello," was all she could manage as she offered a dilapidated grin, raised her hand and wiggled her fingers.

"Uh...hi, Mindy. What are you doing down there?" Archer asked.

"Oh. I'm...looking for my earring." She patted her hands across the floor.

"You mean one of those?" Archer squatted, flicking the gold adornments on Mindy's bejeweled ears with his fingernails.

Mindy's hands flew to her ears and she laughed. "Well, what do you know? Always the last place you look." She laughed again as Archer assisted her to her feet.

"Ah, you must be Archer." Rolf grasped Archer's hand, pumping sturdily. At the same time, Cadbury eagerly greeted Archer by doing his best to crawl up the man's pant leg.

"I am Rolf Schwarzenegger, the rich, important, elderly traveler from Germany." Mindy discreetly kicked his leg and Rolf winced. "I mean *Austria*."

After petting Cadbury, Archer eyed the big, strapping, handsome young hunk. He turned his gaze on Mindy. "So this is the old guy you told me about earlier, huh?"

Mindy felt her face growing hot. She swallowed hard and cleared her throat. "Yes, well...he...uh...the interesting thing is that..." Her mind emptied as fast as a schoolroom at recess.

"Yes, young man," Rolf piped in. "I am much older than I look. Old enough even to be your papa." He winked at Mindy who wanted to wither and die right there on the spot.

"I take special vitamins, eat yogurt and wheat germ, and I work out. For this, I appear to have the childish body of a thirty-five-year-old." He beamed a smile, apparently satisfied Archer was going to buy his cockamamie story without batting an eye.

The expression across Archer's face was half grimace, half twisted smile, as though he wasn't sure whether to laugh or to spit something out. Miraculously, it seemed he hadn't recognized Rolf from the restaurant. Mindy sent up a silent prayer of thanks.

"Is this guy for real?" Archer finally said to Mindy, thumbing toward Rolf.

Mindy blanched as she heard one of Leo's nervous staccato giggles erupt from her lips. "I'm afraid so," she said, offering a sickly smile.

"What do you mean? *Ja*, sure, I am real." Rolf flexed his biceps. "Here, feel this muscle—like iron."

Mindy pressed Rolf's arm down. "Rolf, that's just a figure of speech."

"Oh. Sorry. I still have a little bit of trouble with my English."

Mindy held back a burst of incredulous laughter at his understatement. "Yes, Archer," she said, "Rolf's actually quite a bit older than he looks. Probably something in his genes."

Rolf grasped his suit pants, looking confused. "But I am not wearing my jeans, Mindy. I thought a suit would be better tonight."

Stone faced, Mindy indulged in a long blink. No use shooting him a look meant to kill. It would have little effect on Rolf. He was too busy trying to figure out the genes-jeans issue to notice Mindy's vexation.

"You look awfully familiar, Rolf. Have we met before?" Archer asked through a narrowed, searching gaze. "Someplace recently. Let me think..."

Panic infusing her cells, Mindy slid her fingers behind her back, crossing them.

"No! That was not me you saw at the restaurant last night," Rolf blurted.

"Oh God," Mindy said, letting her head fall against the front door with a thud. "God, God, God," she repeated, banging her head against the door with each repetition.

"Last night. That's it!" Archer practically shrieked as he jabbed a finger at the big German. "The restaurant! You're the face sucker!"

Rolf's features scrunched. "What is this face sucker?"

"For heaven's sake, Archer, don't be ridiculous." Reasonably certain her goose was cooked, Mindy struggled valiantly to salvage the budding relationship with the man of her dreams. "That wasn't Rolf. I mean, how could it be? I told you, he just flew in from Austria today."

"Do I look like an idiot, Mindy?" His chiding tone was steely as Archer crossed his arms over his chest.

"You just arrived today, right, Rolf?" Mindy coached, her smile faltering, the last remnants of confidence evaporating.

Looking flustered, Rolf licked his lips and leaned toward Mindy, cupping his hand against her ear.

"What should I say, Mindy?" he whispered a bit too loudly. "Ow!" he said, rubbing his calf where Mindy had just kicked him. "*Ja*! I just came here today from Austria. I was not the possible face sucker you saw last night." He gave Mindy an exaggerated wink.

Archer shifted, resting his weight on one leg. "There's something really fishy going on around here and I want to know what it is. You're not going to squirm out of it this time, Mindy. Got it?"

"I'm telling you, Archer, that wasn't Rolf you saw last night. That was...my cousin." Oh crap. She couldn't believe her own ears. Talk about desperation! She was a moron. An idiot. A feather-brained nincompoop.

Archer gawked at her, disbelief skewing his features.

Swallowing the lump in her throat, Mindy offered him a sad, sickly, hopeful smile.

"Of course." Raising his arms, Archer let them slap against his sides. "Thus the term, kissing cousins." His smile morphed into a disbelieving glare.

"Yes." She gave an enthusiastic nod. "Exactly. My cousin is the black sheep of the family. Dopey and overly amorous with all of his female cousins." She flashed a hopeful grin.

Archer studied Mindy before shifting his gaze to Rolf. He shook his head. "Nope. Uh-uh." He turned back to Mindy, while pointing at Rolf. "That's him. That's the guy I saw attached to you last night. Come on, what is this? What's going on?"

Rolf stepped forward. "Please, Archer, you must believe Mindy. It could not be me who was doing an attachment to Mindy, because I do not have sexual interest for women."

Archer cocked his head. "Huh?"

"Oh for heaven's sake, Archer," Mindy said. "Rolf is gay."

Archer gave the blue-eyed blond, who could have been a candidate for Mr. Universe, a skeptical appraisal. "It seems you've uncovered a great deal of personal information about your *client,* considering he just flew in from Austria today."

"Eh..." was Mindy's brilliant retort.

"Mindy speaks the truth," Rolf said. "Leo and I are very gay lovers..."

Mindy gasped and Archer's face froze.

"Archer," Mindy jumped in, "let me explain."

"There's nothing to explain. I fully understand the term *gay*, Mindy. However," he eyed the striking German again, "I'm not sure I believe it. I've seen the way this guy looks at you."

As Mindy opened her mouth to protest, the doorbell rang.

She stood stone still, wondering what further travesty awaited just outside her door.

Rolf reached for the doorknob and Mindy whapped his hand away. "Rolf, do *not* touch that doorknob."

"Allow me." Archer yanked the door open before Mindy could stop him.

"Howdy, young fella," Big Jazz said to Archer as he doffed his Stetson. "Is Mindy here?"

Mindy von Grettle proved to herself it was possible for a person to have a near death experience while standing in her foyer greeting guests.

Chapter 23

"THERE'S MY GIRL." Big Jazz picked Mindy up, swinging her around. "Y'all don't mind if I greet the little missus Texas style, do you?"

"The *missus*?" Archer nearly squeaked.

Cadbury barked and growled. He evidently didn't care for the big Texan getting so familiar with his mistress.

Archer looked from Big Jazz to Rolf to Mindy. "What the hell's going on here? Mindy, is this guy your husband?" he asked, motioning to Big Jazz.

"Certainly not." Mindy spit out the words in disgust. "Jasper, put me down this instant!"

Reveling in laughter, Big Jazz complied. "Nope, young fella." He slapped Archer roundly on the back. "I surely tried, but Mindy's heart was stolen by this nice foreign fella here." He nodded toward Rolf and Archer's eyes about popped out of his skull. Mindy gave in to a pained groan. "Name's Jasper Wilson, but everybody calls me Big Jazz. And you are?"

"Archer," he said absently. "Archer Pr—"

"Jasper!" Mindy shrieked before Archer could get the *Priest* part out.

All three men started.

She stepped between Archer and Big Jazz, clinging desperately to the hope that she could somehow salvage the whole sordid, twisted mess. "This is my friend, Archer. He owns a local winery."

"Wine?" Big Jazz gave Archer a lengthy appraisal. "Well, wine's fine for them rich and prissy fancy folk, and for the ladies, of course. But I say, if a man wants a real drink, there's nothing like a good slug of whiskey." Winking, Big Jazz held his hands up almost apologetically. "No offense, mind you, son."

"None taken." Archer shrugged. "To each his own. Now what was that you were saying about Mindy and Rolf?"

"I don't think I have any whiskey or wine in the house," Mindy interrupted, stalling for time, although, at this point, she didn't see how that really even mattered anymore. It was a lost cause.

"But I've got some Godiva chocolate liqueur, some Baileys, dark rum, and Kahlua. And chocolate syrup, of course. I'll mix them all together and you can try it. It's excellent."

The three men curled their lips in revulsion.

"Yup," Big Jazz went on, ignoring Mindy's desperate suggestion, "my little Mindy went and broke my heart when she married this lucky kraut-head here a while back."

"Married."

Mindy wasn't sure if the word Archer uttered was a question or a statement. All she knew was that his face reddened and he looked like he was about to explode, or fall over, or maybe strangle somebody. Maybe a little of each.

"I thought you said you and him were friends, Mindy," Big Jazz said, motioning to Archer and looking puzzled. "How come he don't know about you and Rolf gettin' hitched?"

"Yeah, Mindy. How come?" Archer asked, his voice deadly calm.

Mindy opened her mouth, but nothing came out.

"Oh I get it." Big Jazz nodded. "Guess the newlyweds are still keepin' it a secret. Cousin Leo said old Rolf here had some trouble coming into the country and they had to keep things quiet. Ain't that right, Mindy?"

Mindy's mouth still hung open silently. She ventured a glimpse at Archer, shuddering at his cold, brutal glare.

Life as she knew it was over. Finished. Kaput.

"Best part of all is they're expectin' a little bundle of joy from heaven," Big Jazz offered.

Covering her face, Mindy mumbled feebly, "Stick a fork in me...I'm done. Just take me now, Lord."

"Ain't that right, Rolf?" Big Jazz elbowed the German while reaching over to pat Mindy's belly.

Rolf had the same deer-in-the-headlights look on his face that Mindy expected she had.

"You're pregnant?" Archer's gaze locked on Mindy's midsection and he gaped. "So much for Rolf being gay," he said, pinning Mindy in place with a merciless gaze. "So that was a lie then too, huh, Mindy?"

"Gay!" Big Jazz pounced. "You mean a homo? What in the *hell* are you talkin' about, boy?"

"This guy," Archer said, motioning to Rolf, "and your cousin Leo. I thought they were a couple."

Still awaiting her visit from the Grim Reaper, Mindy uttered a pitiful squeak.

"Whoa! Now hold on there just a danged minute," Big Jazz roared, raising his hands in protest. "You best be careful, 'cause them are fightin' words where I come from." All Big Jazz needed was the set of horns on his head to look like a raging bull.

Nobody moved a muscle.

"Cousin Leo, a pansy?" Big Jazz shuddered. "Look, young fella, there ain't no way one of my own kin is a fairy, you got that? I don't know where you came up with such a harebrained notion, but there ain't nothin' further from the truth. Ya hear?" He gave Rolf's shoulder a pat. "Go ahead and tell him, Rolf."

Glancing from one person to the next, Rolf gulped air like a fish out of water. Mindy glimpsed beads of perspiration streaming in rivulets down his face and neck, soaking his collar.

Rolf cleared his throat. "Leo is the manliest, unflower-like man I have ever known," he insisted, head high and shoulders back. "He has abundant sex with many big-breasted women every day. He is not from another planet and he is not bent."

"Not bent?" Big Jazz removed his Stetson to scratch his head.

"He means Leo's straight," Mindy clarified, somewhat surprised at her apparent ability to comprehend Rolf's fractured English.

Archer turned to Mindy. It didn't take too much imagination to picture his head as a lit stick of dynamite, ready to detonate."

"Well, Mindy?" he said through clenched teeth.

This was all too surreal. Mindy almost felt as if she were floating above the entire scene. She wished to hell she could. Anything but to have to be right there, smack dab in the middle of this horrific mess.

The good news was that she couldn't imagine anything worse happening to her in this lifetime. Nothing.

And then the doorbell rang.

Big Jazz yanked the door open. "Howdy, Cousin Leo. You're just in time to join the party."

"I got your message to meet you here, Jasper. What's this all about?" Leo said, entering Mindy's foyer.

"You gotta set this here friend of Mindy's straight." He gestured toward Archer. "Somehow he's got the notion that you and Mindy's husband are homos. Come on in, cuz."

Mindy felt her brain crackle, crumble and fry, a moment before agonizing shards of red-hot panic shot through her entire being, splitting her skull and disintegrating her on the spot.

Aside from cringing when he saw Archer glaring back at him, Leo stood frozen, fixed to the spot like a statue. He didn't even giggle.

After a small eternity, he said, "Me? Gay? That's ridiculous, Jasper. Preposterous. You know better than that."

"Well, I thought I did." He eyed Leo suspiciously.

"Macho-man Leo is right, Big Jasper. He is ridiculous," Rolf assured, immediately scrambling to Leo's side and securing his arm around his shoulder. "He is the opposite to gay. He is manly and virile in his sex. He wishes he could have sex with Mindy every time he looks at her."

Everyone's attention was momentarily on Rolf, as they slanted him curious looks of wonder, trying to digest his odd assertion.

Mindy groaned. The poor guy was trying so hard to be of help that, regardless of what he'd just said, her heart twisted.

"Well, that ain't hard to believe," Big Jazz said. "I mean, who wouldn't want to have sex with Mindy once they get a gander at that sweet, juicy little body of hers? Heck, I've tried to often enough myself." He guffawed. "No offense, Rolf. In fact, just before you got here, Cousin Leo, we was just tellin' this here Archer fella all about our little Mindy havin' a blessed event soon."

With a swift look to Mindy and the others, a muffled *fuck* escaped Leo's lips.

"Hey, Archer," he said weakly. "How's it going?"

"You mean before or after I entered the Twilight Zone?" Archer responded. "Leo, what the hell's going on? Nobody here seems to know."

"Eh..."

"We've got an Austrian claiming to be your elderly client one minute," Archer said, "your lover the next and, finally, Mindy's husband and the father of her unborn child."

Wide-eyed with a panicked expression of dread across his features, Leo erupted into that atrocious giggle of his. "I can explain everything," Leo said quietly. "A little bit later. Trust me, Archer."

"Is it me, Leo?" Archer clapped his hands against his chest. "Am I the one who's nuts here?" Before Leo could answer, Archer laughed, conking the heel of his hand against his forehead. "Listen to me! I'm asking the nuttiest one in the bunch for logical answers. Oh yeah, I'm losing it. I'm definitely losing it."

Leo sidestepped toward Archer, trying to sling his arm around the man's shoulder but settling for just a hand instead because Archer was too tall.

"Excuse us for just a moment," Leo said, leading Archer away from Mindy, Rolf and Big Jazz.

"Yes," Mindy added, "excuse *us*." There was no way in hell she was about to let Leo get Archer alone so he could concoct yet another harebrained story.

"Archer," Leo said in a scheming whisper, "I guarantee all of this can be fully explained to your satisfaction. I, uh, I know it might seem a little odd—"

"A *little* odd?" Archer barked a laugh. "That's a gross understatement, Leo. What, are you guys a pack of wild swingers or wife-swappers or something? Is that what this is all about?" Mindy gasped at that. "You can count me out because I don't want any part—"

"How could you think such a thing, Archer?" Mindy asked.

Archer's response was a withering glance.

"No, of course we're not," Leo cut in, with a finger to his lips, shushing Archer. Yanking him closer, he whispered in a conspiratorial tone, "It's just that Mindy and I had to come up with a believable story to tell my cousin, Jasper, so he'd think I was this big macho guy. He can't find out I'm gay, Archer. He just can't."

"Right," Mindy chimed in. "And the rest of the story we came up with was to get Big Jazz to finally leave me alone once and for all, see?"

"No."

Licking his lips fretfully, Leo said, "Okay, look, just play along, Archer. I swear I'll explain everything as soon as Jasper leaves, okay? Just follow my lead."

"I suppose you're going to explain everything about the Boris and Natasha thing too."

"That? Oh," Leo waved his hand in a dismissive fashion, "that's easy."

"Go on," Archer said through a challenging smirk.

"Uh, well...go ahead and tell him, Mindy."

"Yes," Archer agreed. "Go ahead and tell me, Mindy."

"Eh...okay. You see, Leo and I were doing a costumed rehearsal for our skit."

Archer just gave her a blank look.

"For the first annual Persimmon Travel Mystery Dinner," Mindy explained.

"We're doing something like a live version of the old Rocky and Bullwinkle cartoon show," Leo added. "That's why we were Boris and Natasha."

"Uh-huh." Archer looked from Mindy to Leo and back again. "And you just happened to choose my sister's real estate office for the rehearsal. The same sister who detests Mindy. The one who makes Mindy gag, right?"

"Exactly." Leo grinned and nodded. "See? I told you it was easy to explain. Mindy and I will tell you about everything else later, Archer. Trust me." He gave Archer a reassuring pat on the back.

Returning his attention to Mindy, Leo gave her a pitiful *I-hope-you-don't-hate-me-too-much* smile. Funny, for some reason, she couldn't even muster the energy or inclination to glare at him anymore. It was as if she had somehow transcended beyond anger. Maybe she was losing her mind. Yes, that would be good. She could just lock herself away inside her head and never have to come out and face Archer Priest again.

She glanced up at Archer who, understandably bewildered, was mumbling to himself as he went back to join Rolf and Big Jazz. Then Mindy looked over at Rolf. The big well-meaning German had turned an odd shade of green and looked as though he wished he'd rather be on a slow boat to the Fatherland than embroiled in this mess. One glance at Big Jazz told Mindy the Texan was having a grand old time enjoying the madcap state of affairs.

"Mindy," Leo whispered, clasping her elbow. "Mindy, honey," he said again when she didn't respond.

"Hmmm?" Mindy was having a hard time concentrating. Being mired in this chaotic web of lies and deceit had taken its toll. She figured the hard drive of her brain had reached maximum capacity and was functioning on standby.

"I'm sorry, Min. I got Jasper's voicemail about him being on his way to your place too late to stop him." Leo did his best to smile, but his attempt was meager at best.

Freeing her elbow from his gasp, Mindy took Leo by the hand and led him back to the foyer to join the others.

"Excuse me, gentlemen, won't you?" she said with what she believed was a pleasant smile. "Just make yourselves at home and get comfortable. I have something to attend to." Humming mindlessly, she swept past the four men standing in her foyer and headed into the kitchen.

"Mindy?" Archer called after her. "Leo, what's wrong with her? She looks like she's zoned out." The kitchen was close enough for Mindy to hear him. She nodded in accord with his assumption.

"She's mega-stressed," Leo said. "We'll have a great laugh over it later. Trust me."

A moment later he was in the kitchen with Mindy.

With Cadbury panting attentively at her heels, Mindy poured Godiva chocolate liqueur into the biggest glass she could find. Baileys, Kahlua, and dark rum followed.

"Jesus, Mindy, you must have a good twelve ounces of booze in that glass," Leo noted. "What the hell are you doing?"

"Killing myself."

"With chocolate liqueur?"

"Can you think of a better way to go?" Unable to manufacture a caustic glare, she tendered a weary expression of defeat and resignation.

"But honey, you'll make yourself awfully sick before you die." Leo tried to take the glass from her. "You'll throw it all up."

With a firm hold on her glass, Mindy went to the refrigerator, retrieved a can of Hershey's chocolate syrup, pouring into her glass.

Slapping his hand to his face and groaning, Leo made another attempt to take the glass from Mindy.

Keeping the tumbler close to her chest, Mindy managed a threatening glare that dared Leo to interfere with her death-by-chocolate plans.

"Chocolate never makes me sick. If this doesn't kill me, I'll finish the job with that bottle of cheap, off-brand chocolate liqueur you foisted on me at Christmastime." She shuddered.

Setting the filled glass on the counter, away from Leo's reach, she dragged over a kitchen chair and stood on it, reaching for the small cabinet above the refrigerator. When she got down, she cradled a decorative cake tin like a precious treasure.

Mindy opened the tin and Cadbury became more attentive than ever as he sniffed the air and licked his chops.

"Aw, you don't want to do this, honey," Leo said, spying the cache of chocolate candy in the tin. "You've come much too far to backslide now. You've got more respect for yourself than that." He reached in to seize a chocolate kiss and Mindy slapped his hand away.

"Respect!? Bullshit. Did you hear what's going on in there?" She pointed toward the living room. "They're in there talking about God knows what, Leo. No, scratch that. Jasper's probably telling Archer about how Rolf supposedly pleasured me under the table in the restaurant!" She slapped her hand against the kitchen counter, rattling the liqueur bottles and her tumbler.

Leo cringed. "Look, Mindy, I—"

"My life is over, Leo." Pointing her index finger at the floor, Mindy twirled it slowly. "It's doing a slow, swirling flush down the toilet. And you, the person singly responsible for this entire catastrophe, have the gall to ask me about self-respect or fear of backsliding?"

Mindy took a deep breath then chugged a good portion of the viscous chocolate mixture before turning back to Leo and heaving a shrug.

"Since my life is ruined," she unwrapped a Snickers bar, "why not eat my way back into the oblivion of obesity? I'll never be able to face Archer Priest again as long as I live after tonight anyway." Shoving as much of the bar into her mouth as she could, Mindy chewed furiously.

"Did I hear my name?" Archer said, coming around the corner.

Mindy eyed Archer and took a swig from her gargantuan tumbler of chocolate elixir. "Go away," she mumbled around her mouthful of chocolate.

"What is that?" Archer gestured to her glass. "It looks like maple syrup."

"Worse. Chocolate liqueur, some other liqueuers, and rum," Leo answered with a tsk. "Laced with chocolate syrup. Followed by a Snickers chaser."

"Jesus." Archer shuddered. "Mindy, you'll make yourself sick with all that sweet syrupy stuff. Not to mention what you'll be doing to...to your baby," he said in a strained voice.

"Baby? Hah!" Mindy glugged again from her glass.

"Archer," Leo said, "you don't understand. Mindy's not really preg—" Leo stopped abruptly when Big Jazz came into the room.

"Uh, Archer's right, Mindy, you don't want to harm the baby." Leo punctuated the sentence with that damned infernal giggle of his.

Mindy curled her lip at Leo. "You're worse than slug-slime, Leo. After my suicide-by-chocolate, I swear to God, I'm coming back to haunt you until the day you die." She swigged from her tumbler again. "I'll gleefully make your life a living hell."

She walked over to Leo, who had that familiar panicky grin plastered on his face, and jabbed her finger hard against his chest. "Don't you *dare* break forth with that maddening giggle of yours again, you hear? And never, ever, think about uttering the words *Trust Me* again. Ever!"

"Feisty little lady you got yourself there, Rolf." Big Jazz elbowed the German, who'd come into the kitchen on Big Jazz's heels.

"*Ja*, my sexy little pregnant wife Mindy is—"

"Shut up, Rolf," Mindy blurted, pointing at him as she downed the last of the liqueur and smacked her lips. "You've already put both feet in your mouth tonight, there's no more room in there."

Immediately clamping his mouth shut, Rolf looked seriously wounded—forlorn, in fact.

"Aw hell. Now see what you made me do, Leo?" Mindy said.

"Me?"

"Yes, you. The poor sweet guy is just trying to help me out of this screwy situation, the one you hatched in that miniscule brain of yours," she knocked on his head, "because he cares for you so much." Mindy's words slurred and she swayed. "And now you made me go and hurt Rolf's feelings. I'm sorry, Rolf. You didn't deserve that."

"I think I'm missin' somethin' here." Big Jazz frowned. "What are y'all talking about, Mindy? You don't mean to tell me that there really *is* something to that hogwash about Cousin Leo and this foreign fella bein'...bein'... Shoot. I can't even bring myself to say it. It makes my belly ache just thinkin' about it."

"Of course not, Jasper," Leo said. "I'm just as straight as you are. Isn't that right, Archer?" He shot a pleading look Archer's way.

Heaving a deep breath, Archer looked at Leo for a small eternity. "Sure," he said finally. He turned to Big Jazz, grinning and clapping the Texan on the shoulder. "I was just joshing with you. Leo's a man's man if ever I saw one. A real lady killer."

Big Jazz looked mighty relieved as he swiped his hand across his forehead and gave forth with a resounding *whew!*

Mouthing a silent *thank you* to Archer, Leo smiled. "Mindy didn't mean anything, Jasper," he said. "It's just the alcohol talking. She gets like this when she drinks." Leo made a show of tsking and shaking his head in dismay. "Poor girl just rambles nonsensically."

"I most certainly do not!" Mindy stated emphatically.

"Yes you do," Leo and Archer chorused back to her.

Mindy gasped. "I resent that, gentlemen. I can handle my alcohol just as well as any of you can."

"Yeah, I forgot," Archer said with a gleam in his eye. "I've caught a glimpse of your amazing fortitude a few times now, as I recall."

"I only got a teensy drunk those other times, Mr. Smarty Pants, because I didn't have any experience with alcohol then." She hiccupped and giggled.

"Like you do now," Archer said.

Mindy nodded confidently. "Exactly." She hiccupped again. "I am a cosmopolitan woman of the world now."

"You know how novice drinkers are, Jasper," Leo said. "Mindy rambles when she's had too much to drink. Like I said before, pay no attention to her."

Big Jazz nodded. "I understand." He chuckled. "Ladies, especially, can't hold their liquor none too well." He turned to Mindy, who was still swaying. "Mindy, honey, I gotta run. I just wanted to stop over here on my way to pick up that cute little filly you and Cousin Leo fixed me up with."

He winked and Mindy knew what was coming next. The final nail in her coffin.

She snatched the bottle of Baileys and turned the neck upside down, chugging from the bottle before adding some to her glass.

"Get ready, Archer," she said. "Because here comes the really good part." Frowning, she splayed her fingers, staring intently as she flexed them repeatedly. "Look...I have bendy fingers," she said with a hiccup. "Hmph...must be the chocolate." She giggled, then frowned again as she caught Archer's gazed locked on her. "Don't look at my bendy fingers, Archer, because you know why?"

Chuckling, Archer put his arm around Mindy's shoulder, rubbing her arm in a comforting manner. "No, why?"

"Because you're going to hate me forever as soon as you hear the good part. Forever. Until eternity." She flexed her fingers some more. "Amen."

"Sweetheart, I might be thoroughly confused and kind of angry, but I promise you I'll never hate you, Mindora von G. Ever. Amen." He watched her fingers opening and closing. "What are you doing with your hands?"

"Checking to see if I'm still alive." Teetering in place, she examined her outstretched fingers for another moment, opening and closing one finger at a time. "Well, it appears my hands and fingers are still working, which means I'm not dead yet. Cheers!" She gulped back half of what she'd poured out, following it with another bite of Snickers.

Archer groaned. "Aw, Mindy, I don't even want to think about how you're going to feel in the morning."

"No problem. I will feel nothing because I will be dead...from *chocolatcide.*" She took another bite of chocolate, making satisfied little sounds as she savored it. "What a way to go!"

Big Jazz guffawed. "She surely is cute and funny when she's tipsy, ain't she?" He elbowed Rolf. "I think you'll be gettin' lucky tonight, Rolf. Know what I mean?"

The silence in the room was deafening. Except for Mindy's hiccup and giggle.

Big Jazz shrugged and continued, "Anyways, I just wanted to thank Mindy and Cousin Leo for makin' me the happiest cowpoke alive, that's all." Winking, he pointed an imaginary pistol at Leo and Mindy.

Licking his lips nervously, Leo placed his hand against his cousin's back. "Why don't I walk you out to your car and you can tell me all about it," he said.

"Heck, no, cousin. I want Mindy to hear this too—whether the little filly is tipsy or not." He laughed. "Now I know this might sound like fast work, but when true love hits, it hits fast and hard, I always say."

"Drumroll please!" Mindy said, pretending to play her imaginary set of drums. "Get ready, Archer, cuz here it comes."

"Yup," Big Jazz went on, "Britney and I spent the afternoon together gettin' to know each other—real good, if ya know what I mean." He elbowed Archer in the ribs and winked. "Leo, Mindy, I want the two of you to be the first to know that I've decided to ask the little lady to be my bride and move to the USSR with me."

"What?" Leo gasped. "After only knowing each other a few hours?" Big Jazz nodded enthusiastically. "Well son of a bitch," Leo muttered, "that was easier than I thought."

"What's that, cousin?"

"Nothing. Forget it, Jasper." Leo grinned. "I'm thrilled for you, cousin. Thrilled!"

"We're shipping Britney to Russia!" Mindy shouted, hoisting her tumbler in the air and taking another swig. "Whooppee!"

"Congratulations to you and Britney, Big Jasper!" Rolf grasped the Texan's hand and pumped hard. "I hope you will be very happy together."

"Thanks, Rolf. Once me and my new lady get set up out there, I'll have to try that sexy little pleasuring-under-the-table trick you were doin' to Mindy at the restaurant last night." Big Jazz jiggled his eyebrows. "She certainly seemed to be enjoyin' that."

Mindy watched the color drain from Leo's face, while Archer uttered an imaginative string of obscenities and pounded his fist against the back of a chair. It didn't bother her a bit. She'd be dead soon anyway.

"So it *was* you making out with Mindy last night, after all," Archer said to Rolf.

Rolf's eyes nearly jiggled as the poor guy nervously looked from Archer to each of the others and stammered.

"Yup, that was Rolf all right." Big Jazz motioned toward the German. "Them two lovebirds couldn't keep their hands off each other all night. Whew, yes indeed, they were goin' at it hot and heavy."

"How much time does it take to drink yourself into a coma?" Mindy asked. She looked skyward. "Hey, come on, God. Why am I still here? Take me. Take me now."

Archer looked from Rolf to Mindy and threw his hands into the air. "That's it. I'm outta here." He turned and started to walk to the front door.

"No! Wait," Rolf called.

"Forget it, Rolf." Archer held up his hand and kept walking. "I'm done."

Rolf grabbed Archer's arm and yanked. Archer was a big man, but no match for Rolf's mega-muscled physique. One mighty tug, and Rolf had tossed Archer right back where he'd been standing a moment before, like he was a rag doll.

"Shit," Archer said with an expression of flat-out amazement.

"It is not what you think, Archer," Rolf offered. "Please...I cannot let Mindy's dreamship sail away. You must let me explain...later. You will stay, *ja*?" Without waiting for an answer, he gave Archer a firm enough push so that Archer fell back and plopped onto one of the kitchen chairs.

"Looks like I'm staying," Archer muttered.

"It doesn't matter anymore, Rolf," Mindy said. "But thanks for trying. And as for you, Archer, go ahead. Leave. See if I care. But when you walk out that door, just remember, you'll never have chocolate-chip-cookie-sex again, ever."

"Aha." Leo slanted Mindy a curious look. "Seems you've been holding out on me, Mindy."

"You guys are a barrel of fun with all your kiddin' around but," Big Jazz glanced at his steer-horn-design watch, "I've gotta go or else I'll be late. I got a big evenin' planned." He clapped his hands together and kicked the air. "Hot diggity-dog!"

Retrieving a business card from his jacket pocket, Big Jazz held it out it to Leo. "Hey, cousin, maybe you can help me out here. I'm driving myself tonight, so I need some directions to the little lady's house. She wrote her address on here and, for the life of me, I can't figure how to get there from Mindy's place."

As the card made its way from Big Jazz to Leo, Archer caught sight of it and gasped. He grabbed the card and studied it.

"Uh-oh..." Leo muttered.

"Britney Priest," Archer read in astonishment. "This is Britney's business card. *This* is the Britney you've been talking about?"

"Well, sure. Dang, that's what I been trying to tell y'all. She's the sweet little filly I been goin' on about all night. You know her?"

"Know her? She's my sister."

Grasping her tumbler, Mindy slid down against the side of the kitchen cabinets, plunking her butt unceremoniously on the kitchen floor. She slurped what was left of the Baileys in her glass, fighting off Cadbury, who wanted his share.

"Bye-bye, Britney," she mumbled, waving.

"Well, fancy that! Ain't this a small world." Big Jazz whacked Archer on the back. "So then you must know Leo here from the days when him and your sister were a hot item, huh?"

Archer's jaw dropped as his stunned gaze slid to Leo.

"Oh God," Leo managed through a pained groan. Slapping his hand to his face, he peeked at Archer through spread fingers.

"Aw, don't worry none, Archer, I know it's all supposed to be hush-hush," Big Jazz said, "so I ain't about to spill the beans. Heck, sometimes former lovers end up despisin' each other like that. I promise I won't never let on to your sister that Leo and Mindy set her and me up together."

Cocking his head, Archer's eyebrows arched with interest. "They did that, huh?" His gaze shifted to the guilty parties.

"Bada bing bada boom!" Mindy called out, followed by her making a crashing cymbals sound.

"Terrific, ain't it?" A broad grin spread across Big Jazz's features. "'Course, I know Britney and Mindy don't get along none too well cause of sharin' the same husband. Funny how things work, ain't it?"

"It's getting funnier by the minute," Archer assured him as his previously perplexed expression morphed into an amused smirk.

"Cousin Leo is Britney's former lover and Mindy is Britney's dead husband's ex-wife." Big Jazz clearly pondered the thought before adding, "Whew, things sure do get mighty complicated."

"With good old Cousin Leo orchestrating things," Archer gave Leo a side-eye glance, "you can bet on it."

"Uh-oh, Leo," Mindy uttered in a failed attempt at a whisper. "Now Archer knows about our big secret plan to ship Britney to Russia."

Leo grabbed another Snickers bar from the tin, unwrapped it and shoved it at Mindy. "Here, stuff this in your piehole and keep quiet." He let forth with a giggle as Archer studied him.

Looking contemplative, Archer stroked his jaw before turning to Big Jazz.

"Hey, Jasper—"

"*Big Jazz.*"

"Right." Archer gave an indifferent shrug. "Were you by any chance at my sister's real estate office this afternoon, driving a Cadillac with a giant steer horn hood ornament?"

"Sure thing, son. Ain't that Caddy a real honey? You should hear the horn. Plays the first few bars of the 'The Yellow Rose of Texas' plain as day."

"Definitely one of a kind," Archer agreed. "I'm curious. Why were you at the real estate office?"

Leo jumped in quickly. "He was there because—"

"Nope." Archer's hand shot up like a crossing guard. "I want to hear it from your cousin, Leo, not you."

"I was afraid of that," Leo muttered.

"It was all Cousin Leo's idea."

"Gee," Archer said, "what a surprise."

"Kinda killed two birds with one stone," Big Jazz continued. "I needed someone to take care of my real estate business before I go to live with them commies in the USSR, and I also needed someone to replace the gapin' hole little Mindy left in my heart when she went and married Rolf. Cousin Leo was kind enough to tell me about this little filly he used to bed." Big Jazz paused. "No disrespect intended to your sister, Archer."

"I understand," Archer said with a nod.

"Anyway, Cousin Leo thought we'd be perfect for each other. And damned if the boy wasn't right. Yeehaa!"

"Yeehaa!" Mindy echoed from the floor. "Give that man a Snickers bar!"

"The added bonus," Big Jazz continued, "is that I hear tell your sister's a sharp little cookie in real estate."

"That she is." A slow grin inched across Archer's lips. "Believe it or not, I think I'm actually beginning to understand what's going on here." A moment later, Archer broke into a rip-roaring bout of laughter. He looked at Leo, who was positively green, and then at Mindy, who was green also, but for entirely different reasons, and he laughed harder.

"Operation Buh-bye Britney," Archer said through his laughter. "Brilliant! I love it."

Mindy and Leo whipped their heads toward Archer and chorused, "You do?"

Rolf expelled a whooshing sigh of relief. "This is good. Everything is happy and okay now, *ja*?" he asked hopefully.

Archer wiped the tears of laughter from his eyes. "You," he said, wagging an outstretched finger at Rolf, "*Mr. Schwarzenegger*, still have some explaining to do. And I can't wait to hear the details." Archer turned back to Big Jazz. "Leo was absolutely right, Big Jazz. I can't think of anyone who'd be more compatible with my sister than you, ol' buddy."

He placed his arm around the Texan's shoulder and gave him a buddy hug. "The two of you were definitely made for each other. An ideal pairing if ever there was one." His grin was so wide his face could hardly contain it. "How long will you be living in Russia?"

"Oh, 'least five years I'm bettin'. They're letting me have the palace for as long as I want it. I just hope your sister sees fit to say yes to my marriage proposal."

"Did you say palace?" Archer asked.

"Yup, they're settin' me up real spiffy, servants and the whole shebang. Them Cossacks know they better treat Big Jazz real good, else he'll take his millions of American dollars right back to the good ol' U. S. of A."

"Does my sister know she'd be living in a palace out there? And that you're a multimillionaire?"

"Billionaire, boy," Big Jazz corrected proudly. "You should have seen the way that little filly's eyes lit up real big and sparkly when she heard that."

"I'll just bet they did." Archer laughed. "Don't worry. If I know my sister, she'll say yes faster than—"

"A Texan can guzzle a keg of moonshine."

"Exactly what I was going to say." Archer nodded.

"Well, hot diggity-dog! Reckon that means you and me'll be family, huh, brother?"

"Yup, I guess it does. Can't tell you how much I'm looking forward to that," Archer assured. "But you can't tell my sister that I know about any of this, Big Jazz. We don't want to get her dander up and have her run out on you like Mindy did, do we...brother?"

"Hell no." Big Jazz stepped around to where Mindy was sitting, bent down and said, "Pardon the profanity, Mindy."

She graced him with a wide, vacant, inebriated smile and nodded. "You are hereby pardoned."

Turning back to Archer, he continued, "I understand how touchy these things can be. Don't worry, your sister Britney ain't never gonna know that you and me met each other here tonight. What the little lady don't know ain't gonna hurt her, right?" He winked at Archer.

"Right." Archer winked back, elbowing Big Jazz in the ribs.

"Right," Mindy echoed gleefully and then hiccupped. "Buh-bye, Britney!"

Chapter 24

Leo

"OKAY, SEE YA, Jasper," Leo called to his cousin as Big Jazz walked to his car. He couldn't believe the big homophobic baboon was finally out of the house. "Don't forget to call me right away and let me know if Britney accepts your proposal. I've got my fingers crossed for you, buddy!"

"Sure as shootin'," Big Jazz replied, aiming invisible six shooters at Leo. "You'll be the first to know, cousin." Once behind the wheel, he blew the car's horn, treating Leo and the entire neighborhood to a few bars of "The Yellow Rose of Texas."

Leo cringed. He couldn't believe Jasper had insisted on giving him that monstrosity of a car when he left for Russia, as a thank-you gift for hooking him up with Britney.

"This honey's gonna be all yours, cousin, faster than a jackrabbit running from a twister."

"I can't wait, Jasper. I'm having heart palpitations just thinking about it."

Flashing a toothy grin, Big Jazz depressed the horn again.

Grinning, Leo nodded his faux-appreciation and gave his cousin a hearty thumbs-up sign. At the same time he muttered beneath his breath, "So long, you racist, bigoted, moronic throwback. You and that little bitch deserve each other." Sporting a self-satisfied smile, he waited until Big Jazz's gaudy, steer-horn-bedecked Cadillac pulled away from the curb before closing the door.

With a sigh of relief, Leo brushed his palms together, as if wiping the entire catastrophe from his hands. "Well, that's that. I knew it would be a cinch." Still grinning from ear-to-ear, he turned, ready to engage in a celebratory little jig, only to find Archer standing a foot away from him.

Arms folded across his chest and a no-nonsense look blazing in his eyes, Archer glared at him.

Handling the situation with his usual aplomb, Leo giggled.

"I think I've got this thing pretty well pieced together," Archer said. "But now you're going to fill me in on all the particulars."

"Sure, Archer, sure. Absolutely." Licking his lips, Leo glanced at his watch. "Hey, what do you know about that?" He chuckled. "I'm late for an appointment. Sorry, gotta go. Call me, we'll do lunch." He reached for the doorknob.

"You're not going anywhere, buddy." Archer seized Leo's arm, steering him back into the family room off the kitchen.

"But my appointment—"

"But nothing. It's after eleven o'clock. There *is* no appointment, so don't even start with me, Leo. The four of us are going to sit here all night if we have to until I get the whole story. Understand?"

"Yeah but, Archer, I—" Leo winced as Archer strengthened his grip. "Okay, okay! You don't have to use brute force. I'm an easygoing kind of guy. I'll tell you anything you want to know."

"That's better," Archer said as they turned the corner. "I don't want to hear any of your elaborate tall tales either. Understand?"

Breathing an audible gasp of mock indignation, Leo clapped a hand to his chest. "Why, Archer, are you suggesting I've been less than truthful with you?"

"I'm suggesting you're a bona fide liar and pretender of the utmost magnitude. In other words, I'm wise to you, Leo."

"Utmost magnitude, huh?" Leo looked up at Archer, cocked his head and flashed his most charming grin. "Thanks for the compliment. I appreciate that."

Archer opened his mouth to speak, paused and broke into laughter. "You're lucky you're so damned likeable, my friend."

"Just keep my likeability quotient in mind while I fill you in on all the details, okay?" Leo said. When they reached the entrance to the family room, he put a finger to his lips and nudged Archer back to keep them hidden.

"Why are we hiding?" Archer asked, annoyance evident in his voice.

"Because Rolf and Mindy are alone in there. Now you'll be able to see for yourself that there's absolutely nothing going on between them," Leo responded. "Come on, let's take a peek."

They leaned forward just enough to catch a glimpse, only to find Rolf at the far side of the room, holding Mindy aloft in his arms, cradling her close.

"Oh Rolf..." Mindy sighed, resting her head against his massive chest.

Archer and Leo exchanged questioning looks. Leo clapped his hand over his mouth to stifle a rising nervous giggle.

"You cannot sleep on the floor, Mindy." Rolf deposited Mindy on the loveseat. "You rest here now. You will feel better soon." He bent to give her a kiss on the forehead.

"You're wonderful, Rolf," she slurred, patting his chest. "You know that?"

"*Danke*, Mindy. I like you very much too."

"It's too bad you're gay. Why are all the good guys always gay?" She frowned. "Except for Leo. He's not a good guy. He's a troublemaker. An evil elf."

"Elf?" Leo whispered to Archer. "I'm not that short."

"Leo doesn't mean to be a gay elf, Mindy. He tries very hard to do the right thing. He loves you like a brother. Leo is a good man with a good heart. He is just a little bit *verrückt*."

Mindy's features screwed. "Ver who?"

Rolf frowned. "In English...in English..." he muttered to himself, clearly searching for the best translation. "Ah, *crazy*. It means crazy," he explained. "Cuckoo." Grinning, he tapped his temple for further clarification.

"Amen to that." Archer laughed and Leo elbowed him.

"Leo needs somebody like me," Rolf continued, "to take good care of him. To protect him and keep him on the outside of trouble. And I need Leo too. He makes me feel *glücklich* inside. Happy," he translated.

"So, that was on the level?" Archer whispered to Leo. "About you and Rolf being a couple?"

"Yeah." Leo beamed a proud smile. "I feel *glücklich* to the max when I'm with him." He winked. "Come on." Tugging on Archer's sleeve, he led the way to the loveseat.

"Are you still with us, Mindy?" Leo asked. "Or have you given up the ghost and gone to the great beyond?"

"Dead or alive, I'm not speaking to you," she answered.

"Everything is good with Big Jasper, *ja*? He does not suspect we are lovers?"

"Whew! Yeah." Leo made an exaggerated wipe of his brow. "Thanks to Archer. I really appreciate you going along with things and not giving me away to my cousin, Archer. It would have been ugly, trust me."

"Ugh!" Mindy slapped her hands over her ears. "I told you never to say those words again, Leo!"

"I'm afraid I wouldn't trust you as far as I could throw you, Leo," Archer said, chuckling. "But I know what you mean. Your good ol' boy cousin sounds intensely homophobic."

"You have *no* idea." Leo shuddered. "The man has a zero tolerance policy. He'd make my life a living hell."

"He'd have to get in line," Mindy muttered.

"*Ja*, Big Jasper thinks gay men should be chopped into sausages," Rolf added. "Then sent on a rocket to another planet." He yanked Leo into a buddy hug. "That's why we must act very macho when Big Jasper is around. It is also why I, how did you say it? Why I was a *face sucker* to Mindy at the restaurant."

Placing his hand on Archer's arm, Rolf transmitted an earnest expression of honesty. "Believe me, Archer. I did not enjoy making sexy kisses with Mindy. It was only my duty to do it."

"Hey!" Mindy propped herself up on the cushioned arm of the loveseat.

"Don't get your garters in a knot, Mindy," Leo said. "You know Rolf didn't mean it that way."

"I'm not wearing any garters. No more grandma underwear either. Anybody wanna see my brand new fancy lace underpants?"

"*Ja*, sure, I would like to see them, Mindy."

Archer elbowed Rolf in the gut. "No you wouldn't."

"Ow. I was just trying to be good manners."

"I'll show you my new underpants later, Rolf," Leo offered with a wink as he patted Rolf's arm. "And just in case you're wondering, Archer, no, they're not lace." He chuckled.

"Whoa." Archer held his hands aloft. "That would definitely come under the heading of TMI, pal."

Rolf cocked his head and opened his mouth. Before he could ask, Leo explained, "It stands for *too much information*."

Giggling, Mindy bent her knees and inched inch her dress up her thighs. "I bought my new bra and panties just for our date tonight, Archer. They're see-through and they come off real easy. They have easy-release tabs." She hiccupped.

"Mindy," Rolf said. "I think maybe this is TMI, pal."

"And that's not all," Mindy continued. "Want to hear a secret?" She brought her fingers to her lips. "Shhhh...the panties I'm wearing are *very* naughty."

"Uh-oh," Leo said.

"They're crotchless," Mindy whispered. "It's all part of my sneaky master seduction plan, Archer."

"Is that so?" Archer raised an eyebrow in amusement. "I'd love to have a look...later."

"Mindy, you wanton harlot," Leo teased, clapping her knees together and tugging her dress back into place.

"Wanton...ooh, I like that. It sounds a lot better than frigid. Besides," Mindy hiccupped, "I really don't think a frigid woman could perform chocolate chip cookie sex the way I did, right, Archer?" A giggle gushed forth. "I don't think I was frigid during our missionary sex either, was I, Archer?"

"Nope. Leo's right, sweetheart. You're definitely a wanton harlot." He covered his face with his hand, laughing. "And you make a mean batch of chocolate chip cookies too," he assured.

Leo raised his hands and blinked. "I'm dying to ask but I won't."

"I don't understand this chocolate chip cookie sex," Rolf said. "Can I ask questions?"

"No," Leo and Archer chorused.

"It's a secret," Mindy said, her finger to her lips. "Isn't it, Archer?"

"Just barely."

"Archer, you just let me know when you want to see my sexy new undies and I'll show them to you. Okay? If you want, I can even do another striptease."

"That's a deal," Archer agreed. "But only if you hum your own background stripper music again."

"She didn't," Leo said with mock astonishment.

"She most certainly did," Archer confirmed.

"After that, Archer, we can try all the rest of those sexual positions you were talking about and decide which ones we like best."

A gleam in his eye, Leo elbowed Archer. "Oh you dog. You rascal, you."

"Definitely TMI, pal," Rolf said, clearly intent on getting plenty of mileage out of his newest favorite American phrase.

All eyes turned to Rolf as his stomach offered a ferocious growl.

"Sorry." Patting his abs, Rolf gave a sheepish smile. "I'm a growing boy. I need food. I think it is all the talk about cookies."

"I'm starving too," Leo said. "Let's order a couple pizzas."

"Sounds good to me," Archer said. "The three of you pranksters can spill your guts while we eat."

"What is *spill your guts*?" Rolf asked.

"He means confess," Leo explained. "Fess up, come clean. Tell the truth."

Rolf wagged a finger at Leo. "See? Didn't I tell you it is always best to tell the truth? Then you don't have to giggle and spill your guts."

"You're right, Rolf. I've learned my lesson. I'm a changed man. From now on, my name will be synonymous with honesty." Leo made a virtuous stance with one hand on his heart and the other held in oath.

Mindy, Archer and Rolf looked at each other and laughed.

Joining the laughter, Leo shrugged. "Okay, so maybe it'll take me a while, but with Rolf's good influence I have a pretty good chance."

"All the lies were for a very good reason." Mindy raised her arms, wiggling her fingers toward Archer in invitation. He sat on the loveseat beside her and she wrapped her arms around his waist, resting her head in his lap.

"I did it because I'm in love with you, Archer," she said, before indulging in a lion-worthy yawn and drifting off to sleep.

Mindy

"OH THIS IS NICE." MINDY cracked her eyes open, realizing her head was resting on Archer's chest, and he had his arm around her. "I'm having one of those wonderful dreams again." She splayed her fingers over his chest, purring as her eyelids fluttered shut again.

"Nope."

"Archer?" Mindy felt the vibration in his chest as he spoke. "Is that really you?"

"In the flesh." He stroked his fingers through her hair, sifting the curls.

Struggling to come out of her fog, Mindy fixed her gaze on him. "Wait a minute..." She remembered something about Archer making Leo confess. The memory made her wince. "No. You can't be here. I remember now. I committed chocolatcide because you hate me for telling all those lies and trying to get rid of your sister."

Archer chuckled. "You made me damn angry there for a while, Mindy, but no, I don't hate you." He brushed a kiss across her lips.

She peered at Archer dreamily. "Then I've died and gone to heaven." Snuggling close to him, she closed her eyes again, relishing the delicious feeling of closeness, even if it wasn't real. "Thank you, God. Please don't ever let me wake up."

"You're not in heaven, babe, you've been asleep here in your own bed for a few hours." Archer tucked the ringlets of her hair that had fallen over her eye behind her ear. "Although, now that I've had a chance to see those sexy undies of yours, maybe it is heaven, after all."

Mindy's eyes popped open and she looked around, recognizing her bedroom. Then she lifted the sheet and gasped. "I'm in my underwear. How did that happen?"

"It wasn't easy. You were dead weight. The guys helped me get you up the stairs, undressed and under the covers."

Mindy gasped. "They saw me in my secret, see-through lace bra and panties?" Slipping off Archer's chest, she hunched down on the mattress and clutched the sheet to her throat. "Oh my God."

"Actually, you'd already given us a good glimpse of those wicked panties while you were still downstairs on the loveseat."

"That's ridiculous, Archer, I—" Brazen loose-legged images floated across her mind and she remembered. Covering her face with her hand, she groaned. "Ohmigod."

"Mmm-hmm. You were quite the little vixen. Thanks to you, I've had a hard-on for so long I think I've broken a personal record."

Her thoughts a blur, Mindy's mind focused on Big Jazz and she groaned. "Please, please tell me Big Jazz wasn't there when I was—" The mournful sound she let out this time was louder and significantly more pained.

"Nope. He'd already left."

"Thank God." She focused on Archer's almost naked body. "You're in your underpants too."

"Yes. But I managed to get that way all by myself." He laughed. "I figured once you woke up you might want to seduce me, so I thought I'd make things easier for you."

"Archer?"

"Hmm?"

"Did, um...did Leo tell you the truth? About everything?" She was reasonably certain he hadn't, because if he had, Archer would have been long gone by now.

Propping up against the pillows with his hands behind his head, Archer smiled, a knowing gleam in his eye. Actually, it was more of a shit-eating grin than a smile.

"You mean how you guys concocted that whole half-baked scheme to ship my sister off to a foreign country so you could charm that hot body of yours into my bed without her interference?"

Mindy winced. "Gee, do you think you could make it sound any more sordid?"

"Leo told me everything, from how he tricked you into going to my winery, to the whole deal with Big Jazz, and the scheme behind the Boris and Natasha masquerade. He also explained how everything was his idea and you were basically an unwilling participant."

"That's true! And you believed everything he told you?"

Archer gave Mindy an *are-you-kidding?* look. "Hell yeah. It's too ridiculous and farfetched to be a lie."

Mindy was flabbergasted. Dumbfounded. "You're not angry about us trying to get rid of Britney?"

"Angry?" Archer broke into laughter. "I've been trying to think of a legal way to get rid of my sister since we were kids. I told Leo I thought his plan was pretty ingenious. A bit convoluted and probably unnecessary, but brilliant all the same. Wish I'd thought of it myself."

"Well I'll be damned."

"You should also know that Leo offered to stay here with you tonight. He told me that, contrary to what I've witnessed, ahem, *several* times," Archer lifted an eyebrow and smirked, "you're not a drinker. He was worried about you. Of course, he also feared for his life. He was pretty sure you'd kill him when you woke up."

"Leo's perceptive if nothing else," Mindy said, fairly certain she would have done bodily harm to her boss if he was there instead of Archer.

"I told him I wanted to be here when you opened your eyes so you'd know everything is okay between us."

"Is it? Okay, I mean?"

"Yes," Archer raised a chastising finger, "but that doesn't mean I'm particularly happy about all the lies."

"I'm sorry, Archer. I really am."

"I know. You couldn't help it," Archer said, the same smug smile taking hold. "Because you're madly in love with me."

Mindy gasped. Bolting upright, she stared down at him, feeling her face redden. Tempted to scrape that self-satisfied smile off his handsome kisser, she said, "No I'm not. Did Leo tell you that?"

"Nope. You did. *I did it because I love you, Archer*," he said, in a bad soprano imitation of her voice. "Sound familiar? Besides, Rolf confirmed it when he told me I'm your *dreamship*."

She sat there gathering her thoughts, trying to recall exactly how much of an ass she'd made of herself earlier. "Oh," she said finally. "I guess I did say that. Although I never said *madly*." Actually, she wasn't all that sure about that. "Did I?"

"No, I tacked that on because I figured you had to be head-over-heels in love with me to go to such mindboggling extremes to win me over. But then, I *am* quite a catch."

"Of all the egotistical—" Mindy slapped his chest and Archer *ooophed*. "And now you're mocking me for saying that I love you. How gallant. Well, for your information, Mr. Priest, that was just the alcohol talking. I didn't mean a word of it."

"Yes you did."

"No. It's not love. Just lust."

"Bullshit. Admit it. You're crazy about me. You can't live without me." He grabbed her hand, placed it over his heart, then dragged her fingers down, tracing his hard pecs and abs, stopping just inside the waistband of his shorts. "Just the feel of my skin against yours makes your lovesick heart go pitter-pat and that shiny pink clit of yours quiver."

"Hah!" As her heart went pitter-pat and her clit quivered, she tore her hand away, turning her back to Archer. Damn if he didn't have her pegged. She'd obviously made a fool of herself fawning all over him and the bastard was getting his kicks out of making her squirm.

"Mindy?"

"Don't talk to me. You're as bad as Big Jazz. Arrogant, insufferable—"

"I love you."

"I said don't—" Stopping short, Mindy turned around and gaped at Archer. "You do?"

"I'm afraid so. Believe me, I've tried like hell not to fall for you but, my dear Mindora von G, I am thoroughly smitten. Besotted. You have succeeded in mesmerizing me beyond all reason. Even though my life's turned into a haphazard, chaotic mess since you came into it, yes, I love you."

Mindy's heart swelled with happiness to the point she was afraid it might burst. Squealing, she flung herself on Archer, squirming against him, hungry to feel the swell of his erection against her flesh. She sprinkled kisses all over his face then locked lips with him, her tongue engaging in an exuberant dance of joy with his.

"Sex!" she shouted once their lips had parted. "Oh Archer, I love you too and I want to have sex with you. Right now. To celebrate."

"Whoa," he cautioned through laughter. "Are you sure? Don't you feel queasy after all that syrupy chocolate stuff you drank? Even if the alcohol content was low, that was one hell of a lot of sugar you downed, honey...along with your Snickers chaser."

"No way." Mindy made a raspberry sound. "You're talking to a bona fide, die-hard chocoholic, Archer. The stuff runs in my veins. I never get sick from chocolate." She grasped his erect cock through his black silk boxers. "What kind of sex are we going to have? Ooh, can I be on top this time?"

"Oh yeah, babe...absolutely. But first, we're gonna play a little bit."

"A man who enjoys foreplay *and* cuddly chats after sex. I hit the jackpot with you, Archer."

"Actually, I lied about being chatty after sex. I'd rather eat pizza."

"I knew you were too good to be true," she teased, tugging at his shorts. "Take these off. I want to see your cock. It's the best one I've ever seen." She watched as Archer yanked off his shorts, letting his beautiful cock bob freely.

"The best one...you mean between me and old Thumbkin? Gee, thanks."

Mindy gave a dismissive wave. "Oh I've seen plenty of cocks. Tons."

Archer gave her a wary look.

"Well, not literally," she clarified. "But I've read about all sorts of cocks in my steamy romance novels. From the in-depth descriptions, I can imagine how they look. Believe me, yours ranks right up there with the best. That's because it's not just long, it's thick too."

Archer traced a fingertip around her breasts, down her belly and through the center of her crotchless panties. Mindy sucked in a breath when his finger slipped into her pussy, wiggling back and forth.

"So you read porn and you're an authority on cocks, hmm? You get more interesting all the time." His finger kept playing inside.

"Ooh, that feels so good." She clamped her thighs tight and sighed. "The romances I read aren't porn. Exactly." A smile spread across her face. "Leo calls them porn with a plot." She laughed. "I missed out on so much with Edward and had a lot to learn about sex. Spicy romance novels were a good way to do that."

"I see. Is that where you learned about doing a striptease?" Archer smoothed his thumb over her clit. A soft moan escaped Mindy's lips as she jerked.

"Nope." Her voice was breathy. "I learned that from watching old movies. Did you really like it?"

"I loved it." His thumb made slow sensuous circles over her clitoris as he finger fucked her. "And the blowing on the cock thing during chocolate chip cookie sex...where did you learn that, sweetheart?"

"Ahem. I can see that, Archer."

"See what?"

"That smirk. I wasn't supposed to blow on you, was I?"

"I liked it. I thought it was very...unique."

"Well," she shrugged, "I guess it doesn't really matter if I did it wrong. Because now I have Archer Priest to teach me all the carnal things I need to know to be a true cosmopolitan woman of the world. At my age I should know all the intricacies about the fine art of sex, don't you think?"

"Only if I'm the one teaching you." Archer removed his finger from inside her, gently pinching her clit.

Her eyes popping wide, nearly crossing at the welcome sensation, Mindy drew up her knees. "The only one." Her breath came out on a lusty sigh as he teased her sweet spot again. "Ohhhh...that-that feels..." The third time he squeezed, Mindy's body stiffened and she lost her mind. Detonating, she cried out

Archer's name while he continued exacting the delicious torment through the last of her body's shudders.

"What I've been missing all these years is an absolute sin," Mindy told him after regaining her senses. "I've been seriously, gravely, hugely deprived." Watching as he sheathed his cock with a condom, she sighed, basking in the thrill of anticipation.

"Think of the fun we'll have getting you all caught up." He brushed his lips across hers, nipping her bottom lip.

"My romance novels have given me a long list of sexy ideas."

"Like dolling yourself up in naughty little undies like these?" He snapped the stretchy band. "I'm glad you bought them just for me. I can't wait to tear them off." His fingers dragged in a slow tease from her shoulders to her breasts, where he pinched and twisted her taut nipples through the lace.

Mindy murmured her delight at his expert touch. "They have tabs."

Archer's fingers stilled. "Your nipples?"

"No," Mindy laughed, "my bra and panties. To get them off faster."

"I approve. Now let's see what's inside this fancy tabbed bra—the one you bought just to impress me so you could sink your womanly clutches into me."

Mindy's snappy retort caught in her throat as Archer drew one bra cup down until her breast popped free. He caught the nipple in his teeth, nipping and tugging before tugging down the other cup. He pinched the pebbled tip of one while suckling the other.

Stroking the inside of his muscular thigh, Mindy cooed with pleasure. "You're better than any romance novel hero I've read about."

"Well I hope so, seeing as how I'm flesh and blood, a-k-a the real deal." Chuckling, he gestured to his body. "Since I've never read a romance novel, I can't compare you to any heroines. All I know is you make me feel alive. You make me think. You make me laugh. And, Jesus Christ, just thinking about you makes me so fucking hot and hard I walk around in a sex-crazed daze most of the time."

Threading his fingers through her hair, Archer's words traveled on a wisp of breath. "You're not only beautiful, Mindora..." She loved the way her name sounded when he spoke it. Like a poem, a perfect note of music. "You're sweet," he kissed the tip of her nose, "adorable," he kissed her forehead, "and addictingly luscious." His tongue pressed against her lips and she gave him access for a hot, heady kiss.

Archer's talented tongue then forged a wet, searing path from her mouth, to the hollow at her throat, to her breast where he lavished attention on one rigid nipple.

"And exquisitely delicious," he added, allowing her breast to pop free of his warm mouth. With the enthusiasm of a boy discovering a new toy, he pinched, plucked and teased at the nipple as the cool air puckered her flesh.

Mindy squirmed at the magic of his mouth and fingers. Snaking her hand between them, she wrapped her fingers around his shaft and indulged in a prolonged throaty sigh. She was so sublimely happy she didn't know whether to laugh or cry.

"I wish we could stay this way forever," she said. "Just the way we are, enjoying each other. Naked, hot, trembly, and enveloped in the heat of passion."

"I can't think of anything sweeter, except for sinking my cock into your juicy pussy."

Before she could blink, Archer had ripped off her panties.

"Archer! The tabs."

"Fuck the tabs. I'll buy you another pair."

"But-but they're crotchless. You could have just—"

"I know, baby, but I couldn't help it. I want you naked. Now."

Mindy yelped as Archer tore her brand new, exceedingly expensive bra from her torso, tossing it aside.

"I'll buy you one of those too," he vowed. "Right now I need to feel that unbelievably tight hole of yours squeezing me as I pump in and out."

Before Mindy could respond, Archer thrust into her, hard and deep, tearing a moan of acute gratification from her throat.

In and out, each slick glide more determined than the last.

"Nothing's ever felt this good." Archer gazed at her with fire in his eyes. "It's like fucking a goddess."

"Each stroke is sublime," Mindy whispered, adoring Archer's description. "Don't stop, Archer...don't stop."

"I'm going to make you quake." He drove hard. "And quiver." He worked his magic again. "With each thrust," he hammered into her, eliciting a shuddering gasp of delight from Mindy, "I'll deliver a potent jolt through that soft, lush body of yours."

A soul-satisfying orgasm was emerging, just from listening to him describe what he planned to do to her.

Their bodies still locked together, Archer rolled them so Mindy sat atop him.

"I didn't forget. Your turn on top, sweetheart." His gifted fingers settled at her swollen clit, manipulating it with enough intensity to rob her of all rational thought.

Determined to make this celebratory fuck as good for Archer as it was for her, Mindy swiveled her hips as she rode him.

"Ah, Christ...look at those beautiful tits swaying above me. Gorgeous." He caught them in his hands, kneading her flesh. "All mine."

Cupping her breasts, as if presenting them on a platter, she said, "You mean these old things?" She gave a throaty chuckle. With Archer's gaze locked on her offering, she bobbled them in her hands like a sexy juggler. "I've noticed you seem fond of them."

"That's an understatement."

Clasping her breasts like a finger bra, she squeezed them, uttering an impassioned moan as she squirmed, pushing herself further down on his dick.

"Do you like it when I make my breasts jiggle for you?" Gingerly bouncing on his groin, she allowed them to move freely.

"Shit..." With a contented groan, Archer bucked his hips, maneuvering so his magnificent cock perfectly abraded all the right places deep inside until Mindy thought she'd go insane.

"I'll take that as a yes," she said, her breathing jagged. Bracing her hands against his chest and squeezing his pecs, she answered his actions with a few of her own, riding him with clockwise circles, then counterclockwise. Watching his expression and listening to the sounds he made, she noted which moves he enjoyed most.

"You learned a lot from those smut books." Clasping his hands on her cool ass cheeks, he slowly trailed his fingers across her thighs.

"I've always been a fast learner," she informed him with a calculated twist of her hips. "My brain is full of so many hot, naughty, dirty little scenarios. I plan to keep you in a constant state of arousal until we test them all."

"I enthusiastically volunteer to be your lab rat, Dr. Porn."

"Excellent. We'll have to go shopping first, unless you already have the stuff I've read about."

"Such as?"

"Butt plugs, nipple clamps, velvet-lined handcuffs. I don't remember the rest right now, but they all sound quite intriguing."

"Damn." Archer's hip action stilled. "I usually hate shopping but this is one shopping trip I'll enjoy. We'll get all the sex toys your amorous little heart desires." He cupped her breasts, playing with them. "I'm looking forward to being your lab rat."

Mindy raised herself high on his dick, slipping down until she collided with the base of his erection. Clamping her inner muscles, she milked his cock with her pussy as she rode. "I like being on top, Archer. It's fun to ride you."

"You're killing me, Min."

She stopped moving. "I'm hurting you?"

"Only in the best possible way." Lifting her by the waist, he held her steady while gliding in and out, wreaking havoc with her senses.

"Have you ever touched yourself, thinking about me?" he asked, watching the in and out suction of cock and pussy.

"Are you kidding?" With a sultry chuckle, Mindy admitted, "I burned out my Duo-Head Maximum Power Thruster vibrator and had to get a new one. Then came my glow-in-the-dark, neon green Wild and Wanton Underwater Wonder. Since then, my arsenal of vibrators has grown considerably...all thanks to you."

"It serves you right after all those middle of the night jerk-off sessions you put me through."

"Good." Mindy smiled. "I like having that kind of power over you."

"You also used your magic powers of seduction to make me fall in love with you. Touch yourself for me now. I want to see your finger swirl around your clit as I fuck you."

Amazed at how at ease she felt with Archer, there was only a slight hesitation before Mindy slid her fingers into place. Meeting the smoldering intensity of his gaze, she treated her clit to sweet, sensual torture as he watched. Pleasuring herself in front of him made the sensations all that much hotter.

In a flash, Archer swapped their positions, with Mindy now on the bottom.

"Wow! That was fast." She was amazed and delighted he had the strength to toss her around so easily. It made her feel downright petite.

"I needed a better look. Men thrive on visuals." Archer grinned. "Do it again. Touch yourself for me. Let me see you play with your breasts too."

Archer loomed over her, a ravenous look in his eyes. Mindy slipped the fingers of one hand to her clit, sliding over the warm, slick flesh, while the fingers of her other hand dallied at her breasts. As her fingers swirled, stroked and tweaked, she luxuriated in the sheer delight of being with Archer...of pleasing him as he watched.

"That's right, sweetheart," Archer coaxed. "Enjoy yourself. Give in to the pleasure. God, you're so incredibly sexy." His hands lovingly roamed her body.

White hot fire ignited deep within Mindy's belly. Her breath came in panting gasps with each sashay across the swollen nub. Pleasuring herself until she purred, she couldn't believe she was doing this in front of anyone...in front of Archer. But it seemed so natural. So right. As if she'd done it before. She had her detailed fantasies to thank for that.

"Ah Christ," Archer ground out. "That's beautiful. So fucking hot. I can feel your fingers. I can feel you stroking yourself." His next thrust jarred her halfway up the bed.

She felt a powerful orgasm building. Staggered that she could come so much, this one promised to be a phenomenal, cataclysmic experience.

His hand on hers, Archer drew her fingers from her pussy, sniffing them. "Sweet, musky. Better than the finest perfume, the most fragrant wine." Bringing her fingers to his mouth, he sucked them, one by one, a deep groan rumbling up from his chest as he did. "Like nectar." He licked his lips. "I love the delicate smell and taste of your sex, Mindy."

At a loss for words, a single tear trickled down Mindy's cheek as she smiled. So this, THIS, is what sex with a loving man was supposed to be. Sheer, unadulterated bliss. Indulging in a prolonged sigh, she lingered on his sensual words...words that made her feel more precious than gold. More desirable than diamonds.

Her entire body thrummed with Archer's next powerful thrust. She was getting close. One glimpse at his expression told her he was about to shatter too.

A strangled sound escaped the back of his throat as they locked gazes.

With a gush of breath, his feral cry vibrated clear to her core, adding an untamed intensity to their lovemaking.

One final swoop of Archer's finger across her engorged clit sent Mindy soaring with him on the wings of passion, crying out her own exclamation of sheer rapture.

"I love you," they chorused, clinging to each other in the throes of joint climax.

Chapter 25

MINDY AWOKE TO the smell of coffee and a note on her pillow. Archer wrote that he'd left early for the winery because there was a problem with one of the vats. He asked her to meet him there for the last wine tour of the day.

The part of the note she liked best was his signature—*all my love, Archer*.

All my love...

She repeated the words, rolling them across her tongue, through her mind, trying to get used to them as she padded down to the kitchen to pour herself a cup of coffee.

Archer Priest loved her. And she loved him. As if that in itself wasn't amazing enough, there was even a decent chance his bitch of a sister could end up on the other side of the planet making nookie with that overbearing asshole Texan. For a good five years at least!

That thought alone was enough to make Mindy want to break out in song.

Yes, life was good. The world seemed lighter, brighter, more buoyant this morning. Mindy didn't even mind the half-dozen messages on her phone from Leo, asking how everything turned out and wanting all the juicy details.

In fact, she felt so magnanimous after spending the night in Archer's arms, making perfect-romance-novel love, she hadn't even entertained any thoughts of eviscerating Leo for all the angst he'd put her through.

Mindy

———●———

"AS THE WINE RESTS, sediment drops from the new wines to the bottom of the tank or barrel," Archer explained to the small tour group as Mindy hung on his every word. "The red wine in barrels absorbs tannin from the wood and the minute amounts of oxygen from the air that will give them character and nudge them toward maturity."

"What's the difference between white zinfandel and red zinfandel?" someone from the tour group asked.

"Well, despite the popularity of white zinfandel," Archer explained, "the grape that all zinfandels are made from is actually red. The red skins are removed to produce a paler blush color wine. The current batch of our zinfandel is made from seventy-year-old vines in California, aged about a year in wood before being bottled."

Naturally, being a vintner, Archer needed to know a great deal about wine but Mindy was still amazed at the depth of his knowledge as she listened to his well-informed answers to the many varied questions the group asked. She never realized how interesting wine and winemaking could be and looked forward to Archer teaching her how to fully appreciate the nuances of the different wines from Archer's Cellars...as well as how to pace herself while drinking them.

Mindy took in her surroundings. Archer's Cellars had the look and feel of something out of an old movie. It was her second visit to the winery but the first time she'd been in the actual wine cellar below the old mansion. Full of tanks, bottles and wood barrels, it was pristinely clean. The cellar was surprisingly cavernous, with gaping areas dug out of the rock.

While the temperature was chilly, it wasn't unpleasant. Besides, Archer's smile flooded her with comforting warmth.

Breathing in, she filled her nostrils with a woody scent laced with pleasing undertones of fruit and herbs. Having smelled this same earthy combination of fragrances on Archer before, it acted like an aphrodisiac on her senses.

Her gaze fell on him again. He wore faded jeans and a denim shirt with sleeves rolled up. The chambray cloth of his shirt strained over his broad shoulders and biceps. That realization had a succulent image of him, shirtless and sweating, flashing into her mind. Against her better judgment, her eyes traveled to his crotch. Her mouth went dry and her lips parted as desire flowed through her, lodging at her clit with a tiny, telltale tremble.

The urge to jump his bones right there in front of the huddled wine novices was almost overwhelming.

She had to get a grip. Rather than feeling sated by their sensational lovemaking sessions, Mindy found herself even more famished. She simply couldn't get enough of the man. An orgasm at the hands of Archer Priest was like a perfect, divine piece of designer chocolate...impossible to have just one.

Mindy blinked.

What in the world has happened to me? Since meeting Archer I've morphed into a wanton woman.

After a couple deep, cleansing breaths, she chanced glancing at him again. She was a mature adult, dammit. She could get through this tour without succumbing to lusty daydreams and wild, carnal imaginings.

Her newly studious self noted that, aside from looking scrumptious, Archer's charm, wit and acumen were evident as he addressed the group. Every so often he directed a special, secret smile toward Mindy, affecting her the same way a magnet attracts iron.

Archer and Becky, his fresh-faced college intern assistant, poured samples from a few of the barrels, using something that looked like a cross between a hypodermic needle and a meat-baster. Mindy tried to pay attention to the fascinating tour. The problem? It wasn't nearly as fascinating as the tour's leader.

Deciding to fully get into the spirit of things, she raised her hand.

"Did you have a question, ma'am?" Archer asked, a silent conversation unfurling between them.

"Yes." Melting at his gaze, Mindy swallowed hard. "What is it that makes so many of your wines award winners?"

"You need quality going in to have quality come out," he answered, his gaze lingering on her. "I can't change grapes, but I can try to steer them in the right direction by reducing acidity through blending."

She loved listening to him talk. Archer took such obvious pride in his wine. It didn't hurt that he was also sable haired, chiseled jawed, and had chocolate chip eyes. How could she help getting all sultry and squirmy watching the gorgeous, generous man who'd forever changed her world?

"My objective," he went on, "is to achieve balance and harmony among the components to provide a pleasant-tasting wine with a pleasing finish."

Listening to Archer enlighten her and the group about the fermented fruits of his labor, Mindy determined she'd make the ultimate sacrifice. She'd give his awful mushroomy-tasting cabernet another chance, without making a single shudder as it slid down her throat. Now *that* was true love.

They strolled to another station where Archer gave demonstrations and answered more questions while Mindy studied the sensuous, sinewy movements of his muscle groupings. She couldn't help being distracted. It wasn't her fault. His mind-melting gaze caused her to be an unruly student.

"And that ends our tour for this afternoon, ladies and gentlemen," Archer said. "I hope you enjoyed learning about how wine is made. Becky will lead you back to the tasting room and wine shop upstairs where you can sample several of our wines along with assorted cheeses and crackers, and make any purchases you might like."

As Mindy followed the group, Archer seized her arm, holding her back.

"Aren't we going upstairs with the rest of them?"

"No, Becky will take care of everything before locking up the winery and going home. We'll have the place to ourselves." Standing behind her, Archer wrapped his arms around her middle, nuzzling her neck. "Oh, the things I'm going to do to you, sweetheart."

Mindy hesitated. "Your mother's not upstairs, is she?"

"Nope, you can breathe easy." Archer laughed. "She's in Florida with friends for a getaway. Come on." There was a twinkle in his eye as he led Mindy to a set of enormous Gothic style doors. "I've got something special to show you."

"Grape etchings?" Mindy teased.

"Better...much better." Unlocking the doors, Archer pushed open the massive, heavy slabs of wood, revealing an underground haven like nothing Mindy had ever seen. It was like a subterranean paradise.

Her hand flew to her throat and she gasped as she surveyed the area's mini-waterfall, abundance of flourishing plants, artful lighting, and exquisite decoration. The room held amazing carved rock furnishings, including a vine-covered bar and stools.

"Holy cow, Archer, this is magnificent. Like something straight out of a fairytale."

"I didn't know it was here when I bought the place years ago," he told her. "Everything down here was a mess and the big oak doors were hidden behind a mountain of debris. After clearing everything out to get the cellar ready for the winery, I discovered the doors and the unexpected chamber behind them. I'm guessing the guy who originally built this place must have had the grotto fixed up as a retreat for himself."

Fingering one of the ornate torches, Mindy said, "I love those lights. They look really old."

"They used to be gaslight torches. Somebody along the way had them converted to electric. I use this room just for me. It's my special little corner of the world, where nothing can bother me and stress doesn't exist. I step in here and all my cares dissolve."

Still eyeing the extraordinary space, Mindy nodded. "I can see exactly why you'd feel that way. This is perfect for relaxation or meditation."

Archer tugged her close. "I've never brought anyone else here before, Mindy," he whispered into her hair.

His admission made her heart swell. She smiled up into those warm, inviting pools of chocolate. "I'm honored you're sharing it with me, Archer."

He lifted her chin, his smile warm, cherishing. "It's because I love you, Mindora von G. With every fiber of my being. Got on those fancy undies? The ones with the easy fuck-me tabs?""

"What?" Caught off guard at his sudden shift from sweet to horny, Mindy laughed.

"Well, do you?"

"Yes. Well, not the same ones you obliterated last night, of course. Why?"

"I want you to take off your clothes and strip down to those wicked undies."

"Now?" She looked around her. "Here?"

"Yup."

"But...but it's cold down here."

"Don't worry, we'll be working up some heat," he assured with a devilish grin. "Now strip like a good little girl." As Mindy complied, Archer shucked off his own clothes.

Goosebumps rose on Mindy's skin as she stood in the cave in only her bra and panties. She scanned the area for something soft, like maybe a hidden futon or bank of pillows, but all she saw was rock formations. Glancing back at Archer, standing there looking unreasonably delicious in nothing but a pair of black silk shorts, Mindy decided it didn't make a damn bit of difference if he wanted to fuck her on the floor, on top of a barrel, or anywhere else.

Standing arms akimbo, Archer surveyed Mindy from head to toe. "No. On second thought, that won't do."

As if they were on a burlesque stage in the middle of a bawdy skit, Archer grabbed her bra and panties, snatching them from her body in one swift yank.

"Oh!"

"Damn, I love doing that. Looks like I'll have to buy you a truckload of those easy fuck-me undies. They're so much fun to rip off your bad girl curves."

Goosebumps vanishing, heat flushed through Mindy.

Now gloriously naked himself and reveling in mischievous laughter, Archer pulled Mindy deeper into the cave, all the way to the back until they'd entered an adjoining room dominated by a giant vat filled with red and deep purple grapes.

"Feel adventurous?"

Glancing from the vat of grapes to Archer, Mindy laughed. "You mean...?"

"Yup. Grape crushing. The old-fashioned way."

Mindy beamed an enthusiastic smile. "I've wanted to do this ever since I saw that old *I Love Lucy* episode where she visits Italy and dances around in the grapes."

"I always liked that episode. That's what gave me the idea. I just put this together this morning." He gestured. "The vat's an old hot tub that was already in here. I cleaned it out and filled it with grapes so we can put a whole new spin on grape crushing."

Mindy decided it was a deliciously naughty idea. "Squishing around naked in a sea of grapes does have a sexy feel to it, doesn't it?"

"We'll find out in a minute."

"How do we do this, Archer?"

"Just like this."

In the next instant, Mindy was in the air, falling into the vat of grapes, with Archer plunging in after her.

"Archer!" she shrieked.

The two of them sat in the vat laughing and fondling each other, while doing their best to right themselves and stand. Finally both on their feet, Mindy danced around, the way Lucy Ricardo had, with hands on her hips. Her unencumbered breasts bounced, drawing Archer's rapt attention.

"Oh baby, give me those jiggly breasts," he growled, following after her, his hands opening and closing in a grabbing motion while he did his own exaggerated grape-stomping dance. "I want to squeeze them, lick them, bite them, suck them."

"The grapes?" Mindy teased.

"Your gorgeous tits. Get ready. I'm coming to get you, Mindy."

"I don't think so. You can't catch me," she teased, prancing around the perimeter of the tub, doing her best to keep her balance in the plump, juicy fruit.

"Oh yes I can," he warned. "And when I do, I'm going to throw you down in those grapes and fuck you silly, back, forth, sideways, *every* way so I can savor every inch of your voluptuous body. My dick's going to drill that pliant pussy of yours so hard that—"

Uttering a loud *whoop* of surprise, Archer slipped, landing on his ass.

Pointing at the fallen Archer, Mindy burst out laughing. Adding insult to injury, she pelted him with handfuls of grapes. Her moment of triumph was fleeting, however, because Archer dove beneath the heap of grapes, yanking Mindy's feet out from under her.

Catching her in his arms as she fell back, he crowed, "Now I've got you, you wicked little temptress. And I'm going to make you pay."

"Go ahead, make me pay. I've been *very* naughty."

They played back and forth, smashing grapes in each other's faces and licking the juice from each other's body parts. Mindy decided there was definitely something to be said for grape-coated cock and balls. It might become her second favorite confection, next to chocolate.

Positioning a single grape at her navel, Archer worked it up Mindy's belly with the tip of his tongue, sidetracking left and right to keep the plump fruit from rolling away. As he nudged the grape through the valley between her breasts, the sensation was tickling and sexy. He succeeded in transporting the grape to the hollow at the base of her throat before curling his tongue and taking the berry into his mouth.

Then he worked his way back down again, this time sans the grape.

"I see your goosebumps are gone," he noted after a lavish lick of her breast. "You taste like spicy hot grape juice." Once the last syllable left his mouth, his busy tongue went back to work, laving her nipple.

Luxuriating in Archer's attention, a melodic sigh escaped Mindy's lips. Romping around nude in the juicy mess she should be cold, freezing...but the heat of passion kept her warm. Inside and out.

"Who knew grapes could be so lust inducing?" she said, her voice soft and low. "You've got me so hot I could probably make mulled wine out of these grapes."

"Hot and Spicy Mulled Mindy. A gold medal winner for sure. I'll have to add a barrel to my private stock."

Wrapping her arms around his neck, she kissed him. "This was a fabulous idea, Archer. I'm having a ball."

He kissed her back, dragging her bottom lip through his teeth. "All this playing around has given me an appetite."

The thought of leaving their wet, carnal playground before making love among the plump, sticky fruit disappointed her. "You mean we're done in here?"

"Not by a long shot." Grabbing her waist tight, he hauled her up and plopped her flat on her back in the grapes. "I've got some serious snacking to do."

A wanton giggle erupted from Mindy's throat. "Archer, you are so smutty!" Before she could utter another word, he spread her thighs and shoved a handful of grapes at her pussy, pushing them inside her, one by one as she gasped. The feeling of being packed with round, squishy fruits was unlike anything she'd ever experienced.

"Oh...this is weird."

"Good weird or bad weird?" Archer busily stuffed her channel with fruit. Before she could answer, he swiped his finger firmly across her clit, eliciting a gasp from Mindy.

"Good weird..." she muttered on a sultry whisper. "Definitely good." His hot tongue swirled around her clit. "Oh...this is too much. I think I'm going to—" Again, Archer thwarted her ability to speak, this time by capturing her swollen nub between his teeth and scraping gently.

Mindy was damn glad they were tucked away in the rock cavern because the prolonged shriek as she shattered would have cracked glass, destroying all those nice bottles of Archer's wine. She couldn't believe how fast she'd come. The waves just kept coming as her inner walls contracted against the grapes, squeezing, crushing. She never wanted it to stop.

And Archer's mouth! Holy shit, he was killing her. Pushing her body beyond its limits. Driving her insane. The pain, the pleasure, the intensity!

"Stop! I can't take anymore, Archer. I think I'm going to have a heart attack. You have to stop."

Pausing in his carnal task, Archer assured, "You're not going to have a heart attack, babe." He gave a husky chuckle. "But if you really want me to stop, I will. You sure that's what you want?" He licked her clit again and her body shuddered clear to her teeth.

"No." Mindy panted, clutching bunches of grapes in her hands, fisting them until they surrendered their juice. "It's heaven. It's hell. It's...oh just go ahead and kill me. I want to die just like this in your arms."

"Let yourself relax and give in to the pleasure, Min, honey." As he sucked her clit, she indulged in a lingering moan. "Let me show you how much I love you."

As his teeth grazed her tortured nub again, Mindy figured she was a goner. A woman could only take so much pleasure before detonating.

"You've been deprived of absolute pleasure for so long, baby. You deserve this."

Bringing one hand to her breast, Archer rolled the nipple firm enough that Mindy felt the sensation in her toes. This, while his magic mouth still toiled at her clit, driving her closer to the brink of insanity, treating her to equal measures of agony and bliss.

She wanted to tell him exactly what he was doing to her. To thank him for so generously treating her to the most intensely pleasurable intimate experience of her life. To let him know her entire arsenal of vibrators were no more than cheap, ineffectual trinkets compared to his expert ministrations. But all she could do was babble nonsensically.

Lost in rapture, Mindy threaded her fingers through Archer's hair, fisting it, pressing his head against her, where it needed to be. Finally, her pleasure core split wide open, transporting her to an inner nirvana of hard, throbbing waves splashing through her senses.

"Yeah...that's it, baby. There's nothing more sensuous than watching you come." Cradling her in his arms as she floated atop the mound of grapes, Archer kissed her sweetly. "Now it's time to get those grapes out of their secret hiding place." Clutching her ass cheeks, he dragged her closer, getting down on his knees, bringing him face to pussy.

"Wait...it's too soon," Mindy told him, barely able to form words at this point. "It's too sensitive down there."

"You mean here?" Archer pressed the tip of his finger against her gleefully worn-out clit.

Crossing her eyes, Mindy let out *whoop*! Her head dropped back into the grapes and she moaned. The indescribable feeling of his finger on her tender flesh sent another jolt through her body. She experienced the sensation clear down to every nerve ending.

It felt terrible. It felt wonderful. She was frightened of the unknown...and ravenous for more.

Bracing her hips high, Archer brought her vulva to his mouth, tonguing out a few grapes. "It's a dirty job but somebody's gotta do it," he teased before removing more grapes and eating them. "Imagine what would happen at your next gynecologist visit if the doc found grapes lodged inside your sweet little pussy." He licked her clit before digging his tongue inside, scooping out another grape.

The idea of trying to explain that to kindly old Dr. Hendricks, who'd been her family doctor since she was a kid, had Mindy laughing while squirming with pleasure.

Then alarm set in.

Ohmigod. What if Archer didn't get them all out? What if a grape or two lingered up there, hidden away, only to be fished out during her next pap smear?

"Oh they need to come out, Archer. All of them. I could *never* explain such a thing to Dr. Hendricks."

"Well, when Doc H asks why you have a little red grape tucked deep in your pretty vagina, you could always claim you went to a spa for their famous grape cure. But their technicians failed to vacuum your innards sufficiently." Archer dutifully returned to his grape-retrieval mission.

Mindy laughed again. How in the hell she could be caught up in giggles at the same time her body was readying for a cataclysmic orgasm was beyond her. She had no idea sex could be so multi-rewarding, so sizzling hot while being such great fun.

Archer inserted two fingers, drawing out more fruit and sliding the sticky wet pulp along her clit before licking it and his fingers clean.

"The taste of you mixed with the grapes is like a fine wine." He swirled a finger inside her, plucking out another fruit. After eating it and licking his lips, he gave a satisfied smile. "I could bottle it for my private stock, labeling it The Tantalizing Taste of Sweet, Musky Sex." He went back for more, again and again, each time doing something different with his tongue, teeth or fingers.

This multitalented man knew how to make her insides thrum.

"I think I've got them all out, but I'd better make sure." Proceeding with caution, Archer thrust his entire hand up her channel, spreading his fingers and exploring. Mindy's body stiffened at the powerfully sweet invasion.

"You-you're touching something up there," she whispered on a sigh, unfamiliar with the new sensation. "Something wonderful."

"Must be the elusive G-spot," he surmised. "Which proves I'm not only a master winemaker, I'm also an amazing lover."

Her eyelids fluttering closed in ecstasy, she murmured, "The most amazing ever."

He moved his fingers back and forth inside her until Mindy felt herself bordering the rim of rapture.

"Archer...ohhh...Archer..." She gazed into his chocolate chip eyes as he hand-screwed her. With an unmistakable look of love, he lowered his head, tenderly kissing her as he fucked her to completion. She was tempted to cry from sheer bliss as he cradled her against him while she trembled. He swallowed her moans as her senses scattered, then whispered soft, intimate words of affection against her ear while she shuddered in his arms.

When it was over, Mindy was spent. She'd ascended to a place of almost mystical scope before finding herself back in her perfectly pleasured body, enfolded in the arms of the man she loved. Adored.

Still caught in a thick fog of passion from her climax, Mindy was surprised to feel Archer at her back, parting her legs with a rear approach, working his fingers deep in her hopefully grape-less hole.

"I can't, Archer," she protested. "Really. It's too soon. Too much. Honestly, I'm spent. I feel like I don't have a single bone left in my body."

Disregarding her protests, his skilled hand performed wonders once again inside her sopping core. Despite being boneless and replete, Mindy moaned out in euphoria, soaking up the ecstasy of Archer pleasuring her, loving her.

Her eyes widened as he splayed her butt cheeks with his free hand. She felt his cock nestling its length in the crease of her ass.

"Archer? Um..."

"I'm playing. You have no idea how much I want my cock inside your tight, hot little butt hole."

Mindy gulped. "I think you've got the wrong hole."

"Nope."

"But-but that's my-my..."

"Your little pink, virgin rosebud."

"My ass," Mindy clarified.

"The sweetest bare ass I've ever seen." Archer dipped his head, touching the tip of his tongue to her anus.

Mindy yelped in surprise.

"Don't tell me you haven't read about this in your steamy romance novels."

She had, actually. But it's something she couldn't imagine happening to her—in an agreeable way, that is.

Archer took his sweet time, licking, kissing and tonguing her. "You'd better get used to the idea that there isn't a single solitary spot on that sumptuous body of yours that I don't find beautiful. Tempting. Tantalizing. Every part of you is precious to me, Mindy. I'm looking forward to hours of in-depth exploration." He licked her hole again and Mindy shivered.

"Are you going to put your cock up my butt?" The notion made her uneasy. "Just, please, whatever you do, Archer, don't stuff any grapes up there, okay?" She almost laughed, giving in when she heard Archer chuckle. The conversation was so strange. Foreign. But then...romance novel heroes seemed to enjoy...butt stuff. So did the heroines. She had to admit the touch of his tongue against her opening provided a definite thrill of sensation gliding up her spine.

"No grapes, don't worry. As for my cock, absolutely. In time. A few weeks. Maybe a month or two. I need to get you ready first."

"Ready how?"

"Like this." Archer slipped one finger inside the crack pressing against the seam of her ass. When he slid his fingertip, wet with grape juice, just inside the opening, she stiffened, startled.

"Oh!"

He pushed his finger a little farther and she tightened, closing her buttocks around his finger. "Jesus, you're so tight in there. I've got to get you ready, pliant, little by little, until your opening can stretch wide enough to accommodate my cock." His finger penetrated to the first knuckle. Mindy gasped then moaned. "Like the way that feels?"

"I'm not sure. I-I think so." The new sensation was entirely unique. There was something deeply erotic about Archer lovingly surveying her most intimate areas. "Yes," she amended. "I do."

He hadn't forgotten about his pussy-pleasuring task. While gently stretching her rectum muscles, lightly tugging at the edges, his other hand fucked her core, repeatedly making contact with her G-spot. The wet, sucking sounds of her drenched center echoed off the cavern walls along with the murmurs of delight she and Archer uttered.

The dual sensations of fullness back and front drove her mad. The addition of Archer's erection gliding up and down her thigh and ass cheek as he pleasured her was the icing on the cake.

Mindy felt the first shudders grip her being. Reaching behind her, grasping onto Archer's arms for dear life, she said, "There's one hell of an avalanche of ecstasy shooting through me, Archer." Sucking in a long, quaking breath, she continued, "I don't know if I'll make it out of this orgasm alive."

She heard Archer's husky chuckle, feeling his hot breath on the back of one shoulder. He planted a tender kiss there before nipping her flesh with his teeth. "Oh I think you'll manage. You're a regular little climax machine, Mindora von G. Damn, it's going to be fun finding all kinds of new ways to fuck you, honey. There's nothing I love more than feeling you convulse in my arms."

She managed a miniscule laugh, which tightened her muscles around his finger in her ass and his fist up her pussy. That was it. The last straw. Spasms jolted through her with such intensity she almost sobbed.

Coming back down to earth, it dawned on her that Archer had unselfishly tended to her needs while ignoring his own. Reaching for his cock, her fingers grazed the marble-hard surface.

"Your turn," she whispered. "Come inside, Archer. Stick your grape-juice-covered cock right in here." She patted the vee between her thighs.

After kissing the tip of her nose, Archer brought Mindy to her feet. "Later. When we're upstairs in my bed."

"Now," she insisted. "You're hard as a rock, Archer."

"No condom." Smiling, he shrugged. "I doubt it would stay on in all this juice, so I decided to make our fun little grape stomping an activity strictly for your pleasure. Believe me, watching your big blue eyes grow wide and your lips form those amazed little O's as you come is plenty satisfying for me, sweetheart."

No way was Mindy about to leave that vat without bringing Archer to climax. An idea crossed her mind and she indulged in a seductive laugh.

"You don't need a condom. Natasha has other ways of making her man come," Mindy informed in her sorry attempt at an eastern European accent. "First, Natasha will suck." Getting on her knees, she stroked Archer's cock with her fingers before giving it a squeeze and clamping her mouth on it.

Humming her pleasure as her lips slid over the silken-hard surface, she treated it to an erotic series of licks and sucking. Gripping the edge of the vat, Archer groaned long and slow as his head fell back.

Letting his cock pop free of her lips, Mindy watched it bob above the grapes. "Mmm, sweet and salty. Natasha likes the grapey taste of her man. Ah, but oral sex is not the only thing Natasha has in her bag of carnal tricks."

"Tell me more." Archer weaved his fingers in Mindy's damp hair, smiling down at her. "I'm *very* interested."

"Natasha will fuck your big, strong cock with her jiggly breasts." As she entertained Archer with a brazen shimmy, Mindy was surprised at her own announcement, not really knowing where the idea came from—probably one of her romance books—but immediately warming to the delicious possibilities.

"Do it. Fuck me with your glorious tits, Natasha."

She heard Archer's sharp intake of breath as she sandwiched his sizeable erection between her breasts, clasping them tight against his cock as she leisurely glided back and forth.

"Natasha sees a tiny pearl of liquid seeping from the tip of your cock," she said, gazing at the grape juice-glazed purple head cruising between her pale breasts. Lowering her head, she licked his salty pre-cum. "Natasha likes Archer's love liquid. Natasha wants to see it spill all over her breasts so she can lick up every creamy drop," she purred.

"Mindy...my God..." A lingering groan of deep gratification rumbled deep in Archer's chest.

Picking up the pace, Mindy slid over him, from tip to root and back again, faster, harder, until Archer's feral growl pierced the silence and his body stiffened. His hands clasped over hers as she held his pulsing cock between her breasts, Archer's gaze was glued to his dick as it spewed ribbons of hot seed all over her breasts.

Humming with pleasure, and the satisfaction that she'd thoroughly pleasured her man, Mindy sucked his depleted cock clean before lifting one breast to her mouth and swooping her tongue over a spot where he'd branded her with his cum.

Cupping her hands, she scooped his semen onto her fingers, bringing it to her lips, lapping it as he watched her, heavy-lidded. She smacked her lips and *ahhhhhed*.

"Natasha knows how to please her man's colossal cock, yes?" Depositing a finger in her mouth, she drew it out slowly between pursed lips with a long, low *mmmmm*.

"Christ almighty..." It took Archer a moment to capture his breath before he could say more. "You know that black wig and the blood-red lipstick you wore, Natasha?"

Mindy nodded.

"Don't throw them out."

Chapter 26

"IT'S THE ONE thing I forgot about from that *I Love Lucy* episode," Mindy said, wincing at her reflection.

"Same here." Archer's dazed expression mirrored hers. "Handling grapes every day, you'd think I would know better."

Turning toward him, hands on hips, she said, "Yes, you would, wouldn't you?"

He gave a sheepish shrug. "I'm sure it will wear off...eventually."

"Good grief, Archer, we look like a couple of...of—"

"Smurfs?" Archer offered, with Mindy growling a *yes*!

Eying the blotchy red, blue and purplish stains all over their bodies, she grumbled, "And look at my hair!" She tugged at the multi-hued, formerly blonde strands. "What am I going to do? How can I go to work like this?"

"There's always your Natasha wig." Archer's eyebrows danced in a rascally waggle. The guy was clearly crazy about her Natasha getup. "Plenty of heavy face makeup, some dark glasses, and a pair of gloves. No one will be the wiser."

"Dream on." Mindy groaned.

"At least we had one hell of a good time." Drawing her close, Archer kissed the top of her towel-dried head.

"The best," Mindy agreed. "Plus all the fun trying to scrub it off each other in the shower."

"You definitely look good in blue, Min."

"It's one of my best colors." She batted her eyelashes. "You're going to have a tough time explaining away that blue cock of yours next time you pee in a public bathroom."

"Guys don't pay attention to each other's dicks when we're in the can."

"Hah!" Mindy snickered. "Yeah right."

"Just wait until your doctor gets a load of your blue vagina and purple asshole." Archer smirked.

Sighing, Mindy cringed at the thought. "Okay, so what do we do now?"

"Maybe if we fuck the night away in my bed some of this will rub off on the sheets." Archer's tone was uncertain at best.

"Definitely worth a try." She knew it wouldn't work but they'd have a great time trying. "My neighbor's watching Cadbury for me tonight, so I don't need to be back."

"So...you were anticipating a night of passion?"

"Purple passion, as it turns out." Laughing, Mindy took Archer's extended hand, following him from the bathroom to the bedroom. Nestling herself on the crisp white sheets, she said, "I've decided making love with you rates just below chocolate. I want you to know it's a very close second."

Archer burst out laughing. "So I come in second to chocolate, huh? Gee, thanks. I'm not sure how I feel about being second fiddle to a Snickers bar."

"Don't be silly." She waved her stained hand through the air. "Obviously you have no idea what a great honor I've just bestowed on you. Believe me, it's extraordinary."

"I don't know," Archer mused. "I think maybe you need to be punished for your emasculating chocolate remarks."

"Oh you do, do you? Just what did you have in mind, Mr. Priest?" she said, full of bravado.

"I could make you stand in the corner."

"You could." Mindy nodded. "But I doubt that would be enough to teach me a lesson."

"You've got a point. You're a *very* bad girl." He rubbed his jaw in contemplation. "I could turn you over my knee and spank your pretty bare ass until it's a charming shade of mottled pink, purple and blue."

Wet heat rippling up from her perfectly pleasured lady parts, Mindy blinked. His surprisingly appealing suggestion caught her completely unawares. She never expected such a pleasurable reaction from the image of Archer slapping her butt. Her mouth fell open and she sputtered.

"Or..." Archer wrapped his hands around her wrists, raising them above her head, tenderly immobilizing them. His voice dropping an octave, he continued, "I could tie you up and have my way with you. Fuck your mouth, your pussy, and your grape-blue-speckled ass until you're boneless, whimpering and completely spent."

Domination. Mindy's thoughts raced to the wild, passionate dream she'd had of a medieval damsel in distress and her bold, sexy knight with the ever-expanding cock. A thrill stole up her spine as a hint of juice trickled down her thigh.

"Come to think of it," her voice grew soft and throaty, "I probably do need to be punished." She swallowed hard. "All over." Her belly churned in excitement and uncertainty.

Leaping off the bed, Archer went to his closet, returning with several silk neckties.

"Trust me?" He drew the slinky fabric between his fingers in a slow glide.

Without a moment's hesitation, she answered, "Yes."

He dragged the top sheet down until it bunched at the foot of the bed. "You know I'd never do anything to hurt you, right?"

She did. She knew it in her heart. Her soul. Unlike her unsavory experience with the bullying, sadistic Edward, any combination of pain and pleasure shared with Archer would be wholly mutual and fully agreeable. And most likely damned pleasant.

"Yes, Archer." Mindy licked her lips with a purr of excitement as he stood over her, his naked blue cock jutting high and proud.

"I knew when I first spotted this antique wrought iron headboard and footboard there was a reason I liked them." He secured Mindy's wrists as she gazed up at him, sucking in ragged little breaths, wondering exactly what he had in mind.

Kneeling on the mattress at her side, Archer's gaze slid over his handiwork, down Mindy's up-stretched arms and to her eyes. "I like the look of that," Archer told her with a slow smile. "My beautiful Mindy, tethered to the headboard of my bed. Helpless and needy."

Never having been tied up before, Mindy found a wild fever of need gripping her being. Impulsively, she curved her body toward him. "What are the rest of the ties for?"

His cocoa eyes dancing with devil lights, the corner of Archer's mouth curved into a roguish grin. "One is for this," he said, surprising Mindy by covering her eyes as he made a blindfold from one of the ties.

"Oh!" A shot of panic rising to the surface at the foreign and unexpected action, Mindy tensed. "But why—"

"Shhh." He placed a finger to her lips. "Just relax while I administer your punishment, sweetheart. Remember, you've been a *very* naughty girl."

"But I want to see you, Archer." Being tied up was one thing, but being blindfolded? No, Mindy didn't think she'd like this one bit.

"Shhh," he admonished again, smoothing his hands from her belly, over her breasts, and up her arms to her bound wrists with agonizing slowness. Retracing his journey, Archer's soothing hands returned to her belly, taking a lingering detour at her breasts, paying homage to each nipple with a flick of his fingers.

A moan of pleasure reverberated in the back of Mindy's throat. She found the sensations especially delightful. She could almost come just from the thought of what he'd done to her already. Her legs and hips writhed and vibrations fluttered at her clit as her mind conjured images of what might come next.

"There's no need to see me. Just picture me in your mind—stained blue." He chuckled.

"Just like the blue djinn," Mindy noted, imagining the flex of muscle as Archer's lean, hard body moved. She could easily visualize the jerk and bob of his engorged blue-stained cock as he studied her, tied to his bed.

Maybe this blindfolded thing wasn't so bad after all.

Kneading her breasts with skillful hands, he said, "What's the blue gin? Sounds like a cocktail." Archer tweaking her nipples effectively silenced her for a moment, except for the lingering moan escaping her lips.

"No, it's a character from *I Dream of Jeannie*, remember?" she said, her voice breathy.

"Nope."

"You never watched those reruns?"

"Uh-uh. I was probably watching football, or outside playing it."

"Well, there was this genie who was part of the blue djinn. As in d-j-i-n-n, as opposed to the alcohol, g-i-n."

"Ah...gotcha."

"I don't remember if he was actually blue or not, but I'll bet he didn't have a big blue cock like yours." Mindy giggled.

"Okay, if it makes you happy, I'll roleplay, being the blue djinn with the big blue cock. As long as I can stick my prized pecker into your pretty purple pussy."

"Perfect plan!" She laughed again. "I love a man who uses alliteration."

"Well whatever that is, I'm glad I apparently have it and know how to use it." Archer laughed as his warm hands caressed her thighs, his fingers digging into her flesh as he leisurely dragged his fingertips down to her ankles. Spreading Mindy's legs wide, Archer secured her ankles to the footboard.

She heard his impassioned groan and felt the brush of his fingertips over her intimate folds, making her shiver.

"You look incredible," he said. "I love how wet you are for me."

"Tell me what you see when you look at me," Mindy whispered, curious at what Archer was getting out of this.

"I see Mindy...the sensuous Mindora von G, in bondage. A veritable feast for the eyes." His hands explored her body as he spoke. "I see a beautiful, desirable woman, all spread out for me like an erotic buffet. Your pussy is all pink, slick and swollen with desire. Trickles of your juice are shimmering on your inner thighs and in your curls."

Mindy heard Archer take in a deep sniff. "I can smell the scent of your arousal. It's more stimulating than fine wine."

"Oh no...I don't believe this."

Archer's hands stilled. "What's wrong?"

"Not a damn thing. It's just...this is all making me so hot I think I'm going to come."

"No, you don't want to do that just yet."

"Oh yes I do." She could hear the tremor in her own voice as she spoke.

"Not until I give you permission."

"Archer Priest..." Mindy groaned. "I had no idea you could be such a hard ass."

She heard his wicked chuckle, then his hands were on her again. Exploring. Caressing. From her ankles to her knees, up her thighs where they lingered as Mindy held her breath. It came out on a sigh as Archer's thumbs grazed along her inner thighs with agonizing slowness...until his exploration came to a halt over her mons.

"If at any time you want me to stop and untie you," Archer told her, "just say the magic word." His hands slipped beneath her, curving over her ass, gently kneading.

"Which is?" Mindy asked through ragged breaths, tensing and giving a little yelp as he stroked the inside of her butt crack.

"Snickers."

Relaxing at the levity in his voice, and the imagined twinkle in his eye, Mindy laughed.

"But once you speak it, everything stops. So use caution."

"Duly noted." What a curious sensation to feel so vulnerable and fully exposed, yet secure enough to luxuriate in Archer's sensual touch.

Leisurely stroking the line of her jaw with a feathery touch, he asked, "Are you comfortable? Anything too tight?"

"I'm fine." Still skittery at the newness of being bound, she squirmed. Testing her bindings, her breasts jiggled with her efforts. As if she'd issued an invitation, Archer's teeth clasped one nipple, tugging. The surprise element of not knowing it was coming made it particularly provocative.

Plucking her nipples like the strings of a violin, he spoke in a whisper that had her insides liquefying. "I could watch those bewitching twin peaks rise and fall for hours. Are you as eager as I am to feel your pretty grape-dyed pussy wrapped around my cock, pulsing with each thrust?"

"I want your epic grapey-blue cock inside me now, Archer. Do it...do it now." She attempted to shimmy.

"Do what, my love?" he teased. "I don't understand."

"Sex," Mindy clarified. "S-E-X. Make love to me...make *sex* to me! Now."

"Like this?" Archer's sensuous lips captured hers, his light stubble abrading the skin around her mouth. His tongue delved inside, penetrating, demanding, just the way she yearned to feel his cock impaling her.

"Mmm, that's *very* nice," Mindy assured as their kiss ended. "But I had something else in mind."

"This perhaps?" Archer's hot tongue speared through her pussy lips, surprising and enthralling her.

Shuddering from a barrage of raw pleasure, Mindy yelped. "Oh! Oh sweet heaven, fuck me, Archer. Don't make me wait any longer." She heard his low teasing chuckle as he licked and slurped his way up her belly.

"Maybe you mean like—"

"No more playing around," she warned, cutting him off. "Let me make it perfectly clear. I want you to fuck me, Archer. As in F.U.C.K. me with your C.O.C.K. Now! Punishment time is over. Let's get this on, Archie boy."

"Ahhh, but you see, my dear, eager Mindora G...waiting, delaying, stalling, is all part of your punishment. Regrettably, I may have to extend your penalty time for using such shocking language."

Steadying her breathing, Mindy warned, "Don't even think about it. You've got me cloaked in a thick cloud of lust and I swear, Archer, I'll go insane if I don't feel you inside me soon." She playfully fought against her bindings. Practically snarling in frustration, she added, "Do I get to do it to you too?"

"What, tie me up?"

"Yup."

"Ehhh..." The hesitation in Archer's voice was evident. "I don't know about that. We'll see."

"I could always tie you up when you're sleeping," she noted.

"Tsk-tsk...bad girl notions will add additional time to your discipline."

Mindy groaned. "Can the prisoner make a request?"

"I suppose so. Perhaps you'd like to request..." his fingers slicked across the crease of her dripping vulva, "this?"

"Ooh...yes." Every nerve ending in her body fired at his touch. "That...and more." She shivered in anticipation. "I want you to give me a screaming orgasm." Mindy tried curving her body toward him, but her movements were limited because of the restraints. "And I want your big blue djinn cock inside me when it's happening."

"Damn...you have no idea how I burn for you, Mindy." His fingers speared inside her soaked channel and she gasped. "You make my blood boil." He finger-fucked her hard with one hand while tugging a nipple with the other.

About to go clear out of her mind, she struggled against her bindings, needing to touch him, to see him—to wind her arms around his neck, threading her fingers through his thick hair. The more she struggled, the more aroused she got.

She moaned on a sigh when Archer's fingers left her core, only to buck when his wet finger drew across her lip.

"Open. I want you to taste yourself. To taste your desire for me."

Shaking her head back and forth, Mindy clamped her lips tight. No, uh-uh. She couldn't do that. Wouldn't. It was...embarrassing. She turned her head away. "I don't think—"

"Open," Archer commanded. "Unless you want to use your magic word and call this all off right now."

Mindy's mouth opened tentatively. Archer placed his finger inside.

"Suck it."

Mindy did. The liquid coating his finger tasted musky, the way her sex smelled when she was aroused. It was interesting. Unusual. Damn, it was downright hot to taste the evidence of her passion, delivered to her lips on Archer's flesh.

Trailing a path from her throat to her breasts, his skilled fingers circled her areolas. She felt her nipples pucker, begging for his attention. Archer didn't disappoint. His hot breath feathered over her breast before he caught one taut nipple in his teeth. He greedily feasted on the sensitive bead while his hands molded the curves and contours of her body.

Treating her to a lavish lick along the path he'd drawn with her juices, Archer said, "The taste of you...every bit of you, is a true aphrodisiac."

A tuneful sigh escaped her lips. "This is so stimulating...tantalizing. I never imagined being tied up and blindfolded could make me feel so erotic. Lustful. It's like all my senses are heightened."

Archer's mouth and hands left her body as she spoke, making Mindy feel lonely. She wiggled on the bed, oddly appreciating the fact she could barely move.

"Where are you, Archer?" She heard rustling sounds. "What are you doing? Talk to me."

"I've got a steel boner because of you, you delinquent girl. You're enticing me with your sweet, juicy body, all spread out for my enjoyment. Such a deliciously bad, bad girl."

Smiling at his words, she focused on the sounds again, reasonably certain he'd ripped open a foil packet and was sheathing himself with a condom. An image of him rolling the cool latex along his long, thick, hot cock made her shiver, clear to her center.

"With each thought of you, with every glance at your lush, made for sin body, you're driving me mad." Mindy felt him get back on the bed. "You're chipping away at my control, inch by inch, woman."

"I'm ready and waiting for some of your inches, Archer," Mindy quipped. "Right here." She vibrated her hips. "Right now." Her self-amused chuckles were cut off as the blue djinn's mighty cock thrust into her depths. High. Hard. Hot.

"Oh holy shit," Mindy cried out on a gasp. "Yessss...this...*this* is what I longed for."

"My thoughts exactly." Archer pounded into her, causing Mindy to become lost in sensations too exquisite to describe. "Christ, you feel good, Min."

As he treated her to a spirited fuck, Mindy feared she'd pass out from sheer bliss. She longed to wrap her legs around him, feel his warm flesh against her skin.

"I crave you, baby. All I can think about is sinking into your luscious hole...your intimate muscles clasping me like a vise."

Clenching instinctively at his evocative words, Mindy's core milked his cock. She could imagine the amorous look in his eyes by the inflection in his voice. They'd be warm, loving, and full of fire as he took her.

"I'm looking at the wet tangle of grapey-purple curls between your thighs as I slide in and out. There isn't a single spot on your body that isn't beautiful, even when it's stained purple and blue."

"I like your unique compliment. I feel the same about your Smurfy body. I just wish I could touch you, Archer. I ache to run my hands all over your hard body...to squeeze your biceps, your pecs, your hard, sexy ass."

"Plenty of time for that later. Right now just enjoy the sensations."

Between murmurs and grunts, Archer's breathing was heavy. The sound of flesh slicking against flesh echoed against the walls as he fucked her, the bedsprings squeaking in time to his thrusts.

Mindy hadn't paid attention to the sounds of lovemaking before, other than their mutual moans, groans and screams. It opened a wealth of new sensations, making their joining even more exceptional.

The sensation of Archer's tongue slicking over her belly, elicited a torrid moan from deep inside her throat. Even the simple action of him licking a supposedly non-erogenous zone built a sense of urgency at her impatient clit.

His hands wrapped around her hips, lifting her bottom from the bed as he drove into her, the adjustment allowing his cock to graze across her clit on the downstroke.

"Oh dear God...I-I can't hold out any longer, Archer."

"Do it," he commanded. "Come for me now, baby. Shudder for me. I want to see you turn all shades of pink and rosy as I fuck you from here to paradise."

Near delirious with passion, Mindy bucked furiously in his hands, longing to draw her legs up, to tighten them as the impending climax ripped through her. Screaming out Archer's name, her body went rigid, trembling as feverish shocks of concentrated pleasure arced through her.

"Oh yeah...yeah...that's it, sweetheart. Beautiful. Christ, Mindy, you're ravishing." Pounding deep inside her, like a thunderous storm reaching its pinnacle, Archer roared out his climax.

Soon the scent of their musk, the spicy tang of their sex, permeated the air. Making love bound and blindfolded taught her to observe new smells, new sounds, and to focus on the deeply stimulating sensation of a lover's intimate touch.

Collapsing against her stretched body, his arms folding around her, Archer provided the perfect end to their lovemaking with his warmth, weight, and her awareness of his rapid pulse. She could stay like this forever.

Moments later it was almost a shock when Archer removed her blindfold. Adjusting to the intrusion of light, Mindy squinted. Once able to fixate on his sated expression, she smiled, indulging in a heartfelt sigh.

Archer...*her* Archer. God, how she loved this amazing man.

"That was incredible. Otherworldly," she said as he unfastened the ties at her ankles. "Spicy, rich, earthy, and satisfying."

"You sound just like a vintner," Archer noted with a warm chuckle.

"Except that I didn't detect any oaky notes," Mindy said with a wink.

"The last thing I'd ever compare your deliciously squirmy body to is something wooden." He winked back at her. "What an exquisitely passionate little package you were, all tied up in silk straps, just for me." He swept a kiss across her lips.

"I can't wait to return the favor so you can experience the thrill of being bound too."

"We'll see." He telegraphed a dubious look. "If there's any tying to be done, I'll be the one doing it in this relationship."

"Are you sure?" Wiggling her toes, Mindy flexed her ankles and bent her knees while Archer moved to her wrists. "It might not be easy tying yourself to the bed," she teased.

"Very funny."

"I thought so. Hey, what happened? I thought you were eager to wheedle your way to first place." Mindy shook her hands once he'd released her wrists.

Archer slanted her a clueless expression. "Huh?"

"Your tactical quest." Her fingers tiptoed from his knee to his groin, resting on his depleted cock, immediately feeling it revive.

"Okay, I'm clueless here. What the heck are you talking about?"

"Your determined quest to replace chocolate as my number one passion."

Belting out a laugh, Archer said, "So we're back to that, are we? Didn't I just get finished punishing you for being such a bad girl?"

"Oh, but I've learned my lesson. Taking me on that sexy journey into bondage, I think you just may have inched your way a notch closer to being number one." With a teasing smile, Mindy fluffed her hair.

"I might know of a way to eke into first place." Archer jumped from the bed, heading for the door. "Be right back."

Chapter 27

MINDY HEARD Archer barreling down the stairs, wondering what he was up to, prancing around down there in the nude. In a few minutes he returned, brandishing a plastic squeeze bottle of chocolate syrup. Jiggling his eyebrows, he hopped back into bed.

Handing the bottle to Mindy, Archer positioned himself flat on his back, spreading his arms and legs wide. "Okay, go ahead. Tie me up. I'm your love slave, almighty Goddess of Chocolate. Do what you will to me with the chocolate syrup. And your tongue. And teeth. And don't forget those bodacious tits."

"All delightfully decadent chocolate-covered possibilities," Mindy purred, licking her lips. "Since chocolate syrup is fat free, I might go wild."

"This bondage thing may not get me the number one spot," Archer noted, "but it sure as hell better make me an equal contender."

"That depends on how well you and your big blue chocolate-covered Smurf cock please me." Grasping Archer's wrists, Mindy wound one of the neckties around them before raising his arms and securing him to the headboard.

"I'm not too crazy about this." Frowning, Archer pulled against his restraints.

"Too bad." She finished tying him, inspecting her work. "I like the way your pecs jump when you fight against your silk chains. Very sexy." She lowered her head, nipping one of his flat, brown nipples with her teeth. As she laved his other nipple, Archer offered a pleasured groan.

"And I love it when your magnificent tits bobble, and when your sweet little cunt constricts, squeezing my cock."

Quietly laughing at his quirky compliment, Mindy realized that, for some reason, she didn't mind when Archer called her breasts tits, or even when he referred to her vagina as a cunt, one of her least favorite words. Whenever Edward had used those coarse terms, she was tempted to stab him in the eye with an ice pick.

She'd learned Archer enjoyed surprising her by using in-your-face terminology every so often. So she decided to boost his pleasure factor by doing some dirty talk herself. It wasn't exactly her strength, but she figured she could fake it, doing a good enough job to make his cock extremely happy.

"Have I told you what a sexy chest you have, Archer?"

"Nope. Tell me all about it." A pleased grin stretching across his face, he made his pecs jump.

She kneaded his chest while licking her lips. "It makes my little pearly pink clit quiver just thinking about your strong, manly chest. All those burly, brawny muscles make my pussy drool." Archer's eyebrows jacked up. "Sometimes when I'm at home thinking about you, I just fuck myself silly with my vibrator, diddling with my sexy bits as I imagine that broad expanse of flesh and muscle crushed and scraping against my curvaceous tits."

"Oh you dirty girl." A deep chuckle arose from his chest. "That can't be my sweet, timid Mindy talking."

"No. This is slutty Mindy. Didn't I ever mention I had a split personality?" she teased.

"The whole Natasha thing kind of clued me in." Archer's grin broadened. "I like it when slutty Mindy gets bold, brazen, and talks dirty."

Binding his ankles, Mindy said, "Then I'll bet you'll like this too." Once finished securing him, she kneeled center stage between his legs, bringing one of her breasts to her mouth, tugging on the nipple with her teeth.

Looking up through her lashes, she saw Archer's jaw drop at the same time his cock jerked.

"Shit," he said. "Damn..."

Cupping both her breasts, she drew out the nipples in long, tugging strokes, tweaking the stiff buds as he watched, loving his animated features and accompanying raw vocabulary.

But Mindy wasn't finished.

"Sometimes I don't use a vibrator at all. I count on my best friend instead."

Archer's expression went blank. "Who?"

Taunting him with a throaty giggle, Mindy said, "Not *who*, silly, *what*."

Archer's quiet laugh was as husky as her giggle. "You're talking about Lieutenant Largo Lovethruster from the planet Dickprobe, aren't you?"

"You remembered! Wow, I'm impressed!"

"Are you kidding? How the hell could I forget that?"

"Nope, it's not Largo. He's my vibrator. I'm talking about my pulsating showerhead, Captain Clitlicker." Mindy almost burst out laughing. She'd just pulled that outrageous name out of her ass. Good grief, she was fast becoming the smut queen.

His eyes bugging, Archer swallowed hard. "Oh my God..."

Glad the impromptu silly name had the desired effect, she told him, "I turn the knob to the full-power pulse setting and aim Captain Clitlicker's steamy stream of water directly at my clit, keeping it there as I think about you fucking me." Mindy closed her eyes and moaned. "Before you know it, *boom*, my body's quaking as my rapturous cries echo off the shower walls."

"Son of a bitch...I want to get my hands on you so bad right now."

"Sometimes," Mindy said, "I just dispense with Largo Lovethruster and Captain Clitlicker and do this instead." He watched intently as her hand snaked down her torso, resting atop her mons. She positioned herself high on her knees, thighs spread, to give Archer the money shot. Then she slipped her finger to her clit, playing with herself.

Turning up the heat, she dropped her head back, moaning as she fingered her clitoris, adding plenty of writhing for the icing on the cake. She was having fun. There was something exceptionally scintillating about masturbating in front of Archer when he was bound and naked.

"Aw, jeez, Mindy, honey..."

"I'll picture you naked," Mindy continued, "your broad, bare chest heaving as you grab me hard into your arms to fuck me senseless." Pinching one of her beading nipples, she said, "I'll imagine your teeth biting my nipples, making me writhe in sweet, pleasured agony." She added a writhing motion.

"You're going to have me coming all over myself in a minute," Archer warned.

Still pleasuring herself, Mindy nailed Archer with a heated gaze. "Oh no you're not, mister. You'll come when I tell you to come, got that?"

"Damn." Archer's hot-blooded expression said it all. "A dominatrix in sheep's clothing. I'm so hot, I swear my blood's boiling"

"In my fantasies," she went on, having the best time ever, "I think about you as I enjoy the delicious sensations at my voluptuous breasts." Swallowing hard, Mindy found herself growing closer to orgasm. "Nipple stimulation drives me crazy. When combined with the powerful tingling at my clit, my insides swirl, simmer, take control of my mind. I keep swirling over my eager clitoris and it keeps inching me closer…closer…" she sucked in a deep breath, "closer to climax."

"Wait!" Archer urged. "Come in my mouth, Mindy."

Almost at the point of no return, Mindy's eyes widened and her hands stilled. "What?"

"Do it. Bring that juicy little pussy of yours here, baby. Sit on my face."

Mindy hesitated. She couldn't do that. She'd suffocate him. Crush him to death. Good grief, sitting on his face would be downright…slutty.

"Give me the pleasure of licking you to completion, sweetheart."

Scorching hot and needing to come almost more than she needed to take her next breath, slutty Mindy did as Archer asked.

As soon as she was in position, Archer freed his hands from the headboard, grasping her hips, positioning her just right.

"Hey!" Mindy gasped. "How did you do that?" Not only was she amazed he'd freed himself without so much as a grunt, but his powerful arms held her steady, as if she weighed no more than, well, a Snickers bar.

"You suck at tying knots," he told her with a teasing chuckle. "You tie knots like a girl. I could have freed my wrists anytime I wanted to." The next thing that came out of his mouth was his tongue, hot and wet, as he boldly swiped it across Mindy's engorged clit.

"Yikes…that feels soooo good," she said, completely forgetting she'd intended to admonish him. "Again. Do it again. I'm almost there, Archer."

She about died when he took her clit between his teeth and nibbled her straight to nirvana. Through shrieks, pants and gasps, she trembled and shuddered as Archer held her over his mouth, sucking her juices down his throat.

"So fucking tasty." Setting Mindy on his chest, he looked up into her eyes. "Babe, you are so hot. So amazingly sexy. I can't imagine we'll ever get bored in the bedroom."

Limp and sated, Mindy gave him a dreamy smile. "Who says we have to limit our activities to the bedroom?" she offered, amazed she could speak after that skyrocketing whirlwind of pleasure. "I must admit, I had a heck of a good time in that vat of grapes." She smiled at the recollection. "Blue tint and all."

"Me too," Archer agreed. "I'd be happy fucking you anywhere, anytime, sweetheart."

"And now, as for you, Archer Priest, you dirty, lowdown, lying snake in the grass," Mindy teased, gathering his wrists again. "This time I'm showing no mercy. The only way you'll get out of these knots is by me slicing your silk ties off with a knife."

"Go ahead, do your worst," Archer said with a cavalier smile. "Punish me to your heart's content."

"My plan exactly."

"Absolutely. I deserve it."

"I see you snickering. You think you're going to be able to get away again, don't you? Hah!"

"The thought never crossed my mind."

"Mmm-hmm. You know, you look really hot like this," Mindy noted. "Like Tarzan, tied up in the jungle by the evil ivory hunters and left for the lions to devour." Removing the cap from the bottle of chocolate syrup, she glazed Archer's grape-stained cock. "I'll be the lion," she announced, licking her lips a moment before trailing her tongue from the root of his cock to the swollen cap of the head, where she dotted a kiss.

Then she paused to put his blindfold in place.

"Whoa, wait a minute," Archer protested. "Skip the blindfold, okay? I want to watch."

"Too bad. Just relax and enjoy the sensations. You'll like it."

"But men are visual creatures, Min. Half the—"

Wasting no time, Mindy clamped her mouth on his cock and sucked.

Archer's breath grew ragged. "Half the enjoyment is in the observing," he finished

"Observe this." Gently massaging his balls, she scraped her teeth lightly over the sides of his cock, causing his thighs to tense and his shaft to jerk. Her tongue swirled in slow, circles, torturing him sweetly, she hoped.

"Oh that mouth of yours..." Archer said on a groan. "Your body isn't the only thing made for sin."

Mindy flicked her tongue over the top of his shaft, capturing a little pearl of pre-cum before digging the tip of her tongue into the tiny hole at the summit.

"Does Tarzan like?" she asked after another wicked lick across the small opening.

Tensing his muscles, Archer wailed a classic Tarzan yell loud enough to rattle the picture frames on the wall. "Damn right. Tarzan like, *very* much."

Pausing from nipping the soft flesh covering his marble-hard column, Mindy asked, "You know what this lioness likes?"

"Tell me. Fuck, I wish I could see you right now."

Mindy raked his chest and abs with her nails, hard enough for a sexy jolt, but soft enough not to leave scratch marks. "This lioness likes the salty taste of cum sliding down the back of her throat as she sucks Tarzan's mighty cock."

"Aw...fuck me," Archer groaned.

"Exactly."

"You're killing me, Mindy."

"This lioness doesn't kill," Mindy informed. "She just likes to play with her meat and maul it a little bit." She leaned in close, spreading his thighs. Her hands snaked beneath him, clutching

Archer's ass cheeks and digging in her fingers. She licked the sensitive patch of skin between his balls and ass.

As he growled, she felt his butt muscles tighten in her hands and decided it was a good time to finish the job of pleasuring the big, beautiful, bound hunk of man before her.

Inch by inch she swallowed as much cock as she could, until it collided with the back of her throat. Mindy sucked it, licked it, worshipped it, fucked it until her lips and cheeks were sore. She cupped his sac with her fingers, rolling it gently as she milked his cock.

"I wish I could sink my fingers into your hair now," Archer said, his voice coming out like a croak. "I want to hold your pretty head close to me as you fuck me with that amazing mouth of yours."

Mindy could tell he was getting close. Listening to his grunts, groans and murmurs, she watched Archer's head shift from side to side as his muscles tensed and tightened.

A moment later, his body rigid and a pleasured grimace across his mouth, Archer howled a blistering curse as his hips bucked against her and his hot semen flooded the cavern of her mouth and throat.

Once she'd finished catching, savoring and swallowing every last drop of his cum, Mindy sat back on her heels, quite pleased with herself as she watched the rise and fall of Archer's chest. She only hoped his experience was half as stimulating as the one he'd given her.

"I enjoyed that immensely," she told him, removing his blindfold. "That was so pleasurable, it just brought you one step closer to claiming first place on my chocolate bliss-o-meter."

As Archer opened his mouth to answer, his phone rang on his nightstand.

The rude interruption had them both groaning.

Glancing at the display on his phone, he said, "Jeez, it's just past midnight...and I don't recognize the number." He shook his head. "I'm letting it go to voicemail. Now why don't you untie me like a good little girl?"

Leaning over, Mindy caught a glimpse of the number on Archer's phone. "Oh my gosh, that's Leo. I wonder if something's wrong."

"Please don't answer the—"

"Hello? Leo? Is everything okay?" Mindy put Leo on speakerphone as Archer groaned.

"I thought I might catch you two together." Leo giggled.

"Aw hell," Archer muttered.

"I've got important news about Jasper and Britney."

Mindy bolted up on her knees while Archer struggled with his bindings.

"Get me out of this," he demanded.

Mindy couldn't help giggling at the fearsome scowl across Archer's features. "Gee, why don't you just slip out of those girly knots all by yourself, Tarzan?"

The no-nonsense glare he transmitted gave her second thoughts about any further glibness.

"Tarzan?" Leo said. "What's going on?"

"Nothing. Hold on a minute, Leo." Mindy fiddled with the ties at Archer's wrists, grunting and groaning as she tried to undo her handiwork. It was useless. She'd clearly succeeded in tying a series of manly knots at Archer's wrists.

"Archer? Mindy?" Leo's voice called out again.

"Damn. Get these damned ties off me!" Archer yanked so hard, Mindy half-expected the headboard to come flying overhead.

"Ties? Well that sounds interesting," Leo noted while Archer's eyes narrowed at the intrusion.

"There's a jackknife in my nightstand drawer," Archer told Mindy.

"Okay." Scrambling over him, she reached the edge of the mattress before realizing it and fell off the bed, landing on a heap of sheets and the comforter on the floor.

"Whoooop!" she warbled, landing in a sprawl.

"Yeah, Leo," Archer called out. "What's up?"

"What the heck are you two doing?"

"None of your business, Leo," Archer said.

"Good," Leo laughed, "I'm glad you two are having a fun time. Am I on speakerphone?"

"Yup," Archer said, still tugging at his bindings. "Go ahead, Leo."

"Hey, why don't we do facetime?" Leo suggested

'No!" Mindy and Archer chorused.

"Okay, okay. Hey, Mindy?"

Half sighing and half laughing, Mindy answered, "Yes, Leo." Standing, she instinctively pulled the sheet up, covering her exposed breasts, bunching the fabric in her fist.

"I kind of figured I might catch you two together there. My psychic feelings told me—"

Archer turned to Mindy and whispered, "Get the knife out and cut off these damn straps."

"Straps?" Leo said. "Ooh, sounds like some naughty bondage fun."

"Shut up, Leo," Archer said as Mindy got the knife and opened it. The blade whooshed out, startling her, causing her to drop her bunched up sheet.

"Wow, this thing is lethal. Why do you keep it in your nightstand?"

"Just untie me, for chrissakes," Archer demanded, rattling the headboard as he yanked at his bindings again.

"I have to be careful, Archer. I don't want to slice your wrists."

"Oh yeah." Leo chuckled. "Some good times were had."

"Never mind, Leo." Tsking, Mindy felt her cheeks flush. "What about Britney and Jasper?"

"She said yes, Mindy. Britney said yes!"

"You mean, my sister and your cousin—" Archer started.

"Exactly! Jasper, Big Jazz, your soon to be brother-in-law, just called me. He was on his way to the airport to catch a flight for Texas. He and Britney leave for Russia in, get this, guys, in two weeks! Yeeehaaa!"

His hands finally free, Archer telegraphed a mile-wide grin, which Mindy echoed. "Yeeehaaa!" they dueted back to Leo.

"Remember, Archer, you have to act completely surprised when Britney tells you her big news about marrying Jasper and moving overseas."

"I'll put on a performance that'll make you proud, Leo." Archer worked at the knots at one ankle as Mindy worked at the other.

"Good boy. Hey Mindy, I've penciled in a two-week vacation for you starting the day after Britney leaves for Russia. You can take a few extra days if you need to, but no more than three weeks, okay? That starts cutting into our busy time."

"Vacation?" Cocking her head, Mindy frowned. "Why, Leo? I wasn't planning to take a—"

"For your honeymoon, of course."

"Honeymoon!" Mindy gasped. "What honeymoon?"

"Oops." Leo broke into his patented nervous giggle. "Archer, haven't you...uh...*talked* to Mindy yet?"

Archer looked to Mindy, grinned and scratched his head. "Uh...no. Not yet, Leo."

Mindy swallowed a scream strong enough to crack those lovely old leaded-glass windows in Archer's bedroom. Trying desperately not to look too eager, and to keep her heart from leaping out of her throat, she asked, "Archer, what's Leo talking about?"

"I was planning to wait until we had breakfast together, but thanks to your *bigmouth boss*," Archer cupped his hands over his mouth to amplify the words," I guess I'll have to change my plans." Sitting at the edge of the bed, he raked his fingers through his hair. "I swear to God, Leo," he said, laughing. "You're going to be worse than an in-law."

"Don't worry, Archer," Leo assured. "You'll be used to me before you know it. Won't he, Mindy?"

There was silence as Mindy looked skyward, expelling a noisy sigh.

"Mindy?" Leo's giggle pierced the air.

"Right, Leo," she said finally, shrugging as Archer smirked.

"Since you basically orchestrated this whole relationship with Mindy and me," Archer said, "I suppose it's only fitting that you hear the proposal, Leo."

Ears perked, Mindy sat ramrod-straight. "Proposal?"

"Yes!" Leo said. "*Yes!*"

Archer rose from the bed and paused, looking down at his naked cock. "Wait, there's something I have to do first."

"What?" Leo said. "What?! You're killing me here."

"None of your beeswax, Leo." Archer slipped into his jeans. Grabbing his shirt, he yanked that on as well. "There. That's better." He beamed a broad grin. "Somehow it just wouldn't seem right the other way."

"What other way?" Leo asked. "What's going on there? Archer? Mindy?"

"Oh gosh," Mindy said. "Just a minute." Gathering the top sheet, she wrapped it around herself, flinging one end over her shoulder. Sitting there naked and blotchy blue-purple just didn't seem apropos when she was about to get proposed to.

"You look like a Greek goddess, Mindy," Archer told her.

"Thank you. Okay, I'm ready." She sat back down on the edge of the bed, feeling like a kid on Christmas morning.

Getting down on one knee, Archer cleared his throat.

"Ohmigod," Mindy whispered, her eyes filling with tears as he took her hand in his and cleared his throat again.

"Mindy Klopenshaw von Grettle, I—"

"Oh boy, she even told you her maiden name?" Leo asked. "Excellent! That means you really rate, Archer."

Rolling his eyes in frustration, Archer said, "How about letting me get through this without you interrupting, okay, Leo?"

"Of course. Absolutely. My lips are sealed. Go ahead Archie."

"Archie?" Archer groused and Mindy giggled.

"You just go ahead and ignore Leo," Mindy encouraged.

Nodding, Archer started again, "Mindy Klopenshaw von Grettle, I love you. I can't live without you. And I can't imagine feeling this way about anyone else in this lifetime or any other. You are the woman of my dreams, of my heart, my soul."

"Oh that was good, Archer," Leo said. "Really good." The sound of a weepy Leo blowing his nose came across loud and clear.

Archer closed his eyes in a long blink and sort of smiled. It seemed to Mindy as though he might be counting to ten.

"Leo?" Archer said.

"Yeah, buddy?"

"Shut up."

"Your wish is my command. Go ahead."

Archer cleared his throat for the umpteenth time and gazed into Mindy's eyes. "You and I are like the components of a fine wine, Min. Blended together, I know we can achieve that special balance and harmony that will provide our relationship with body, substance, smoothness, character. And, of course, a pleasing finish." Archer grinned.

"And don't forget *great legs*," Mindy said with a wink, remembering her wine gaffe during their picnic lunch.

Laughing, Archer squeezed one of Mindy's calves. "Great legs. Definitely."

Leo expelled an audible sigh, indicating his impatience. Mindy and Archer snickered.

"What I'm trying to say, Mindy, is," he paused and cleared his throat again. Mindy had never seen him so nervous.

"Yes, Archer?"

"I want to ask you if—"

"Oh for heaven's sake, Archer, spit it out already!" Leo cut in. "The man's asking you to marry him, Mindy. Say yes before I keel over from old age, will you?"

Archer slapped his hand to his forehead and Mindy burst out laughing.

"Are you, Archer? Asking me to marry you?"

Archer nodded. "And doing a damn piss-poor job of it apparently."

"Oh no. It was perfect, Archer. Just perfect." Mindy threw her arms around his neck and squealed. "Yes! Yes, Archer. Yes, yes, yes!"

"Finally!" Leo said. "See, Mindy? What did I tell you? Maybe now you'll believe I'm psychic. I told you my predictions always come true and that you and Archer would end up together, didn't I?"

"Yeah, with plenty of cockeyed finagling from you, Leo," Archer said.

"Well, it worked, didn't it? It was my responsibility to get you two together. Anyway," Leo continued, "congratulations, kids. I'll get busy and set up the wedding arrangements at that cute little chapel with the justice of the peace two blocks from your winery. You'll get married the day after Britney and Jasper leave for Russia. We'll—"

"Whoa!" Mindy said. "Slow down, Leo. The man just finished proposing and you're already planning our wedding? What if we want a long engagement?"

"Trust me, that's not a concern, darling," he assured her. "We'll have to keep the wedding relatively small because of the short notice and, of course, we don't want Britney to get wind of anything before she leaves. Rolf and his sister Marta have offered to have the reception at Bavaria Haus. With a live polka music band, Mindy! We don't have to worry about wine because you can provide that, Archer. And—"

"Leo, stop," Mindy cut in. "I really think Archer should have some say in all this."

"Oh, Archer and I already worked out the details when you were passed out after downing that killer chocolate concoction." Leo laughed.

"I wasn't passed out, I-I was sleeping," Mindy objected.

"Yeah, right," Leo and Archer chorused.

"Anyway," Leo continued, "we decided it was best to get you guys hitched as soon as we ship Britney out of here. We don't want to wait too long because if she comes back for some reason, she might try to screw things up. This is for the best, Mindy. Really. Trust me."

Mindy's jaw dropped as she turned to her new fiancé. "You and Leo got together and planned this all without consulting me? Before you even proposed, or knew I'd say yes?"

"Uh...well, yeah, sort of, I guess." Archer looked like a deer caught in the headlights. It was the undeniably clueless expression men get when put on the spot by a woman. "See, Leo was eager to make the plans, so I told him to go ahead and run with it. I wasn't worried about you saying no to my proposal, so that wasn't a concern."

Mindy huffed, balled her fists and planted them on her hips. "Is that so?

"Are you kidding? After all the trouble you went to just to hook me? No chance in hell you'd say no, sweetheart." Devilish, teasing laughter erupted from Archer's lips.

Mindy rose abruptly and shoved Archer's shoulder, making him lose his balance on the one knee and land on his ass. "So you and my boss just decided to plan out my wedding and my whole life for me without even asking me for input."

"You're absolutely right, Mindy," Leo said. "We definitely should have asked for your input. Barcelona, London or Frankfurt?"

Mindy skewed her features. "Huh?"

"You want to be asked for your input, Min, so I'm asking. Which of those three places do you want to go for your honeymoon?"

Mindy slumped back on the edge of the bed, dazed and bewildered. "Well, let's see. I love London, but I've always wanted to go to Germany...hmmm, I guess maybe—"

"Barcelona?" Leo said. "Good. Just what I was thinking. Spain is great this time of year. I've got this terrific little villa lined up there for you guys with a gorgeous hand-painted ceramic tile veranda overlooking the city. The neighboring buildings are a few hundred years old with magnificent larger-than-life sculptures and columns. It's quiet, full of history, secluded, the food is phenomenal, and I hear the villa's master bedroom suite is to die for. Good choice, Mindy. You'll love it."

Still on the floor, Archer peered at Mindy, broadcasting a charming little-boy smile. "Sounds romantic to me, Mindy. What do you think?"

"Do I have a choice?" Mindy threw up her hands. "Sure. Why not?" She paused for a moment and then it struck her. She gaped at Archer, her heart racing. "Oh my God. Oh. My. God!"

"What?" Archer and Leo said together.

"This all happened so fast and I just now realized we're talking about the two of us actually being husband and wife and spending our honeymoon in Spain." She indulged in a dreamy sigh. "I feel just like a princess in a storybook—after the ugly old witch gets her comeuppance and takes off for Russia with the horny Texas toad."

Beaming a grin, she snaked herself down, sitting on the floor next to Archer, giving him a hug. "I don't care where we go or when, as long as we're together, Archer. So, Leo," she raised her voice so he'd be sure to hear, "you can just go right ahead and take care of whatever plans you please."

"Great! It just so happens I've already made the reservations for air and hotel, plus a car to use once you're in Barcelona. This is great, isn't it?" Leo gushed. "You two must be feeling on top of the world right now, right?"

Appraising their stained, speckled bodies, Mindy let out a mischievous giggle. "Actually, we're kind of blue at the moment, Leo."

"Blue? *Blue*! Are you insane? How can you possibly be feeling blue? You just got engaged for chrissakes."

"I didn't say we were *feeling* blue. We're just blue," Mindy clarified through another impish giggle.

"Literally," Archer added, squeezing Mindy tight.

"You two aren't making any sense," Leo said with a tsk. "I'm chalking it up to pre-wedding jitters. Hey Archer, you busy after breakfast?"

"That depends." Archer slanted his phone an apprehensive look. "Why?"

"I was wondering if you wouldn't mind giving me and Rolf a hand. We're moving him into my place."

"That's wonderful, Leo!" Mindy said. "Rolf's a wonderful person, and he's good for you too. You need someone to help keep you on the straight and narrow."

"What can I say?" Leo said with a laugh. "The big naïve lummox obviously needs someone to take care of him and show him the ropes here in the states, so I figured I may as well volunteer for the job."

"I'd be glad to help, Leo," Archer said, giving Mindy a smile.

"Excellent. Tomorrow night you and your *fiancée*," Leo obviously relished saying the word, "can join Rolf and me for cocktails. The four of us have tons to celebrate. Rolf and I plan to start moving his stuff about ten o'clock in the morning, Archer. How soon can you be here?"

Archer looked at Mindy and picked up the bottle of chocolate syrup from the nightstand. "As soon as I manage to replace chocolate as the number one love of Mindy's life."

"At that rate you'll never get here." Leo laughed. "Let's not get carried away, Archer. I know Mindy loves you but—"

"I'm ending the call now, Leo. I'll be there in time," Archer said, slipping out of his jeans and shirt. He jumped back into the bed and squirted chocolate all over himself, giving extra attention to his cock as it saluted the ceiling.

Eyeing Archer with a lusty appraisal, Mindy licked her lips. She had no doubt her future husband would succeed in his mission.

"But—" Leo began again.

"*Trust me*," Archer said, disconnecting the call.

~<>~

TURN THE PAGE TO READ Chapter 1 of TRAINED BY THE GREEK, book 1 of the Drakos Brothers series. This hot and spicy hilarious romantic comedy will be available in the summer of 2024...

Trained by the Greek: Chapter 1

"**I** SWEAR, I'M NOT a terrorist," Riley McNiven promised the airport security agent detaining her after she walked through the scanner, causing it to buzz. She tried making light of the situation by adding a little laughter. Unfortunately, he was devoid of humor. Hands raised, she added, "Honest. It's just..." she lowered her voice to a whisper, "my bra."

"Your what?" the scowling agent asked.

Frustrated and still half asleep at three a.m., she tsked, leaned closer, and answered a little louder. "My bra."

"Did you say your bra? Like brassiere?" the guy boomed.

Riley's sleep-deprived eyes popped wide as his words echoed off the airport walls. Cringing at his volume, she glanced at the dozens of people in adjacent lines, waiting to pass through the security checkpoint. The sixty-ish security guy looked clueless as well as humorless. A pair of hearing aids indicated a hearing problem.

"Yes," she answered with more vehemence than she'd intended. "My bra." Snapping the strap at her shoulder, she succumbed to a spurt of nervous laughter. Not that anything was even remotely funny. Laughter was just Riley's default mechanism when she was angsty.

"You're wearing a bra with metal in it, ma'am?" he asked, neither cognizant nor caring about her discomfort at the unwanted attention.

"Well...it's possible. I'm not really sure. I mean, I didn't think so at first, because I thought it was probably some sort of space age plastic-like material that—" Suddenly aware her tranquilizers had kicked in, making her feel thick-headed and loopy, Riley went silent.

"Yes ma'am?" He gave her the side-eye. "Material that...?"

Although mindful that she tended to babble when tense or nervous, she was unable to keep her big fat motormouth shut.

"Bends. Material that bends," she explained, with accompanying gestures, "keeping its shape like metal underwires. But I, um, didn't bother reading the pamphlet that came with the bra. I mean, who bothers reading a whole pamphlet about underwear? I'll bet you haven't, have you?" She gushed nervous laughter, praying to spot a scrap of duct tape to plaster over her mouth.

"It's new," she went on. "I just got it. I haven't worn underwires in years because they're so restrictive and uncomfortable the way they dig in all over, pinching and binding, you know?"

"No ma'am." Security guy eyeballed her like she was from Mars. A guilty, mouthy Martian terrorist without an off button.

"So," Riley shrugged, "since I haven't worn an underwire bra for so long," she paused just long enough to giggle while sweat beaded on her upper lip, "I didn't stop to think there might be metal underwires in my new bra and—"

"Female security attendant needed for full body pat down," security guy said into a mouthpiece.

That shut Riley up fast.

For half a minute.

"A full body..." She gasped. "Oh, I don't really think that's necessary, do you..." she leaned forward, looking at his name badge, "Bob? I'm sure lots of women here are unintentionally, or maybe even intentionally, wearing bras with metal underwires for, you know, lift and support, kind of like men's athletic supporters. Do they have metal in them? Probably not but that doesn't mean women should be searched like we're terrorists with explosive materials sewn into our bras. Is that something terrorists do?"

"Explosives?" Security guy's eyebrows knitted impossibly close. Aw hell.

"I didn't mean to say *explosives*. They tell you never to use that word in an airport or on a plane. The last thing I want is to make anyone nervous. It's not my fault, Bob, it's the pills. I never even think about explosives much less talk about them...unless it's the fourth of July. Who talks about explosives, unless they're terrorists, or people who manufacture bombs?"

Her hands shooting up, Riley clarified, "Okay, I didn't mean to bring up bombs, another taboo word, either but you're making me *really* nervous, Bob. I think I've already established that I'm not a terrorist. I'm just a woman who was foolish enough not to read the pamphlet that came with her pricey new bra, or check for metal in it before coming to the airport. I'm certainly not a threat to anyone." *Giggle.*

Security guy could pass for a statue the way he stood stock still staring at her like she was a lethal bra-wearing terrorist.

"I'm just a caterer, for heaven's sake. It's not like I carry my chef's knife around with me, or forks, or vegetable peelers, or anything metal like that. The whole buzzer thing was probably a mistake, Bob. A fluke. I'm sure your space-age atomic gamma ray scanner just went off in error. Here, let me walk through again, you'll see."

BUZZ!

Damn.

"Do you have any other metal on you, ma'am?" security guy asked. "Knife, fork, potato peelers, or other possible weapons?"

"Don't be silly, of course not. I don't walk around with cooking utensils on my person. A fork? Seriously?" Riley hoped the tiny river of nervous perspiration trickling down her temple didn't make her look like a guilty terrorist. "Like I'm planning a deadly forking attack on a plane full of passengers before using my vegetable peeler to skin them all?" The thought made her shudder. "Aw, come on, Bob. Really? Do I look like a forking peeler kind of woman to you?"

The sound of deep male chuckling behind her caught Riley's attention. Turning, she frowned as she spotted the passenger, a tall, gloriously handsome man with dark hair and eyes.

"Excuse me..." she narrowed one eye, "are you laughing at me?"

Lifting both hands in surrender, the handsome hunk laughingly claimed, "No, no. Sorry. I didn't mean to laugh." His voice was deep and foreign. Mediterranean something or other. If Riley wasn't already happily engaged, she might have batted her eyelashes and struck up a conversation but this clearly wasn't the time because, once again, security guy called for a female attendant in his thunderous voice.

Riley's shoulders sagged along with her boobs.

"It's going to be all right," handsome Mediterranean guy assured in his delicious r-rolling accent. "I'm sure they don't think you're a terrorist but perhaps..." He smiled while hesitating.

"Perhaps?" Riley nudged.

"Perhaps you might want to stop talking so much." He made a chatting motion with his fingers. "I think you are, how do you say...digging a trench for yourself."

"Digging a hole." Riley nodded. "Yup, you're right. Four o'clock in the morning is an ungodly hour for a flight but it was the only choice I had for my travel schedule. I may be somewhat overtired because I only got about two hours of sleep. Plus I took a tranquilizer, well, two actually, that's made me very...tranquil." She smiled up at him. Boy he was attractive.

"I understand. For me as well."

"You took two tranquilizers too?"

The tone of his laughter was enticing. Almost seductive. No, no, no...absently shaking her head from side to side, Riley recognized those as probable double tranquilizer thoughts. She was sure the sound was like any other ordinary man's deeply provocative, sensuous, sexy laughter.

She blinked. Nowhere was *lewd thinking* listed as a possible side effect of her tranquilizers.

"No," he told her, "I mean I'm tired because I got little sleep."

"Oh. Where are you going?" Riley felt compelled to ask handsome Mediterranean guy, purely out of general curiosity because she was very happily engaged to Victor.

"To my home in Greece."

"Oh, that's a really long flight too." So handsome Mediterranean guy was actually handsome Greek guy.

"And you?"

"As long as they don't haul me off to a cell for terrorists," she made a goofy face, "first I'm going to New York to visit my best friend, Sophie, before flying to London to surprise Victor, my fiancé."

Airport security guy cleared his throat. Riley had almost forgotten he was there.

"Agent Harper will be here in a moment, as soon as she's finished with another passenger."

Glancing at the wall clock, Riley told the agent, "It was three o'clock when I reached the security scanner. Three o'clock when my travel day went to hell. Going through security has always been my least favorite step, but this embarrassing experience has transcended any other."

"I understand, ma'am. In the future you should avoid wearing anything with metal."

"I thought that's what I did but, nope. Paying nearly seventy bucks for a bra was outrageous. At that price, I'd expect this big-ticket undergarment to magically get me out of this embarrassing mess," she griped. "But no such luck. Here I am, a suspected terrorist in my own hometown, holding up a long line of people waiting to go through the scanner."

"No one said anything about you being a suspected—"

"This bra was highly recommended by a popular online influencer for providing excellent lift and separation for larger-busted women, Bob. I not only bought the spiel, I bought the exceedingly pricey bra too. You know why?"

Bob, who was now accompanied by another security agent, offered a blank stare.

"Because a nurse friend warned me I needed to replace my cheapie bras with ones that offered better support since my tatas might soon be venturing south, due to their size and because I'm fast approaching forty." She frowned. "I don't think I look like I'm thirty-seven, do you?"

Both security guys shook their heads negatively.

"Not at all," handsome Greek guy chimed in.

Riley knew, she really, absolutely, positively knew, she was yakety-yakking to excess but she just. Could. Not. Stop.

"Thank you," she said to the men. "Finally giving in, I went to an upscale lingerie shop for my first bra fitting in years. I swear, if I could surgically attach my fancy new bra to my body, I would. Not only does it lift and separate as promised, the fit is close and comfortable, as if tailor made. That's why it's so hard to believe it has metal underwires, because it's soooo comfy."

She noticed three pairs of eyes suddenly locked onto her chest...and still she couldn't shut the hell up. She wondered briefly if the doctor had made an error, prescribing jackass pills instead of tranquilizers.

"I think it makes me look fifteen years younger too. You know, like slathering lotion all over your hands," she gestured a scrubbing motion before spreading her fingers wide, "enjoying that they look fifteen years younger for the next ten minutes, except my costly new bra makes me look younger for the whole time I wear it. Since you didn't know me before I started wearing it you wouldn't know, so you'll just have to trust me on the age thing."

Agent Harper stepped in front of Riley, snapping on a pair of blue plastic gloves. Riley offered her biggest, most innocent non-terrorist smile, quickly spoiling the effect by laughing, perspiring, and biting the peeling cracked skin on her lip, making it bleed.

"So, naturally," Riley continued her jackassery, "before heading to PDX for my insanely early flight, I put on my luxurious new bra, along with my standard, comfortable air travel outfit, consisting of jeans and a hoody." She motioned to her outfit.

"Everything went perfectly until I stepped through the security scanner, which made PDX security think I must be a terrorist, even though I'm just an innocent caterer traveling to London, via New York."

"You're traveling outside the country," Agent Harper said as more of a statement than a question as her eyebrows inched down.

"Yes but you don't have to worry because I don't have anything against London or anyone living there...or my fiancé who's there temporarily finishing his latest novel. Victor is a published author."

Riley smiled and Agent Harper grunted.

As the woman calmly explained exactly what she was going to do, Riley felt sure everyone was looking at her, including the hunky Greek behind her. She wanted to cry. She wanted to laugh. So she did both, before babbling more details of her expensive new bra. She could see people a few feet away cringing as she just kept talking and talking and digging a deeper hole for herself. Or trench. She decided Greek guy's phraseology was more apropos.

Why couldn't she be like normal people who got tongue-tied and went mute when scared or nervous? She was making a terrible impression on everyone and she damn well knew it. The only upside is that she'd never have to see any of these people again for the rest of her life...unless she was incarcerated for being a terrorist, in which case she might have to see the security agents at her trial.

"I don't have to take off my clothes in front of everybody, do I? You're not going to make me take off my bra, are you, Agent Harper? Are there security cameras here?" She gazed all around. "I don't want to be undressed on camera. What if the video got into the wrong hands and went viral on social media and I became infamous for being an airport stripper? I'm not a stripper, I'm a caterer."

"No, ma'am, you don't need to disrobe," Agent Harper told her flatly. "You're on the verge of getting hysterical. Please try to relax."

"Hysterical...me? No, no, I'm not hysterical," Riley pledged, her voice on the verge of hysteria as she waved her hands through the air. "I'm just nervous. Honest. I mean, it's just after three in the morning, wouldn't you be nervous if a stranger wearing plastic gloves told you to take off your clothes in front of hundreds of people in the airport security area so she could pat you down like a common criminal?"

There was nothing funny about it, but Riley giggled nonetheless.

The agent eyed her, probably deciding whether or not it was the stealthy hilarity-tinged giggle of a terrorist.

"I'm not a terrorist," Riley repeated for the umpteenth time. "I'm sure even terrorists say that but I mean it. I'm not one of them. I might look and sound a little terrorist-like because my relaxation medication just kicked in and aside from making me sleepy, it makes me feel sort of loony...not that I have any mental or emotional issues. I don't...except for being a diehard chocoholic.

And the tranquilizers make me giggle." *Giggle.* Holding up two fingers, she added, "Twice as much giggling with two pills." *Giggle.*

Riley heard Greek guy chuckle and mutter something in what she assumed was Greek. Not being the most confident girl on the block, she'd always found herself bashful around striking men like the Greek. She worried they'd think she was dull and uninteresting. But she'd never had to worry about them pegging her as a blathering idiot before. She could imagine him snort-laughing about the crazy American woman at the airport once he got home to his wife and kids in Greece.

Clearly incapable of turning off her idiotic jabbering, Riley went on, "You see, Agent Harper, when I timed taking my tranquilizer pill long before the crack of dawn this morning I'd assumed I'd already be tucked into my seat on the plane by now, getting all cozy and relaxed, reading my book and it wouldn't matter if my pill kicked in because I could just drift off to sleep. But this security thing is taking so much time that I—"

"You don't have to get undressed, ma'am. I already explained that I'm just going to pat you down. It's standard operating procedure. Now please step to the side so we can commence and let the other passengers get through." She gestured, waving her arm.

Stepping out of line to her right and over to an area with a short blue curtain that wasn't private enough to conceal anything, Riley asked, "Right here...in front of everybody?"

"It'll just take a minute, ma'am." The agent pulled the non-discreet curtain around them.

"When you call me ma'am it makes me feel old. Like somebody's grandma. I'm not even a mom." *Giggle.* "You can just call me Riley." She projected her least saboteur-like smile. "That's my name. Riley McNiven. Do you want to see my ID photo?"

"No ma'am, that's not necessary."

"I look just like it, auburn hair, pale skin, and freckles, except there aren't any freckles showing in my picture because I usually cover them up with makeup, but I didn't have time to put on any makeup this morning, which is why you can see them now. See?" She turned her face left and right. "But I'm not too sure about this patting down thing, Agent Harper, because everybody is looking."

"I've closed the privacy curtain. No one is looking."

Giggle.

The rest was kind of a blur, except for the part where Riley asked the woman why she had to pat her between the legs and on her butt when that's clearly not where her bra was. It's possible some of what Riley thought was happening might possibly be an ever-so-slight exaggeration of the truth on her part.

Because of the tranquilizer pills.

The doctor prescribed them because Riley had a fear of flying and became agitated on flights. Maybe a teensy anxious...and panicky. A medication minimalist, she steered clear of unnecessary medications, especially things like tranquilizers. This was only the second time she'd taken one. It worked great the first time, with her happily drifting off to dreamland in no time, just as she started feeling loopy.

Since the doctor said she could take two pills if needed, and the cross-country flight from Portland to New York was godawful long, Riley took two.

Finally, *finally*, her pat-down ordeal was finished. She made it beyond the checkpoint to the section where her plane was boarding, and got on the plane without any further problems, except for the PTMD (Post Traumatic Mortification Disorder) she experienced during the flight.

Riley feared the mortifying event of being branded a babbling public nuisance while under the influence of tranquilizers would scar her life. Everyone, from the airport security team, to all the people in line, to the passenger sitting next to her for the entire flight to New York—the hunky, handsome Greek guy who'd been behind her in line—must be laughing their asses off.

Sometimes life could be so unfair.

She was fairly certain she talked his ear off, all the way to New York...but she couldn't remember a damn thing either of them had said. Except for his name.

Mortified to the bone at what he must think of her, Riley was comforted that she and walking, talking Greek god, Jordan Drakos, would never cross paths again.

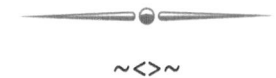

~<>~

And So, Dear Reader,

You've finished reading Don't Even Think About It, a Daisy Dexter Dobbs standalone book that (*fingers crossed and hopeful sigh*) you were sorry to see end. Meanwhile I, author DDD, am gleefully clacking away at my keyboard, writing yet another sensational, utterly phenomenal (*please don't burst my bubble*) book. I'd like to conclude our time together with a heartfelt THANK YOU for choosing to read this standalone book.

I hope you got as much fun and enjoyment out of reading this spicy screwball romantic comedy as I did writing it. Creating these characters and their zany scenarios was pure joy for me.

I'm often asked why I choose to write romcoms with often ridiculous situations. If I find myself laughing while I write, that tells me the story will bring laughter to others as well, maybe at a time when they need it most. If I can accomplish that through my writing, wow, I'm one very happy, very fortunate woman indeed!

Laughter is wonderful medicine. It infuses us with hope, helps us feel better, and allows us to manage problems with a more optimistic approach. The world seems brighter, and we're able to see light at the end of the tunnel. At least that's what laughter accomplishes for me. Finding ways to laugh (often at myself—which admittedly happens far too often) makes managing my advanced AS (ankylosing spondylitis) condition much easier.

"From the moment I picked your book up until I laid it down, I was convulsed with laughter. Someday I intend reading it."
–Groucho Marx

~<>~

If you enjoyed Don't Even Think About It I'd be delighted if you left a positive review or rating on the site where you purchased it. (Not that I check daily for new reviews. Or ever Google myself. Or do anything else indicating I'm an insecure creative person craving validation. Nope, nothing like that.) Your review can be long, short, or just a star rating. Reviews help other readers find my books, and keep my stories from getting lost in a site's complicated algorithms. Plus, it gives me encouragement to keep on writing!

Speaking of other readers, you can help them find this book by recommending it to your friends, neighbors, relatives, coworkers, your dentist, doctor, mail carrier, all the strangers you meet in the grocery store, at the mall, the neighborhood pub, your favorite coffee shop, and, of course, everyone you know online. (I'm ready with additional suggestions if needed.)

Thanks again! Wishing you love, laughter, romance and happy reading!

—*Daisy Dexter Dobbs*

~<>~

DAISY DEXTER DOBBS BOOK LIST

SERIES

Heartwishes

Small town Contemporary Romance / Romantic Comedy (mild to medium spice level)

Family legend says the magical heartwish ring was given to the matriarch of a Viking king by Odin, the most powerful of Norse gods. It must be held against the heart when making a sincere heartwish and will remain on the finger until it's time to pass it on. Though the mind may be cluttered and uncertain, the heart knows the right wish to make. Always trust your heart.

(Can be read as standalones but better appreciated when read in order so you can get to know all the characters and fall in love with the Malones!)

The Viking's Heartwish (Book 1: Delaney and Varik)

The Genie's Heartwish (Book 2: Laila and Zak)

The Firefighter's Heartwish (Book 3: Gard and Sabrina)

The Knitter's Heartwish (Book 4: Reen and Drake)

The Nymph's Heartwish (Book 5: Nevan and Aladee)

The Psychic's Heartwish (Book 6: Kady and Rylan)

The Daughter's Heartwish (Book 7: Bekka and Jamie – coming soon)

And at least 2 more Heartwishes titles are planned

∼<>∼

The Drakos Brothers

(releasing summer of 2024)

Small town Contemporary Romance / Romantic Comedy
(scorching-hot spice level)
Bold, opinionated Greek men, the Drakos brothers star in this
hot, hot, HOT laugh out loud romantic comedy series featuring
lots of hunky, delicious Greek men and the women who capture
their alpha male hearts. (Can be read as standalones but better
appreciated when read in order so you can get to know all the
characters.)
Trained by the Greek (Book 1: Jordan and Riley)
Vexed by the Greek (Book 2: Dino and Sophie)
Bossed by the Greek (Book 3: Sebastian and Ardine)
Conned by the Greek (Book 4: Benedict and Angel)
(additional stories for more brothers coming)
~<>~

————◉————

STANDALONES
Don't Even Think About It (Mindy and Archer)
Laugh-out-loud Romantic Comedy (scorching-hot spice level)
Avowed chocoholic Mindy handles her topsy-turvy life with as
much grace and aplomb as possible—by attempting chocolatcide.
This steamy, spicy, laugh-out-loud, award-winning romantic
comedy novel is brimming with love, snappy banter, sexy inventive
scenes that sizzle, and numerous naughty words.
~<>~
MORE SERIES AND STANDALONES
COMING SOON FROM DAISY
Daisy has written close to 100 novels and numerous novellas and
short stories over the last few decades. She certainly can't have
novels full of pay phones, answering machines, landlines, no email,
or the internet, or social media now, can she? Nope, nope, nope.
Of course not. So now that she has the rights back to all of her

books and stories from her previous publishers, she's been hard at work rewriting and updating her books for release as an indie author. Revisiting umpteen stories featuring gorgeous, handsome, oh-so-sexy hunks is a tough job, but somebody's gotta do it. So here's a sneak peek at just some of the dozens of titles Daisy's been maniacally, um, I mean, *diligently*, working on (check her website and newsletter for updates!).

(NOTE: many of these are working titles and may change upon publication.)

~<>~

VISIT DaisyDexterDobbs.com[1] for a full, up-to-date listing of Daisy's books. Sign up for Daisy's newsletter and mailing list to get notifications for new book releases, contests, and more.

~<>~

---

1. https://www.daisydexterdobbs.com

About the Author

A born storyteller, Daisy Dexter Dobbs started writing stories at five, satisfying her inner ham by reading them aloud, using a toilet plunger as a microphone. Today, Daisy creates written voyages of the imagination, infused with love, laugh-out-loud comedy, friendships, family and guaranteed happy endings. Some of her books include paranormal and fantasy elements. And some books are scorching HOT on the spice scale.

Having worked at more than 40 different jobs provides Daisy with a ridiculous amount of questionable experience to draw on for her characters. She's been: a ghostwriter for politicians; a library art director; a weight loss counselor; mayor's executive secretary; a Realtor; travel agent; editor; and a butcher's meat wrapper, quitting after she spotted a big eyeball coming toward her on the conveyor.

A Chicago native, Daisy and her husband, now live in the Pacific Northwest. Happily, Daisy no longer feels the need to use a bathroom plunger as a microphone when entertaining.

You can find Daisy here:
Facebook: DaisyDexterDobbs
Instagram: DaisyDexterDobbs
TikTok: @daisydexterdobbs
Amazon: Daisy Dexter Dobbs
Goodreads: daisydexterdobbs
BookBub: Daisy-Dexter-Dobbs
Twitter/X: DaisyDDobbs
Threads: @DaisyDexterDobbs
Pinterest: DaisyDDobbs
Email: DaisyDexterDobbs@gmail.com
Read more at www.DaisyDexterDobbs.com.